HOUSE CALL

Ponder House Press
2565 Lake Circle
Jackson MS 39211-6625

Library of Congress Catalog Card Number: TXu1-244-033

Copyright © 2005 Darden North, MD

Layout and Design by The Gibbes Company

ISBN 978-0-9771126-2-3

First Printing

To Sally:

Let's make a deal.

Prologue

Its metal casing rusted by years of moisture, the glass doorknob creaked as it turned slowly to the right. Steaming water pouring from the nearby faucet masked this sound as well as that of the approaching footsteps, soft as they crossed the damp tile floor.

Taylor firmly squeezed the plastic bottle, releasing salon conditioner in streaks over her freshly shampooed hair. Leaning forward to rinse, she felt a firm hand grab the highlighted strands. With her head angled severely backwards, screaming was impossible, particularly as the conditioner rolled down onto her face and mouth. Now almost entirely submerged in the slippery bathtub, Taylor Richards could not struggle but only gag and cough.

Moments later her chest exploded, tearing and burning, as the thrusts between her ribs were swift and repeated. Blood pouring from the punctures mixed with the soapy water, forming a red scum on the sides of the porcelain tub.

Glancing hopelessly at the bathroom ceiling through a ruddy mist, Taylor lost consciousness as her face was submerged. She was not aware of the final snap and slash to her neck that severed the carotid arteries and trachea. A few bubbles of air escaped from this artificial opening, rising quickly to the surface of the tub water. Satisfied, the departing visitor hurriedly rinsed the instrument under the faucet, leaving the water to flow at a mere stream.

As the soapy, crimson liquid eventually topped the brim of the bathtub, it spilled onto the tile floor as Taylor's body rocked to stillness.

Contents

HOUSE
CALL

◆ ◆ ◆

DARDEN NORTH, MD

Chapter

1

...

THE LAST DAY

"OK, Shugga, keep your legs back. That's nice. Wide apart. Let me get a good feel. Yes, that feels exactly right. No, not too tight. Remember what we talked about. There, that's it! Get ready. One's coming now. It's coming. It's coming. Can't you feel the rhythm? Ohhh!"

"This place never closes, just like Wal-Mart," Taylor grumbled as she slid her employee badge through the check-in slot by the time clock. *06:42.*

"Push...Pushh...Pushhh...Push,Push,Push,Push,Push... Pushhhh...Pushhhhh......Wait now! Don't Push, DON'T PUSH. I see the head crowning. Lots of dark hair. Great job! I'll get the techs to set up for delivery, and we need to call the doctor. STAT."

These vehement coaching efforts of a fellow labor and delivery nurse easily penetrated the wall from the adjacent room. Despite the huffing and puffing of the parturient patient, there was no way to miss the cheerleading augmented by the bedside family members. Hearing the nurse's urgent call for the obstetrician, Taylor could envision the sweat forming on her comrade's brow, adding to that already pouring from the patient.

The day was Friday, and unlike most professional work situations, the week was not over for this registered nurse, nor for the others like her. As Taylor re-clipped her employee badge to her scrub suit, she tried to look past the monotony she felt. Pulling a hospital-nursing shift on any day had grown almost unbearable for Taylor Richards. Having more combined practical experience than most of the newer hospital nurses, the thirty-three year old was nearing burnout. Besides, her volunteer time spent taking blood pressures and treating colds at the homeless shelter had almost become more rewarding to her.

"Why do I stay here? Stay in this? I ought to just walk back out the front door," she groaned loudly and carelessly enough to be heard by the young physician approaching from behind. Knox Chamblee was not purposefully following Taylor but was enjoying the walk nonetheless.

"Hey, I heard that," he retorted playfully. "A bad attitude like that won't win many Brownie points with the nursing supervisor, you know."

Despite the fact that the route to the nurses' locker room led along the hall directly in front of the doctors' lounge, Taylor had failed to notice the door opening as Dr. Knox Chamblee exited from his complimentary breakfast. Conversely, as the nurse stomped down the corridor, Chamblee could not miss the blonde hair tossed side-to-side almost in rhythm with her steps.

"Oh, hi. I'm just having a bad day, I guess," Taylor responded, exaggerating her embarrassment over being overheard.

Believing himself to be only slightly younger than Taylor Richards, Dr. Chamblee had on several occasions entertained the idea of asking this girl out. However, despite her great looks and the tight butt walking in front of him, Knox had been steered away by his office secretary. She warned him that Taylor carried tons of emotional garbage, heaped on by her ex.

"Stupid."

"Excuse me?" Knox called to her, pretending to be indignant as he stopped in the middle of the hall, still watching Taylor hike toward the nurses' locker room.

"Wasn't talking to you, Doc. Don't be paranoid. I was berating myself," Taylor explained rather flippantly, while slowing her pace a bit and turning her head back toward Knox. "You're kinda cute, you know."

"So are y......," Knox responded to the vanishing spectacle as he stood in the walkway watching Taylor disappear down the next corridor. "I need to ask my secretary some more questions about that girl. That shape could overrule most emotional problems," he mumbled to himself.

Disappointed that his only surgery case for the day had cancelled at the last minute, Knox decided to drive over to the office to digest his doctors' lounge breakfast. Not until this morning's arrival at the hospital did he learn of the patient's message received the preceding night by the answering service: "Tell the doctor that I just can't go through with it. I'm afraid of being put to sleep." Blindly turning around, he almost knocked over the thick, yellow-and-black plastic *Wet Floor* sign that had materialized behind him. Trying not to appear annoyed, Knox nodded at the custodian who was tackling the corridor's flooring with a mop and bucket.

"Sorry, Doc," the janitor seemed to force an apology without looking up at Knox, as though the Grace Community Hospital employee had expected to be in the doctor's way.

"When I had the chance, I should have accepted that pharmaceutical rep job," Taylor blurted out when she reached the nurses' lounge alone; but the slamming of her locker door muffled her aggravation. "After all, he is good-looking." Taylor stopped for a minute to check her makeup in the long mirror mounted over the sinks. Before her divorce the regional salesman with Peyton-Rose Pharmaceuticals had actively recruited her to fill a local detail position. While the job offer had been legitimately presented to her, even in writing, the still-married Taylor found his illegitimate overtures to her disgusting.

Nowadays, Taylor felt more and more trapped in her present nursing position. Having reached such a high level of seniority in her field, despite working only fourteen years as a registered nurse, her salary was rumored to be one of the largest in the city and most likely could not be duplicated. Earlier, she had considered transferring to the hospital's new Critical Care Unit filled with really sick patients but decided against the gloomy position.

Walking back toward the nursing station, Taylor reminded herself of the joyous endings in obstetrics: young healthy patients, beaming families, gratified nurses. Yes, her exhausting occupation should be satisfying. Sitting at the workstation, she stared into the reflection on the glass surface of the central fetal heart rate monitor. Gone was the happy, energetic, attractive female in her early thirties. Instead, the likeness was distorted by the jerky white lines of an electronic fetal heart rate pattern, making her seem prematurely wrinkled and thoroughly worn out.

Believing that her facial appearance and attitude had suddenly transformed the rest of her smooth, tight body into that of an old woman, Taylor decided, "I should fix up more, like I used to, and go to the gym more often." Taylor thought about Dr. Chamblee as she reached down into her jacket pocket for some lipstick.

"Whose dusty white Suburban is in my parking spot?" Dr. Hawes broke Taylor out of her trance. The abruptness of the most senior female physician on the hospital staff demanded Taylor's immediate attention as well as that of the other nurses who had gathered for morning report. "That place is reserved for me. I fought long and hard to get that assigned parking space, and it's mine." Hawes' spacious location on the garage's first level provided a comfortable home for her black BMW, sparing it from door-opening nicks as well as the elements. During the preceding night, the ignorant and anxious partner of a patient had ignored the *Dr. Hawes* marker and hastily usurped her authority with his SUV.

"We'll get security to have it moved, Doctor." This pacifying remark came from one of the coherent nurses left from last night's shift, who planned to find the culprit quietly and ask him to park in the visitors' lot.

Nodding with approval and expectation, Hawes shifted gears and continued the storm. "Whoever is taking care of Priscilla Buckwalter — I need you to come with me now. Right now!"

Today's performance had been another dramatic example of classic *Elizabeth Aslyn Hawes, MD*. Her 7:00 a.m. interruption on the Labor and Delivery Unit during the nurses' shift change brought the patient care report there to a grinding halt. Certain that she was aging prematurely because of working with this demanding woman, Taylor had privately renamed Dr. Hawes, *Dr. Haughty*. Most, if not all, of the other nurses shared Taylor's unfavorable opinion of her. In fact, with few exceptions, the African-American nurses and Dr. Hawes shared a particular mutual dislike.

The bright aspect of Taylor's being laid off from her previous job at the Montclair Center for Women's Medical and Surgical Services was that Dr. Hawes had been one of its partnered physicians. "Nothing personal," the office manager insisted when terminating her. "Taylor, you've done a great job. Really, you have. It's just that with all the cuts in medical insurance payments to the doctors, we've got to lower our practice overhead somehow. I'm sorry, but one way is to have cheaper employees."

The office manager's outstanding reference landed Taylor in her current registered nurse position at Grace Community Hospital. Now as she stood next in line for a patient assignment, she would receive a tortured reminder of her previous job; her new patient's attending physician was the overbearing Dr. Hawes. Trying to be optimistic, Taylor was grateful that this would be Priscilla Buckwalter's fourth baby, meaning a mercifully quick delivery and less time to work with Hawes. She dreaded watching Dr. Hawes' predictable, syrupy demeanor toward the patient, a sharp distinction to her treatment of the nursing staff.

Taylor's most memorable experience with Hawes had been several months ago. Having to work an 11p to 7a shift was uncommon for a nurse with Taylor's seniority, but she was filling in at the last minute for a much younger nurse with a sick child. While observing one of Dr. Hawes' patients for possible progression of labor, it became obvious that an active pattern had developed, so she appropriately paged Hawes.

"This is Dr. Hawes. Why did someone page me?" Hawes responded customarily with prompt but irritated inflection.

"I did. You have Sophia Currie here. She's six centimeters and wants an epidural."

"Who is this?" There was no way to miss the woman's annoyance at being bothered.

"Dr. Hawes, this is Taylor, Taylor Richards."

"Well, it helps if you identify yourself over the phone. That's really common professional courtesy. Hard to keep all you nurses straight, you know. Anyway, I'm not on. Gwinn is."

Minimizing the fetal monitor pattern on the computer screen, Taylor quickly accessed the physicians' call schedule for the month. Much to her relief, she found *E Hawes* clearly displayed next to the date. Trying not to sound too self-satisfied, Taylor countered, "I'm sorry, Dr. Hawes, but our schedule has you on call for Dr. Gwinn."

Simultaneously Taylor could nearly feel the heat emanating from the telephone receiver, as Dr. Hawes' face tightened in radiant scarlet.

"Huh, well, I see now that you're right. Verified that call change on my hand-held. OK. Be right there. Tell anesthesia to go ahead and start the epidural... Please."

Twenty minutes later the striking Dr. Hawes arrived clad in an evening gown complete with double stranded pearls and ranch mink stroller. Her dark hair crowned the ensemble in a high, tight, elegant bun. Taylor remembered how she and the other RN on duty watched in dismay as Dr. Hawes whisked off her fur coat, draping it over a nearby medical supply cart. Donning a pair of sterile gloves retrieved off the cart and referring to the patient's amniotic fluid sac, the doctor then announced, "O.K., ladies, let's break water!"

An avid fan of old TV shows and re-runs, the other nurse whispered, "Taylor, she looks just like Emma Peele."

Taylor thought at the time that most doctors would have at least changed clothes first before coming to the hospital dressed so ostentatiously. Also, that night Dr. Hawes reeked strongly of perfume, not something she usually wore, and her breath was overpowering with artificial freshener. As immaculate and boisterous as she appeared that evening, Hawes should have been holding a martini rather than the tool she was to employ in rupturing the amniotic sac.

Shortly after the amniotomy, and while Taylor replaced Mrs. Currie's soaked sheets, Dr. Hawes appropriately changed into a scrub suit, leaving most of her finery in the female doctors' locker room except for the mink stroller still resting on the cart at the nurses' workstation. While the confident doctor delivered the baby, Taylor and her co-worker sneaked a quick try-on, each admiring the improvement expensive fur brings to a nurse's uniform.

After her expert physician's performance, Dr. Hawes re-gowned and applied the pearls and mink — then disappeared. Taylor could almost envision her skid marks in the pavement as the BMW whisked her away from the hospital, evidently to return to a party. After that incident the other nurses quietly referred to Elizabeth Hawes as *Queen Elizabeth*. This surreptitious nickname had stuck despite the fact that Dr. Hawes now asked to be addressed as *Dr. Aslyn Hawes*. While most believed that Hawes had revised her professional salutation to invoke a more youthful flair, in truth the change arose from her overhearing some nurses laughingly employ the regal moniker. Aslyn now held an even greater disdain for those individuals.

Nevertheless here during the daylight hours, Dr. Hawes was dressed in the usual scrub suit and monogrammed white lab jacket with thick, dark hair resting more casually on her shoulders in a manner that remained perfectly coiffured. "Ladies, I don't suppose any other patients besides Priscilla dropped in for me during the night?" she asked. "No labor inductions scheduled today since I'm not on call. Sure of it."

"No, Dr. Hawes, Buckwalter in labor room eleven is the only one," Taylor answered as she handed over the written patient record. Eleven was one of the full-service rooms recently renovated into an ultra modern suite to include all the amenities, right in line with the latest hospital marketing fad. Taylor remembered that the *Queen* could be easily provoked into a semi-tirade if any of her *subjects* were not assigned to one of these new spaces. But to give Hawes credit, she insisted upon this privilege for all of her patients, no matter who they were or to what social class they belonged.

"Priscilla Buckwalter, a gravida four, three centimeters dilated in the office on last visit. That's what Chamblee's note says. He was the only one available to see some patients for me last week when I was out of the office at a meeting." The Queen then pronounced confidently, "Priscilla will go quickly. Doesn't want her tubes tied today. So I'm sure she'll be back for a fifth!" Taylor could almost envision Dr. Haughty holding a scepter.

Listening to Hawes' disapproving tone in reference to Chamblee, Taylor countered her lack of subtlety. "Yes, Priscilla mentioned that she had seen Dr. Chamblee at her last visit and that she had been a little nervous about seeing a male doctor. But she told me that he had been very nice. Really genteel. Showed a good bedside manner."

Dr. Hawes never looked up from the patient's chart while Nurse Richards shared the compliments regarding the young associate physician. "Well, Taylor, if you're through talking about Knox Chamblee, let's go take care of Mrs. Buckwalter," Hawes demanded as she stepped quickly toward the patient's room. "I guess that, for some reason, Priscilla has...has some kind of crush on him." As though to denounce the whole incident, Hawes shook her head and uttered, "Entirely, just completely, unprofessional of him."

Unknown to Taylor, Aslyn Hawes had possessed great reservations about hiring Knox Chamblee into her practice. She considered him too good-looking to be an obstetrician and gynecologist. True, he had been well thought of during his residency at the university, earning the professors' approval as a qualified surgeon and capable physician. Her senior partner, Cullen Gwinn, had in her opinion overly extolled the candidate's virtues as he pushed Knox successfully through the Center's interview process.

But in the eyes of Dr. Aslyn Hawes, Chamblee was just an average male OB/GYN. He was not originally from Montclair and vicinity, so he had no family ties, professional friendships, or other connections to endear him to referring physicians. Being single, there was no cute wife to run around town, indirectly promoting her husband's practice in the social circles. Under the circumstances, Aslyn doubted if Knox would ever produce enough patient business to qualify as a financial partner in the group.

Mistakenly believing that her avoidance of him was not obvious, she would turn the opposite way if she suspected that they might pass each other in the hall. In the rare event that she felt it necessary to consult with him about a patient, she would send him e-mail or pass the message via a nurse.

To the contrary, Dr. Hawes was thrilled over the other recently acquired physician associate who preceded Knox Chamblee. In Aslyn's mind the practice had been fortunate in stealing her from the competing practice across town, tantalizing the conquest with a better benefits package. But, to Aslyn's annoyance, the new female associate turned out to be much too fertile and was already out on maternity leave.

Anyway, she temporarily dismissed the thoughts of the young associates in her practice as she entered the patient's labor room. Walking through the doorway, Hawes turned her majestic head slightly to glance behind her, verifying that Nurse Richards was on her heels. Taylor tried to ignore that almost insulting gesture.

After Taylor assisted Dr. Hawes in putting on sterile examining gloves, Aslyn performed a cervical exam. "My goodness, Priscilla, you're already ten centimeters dilated. And the baby's way down. Great. You're very near to delivery!" Taylor immediately interpreted the arrogant, disapproving glare directed toward her by the doctor as, "How come you didn't know that this patient was ready to push the baby out? Were you not paying attention to my special patient before I got here?"

Luckily for all, Priscilla had already welcomed the anesthesiologist's epidural and promptly experienced the joyous and painless delivery of her fourth healthy child. Judging which person in the delivery room was now the happiest would have been difficult: Priscilla's husband who hoped that, since his wife had now birthed a female to add to their testosterone-dominated brood, she might stop getting pregnant; Dr. Aslyn Hawes, whose day would now proceed more smoothly following the quick, easy delivery; or Taylor Richards who was temporarily freed from her nemesis.

Chapter
2
•••
THE DUTY

His one elective surgery case for the week cancelled. No deliveries in the last two weeks. No recent medical hospital admissions either. Not a single one. Leaving Grace Community by car for his nearby office, Knox Chamblee wondered if maybe an advertising billboard on the interstate would help him develop a full clientele. "Heck, I'd be happy for a half load or even an eighth," he explained to the dashboard CD player.

Knox could envision his picture, a large color one of his smiling face, posted high above a highway exit marker holding a metal speculum with the slogan:

One Stop...Pap Smear - Breast Exam - Cholesterol Check

After all, this method had worked well for the lawyers.

"My surgery cancelled. No hospital rounds to make. Time to head straight to the office to play with ourselves."

When Knox was offered this practice opportunity, he jumped on it since he had already waited much longer for a concrete job prospect than his female peers. The most senior doctor at the Center, Cullen Gwinn, and the administrator promptly huddled with him, devising a schedule to build a quick patient base by offering consultations and exams at hours traditionally unavailable. Unfortunately for the young obstetrician and gynecologist, this studied arrangement had not been fruitful.

As Knox entered the building, he pulled up his day's office schedule on the computer terminal. "Eighteen months of practice, and this is all that has been scheduled for me to see," he thought as the LCD monitor flashed *APPOINTMENT AVAILABLE, APPOINTMENT AVAILABLE, APPOINTMENT AVAILABLE* in so many patient time slots that it resembled twinkling white lights on a Christmas tree. Knox understood that Fridays could be relatively slow in the Center for most of the doctors although the potential for medical activity at the hospital could be heavy. Today's depressing reality for Knox was that he was not busy at either facility.

"Well, my chief resident was right; he always was," Knox decided, as he again studied the day's miserable excuse for an office patient schedule. *"Boy, you won't be busy at first."* Somehow the list appeared even more pitiful on paper when spit out by the nearby laser printer.

Now entering the third quarter of his second year at the Center and feeling no momentum to his work, Knox began to worry that a third-year employment contract actually might not be extended to him. A welcomed first and second year post-residency salary had been guaranteed by the Montclair Center for Women's Medical and Surgical Services. However, with contract renewal at the beginning of the third year at the Center, his income would be determined directly by the patient services that he personally provided. Unaware that his predicament had provided a lively agenda item for the physician board meeting the night before, Knox planned to work on that third year later as his mind wandered.

"Elizabeth, uh, I mean, Aslyn, you were as much a part in hiring him as I was," Cullen Gwinn argued at the board meeting.

"Cullen, you pushed the boy through. You know you did. It was your God-awful mistake. For heaven's sake, go ahead and admit it!"

"Wait a damn minute! Everyone of us here..." Dr. Cullen Gwinn responded while trying to read the circle of faces around him. Stonewalling, just like a poker game. "We all interviewed Knox Chamblee. His qualifications and abilities are as good, as outstanding, as anybody's."

Cullen again looked around into the eyes of the other physician executive board members, still finding no sign of support for his argument. Most notably, Dr. Marshall Langley turned his own attention to the thin and thick crust specimens from Pizza Hut displayed on the conference table, the traditional dinner fare for the monthly meeting.

"Cullen Gwinn, you essentially ramrodded that guy down our throats!" Dr. Hawes retorted as she stood from her leather chair so abruptly that mineral water almost flew from the bottle in her hand. "He may be fairly likeable, but he just cannot put enough money on the books. This isn't about quality of care or malpractice concerns. The bottom line is this: Chamblee is a drain, a financial drain on this practice."

Gwinn still believed strongly in the potential of Knox Chamblee's practice success and remained steadfast in his support of him. However, he along with the other physicians had dreaded this item on the meeting's agenda: a possible change in employment status for the newest physician associate of the Montclair Center for Women's Medical and Surgical Services. He glanced over to the office manager, but Nell Lowery would not turn her attention away from the duty of recording secretary. Even Faye Edmund, a maturing physician partner, was showing no tendency toward entering the debate, pro or con. Dr. Gwinn remained alone in voicing support for Knox.

"Come on, Aslyn, you yourself just said that he was friendly. I think you actually used *likeable*. Don't you remember that we even went so far as to have our office secretaries interview Knox, some one-on-one, before we offered him a contract?"

"Yeah, I do remember that," Dr. Edmund startled Cullen with

this sudden recollection and interruption. "Heather especially liked his personality and looks. After meeting him, she described Knox to me as *a real piece.* Said he was so adorable that patients wouldn't be able to resist using him as their gynecologist."

"Only that Heather What's-Her-Name would be that crude. Imagine, wanting to get an orgasm from a Pap smear," Hawes somberly summarized.

Hearing this comment regarding Heather's criteria for physician selection, Marshall Langley spewed his chewed pizza mixture onto the paper plate adjacent to his agenda book. The combination of Italian sausage, goat cheese, and Mediterranean olives was no longer recognizable. Once he stopped choking, his laughter became uncontrollable.

Cullen stared coolly at his noisy partner and then redirected the dialogue to Dr. Hawes. "Aslyn, the Center has not actually lost any money on Dr. Chamblee, nor have we made any. He just needs a chance to..."

"What do you mean needs a chance? Please get it through your thick skull, Cullen. He's had a chance, eighteen months worth. Look, I asked Nell to print out his total production and collection receipts. The simple truth is this: Chamblee's financial figures just don't approach those of other new associates before him. They're nowhere close!"

"Now, now, wait a minute. Several weeks ago that medical consultant firm completed the survey about physician productivity and office staffing. Since you all wanted it, and we've given them sixteen thousand plus to do it, let's just hold on and see what they have to say."

Remembering his personal objection to hiring the Perkins and Unger firm, Cullen continued, "Nell, when are the results of that almighty P & U survey due?"

"Any day now, as far as I can tell. All I know is that the check I sent them has cleared."

Aslyn Hawes became noticeably silent. During the consultants' survey she had developed a friendship with one of the examiners. That rapport earned her the opportunity to review the firm's preliminary findings and recommendations before the final draft. As promised, the sneak preview had been exclusively emailed to her today.

A text message suddenly scrolled across the screen of Dr. Gwinn's two-way pager, alerting him to a deteriorating fetal heart rate pattern. Being on call that night for the group and now distracted from the meeting's business, Cullen left the gathering immediately and reported back to the hospital.

A shrill buzzing noise from the Center's intercom system interrupted his daydreaming and was immediately followed by a scratchy but friendly voice. "Dr. Chamblee, you do know that you are on unreferred this month, don't you? And on private call today for the Center?"

"Sure, I knew about the unreferred hospital call but not the other. What gives, Heather?" Knox responded into the speakerphone in the artificially low, husky voice that he knew she wanted to hear. Surprised by this potential burden of covering for the entire Center's absent doctors, he added, "I thought I wouldn't be busy today, but you've really dropped a bomb on me, Captain." Knox assumed that Heather was most likely responsible for the physician scheduling error and desperately needed the available doctor with the lowest seniority to make it right.

"OOOOhhhhhhh, but you're young and virile, 'Mr. President.' You can handle it." Heather's Marilyn Monroe imitation sounded fairly authentic today. Chamblee realized on his first day of employment in Montclair that this appointment secretary was fond of him. She was twenty-five years his senior and the only female of her generation that he had ever met named *Heather*.

"Anyway, Dr. Gwinn and the wife decided to take a long weekend. Nell mentioned something about their flying down to Point Clear on a swanky private jet."

"Seems too much like a spendthrift, not like the Dr. Gwinn

I know."

After one long, emphysemic smoker's breath Heather continued. "It's a treat from some corporation exec-types. You know, they own a bunch of hospitals."

"And most probably want to own more. That should be an interesting adventure. Lots of wining and dining, I imagine."

"Don't worry, Honey, your day will come. Anyhow, let's get back to the real world." Heather was interrupted as the surrounding phone lines began to blink in rapid succession. "Geeze, they're always ringing off the hook. Better go before Nell catches me wasting time yapping, even if it's with you. Remember, Hon, since the boss is gone today, see his hospital patients. Just wanted to remind you 'cause it's my job."

"*Remind* is not the word. How about *surprise*?" Knox said to himself.

"Oh, and in case you haven't noticed this, Sweetie, you'll have plenty of time to make hospital rounds on Dr. Gwinn's patients. You're free over here until your 10:45 appointment; that is, if she shows up."

"Heather, I'm happy to take this call for you; I mean Dr. Gwinn. You're a regular little guardian angel, you know," he chuckled.

"You're welcome, Sweetie. I always try to take care of my doctors. Have a blessed day." After Heather's jolt to his usually leisurely timetable, Knox grabbed his white lab coat as he quickly rose from the physician workstation. Lightly starched and complete with pink and blue monogramming, the garment bore the distinctive marketing symbol of the Montclair Center for Women's Medical and Surgical Services. Like the other doctors of the Center, Knox wore this coat constantly during the day except when scrubbing at the hospital for surgery or when delivering a baby. This custom, of course, meant that he kept the coat on most of the time.

Since the Center was close to the hospital, Knox trotted over to Grace Community, entering through the *EMERGENCY ENTRANCE ONLY* side door. Despite growing concern over baby snatching, the hospital still provided this convenient physician entryway. Reaching the nursing station promptly,

Chamblee was met with medical bedlam.

"Just you look at this place, Dr. Chamblee! It's gone to Hell in a handbag. One of Dr. Gwinn's labor inductions scheduled for later just moseyed on in today, blowin' and goin'. The two health department unreferreds were supposed to go to the University but graced our presence instead. Ya know why? Of course, they heard our rooms are nicer."

"OK, Marg, what nurse is taking care of Dr. Gwinn's private patient?" Knox responded to the cries of Margina Baker, the unit nurse in charge.

Dripping in drama, Margina ignored him; she was not finished with her tirade. "Also, at the start of the shift we already had four patients in active labor. Only one of them was making any progress, but she delivered real quickly once Dr. Hawes got here. Taylor is still tied up in there with recovery."

The delivered patients were not the issue. Even though Knox needed more information about the undelivered ones, he safely leaned back and listened to the show.

The strain in her voice was building, "Two of our nurses scheduled for later in the day called in sick. And we were already shorthanded." Margina's heavy facial features seemed to vibrate as she stopped her ranting briefly to ponder the nightmare, grinding her teeth in frustration. Knox stared in amazement, giving up on interrupting her. He decided that if nurses still wore those tight, little starched white hats, Margina's would have popped off her head by now.

"One of the unreferred patients is a severe toxemic with her blood pressure out the roof. Oh, Lord," she rose her hands up toward the ceiling, "could just seize, seize just anytime. Also another pregnant one was sent up from ER with some sort of abdominal pain."

Knox tried again to interrupt with questions, but the effort was fruitless.

"And, Dr. Chamblee, right before you walked in, a nurse from your Center called. She's sending over another one of Dr. Gwinn's drop-ins. The chick thinks she's in premature labor."

Sharing Marg's dismay, Knox walked over and looked at the

chalkboard plainly displayed in the Labor and Delivery nursing workstation. The board, which had been retrieved earlier during the shift from a storage room, served as a centralized conglomerate display of individual medical information and now represented a HIPPA violation.

Nevertheless, for the sake of monitoring the stability of the patients, or perhaps the lack thereof, Chamblee agreed with Margina's breaking the rules. Today they would rely on their old friend, the Board, as it had been affectionately called, instead of a computer display. That expansive, black common-sense tool had at one time been a fixture for all L & D units before a keyboard and mouse replaced chalk and eraser.

Dr. Chamblee's priority for this mess was to get through the trenches without disaster for the patients or the staff. He fought feeling overwhelmed but was certain that the highly trained and usually ample nursing staff would enable him to manage the problems.

Knox's confidence was short-lived.

"Like I told you already, the real kicker for today is going to be the shortage of nursing staff. Taylor is here, and I'm going to get her to work most of a double like she did last night."

Taylor Richards walked up hurriedly to join the discussion. "Marg and Dr. Chamblee, you won't believe this, or maybe you will." She continued in a hushed tone as though she were gossiping. "While you two were looking at the board, Dr. Ricks called from the North Montclair Women's Clinic."

"Oh, gosh, Taylor, we can always count on him to muck things up even more than they are already. What's he sending?" panicked Margina.

"Get this: he said that he was rushing over a set of twins by ambulance, planning to let them labor, then deliver vaginally." Taylor groaned.

Margina gestured as though she might swoon. "We don't have enough nurses today to take care of all of these patients, I tell you. We just don't!"

"Can't the hospital nursing supervisor do something about

getting some more help in here?" Knox inquired of Taylor, as Margina paced around the nursing station too frustrated to pay any attention to him. Without answering, Taylor suddenly disappeared, running down the hall to check on a patient who was vomiting. "Aren't there some standby or on-call nurses?" Knox asked almost rhetorically, knowing the answer was no because of hospital cost-cutting measures. That economic belt tightening was tolerable on a regular day, perhaps, but not on a day like this one.

Knox came up dry in his search for another nurse to help him get oriented. The only one available was the still ranting-and-raving Margina. Understanding that because of today's call assignment he could pull twenty-four hours straight of hands-on hospital duty, he urgently needed control of these first few hours and nursing help from a knowledgeable person who still had her senses.

"Is Dr. Hawes in the suite?" he successfully interrupted Margina. "I'm going to need some physician help, too."

"Like I said before, she was in with the patient in room eleven but busted out of here as soon as the baby was delivered. No episiotomy to sew up, so nothing to slow her down. After she had done the congrats, Dr. Hawes practically ran out of the unit, saying something about an errand to run before going to the office."

Margina lowered her voice a bit. "I don't think Taylor was too thrilled about having to work with Dr. Hawes."

Knox knew that most of the nurses tried to avoid working with Hawes, telling him that they really disliked her, finding her often abrasive to them. Dr. Chamblee shared many of these unfavorable sentiments but never professionally agreed with their fussing. After all, Hawes was one of the senior partners in his practice, one of his future partners.

If he had felt more comfortable working side by side with Dr. Hawes, Knox would have been better prepared to ask for her assistance. Besides, any physician would understand the need for help in managing even one of the obstetrical patients presently dumped on him. Knox smiled as he pictured Dr.

Hawes' vivid response to his request to take over one of the unreferred patients: eyebrows and eyelashes lifting as her eyes opened wide with surprise, almost in indignation, chin tilted high.

"Why should I do someone else's work?" she would probably curse under her breath or better yet say audibly while her back stiffened. "What do you think I, I mean we, pay you for?" she might think or declare to him. "Besides, aren't you the one on call anyway, Chamblee? I can't stay over here at the hospital today. Of course not!" Aslyn Hawes would continue for several minutes with this oration, as Knox knew he would sink further into the hospital's slab foundation.

"You know, Dr. Chamblee, that I'm scheduled to be in the office all morning and afternoon, and my patients are too important to be left waiting," he imagined she would loudly object while stomping away, stomping the best she could in expensive stiletto heels.

Risking further annihilation by requesting her aid was not a wise option for Knox. Unfortunately, there were no other alternatives. Marshall Langley had given up OB; Erin was on maternity leave; and Faye was out of town, as was Dr. Gwinn. In any case, he suspected that Aslyn Hawes enjoyed the concept of benefiting financially from the hired help without lifting a finger.

As Margina was beginning to complain vehemently about how certain nurses more often than others were prone to leave her shorthanded by calling in sick, the main hospital supervisor mercifully walked through the mechanical doors into the nursing station. Knox was not certain whether her stern look or gruff authoritative voice was more of an admonishment of Margina's behavior or a reaction to the extensive list of patients on the large chalkboard.

"Look, Marg, settle down. I've been able to reach Lottie Starnes. And she can be here in about thirty minutes."

Hearing but not wanting to believe this solution, Margina ceased her ranting and, despite her ebony complexion, turned almost pale in reaction.

"I know that Lottie is an agency nurse and sometimes hard to get along with, but she is the best I can do. Marg, you and the others will just have to do your best to work with her." For the moment Margina remained speechless.

"Besides, Margina, you're not doing much to promote a comfortable feeling of our young doctor here toward our wonderful hospital," the supervisor declared while pointing her clipboard toward Dr. Chamblee. "Since the other units seem to be fairly quiet, I can stay back here for awhile and assist y'all until Miss Starnes gets here and gets herself oriented to that board. By the way, we're lucky Mr. Rutledge is away. That man would have a hissy if he knew we were violating all that patient privacy," she chuckled as she pointed her finger at the now infamous chalkboard, prominently propped up in the middle of the area.

The prospect of receiving some nursing help seemed to placate and organize Margina, although she did not think Lottie all that dependable. Just as some element of tranquility began to creep over the unit, the double doors at the opposite end of the hall flew open. From the direction of the ambulance drop-off dashed a gurney loaded with a screaming woman and tiny Dr. Ricks kneeling between her legs. Taylor was running alongside carrying a crying infant wrapped in bloody sheets while two EMTs propelled the gurney toward the emergency Cesarean section room.

"Cord prolapse! Second twin, presenting breech. I'm holding up the butt, trying to relieve cord pressure. Ambulance driver delivered Twin A. I met them in the parking lot." Ricks bellowed with great drama to the gawking group standing at the nurses' station. While almost spinning off the gurney as it passed the shocked spectators and rounded the corner of the hall, he demanded, "Call anesthesia, for God's sake!"

The hospital nursing supervisor followed the speeding doctor, mother, and soon-to-be newborn as she shouted orders for anesthesia assistance into the cellular device popped from her belt. "Taylor, hand off the first baby to the nursery and scrub with Dr. Ricks. I'll pass instruments," the supervisor barked further without the need of technology.

Once the commotion had disappeared, Knox reasoned that he

had to move forward with his own dilemmas. Simple arithmetic determined that, as the last hour had unfolded, he had assumed charge of four of the present L & D patients. "Come on, Margina, let's check on each of these ladies," he motioned as she followed him down the hall.

The Labor and Delivery Unit of Montclair's Grace Community Hospital had undergone an extensive renovation two years earlier. That much needed modernization was another factor that had attracted Knox to begin his practice in association with this medical staff. The unit was organized into six patient observation rooms, ten labor and delivery-recovery rooms, and four cesarean delivery or other operative-use rooms. The ten labor and delivery-recovery rooms were more commonly referred to as *LDRs*. It was into one of these LDRs that he and Margina entered first in their patient rounds.

Behind the partition that greeted them were the unmistakable groans and heavy breathing that even a green third-year medical student could equate with a pregnant woman in active labor. "Earlier, I tried to talk Mrs. Peterson here into an epidural that would help her tolerate labor better," Margina whispered to Knox as she shut the door and pulled back the curtain. This exposed Christina Peterson sitting up in her bed in a knee-chest position, panting.

Since admission to the hospital, Christina had been adamant against a Cesarean section as well as an epidural for anesthesia. Various positions had been attempted (many of which had been the patient's idea) to encourage the unborn baby boy's head to descend further into the mother's pelvis. Margina had hoped that this particular position would result in successful rotation of the fetal head and a vaginal delivery.

"Christina, it seems that you are working very hard," Knox interjected between the audible pants coming from the labor bed. "Hi, I'm Dr. Chamblee," he explained as he moved further around the privacy curtain to directly face her bed. Scattered about the woman's room among the flower arrangements, potted plants, and baby clothes, Knox noted several digital cameras, including video, as well as two or three cell phones and pagers. A multi-function Sony device emitted soothing mood music from the built-in cabinet. The other shelves were decorated with expensively framed photos of small children and a dog. The current *Architectural Digest* rested under the latest Grisham novel, lying open on a side table.

"But, but, ugghh, ugghh, where is Dr. Gwinn?" Mrs. Peterson groaned as she looked up at Knox through a Stadol haze, the disappointment obvious on her face. Despite the patient's being in active labor, her makeup and hairstyle were still nearly perfect.

"I'm one of Dr. Gwinn's partners, filling in for him while he is away," he explained, using the word *partners* loosely. The technicalities of the physician business arrangement of the practice were not important at the moment.

"Yes, Doctor, I'm sure that you are quite competent; but, but, I want Dr. Gwinn to deliver my baby," Mrs. Peterson demanded between practiced breathing motions. "That's, that's, what I've paid for. Ah, Ahh, Ahhh, Ahhhh!"

As copious tears began to roll down the patient's face, sinking into her gaping mouth, Margina rolled her own eyes in disbelief. Keeping her facial expression outside of Christina's visual field, the well-seasoned nurse was continually amazed by the antics of what she termed *a histrionic Republican white girl*. At this point of the pregnancy, why would the socialite really care who received the physical honor of delivering the next Peterson baby?

Knox, accustomed to hearing this comment from other patients while taking call and substituting for the other doctors, gave his standard reply. "I'm sure that you would prefer to have Dr. Gwinn attend your delivery; however, he is unavailable. He's out-of-town."

"Yes, but please. We both want Cullen here," Mr. Peterson interrupted, as he stood from the comfortable-appearing position on the couch, his costly shirt and trousers still neatly pressed.

"Sorry, but Dr. Gwinn has left me in charge of his patients. I'm today's on-call physician."

"Yes, but why can't we call Cullen? I'm...huh, huhh, huhhh... so disappointed. Anyway, he was expecting to induce me on Monday." Mrs. Peterson managed to get out between heavy breaths as her pleading husband nodded in agreement.

"Like I said, Dr. Gwinn is out-of-town, in fact, in another state. Actually, he's gone for the whole weekend. I'm sure he regrets not being here in Montclair and normally would have stayed all day and night with you if necessary to get your child safely delivered."

There was no opportunity for rebuttal as the next contraction overwhelmed Christina. Likewise, her sympathetic husband, who was now standing across from Knox on the other side of the labor bed, diverted his attention away from this fill-in doctor and concentrated on the intensity of his wife's pain.

At the conclusion of the forceful uterine contraction, Mrs. Peterson agreed to a vaginal exam by Dr. Chamblee, during which he determined her cervix to be eight centimeters dilated. Before the next contraction the Petersons then embraced and kissed, overjoyed that only two centimeters remained before their planned natural delivery.

Suddenly, the Petersons no longer seemed to be concerned about Dr. Gwinn's whereabouts.

Assuring them that he would be readily available to care for them as necessary, Knox exited the room with Margina, carrying Mrs. Peterson's hospital chart into the hall to scribble a progress note. It became obvious to both Knox and Margina that at this point the Petersons now appeared comfortable with the prospect of his medical management. His being able to give them such reassuring news about her progress had no doubt helped to win their confidence. In fact, as the nurse and doctor left the Petersons' LDR, Christina and her husband quickly decided that this new physician had seemed extremely patient and kind. They believed that they might grow to like and trust him as much as Cullen Gwinn, if not better.

"Now that we've gotten through that, Dr. Chamblee, the really pressing problem patient is in the next labor room," Margina proclaimed as she motioned for Knox to follow her down the fake oak-floored corridor. While Knox felt that the one he had just evaluated had the makings of a quandary, he knew that Margina was probably referring to a medical, not a social problem.

Margina continued her report. "Dr. Stewart admitted this next patient last night directly from ER. As you might imagine, the girl doesn't have a regular doctor here. Her complaint was vague abdominal pain and slight shortness of breath. And, of course, she's pregnant."

Knox completed Peterson's chart note and returned the record to the storage rack, face down, now planning to direct all of his attention to Margina.

"She's Vietnamese and doesn't speak English well, not at all. Neither does the boyfriend. We've been observing her closely because the fetus is premature, but she's not in labor. And imagine this: they didn't even know the poor thing was pregnant until the ER got an abdominal x-ray. The radiology tech was flabbergasted when he developed the film."

"Yeah, I know. He saw a fully formed fetal skeleton. Sure, we had that happen all the time during my residency. Fourteen year-olds trying to hide their pregnancies from their parents. Mom and Dad bring their innocent daughter to the ER, thinking that she has appendicitis. But the worm they should have been worrying about was not an appendix. Anyway, I'm sure they got an ultrasound. What did it show?"

"Thirty-one weeks gestation, normal fluid, surprisingly no growth retardation."

Hoping the story would get simpler but instead meeting disappointment, Knox listened intently to Margina.

"They watched the patient overnight in observation. But Dr. Stewart told the night nurses to have the unreferred OB call doctor - and that's you, lucky you - look at the poor girl again this morning for possible admission. The general surgeon Stewart consulted to see her hasn't shown up yet," Margina sighed. "Oh, and one more thing. The gallbladder sono she ordered also hasn't been done."

Dr. Britton Stewart was considered by the hospital staff to be an extremely conscientious emergency room physician. Knox was sorry that Britton had not asserted her obsessive compulsions by getting the general surgeon and radiologist in last night to evaluate this diagnostic puzzle.

When Knox met Britton at his first hospital staff meeting several months ago, she looked like the archetypal attractive female physician, archetypal in that she did her best not to look too attractive. To that end, while working Stewart fashioned her long, black hair into a ponytail and wore minimal make-up, if any at all. Her sparkling clean blue and white New Balance tennis shoes complemented the remainder of her ER physician uniform, which was a neatly pressed blue scrub suit. On occasion a colorful seasonal pin, such as a pumpkin, Christmas tree, American flag, or Easter Bunny decorated the flap of her top left pocket.

Knox later discovered that Stewart could look much more appealing than her working outfit suggested. The makeover was obvious one evening when he ran into her and a lawyer boyfriend at a restaurant. After meeting her unimpressive dinner partner and while leaving with his take-out, Knox judged that Britton's skimpy, street-clothes could easily earn her an improved boyfriend.

Pulling his mind back to the upcoming patient, Knox directed Margina, "Have the unit secretary call the answering service. Change the general surgery consultation to *urgent*."

As Margina turned and walked back to the nurses' station, Knox picked up the chart from the rack outside the patient's labor room, finding the record purposefully turned over to protect her privacy. "HIPPA, again," Knox remarked under his breath. Glancing over the Vietnamese girl's chart, Knox found that the nineteen year-old's intermittent abdominal pain had originated just below the sternum and was associated with mild shortness of breath. The problems had originally led this unfortunate young woman and her boyfriend to the local hospital in Pershing County; nonetheless, the pain and breathing symptoms were
resolved after a short observation period and without a diagnosis of pregnancy.

Reading on through Stewart's notes, Knox doubted if the patient and her partner spoke good English to the smart ER doctor. "At any rate, Britton probably speaks Vietnamese," he sarcastically said to himself. Stewart detailed that when the pain recurred more acutely than before, the boyfriend rushed the agonizing woman from her job at the nail salon back to the nearby hospital. The Pershing County ER nurses' mixture of antacids, slyly called the *County Cocktail* or CC, did not help her; so the two then sped to the Grace Community Emergency Room.

"I want Zoe to see real doctor — not quack," her partner Phan had pleaded to Stewart upon their arrival to Grace. According to him, the episodic pain was becoming much more severe. "Doc, she say it torture her, make it hard to breathe," he had added. "Please help my Zoe."

Knox was still reviewing the chart and had not yet walked from the hall into Zoe's room when Margina returned from speaking with the physician paging service. "The girls at Answer Quik! promised me that they would re-page the surgeon on call for us. But they think he's tied up with an aortic aneurysm case over at Lutheran."

As Knox began to replace Zoe Nguyen's chart on the door's exterior, the door pulled back abruptly, causing the chart to miss its holder. The binder of the medical record broke when it hit the shiny floor of the hall, spilling the pages into random order. A diminutive, dark-skinned young man rushed out of the room, almost knocking over the startled physician.

"Zoe sicker. Help her! Where is doctor?" he screamed.

Knox darted into the room as Margina followed. They encountered a markedly pale pregnant woman attached to an intravenous line and breathing with only shallow respirations. Margina promptly increased the woman's IV fluid infusion rate while Knox put an activated oxygen facemask on her.

"Can you hear me, Miss Nguyen? Are you hurting more? Tell me where it hurts the most," Knox earnestly questioned her in slow, deliberate English, omitting as much Southern accent as possible. Simultaneously, he checked her carotid arterial pulse.

Weakly, Zoe Nguyen pointed to her swollen abdomen and chest but appeared to be in too much discomfort to speak.

"Dr. Chamblee, her blood pressure is 60 over 30, and her baseline had been running about 100 over 60!" Margina blurted. "I'm going to put her in Trendelenburg," Margina announced as she began to lower the patient's head to a level below her feet by pushing the electric controls on the side of the bed.

While nodding approval to the labor nurse, Knox surveyed the fetal monitor strips. Over the last three minutes, the fetal heart rate pattern had dramatically decreased from a normal range of one hundred thirty-two beats per minute to an ominous forty beats per minute, a universally recognized pattern of fetal distress.

Next, Margina attached a pulse oximeter to the tip of Zoe's forefinger to monitor her blood oxygen saturation. "Her sats are very low, Doctor!" Margina warned. Knox hardly noticed these objective measurements because he was drawn to the patient's dark, cyanotic facial pallor and her suddenly faint, barely palpable pulse. He nodded in agreement to his assistant that his patient was highly unstable.

Knox's mind began to race with the diagnostic possibilities; however, he realized that regardless of the conclusion, the treatment must be the same. He must stabilize Zoe's blood pressure and lung function quickly for the sake of both patients. As he drew on his knowledge of cardiopulmonary resuscitation, he called for a variety of other medications and equipment.

"Go ahead and call a CODE, Margina, and get every spare body you can find to come in here and help us," he said forcibly while suppressing his panic. As he darted away from the nurse and looked back toward the gravid patient, he found Zoe's glassy, fixed stare.

"Dr. Chamblee, she has no blood pressure!" Margina's alarming declaration served only to boost his own adrenaline level. She pushed the nurse call button and instructed the unit secretary to call the "Code Blue" to summon the entire hospital cardiac resuscitation team. Concurrently, Knox was not surprised by the sustained low fetal heart rate he again noted as he rechecked the fetal monitoring pattern on the computer screen by the bed. Based on the mother's dying condition, Chamblee knew that this still viable, unborn baby would not survive in utero much longer. Knox's additional concern was that should the baby survive, its brain and other organs could suffer from oxygen deprivation — consequences ranging from cerebral palsy to renal failure.

The mother was in a morbid state, likely an irreversible one, but at least there was a slim chance the baby could be saved.

Silently, but with immediate method, Knox reassessed the estimates of the baby's gestational age. He weighed the information he had reviewed in the chart notes in comparison to the physical size of Zoe's abdomen. He knew that the baby should be large enough and have sufficient lung maturity with artificial support to survive outside of the womb...if delivered NOW!

"Get me a surgical set-up!" he yelled to Lottie Starnes, the first person to run into the room in response to Margina's distress call. "We're going to do a STAT section!" he announced urgently while trying not to shout anymore. He knew, as did Margina, that this procedure would likely not only be an emergency C-section but also a post-mortem one.

Feeling a pair of terrified eyes staring at him, Knox instinctively turned to his side. Only the wall behind him now supported the extremely weak-appearing boyfriend. "Doctor, what is de madder with my girlfriend?" Phan pleaded.

"I'm not exactly sure, Sir," Knox hurriedly replied, trying not to be abrupt, "but we must deliver your baby immediately if it is going to have a chance, any chance at all."

"But, but, what about my...my Zoe?"

"We are going to try to save your girlfriend also, if we can." Knox knew, as did the increasing numbers of medical personnel now flying into the room transporting various supplies and equipment, that the possibility of successfully resuscitating Zoe Nguyen was dismal. They were, in actuality, going to perform a postmortem Cesarean section, an operation on a dead patient designed to save the as yet unborn one. The scrub techs joining the foray had rushed a major surgical instrument set-up into the labor room. They were quickly preparing for the C-section which would be done just like a routine one, only with much greater speed and without the need of anesthesia.

Staring directly into the dark eyes of Zoe's boyfriend, the doctor summarized, "We must do a C-section right now on your girlfriend to deliver your baby right here in this room. Zoe is unconscious. Unfortunately, her heart is not beating anymore. She will not even know that we are operating on her."

"What? What? What is *operate*?" The boyfriend could barely talk as though he were himself in the process of choking.

The surgical team practically had everything ready for Knox to begin Zoe's procedure.

"She previously signed a piece of paper giving us permission to deliver your baby through her vagina or, if necessary, through a cut in her abdomen by Cesarean section. (Actually, Knox had not seen such a permit. Instead, he only assumed that such a document had been executed according to the hospital's practice standards.) If you understand what I am telling you, I want you to say yes with everyone here watching and listening to us. It is very important that you understand what I am trying to explain to you."

Finishing his verbal informed consent presentation to the man who looked totally oblivious to the proceedings before him, Knox firmly added, "Since you came to our hospital to let us take care of you, we have to proceed with this emergency surgery and delivery now!"

Zoe's companion nodded and weakly responded, "Yes," as he fell against the wall behind him, sliding slowly down to the floor, coming to rest in a faint with his head upright and eyes open. That was the best informed consent that Knox could expect. The orderly, who had also entered the room as the CODE was called, wheeled the unconscious father-to-be away on a stretcher, storing the cargo in an alcove down the hall.

At the same time as counseling the boyfriend, Knox had donned a pair of sterile latex surgical gloves and also prepared mentally to begin the surgical case. Despite all the commotion and excitement in the labor room that was now transformed into a small, makeshift operating suite, he still was able to keep his wits about the dire situation. He could not help thinking that somewhere out there existed a plaintiff's lawyer standing by ready to sue him over this situation regardless of the outcome. Maintaining a practical approach, Knox knew that his job was to manage this emergency the best way he could. And that was what he was going to do.

"Hand me a number eleven!" Knox demanded. Margina then removed the scalpel from the surgical tray, passing it quickly but carefully to Knox. She had managed to splash some disinfecting fluid over the patient's abdomen at the surgical site and likewise put on a pair of gloves. The attendant who had tucked Phan safely away rushed back into the room and activated the procedure lights, which lowered automatically out of the ceiling. The lights did not precisely shine on the surgical area but were better than nothing. Knox had done so many C-sections as a resident that he had always believed he could do one in the dark. As the rest of the resuscitation team crowded into the room, the obstetrical surgeon began the procedure.

Margina did her best to assist Dr. Chamblee surgically without getting her fingers in the way of his rapidly advancing scalpel. She watched in awe as Knox sliced through the layers of the abdominal wall, entering the peritoneal cavity in one decisive stroke. Fortunately, increased adrenaline in a surgeon's body is a powerful chemical accelerant. As everyone in the room understood, a few seconds' delay in delivery could be the difference between healthy survival and tragic death for the baby.

The gravid uterus quickly appeared in the relatively bloodless surgical field. "Dead people don't bleed," Knox thought to himself and wondered if Margina had made the same assessment. Surprisingly, in his precise haste Knox had entered Zoe's abdomen without apparent injury to the intestine, bladder, or any other essential structure.

With his stamina bolstered by a surge of adrenaline, this doctor was able to work faster than expected; each surgical motion was deliberate, effective, and almost automatic. In less than seconds, the following stroke of the scalpel sliced all the way through the uterine muscle, missing the patient's bladder by a few centimeters. Then with his fingers, Chamblee widened the uterine opening, enabling him easily to grasp the baby's head. He was relieved not to find a buttocks, arm, or leg presentation because any of those unstable fetal positions could have added to delivery time. As Knox correctly lifted the infant's head, swiftly bringing it through the uterine incision, he instructed Margina to apply pressure internally directly to the top of Zoe's uterus.

"OK, push, Margina!" His command was needless as she applied a burly thrust almost in reflex that propelled the newborn from the womb.

Rapidly suctioning the dark, greenish-brown amniotic fluid from the baby's oral and pharyngeal cavities with a special device, Knox assumed from Margina's forceful stroke and tense facial muscles that her adrenaline volume was also soaring. Not a surprise to anyone, this slimy amniotic fluid stained with meconium was a result of the baby's bowel movement passed inside the uterine cavity. A response to decreased fetal oxygen supply, the meconium also served as one more mark of the mother's own deteriorated physical condition.

The umbilical cord now clamped and severed, Knox quickly handed the floppy baby to the neonatologist and his nursery team standing by. The obstetrician was relieved to see that the initially motionless child was making attempts at respiration while beginning to move its arms and legs.

"Did anyone notice the baby's sex?" he asked as the neonatologist and his assistants bolted out of the makeshift Cesarean section room, carrying the infant to the resuscitation station across the hall. Lottie Starnes, RN, who had thrown up several times in the corner of the room during the procedure, ran out with them.

"It's a boy!" Margina joyfully answered. "I noticed because his thing almost got in the way of the umbilical cord clamp."

Everyone in the room could sense the relief felt by everyone else that the baby was out and alive. The neonatologist would, they hoped, soon send a reassuring update about the baby's condition. Knox's anticipation that the mother's status might begin to improve after the infant was delivered proved fruitless. Tragically, the efforts of the maternal resuscitation team had been unsuccessful. The brightness of the flat green-colored line on the adult cardiac monitor overhead was a dismal contrast to Zoe's now even darker, cyanotic, and cool skin.

Closing the surgical wound as cosmetically as possible while Margina continued to assist, Knox prepared himself more emotionally than physically to talk with Zoe's partner and any family members who might have arrived. He hoped that some of them might speak better English. Reporting the news of this young woman's death would be gut wrenching, made more difficult by the language barrier.

"Why doesn't medical school curriculum encourage learning even the simplest phrases in foreign languages," he wondered. "It wouldn't detract much from the present curriculum to teach some phrases like: *Open wide! Where does it hurt? What is your name? When was your last period?* " he almost proposed. Knox then began to think about what a time-consuming medical records nightmare this emergency would become. Charting all of these events would not be enjoyable, of course, except for the team's success in saving the baby.

Grace Community Hospital was a relatively small treatment center but was still afflicted by the rigors of a full-service medical facility. Much like its larger counterparts across town, the hospital's practice of medicine was becoming a system of rituals or allowances. For instance, whenever a physician tried to interject a facet of art into the science of medicine, another helpful medical caregiver would suggest referral to a procedural manual, particularly when the medical or surgical events were unusual. Documents termed *critical pathways* had been authored by appointed members of the medical staff and then approved by the board of directors as recipes for treating and managing certain medical diseases or surgical cases. Sometimes these documents were referred to as *protocols*.

Similar manuals had been written to direct the management of certain situations, ranging from firing an undesirable employee to comforting a bereaved family. Some of the more senior doctors resented these manuals, alluding to the use of protocols, critical pathways, or other directives as cookbook medicine. While Knox had a similar opinion of these documents, he found that in tense or stressful patient-care situations it could be much easier to fill out a form or refer to protocols rather than do a lot of second-guessing.

"Dr. Chamblee, will you fill out this maternal death register form? It's required by law, you know," interjected Dorothula Rivers, the helpful L&D unit secretary now on duty. As he walked down the hall from the temporary Cesarean section room, Dorothula handed him the long form printed on the front and back of a yellow sheet of paper as though she had simply torn one out of special, pre-printed tablet.

"Also, Baby, the nursing supervisor wanted me to remind you that we need a social work consult." She lowered her voice to a whisper. "It's required whenever there's a death. But I'm sure that you already know that." Dorothula raised her eyebrows as she hesitated slightly. "I hope that Sibley Paige is taking social work calls today."

Believing that he caught a wink from Dorothula in reference to the social work consult, Knox replied exhaustedly, "I'll fill out the form, Thula, but actually this will probably not be the official death certificate. The coroner completes that." Miss Rivers always tried to be helpful. Knox liked her, as did everyone else at the hospital. She had been extremely kind in referring some patients to him and in consistently showering him with compliments about his method of patient care, no matter how few those patients might be.

"Sure, let's go ahead and put in the consult. Since it's fairly early in the day, the social worker should be able to get out here to help me comfort Zoe's boyfriend and any other family that may have shown up by then." Knox doubted that he would be lucky enough for Sibly Paige to be fluent in Vietnamese.

Although he longed to relax in the doctors' lounge with a Diet Coke and a doughnut, Knox headed for an empty chair at the doctors' workstation to begin the necessary care summary.

However, he was deterred from the dictation after spotting the reviving Phan, lying out of the way on the hall stretcher where he had been monitored by one of the nurse's aides. Walking over to check on him, Knox realized that any guy in the same devastating situation would have difficulty in dealing with a newborn, especially a premature one. Since the neonatologist had reported that the baby should survive neurologically and physically intact, he would be ready for discharge to the family in a few weeks. Knox hoped for Phan's sake that the new father would remain supportive in adjusting to paternal life or at least seek help from someone experienced in childcare.

Standing by the stretcher and feeling Phan's steady pulse, Knox asked him how he was feeling after passing out. As the new father looked worriedly up at him, he answered, "I...OK, tank you." He then asked tearfully, "But, Doc, my...my... Zoe. She make it?" Without giving the sad-looking doctor a chance to reply, he continued, "I know she didn't. But baby did. I know baby did, right?"

There are moments when a physician finds maintaining composure difficult. "Congratulations. You have a baby boy. He is kinda small and a little early, but his doctor tells me that he is going to be OK."

With that reassurance the gentle, teary-eyed man turned his head away. For further consolation Knox left Phan to the nearby nurse and hospital chaplain and returned to the dictation area. He sat there silently for a few moments, then picked up the medical record of his now deceased patient, preparing to dictate. His review of the recorded facts and his soul-searching could find no alternative to the patient management and outcome that had just unfolded. He also felt confident that his medical peers would assume the same. What acute terminal event had caused the catastrophe? A pulmonary embolism, stroke, MI? He was not sure. They would all have to wait for the autopsy, assuming that the family would consent.

"You're in luck, Dr. Chamblee!" Dorothula's proclamation demanded Knox's attention. "Sibley Paige is taking social work consults today." Supporting the attending physician as well as bereaved family members was a trademark of the young, but well trained, Miss Paige.

Although Knox had passed Sibley in the hospital hallways during his brief patient rounds, he had never met her professionally or otherwise. In contrast, he had studied her full-length photo published in one of the hospital's community service brochures. Her facial features and well proportioned athletic but feminine body were striking. No doubt, she had been an easy choice for the Marketing Department. Knox was now looking forward to meeting Sibley Paige, but the introductions would be shadowed by sadness.

"Dr. Chamblee, come back to Peterson's room, quick. Downed heart tones. She's about to precipt, " Taylor Richards almost shouted as she ran up to where Knox was sitting; she looked down at him, puzzled, as though she had interrupted a daydream. After having been freed from the Dr. Ricks nightmare, which somehow produced two healthy identical babies and a surviving mother, Taylor had assumed the nursing care of the Peterson couple. However, with all the excitement surrounding the delivery of the twins and Zoe's tragedy, there had been minimal time left for Christina Peterson. Glancing up at Taylor, Knox tossed aside his paperwork and immediately followed.

"Jesus! It's coming out. It's coming out, now!" Peterson was standing in her bed, nearly naked, screaming and panting simultaneously. Her make-up was smeared and her hair amassed in sweaty ringlets. Quickly she noticed Knox, who was trying not to see the humor in the ambiguity before him. "Oh, well! There you are, Dr. Chamblee. Where in the Hell have you been?"

"Breathe, breathe, breathe, Christina. Get back down in the bed. Let the doctor check you." With forced composure, her horrified husband patted the back of her legs.

"Get your stinking hands off me, you bastard!"

Near the extreme of hyperventilation, Mrs. Peterson began to pant even more rapidly while looking down toward her pelvic area. "Get it out! Get it out! Aughhhhhhhh! Well, damnit, can't you hear me? Get it out! Get it out right now!"

Taylor tried not to appear frantic, especially in front of a man she desired to impress. "Dr. Chamblee, she still has refused an epidural from the anesthesiologist. Said she wanted to go local instead," Taylor whispered to Knox, even though whispering was unnecessary.

"It's comin', help me, please! G--D------, Doctor, can't you hear me? Shit!"

"Sounds like she's going vocal to me," Knox declared under his breath as he reached for a sterile exam glove.

Chapter
3
•••
THE RIDE HOME

"Taking care of that Peterson woman may have been the worst part of both shifts," she said although there was no one standing around to hear. Having returned to the time clock station, she again slid the magnetic strip of her hospital badge through the portal. Nine forty-five p.m. was stamped on the card spit from the adjacent wall-mounted printer. Because the demanding day had consisted of one horrendioma after the other but had now slowed to a snail's pace, Margina agreed to let Taylor leave before the end of her scheduled double shift.

Being single and now self-supporting, Taylor originally accepted the day's extra work because she needed the money to maintain a lifestyle beyond that of a nursing salary. Before she married Chip, she had used her official time off to increase her income through private-duty nursing of invalids or other hospice patients. However, after she married, she stopped moonlighting but had resumed it once divorced.

Leaving the hospital, Taylor Richards began the usually monotonous drive home to the Booker Street section of town. Exhausted, she hoped that a large black coffee from her favorite convenience store would get her home. Before exiting the 24-hour mart, she noticed that the fuel gauge of her Saab registered under a fourth of a tank; so she drove around to fill up at the self-serve island.

After several hot swallows of coffee, Taylor felt revived as she drove away from the gasoline pump and chose the shortest route home. This meant using the new inner city overpass section of the interstate. The relatively steep decline from the top of the overpass made holding to the 50-mph speed limit a challenge, even for her aging vehicle. A construction detour soon forced her from the interstate, throwing Richards into a busy thoroughfare where she was caught by a red light.

Finally moving through the intersection, she returned to the interstate only to find the traffic congested a few miles later, coming to an eventual halt. Taylor sat patiently in her car for a few moments, sipping on the cooling contents of the Styrofoam cup and listening to Delilah spout wisdom and encouragement over the radio. A few of the other people occupying the snarled vehicles began to leave their cars and walk ahead to investigate the delay. The lighting along the massive concrete structure was enough to see the facial features of each snooping person as they passed Taylor's car. Since even January nights in the Deep South can be pleasant enough to venture outdoors, Taylor decided that a walk along the motionless interstate was the evenings only opportunity for a stroll.

Feeling safety in numbers, she exited the security of her car to join the inquisitive crowd, taking her cell phone, keys, and wallet. The expressway was illuminated to a degree that she almost lost the sensation of nighttime. Walking past a couple of chatty, older women who were standing outside by their car, she noticed they were enjoying boiled peanuts and throwing the shells over the railing down onto the underpass. A slightly younger woman hovering near them was swallowing her peanuts unshelled, elephant style.

As Taylor ambled by the three women, she was quickly reminded of an incident shortly after she graduated from nursing school. While working at her first salaried position in an assisted-living facility, she used the Heimlich maneuver to resuscitate a physician on rounds who was also eating whole peanuts.

Unavoidably, Taylor's attention was drawn toward the flashing lights coming from two squad cars up ahead. As she approached the throng of prying onlookers, it appeared as though the revolving blue streams emitted by the investigating vehicles had hypnotized everyone. The police cars were blocking an enormous gaping hole in the twisted metal side railing that once neatly protected this sharpest curve of Interstate 79.

"Most cars would have caught fire. Flipping through a railing this high up and hitting that stone retainer wall over there," remarked the man standing closest to the distorted barrier. As he stood with seeming authority in the middle of a pile of glass shards and scraps of painted metal, he spoke to no one in particular. The captivated onlookers listened to him as though his grease-stained mechanic's uniform led credence to his statements.

"Yep. Saw it happen; sure did," he added, while waving his arms enthusiastically toward the mangled car now lying below them. The official police report would later detail that the out-of-control, speeding convertible tore through the railing as it flipped backwards, impacting the old brick and stone wall sixty feet below.

"I seen the convertible's bumper hit the wall first. Then the car flipped over backwards, crushing that guy's head," declared the self-appointed tour guide as he pointed to the victim being extracted from the wreckage. "The windshield smacked first into the riverbank. Then that sucker flipped again! Stuck right side up in that soft mush. Looks like just a pile of twisted painted metal, don't it?" he inquired morbidly, scanning the crowd as though expecting an answer from a class of students.

Receiving no response except for a few stares, the lecturer continued. "I just don't understand it. That thang was travelin' so fast it should've blowed up, like in a fireball, or bounced into the river itself!"

He then turned to Taylor, who was standing immediately behind him, as though to single her out for agreement. She quickly glanced away without a response but sensed his disappointment that no inferno had already erupted from the already gruesome spectacle. Not receiving the expected response from the pretty blonde behind him, the master of ceremonies moved on to detail individually the others in his audience.

Taylor then looked down off the overpass, noting that the ambulance had been able to reach the crash site by using the boat-launching ramp access road. She remembered that while in nursing school she and Chip used to launch his father's aluminum johnboat at that ramp. They would then troll downstream, following the slow river current to fish near the old highway bridge.

The paramedics maneuvered a gurney through the tall weeds, scrub brush, and trashed appliances to reach the victim. Directing her attention to the rescue effort, Taylor watched as a white sheet was being placed over the nearly decapitated body. As the victim was pushed into the rear of the ambulance, Taylor had a hollow, powerless feeling about the tragedy and felt no solace even in the fact that the deceased was unknown to her.

"Makes my guts churn, just lookin' at this," commented the peanut-swallowing woman, who had walked up to stand aside Taylor. "Honey, you look like a nurse. At least, you're dressed like one," she added as she curiously surveyed Taylor's uniform and hospital identification badge. Talking through peanut shell shards stuck between her front teeth, she inquired, "Does this kind of gory stuff get to you, too? Like make you wanna puke?"

Taylor ignored her.

After experiencing all of this commotion and tragedy unexpectedly on a simple drive home, Taylor felt even more exhausted now than when she left the grind at work. Suddenly she was ashamed of staring at the bloody scene below as though she were merely a gore monger, no better than any of the other common people standing around gawking. Her guilty

thoughts were abruptly interrupted when a motorcycle
cop brushed by to unclog the traffic congestion and disperse
the crowd.

Sprinting back to her car, Taylor quickly unlocked the
driver's door and practically jumped back into her seat. Once
locked in, she fastened the seat belt, started the engine, and
tried to remain patient as the line of vehicles began to creep
ahead. Gruesome human curiosity directed most of the other
drivers to slow for one last look while passing the actual
accident scene. Surely, she hoped, the rest of her late drive
home would be smooth and uninterrupted.

Proceeding as though it were on autopilot, the Saab took exit
24 off the interstate onto the frontage road; then right onto
River Road; three miles to Booker Street; eighth house at the
bottom of the hill. Shortly after pulling into her driveway,
Taylor stopped to pick up the newspaper. It had not been there
when she left for work that morning. Sleep deprived, Taylor
carelessly tossed the daily across to the front passenger side.
The black tire depression marking one side of the folded front
page went unnoticed.

"I can't believe I forgot to close that damn door again!" she
cursed as she pulled into the garage, which was attached to the
main frame of her 1940s Tudor-style home. Thinking back
about how she had left for work that day in her usual mad rush,
she remembered her mother's often ignored advice. "They
don't pay you enough at that hospital for you
to break your neck."

After lowering the noisy garage door by remote control,
Taylor felt secure. It was uncommon for houses in that
neighborhood to have garage doors, much less automatic
electric ones like hers. Chip had ordered it over the Internet,
then installed it himself as an anniversary present. When
the division of property granted Chip no rights to their house,
he sarcastically requested ownership of at least the garage door
and the windshield visor remote. The judge
who handled the divorce proceedings took great pleasure in
turning down the request.

Rummaging through her purse, Taylor thought back on the highlights of their fairly brief, somewhat notorious marriage. "That bastard!" she uttered, as she found the house keys under some Kleenex. Her mother often used the same descriptor for Chip Richards.

Taylor held the keys in her right hand as she left the car, a self-defense tactic taught by the security department to all of the hospital employees. She also grasped her white nurse's jacket and purse along with the newspaper as she shut the door to the Saab. Fumbling with the tired, nearly stuck deadbolt lock, she eventually entered her kitchen through the laundry room. A knock at the front door startled Taylor, and at first she decided to ignore it. When the noise persisted, Taylor assumed someone's drunken date had stumbled onto the wrong house. Annoyed and physically drained, Nurse Richards firmly told the whoever-it-was to get lost.

By the time Taylor finally reached her bedroom, she had stripped down to her bra and panties. Dropping her things on the bed, she noticed that her newspaper was marred with tire marks. Having seen the teenage delivery boy use her driveway as a turnaround, she determined that he was the culprit.

"If I can only stay awake long enough to run the bath water," she moaned while removing the rest of her clothes.

At the end of the hall leading from Taylor's kitchen was the single, over-sized bathroom. It was enlarged as part of a mid-1980s renovation that included engulfing part of an adjacent unused sewing room. The strangely shaped bathroom now had three entrances, one of which was from her bedroom. While stuffing the rubber stopper into the bathtub drain and turning the water nozzles, Taylor wondered again why the previous owner had not replaced the ancient bathtub with a Jacuzzi. Pulsating jets of hot water would have been particularly soothing after the grueling work schedule of the last two days. Instead she would have to settle tonight for the respite of several scented candles that she retrieved from a cabinet, placed along the front rim of the tub, and lit carefully.

While Chip lived with her, he normally was at home by the time she returned from work, except for an occasional boys' night out. Those night-out occasions became more and more frequent as their marriage unraveled. In the thrilling infancy of their living together, Chip would wait up for Taylor even after one of her crazy late-hour nursing shifts. He would also treat her to a light breakfast when she had to be dressed for work early the next morning. Thinking back about that once cherished but now dissolved relationship, Taylor began to sense her ex-husband's caresses as she returned nude into the warming bathroom. Despite her desire for his touches at the end of this tiring, stressful day, Taylor forced herself to remember that Chip had found other comfort in girlfriends, poker games, and nightclubs.

Since the tub was still filling, Taylor removed the terry cloth robe from the door hook and slipped it over her thin, but well-proportioned body. Pulling a stool over to the tub, she poured vanilla-scented bath gel under the faucet and soaked her swollen feet in the slowly rising, steamy bathwater. Reliving her taxing day at work only served to scramble her worries over personal problems. Certainly, coming across that fatal motor vehicle accident on the way home had not helped to clear her mind. She now wished even more for another chance to lose herself in one of Chip's hot, penetrating neck massages.

"Chip is gone," she blurted out, her voice hollow in the roomy bathroom with its high ceilings and wood plank floors. "I don't have him anymore and don't need him!" she added with emphasis while holding herself in her own arms. Her voice could not reassure her or erase the loneliness she suddenly felt. During this and other empty moments, she wished for that ultimate physical pleasure and sensual novelty which had been her first attraction to her former husband.

Shortly after the separation and ensuing divorce, all traces of Chip Richards were quickly erased from the house except for a few wedding gifts from his family, who had insisted Taylor keep them. Her salvation through the whole mess had been the exposure of Chip's drug dealings and subsequent arrest. Almost everyone who knew the couple sided with Taylor, believing that Chip's incarceration was too short. After being rescued from the correctional facility by his attorney father, her ex-husband promptly moved to Birmingham with a leftover Ole Miss girlfriend. Taylor had recently heard that the girl was now pregnant.

Despite becoming more and more demanding, Taylor knew that her nursing career had been her salvation, a definite diversion from marital troubles. As she slipped out of the thick white covering, letting it fall limp to the damp floor, her thoughts drifted back to the day's work ordeal. Not only did she begin to sort through the day's challenging patients, but Taylor also mulled over the small conference she and some of the other nurses had attended earlier. As someone from administration hinted at possible business deals between the hospital owners, medical insurance companies, and doctors, Taylor saw increasing signs of personalized healthcare deterioration. The prospect of losing the professional intimacy once cherished by her field depressed Taylor. She viewed these changes as a trickle down effect from physicians' legal and financial tribulations.

Slipping her smooth body into the rising hot water, Taylor remembered what the assistant hospital administrator had announced in trying to end speculation about the future of medical care. Most of the department heads and other nurses at the meeting felt, as did Taylor, that this directive was just a hint of trouble ahead: "We're going to have to become more productive. Utilize our hospital staff better. And optimize patient care." It became obvious to every meeting attendee that individual nursing loads were going to become heavier, sustaining profits for the hospital.

While Taylor realized that this new policy meant nursing layoffs, she felt secure in her own employment but was concerned about the nurses who had no longevity. She attempted to fight back negative thoughts, relying on the warmth and relaxation that engulfed her. Despite her immersion in the fragrant, nearly filled tub, she lost the struggle. The hot, soothing aroma of the bath gel could not distract her from the more personal unpleasantness which began to whirl around in her head. As she leaned back to let the tub rim massage her tense neck, Taylor reflected on the final miserable days spent with her ex-husband. Within the cloud of steam rising from the water's surface, Taylor could envision his handsomely chiseled but insincere features. Laughing aloud, she compared the marked difference in the success and failure of her professional and marital careers.

Fortunately, the divorce decree had granted Taylor the house and the meager equity attached to it. Having become infatuated with the quaint cottage right after a realtor located it, she had easily convinced Chip that they really needed no more space than that of the two-bedroom, one-bath dwelling. Chip was in agreement that the extra bedroom would serve well as a future nursery. Still working together as a team to decorate the home, Taylor and her mom had become consumed with the never-ending project.

Located centrally at the end of the main hall, the bathroom was situated between the two bedrooms. This arrangement allowed persons in either room to have access to the toilet directly without first having to pass through the hall. The second bedroom, which was located toward the rear of her house, had not been used for guests and had never materialized into that nursery. Having been transformed into a study or project area, the extra bedroom had become almost an extension of Taylor's bedroom. The treadmill she received as her last birthday present from her parents stood out of the way, covered in dust.

Lying in the tub soaking, Taylor gazed around the oversized bathroom, which she and Chip had agreed was an attractive feature of the house. The walls now needed painting, she decided, or maybe a trendy wallpaper. She realized that the thirty year-old bathroom fixtures could be updated as well.

A soothing sauna was created in this usually drafty room by keeping the three bathroom doors closed. Her ex-husband had seemed to enjoy this same satisfying experience here, especially when they were in the tub together. As she washed her thick, blonde hair and rinsed out the shampoo under the faucet,

Taylor returned to the intoxication of their early relationship. Concentrating on that closeness, she reached blindly for the bottle of conditioner and missed the whiff of cooler air coming from behind.

Chapter

4

• • •

THE EARLY WEEKEND

"Cullen, why didn't you swap last night's call with somebody? Or cancel this trip?" queried his wife after he hit the snooze alarm for the third time. "One more push, and we'll be late for the airport limo."

"Mad, there was no way out of last night's call. Everybody except Chamblee and Hawes was out-of-town for a long weekend or on leave from the practice. Anyway, that poor young guy's already got to take calls today and tonight, and I suspect that he'll be busy since it's Friday. I couldn't have asked him to do two in a row."

"What about Elizabeth? Why couldn't she take the call?"

"No, no, I really didn't want to ask Elizabeth. Incidentally, the woman has decided to go by *Aslyn* for some unknown reason. She and I haven't been seeing eye-to-eye about some business issues lately, you might say. So I didn't want to ask her for a favor at all, by either name, and there was just no way to cancel out of this trip. Too much of an obligation."

"Well, I have been looking forward to going to Point Clear," Madelyn confessed.

Joining the others on the Citation that morning was a customary extravagance for the host company but a novelty for Cullen and Madelyn Gwinn. Accepting the invitation to jet down rather than drive to Point Clear, Alabama, fit Cullen's desire to minimize non-productive time away from his medical practice. At any rate, after last night's tumultuous physician call, he would not have been in any shape to drive.

Without even asking about the travel arrangements, Madelyn had quickly accepted the invitation to accompany her husband on this short medical-business meeting. She did not want to miss a moment of much needed time away with him, even if only for several days. Generally, these shorter trips were more relaxing to her than longer excursions abroad or within the States, and she was certain that her husband of twenty-two years felt the same.

There were other reasons Madelyn did not want to miss this chance to get away. Serving for the past twelve months as president of the Montclair Humanitarian Alliance, she had faced an exhausting challenge. By tolerating mountains of stress, she had maintained the Alliance as a major benefactor to local charities. However, her method of stress management was to eat her way though organizing various raffles, auctions, and merchandise shows. Mrs. Gwinn had completed her term greatly satisfied with presidential accomplishments but also unpleasantly plump. However, her dear husband had helped her out of that predicament.

During the recent weeks, the culmination of her charity work had literally become a headache as the almost blinding pain began without warning. Relaxing to let the headaches pass was not an option for Madelyn since long, late pro bono hours were needed to complete the volumes of paperwork necessary for her successor. The president-elect, Tricia Pennington, was due various activity summaries, financial reports, and *this would work better next time if we would just* ... documents. Attributing the headaches to tension, fatigue, and a certain degree of worry that Pennington was going to fall flat on her face, Madelyn swallowed Advil like candy to keep the pain tolerable.

Despite the strain of the last twelve months, Madelyn Gwinn had found great satisfaction serving as the head of what she and many others considered to be an important contribution to the community. Becoming Alliance president was a position that many socially astute women in the Montclair strove to attain, but, of course, most never reached. Speculation by the envious was that Mrs. Cullen Gwinn had bypassed some of the lowly committee work required of previous Alliance presidents, all because of her husband's reputation.

Flying over Hattiesburg, Madelyn promised herself that during this getaway she would toss her worries over charitable organizations, putting the pettiness aside. From her standpoint this excursion was a perk for a long-suffering physician's wife whose husband was to make good on his own pledge. He had agreed to devote time to her wishes and not spend the entire short vacation in medical meetings. Simply hearing that she and Cullen would be flying all-expenses-paid to the Grand Hotel with some hospital-executive types was not in itself attractive to Madelyn. After all, Dr. and Mrs. Gwinn could splurge for a similar trip but maybe without the private plane. However, Cullen had insisted that they accept the free flight to Point Clear and then book a rental car for Madelyn's shopping excursion to the quaint boutiques in nearby Fairhope, Alabama.

Of the three suited gentlemen who greeted them at the airport hangar in Montclair, the only name with which Madelyn was familiar was *Jay Rutledge*. As Cullen reintroduced her to him, she remarked without jest, "Oh, yes, you're the administrator of Cullen's hospital." Making a mental note of the names of the other two men, she categorized them as non-southern business types, somewhat overbearing.

Delighted to find no other female companions flying with them, Mrs. Gwinn planned to arrange her own uninterrupted agenda. She would not miss feeling obligated to go to lunch with other wives while the men were busy. Madelyn loathed to go shopping with other women who did not necessarily have her same tastes in clothes or home decorating.

The highly-paid pilot managed a smooth flight to Point Clear, terminating with an uneventful landing at the regional airport. Next, the party was transferred by Expedition limousine to the Grand Hotel, approximately forty miles away. The charming, antiqued appearance of the hotel's central structure had been maintained despite a new owner's major overhaul of the property. The expansion also included the remodeling of other oceanfront rooms as well as the removal of some adjacent, dated cottages. Much to Madelyn's disappointment, the accommodations provided by the meeting's organizers consisted of the attached ocean front rooms, not the original historic section of the hotel with its ambiance of antiques, leather chairs, and live music.

While checking in at the front desk of the elaborate yet comfortable lobby, Cullen tried to moderate her displeasure over the accommodations, whispering, "Darling, they've put us up in some rooms nearer to a meeting area. That'll probably save some time. If we can get the business over quicker, then there'll be more time for the golf course, sailboats, the beach, shopping, and stuff," he reasoned with her fairly successfully. "I just hope that this great weather holds up while we're here," her husband added, referring to the often-unpredictable winter of the South.

Nodding indifferently to his explanations, Madelyn looked around, noticing beyond the lobby the formal dining room of the hotel. She remembered that adjacent to the main seating area would be the dance floor where she had once done a salsa with a famous journalist. "After we unpack and change, we're to meet Rutledge and those Global Healthcare guys for cocktails before dinner." Madelyn wished again that they would be gathering in the ambiance of the main building itself complete with antiques, leather chairs, and live music. "They told me that we would then walk over to the hotel dining room for dinner."

"Cullen, let's don't stay out late. I'm extremely exhausted. You've been so very busy lately that you must be tired, too."

"Jay assured me that tonight's dinner should be relaxing business discussions kept to a minimum."

Slightly later while they were dressing for the evening, Cullen resumed his attempts to pacify her, "I really don't want you to be bored by all the weekend's proceedings. I assumed that the others were also bringing along spouses or girlfriends," Cullen explained as he zipped up the back of her Escada cocktail dress, which coordinated well with the Chanel bag she was planning to use.

"I'll just have a couple of quick gin-and-tonics as soon as we join them," Madelyn responded in a joking manner although she knew full well that G&T's had gotten her through many a dull or nasty power point dinner presentation. Fastening a diamond and pearl bracelet on her left forearm while Cullen straightened his tie, she reminded him, "And there was that dinner talk in New York. Some Canadian doctor with a lot of nasal hairs showed pictures of tumors coming out of vaginas. Didn't set well at all with the tiramisu."

In contrast to this aversion to medical seminars, Madelyn had recently enjoyed a few info-talk presentations by some of her husband's psychiatrist friends. Silently, she played a matching game of association of her friends and acquaintances to the crazy diseases the psychiatrists described. During one recent meeting in Montclair, she burst into embarrassed laughter when one doctor pegged her late mother.

Soon afterwards in private, Cullen wryly remarked to her, "Madelyn, your comical outburst during that doctor's talk. That's probably one of the reasons some of the drug companies don't invite physicians' spouses anymore to those dinner lectures!"

Returning her thoughts to inclusion in this evening's dinner, Madelyn was glad to be here with her busy husband. "I'll be fine, Honey. I may even excuse myself from the table early, before dessert, so that you all can discuss whatever it is you need to talk about. I can just come back to the room, get in the whirlpool, and relax. Like to get up kind of early in the morning. Exercise. Walk along the boardwalk. Hope tomorrow's meetings won't keep you from joining me."

Cullen hated to disappoint her. "Unfortunately, our 7:00 tee-off will knock me out of the morning walk. We should be finished with eighteen by around one. Let's meet at the golf course restaurant for lunch and decide then about what to do for the rest of the day."

Madelyn knew that she really could not object to those plans. She had even encouraged Cullen several years ago to pursue a better golf game. "After all, that's what men usually do on these sorts of trips, don't they?" she thought to herself.

"That'll work out fine," she responded. "While you're playing golf, I might get a massage and pedicure after I walk. My feet will probably be hurting by that time." Thinking that the hospital company was likely picking up all the extra expenses, she added, "I may also get a manicure."

Cullen then kissed his wife, marring her fresh lipstick, much to her half-jokingly displeasure. "You're really being understanding about this. Why don't you take advantage of the hotel's sauna and workout facility while I'm gone? Just charge everything to the room."

"I planned to!" she interjected.

"This is really an important weekend for us," he semi-whispered into her ear as he kissed her neck from behind and put his hands on her waist. "It could affect the status and profitability of the hospital. You know that I...we...have a large financial stake in the continued success of Grace." Cullen moved his hands up to cup her breasts. "There's a great deal of financial and other kinds of restructuring going on these days in the medical industry. Some for profit, some to ward off lawsuits. Of course, we don't want to be left out because I'd like to retire some day. And these people from Global might help me get there quicker." He summarized while squeezing Madelyn's bosom slightly, "We're lucky because they don't often show interest in buying medical facilities in the South."

Madelyn wanted to believe that Cullen would cut back his workload and have more civilized hours. However, each time she broached the subject of his retiring at least the obstetrical part of his practice, he retorted with, "As long as they're still having 'em and think I'm young enough to deliver 'em, I'm going to keep doing it!"

"These guys from Global may be exactly the company we need to rescue the hospital from its miserable financial shape," Cullen summarized as though his statement was the conclusion of a major mental exercise.

Suddenly Madelyn regretted that she and her husband were now involved in another discussion of hospital business. An aura of tension arose from him, replacing his relaxed touch. "You've heard me cuss and complain about that son-of-a-bitch ex-administrator we had," Cullen continued. "Don't know why it took us that long to dump him! It's hard to fire an employee these days without being sued. The hospital board was fortunate. Finally, he gave us a concrete excuse to fire him. Stealing narcotics from the pharmacy will do it every time."

Madelyn remembered when the hospital announced the hiring of the replacement administrator. Surprised, she later read newspaper accounts praising the previous one. In fact, her chairman-of-the-hospital-board husband was quoted specifically extolling the attributes of the narcotic thief. Cullen credited the man with leading Grace Community Hospital through many years of physical growth in expanding medical services, thereby benefiting even the entire state. After reading the impressive front-page business section article about the outstanding, hard working, well educated, but secretly drug-addicted administrator, she wondered why the hospital board had not thrown itself in front of his moving vehicle as he left.

Touching up her lipstick, Madelyn admired the end result in the mirror. Cullen complimented her hair and expensive-looking ensemble but gently insisted, "We really need to head over to the restaurant. Our cocktail get-together is probably already over." With a greater urgency, "The sit down dinner is such a small group. I don't wanna be late."

Cut short by the loud ringing of the landline, Cullen answered by pushing the speakerphone control. It was Rutledge, the present hospital administrator. "Cullen, the three of us are going to go ahead and walk on over to the cocktail lounge. We'll wait for you and Mrs. Gwinn before they seat us in the restaurant," he explained. "Please take your time. There's no hurry." Cullen had begun to note a difference in demeanor between Rutledge and his predecessor, both in professional and personal aspects. Rutledge seemed to be more social, particularly in his involvement with the physician medical staff.

The cocktail lounge was located off a corridor leading from the original part of the historic hotel. Since the early January weather had remained pleasant, Madelyn and Cullen enjoyed a comfortable stroll as they left their room and moved through the dense gardens toward the central part of the resort. Slowly following the stone walk along the lagoon relaxed them both, and Madelyn began to wish again for dinnertime alone with her husband.

"If only he did not have to meet with those guys, and we could be by ourselves," Madelyn thought. But after their discussion while dressing, the real business reason for this trip had been reinforced. Naturally, she would again play along, being a talkative, engaging doctor's wife as she had done many times before. She and her husband would eventually have private time; she would make sure of it. Cullen could always be a lot of fun when he relaxed and let go.

"Mrs. Gwinn, you look lovely." Mitch Piazza, the president of Global Healthcare, welcomed Madelyn and Cullen to the cocktail lounge that overlooked the lighted croquet court. "Belinda regretted that she couldn't come with me. She's back in Cincinnati in charge of the stage scenery for our son's school musical. He has the starring role, you know. Not sure where he got his great singing voice!"

"I'm sure you and your wife are very proud of him." Madelyn responded almost automatically as she moved slightly away to circulate around the room.

Piazza gently pulled her back by the left arm. "Perhaps Bee can join me on another trip down here since she hasn't visited the South. You're certain to like her; and she, you. You guys would find many things in common."

While Madelyn forced a continued smile at Piazza, she was certain she would find no fascination in carting a woman from

Cincinnati around Montclair or anywhere else for that matter. "Oh, that would be nice. I'm sure my husband will let me know if she comes," Madelyn's reply forced sincerity. The man still holding her left arm with a slight squeeze above the elbow apparently had started his cocktail hour long before the others. While his breath and mannerisms bordered on intoxication, this persona easily blended with the gold chain circling his neck and the thinner one wrapped round his left wrist, where most men would sport a watch.

Mr. Piazza's visible jewelry ensemble was completed by a heavy gold wedding band, supporting at least a karat and a half diamond embedded in its center. Madelyn assumed that he was wearing a thong under his flat front polyester blend trousers — if he had any underwear on at all -- that probably matched his double-breasted coat. As she tried to nod in agreement while gently moving away from this zealot, she was yet more confident that she and Bee had dissimilar tastes.

Remembering that he was the president of Global Healthcare, Madelyn decided to redirect the conversation along that venue. "Naturally, Mr. Piazza," she added as she finally broke clear of his grasp, "you would think that I run around all day giving 'Ole South' tours since my husband spends a great deal of time away from me at his office and hospital. But I'm working on him. He needs to stay at home with me more often."

"Well, I'm sure he does want to stay home with such a gorgeous woman," he reached out to try to retake Madelyn's arm; but she turned slightly, and Piazza missed.

Leaning forward and whispering emphatically almost in his ear, she suggested, "Perhaps you all can make some fantastic business arrangement with Cullen during this meeting. Come up with some really nice deal that will make him tons and tons and tons of money. Maybe then he can cut back on his hours."

"Why, yes," Mitch Piazza responded, uncertain of Madelyn's sincerity about entertaining his wife or being interested in any of the hospital business dealings. Abruptly, he seemed to acquire a degree of sobriety. "Your husband has almost single-handedly built Grace Community Hospital and its reputation. That's why we have wanted to get to know him and you better. Of course, your husband is highly respected in the medical community even outside the reaches of Montclair. I must say, however, that if you typically dress at home like you are tonight, you should have no trouble keeping him there with you."

Seeming to ignore Piazza's last innuendo, Madelyn took a sip of her drink, wet her lips with it, and then swallowed slowly. "As you might imagine, Cullen leaves for the hospital before 6:30 or 7:00 o'clock every day, Monday though Friday, and then has a meeting, delivery, emergency surgery, or a hospital call nearly every night. That steady pace consistently puts him home late."

As Cullen auspiciously walked over from the bar as though to rescue her, she rolled on slyly, "I do hope to have him to myself a little while we're down here this weekend, Mr., ah, Piazza," Madelyn affectionately squeezed her husband's waist with her free arm and kissed his cheek firmly as he approached carting two fresh Tanquerays and tonic. Although Cullen clearly understood that most men near his age, or even younger, envied him for having such a well-preserved wife, he had never known her to display such a public show of affection.

"I'm not sure that you've gotten to know our corporate medical director, Dr. Blake Shaffer," Mitch Piazza suggested as he escorted Madelyn across the room while Cullen followed. "I know that the jet and limo rides were really rushed." Tall and slightly gray-haired, Shaffer was standing near a couch, engrossed with an attractive female server.

"Dr. Shaffer has been with Global Healthcare for three years since retiring from his orthopedic surgery practice in Wisconsin," Piazza explained. "He keeps us abreast of current medical trends and issues. This has helped Global continue to expand its service area and become the third largest healthcare organization in the world." With a certain degree of pride he stiffened as he announced, "We now own or manage more hospitals and medical clinics than I can list without checking my palm pilot!"

Appearing to be in his early sixties, Blake Shaffer, MD, still held the physique expected of an orthopedic surgeon: tall stature, determined facial features, wide shoulders, strong-looking hands. Madelyn thought him almost statuesque except that his posture was a bit stooped, and those hands of strength displayed a faint tremor. His ruddy complexion and prominent facial veins along with the slightly protruding belly were not simply the effects of aging but soft, good living. Piazza motioned for Dr. Shaffer to join them, which he did after the server in the mini-skirt handed him his second scotch and water refill.

"Yes, Mitch, I have wanted to meet Mrs. Gwinn officially. A lovely lady always brightens one of these events."

"Mrs. Cullen Gwinn, this is Dr. Blake Shaffer," Mitch Piazza offered formally. "Blake, weren't we delighted that Mrs. Gwinn — or can we call you *Madelyn* — could accompany Dr. Gwinn to Point Clear?"

To foster the impression of a genteel, well-bred Southern gal, she just smiled and nodded her permission. "My husband doesn't always bring me along on medical trips. Incidentally, do you have a family, Dr. Shaffer?" Madelyn Gwinn possessed a talent for small talk, even though forced. The art was acquired while attending a multitude of Humanitarian Alliance luncheons and country club
bridge tournaments.

"My wife and I divorced three years ago, shortly after I joined Global as their medical advisor. We had one son," he replied.

Deciding not to pursue the apparent sensitive family issue, Madelyn was swiftly rescued as Cullen made efforts to break into the conversation. However, before she could slip away, Piazza chided, "Dr. Gwinn, your lovely wife tells me that your busy workload back in Montclair often leaves her home alone."

"Yes, I'm afraid she's right. Guilty as charged. But even though we don't have any children ourselves to keep her occupied, Madelyn stays extremely busy. In fact she was recently president of her woman's club." Cullen always referred to the Alliance as a woman's club, semantics that often annoyed his wife. "She seems to find her community activities and charity events rewarding, devoting countless hours and quanta of energy to make those functions a success," Dr. Gwinn seemed to brag.

"Cullen, please!" Madelyn interjected. "You make me sound like a martyr."

"Often I can't get her to leave town because of a community fund-raiser like a 'Friends of the Something or Other Banquet,' " he detailed with slight sarcasm while smiling over to his wife. "She just completed her year as president of the women's club, then turned around and signed on to be some sort of permanent advisor," Cullen added, but failed to explain that Madelyn had accepted that follow-up position to spite her critics. "Needless to say, the service jobs don't pay the light bill, and donation of time to charity doesn't help a guy on his income taxes!" he joked.

"Cullen's exaggerating, gentlemen. My husband has always been supportive of my community activities. In the beginning he found that my charity work even made him appear civic-minded. Ask him about the time the Soup Shelter tapped him as 'Doc of the Month'." For a while the homeless had their own personal physician," she chided while planting a dry kiss on Cullen's now flushed cheek.

Piazza secretly darted his eyes toward Shaffer as though to say, "Typical," in reference to Madelyn and her mannerisms as she successfully broke away from the group.

Taking a view different from his associate that Mrs. Gwinn's comments were not simply idle chatter, Shaffer clarified the issue. "Back in the old days, donation of your professional time to charitable organizations and the like was a precursor to medical marketing, but nobody called it that. My old orthopedics group would give free physicals to local high school athletes and serve as the team doctor on a rotating basis. People saw us out helping the town and its kids for free. Brought in loads of new patients, relatives of the athletes or teachers or just game spectators. Sadly, these days goodwill just doesn't pay off anymore. The HMOs and our 'friends' the

PPOs direct the patients to wherever they want them to go."

"And then there's the liability issue of the medical care," Cullen added.

Madelyn glanced back at the conversing men as she moved through the expansive mahogany arches to the outside porch and patio area. She noticed that tall outdoor heaters, resembling immense mushrooms, stood waiting in case the weather turned cooler. Having found that discussion tiring, she began to wish for more idle cocktail chatter. "Poor Cullen," she said to herself, "I hope he finds all that B.S. interesting."

Dr. Shaffer continued with his shrinking but captive audience, "As you know, the Health Maintenance Organizations and Preferred Provider Organizations promote the physicians and hospitals included in their medical plans as the highest quality healthcare available. Dr. Gwinn, they develop these medical care provider packages for businesses purely as cost saving measures. While the businesses want to believe that they are granting their employees the highest quality medical care available, they want it to be cheap, cheap, cheap, you know, at a dramatic discount. These HMOs and PPOs are forcing medical care providers such as our hospitals and doctors like you, Cullen, to cut their fees unrealistically. However, these savings are not always passed along to the lives they cover."

"All of us lowly MDs out in private practice understand all of that. We're all working harder, making less," Cullen remarked. "You, of course, would not have a job if all of this managed care stuff had not developed. In fact, I don't think that Global Healthcare itself would exist if the medical economic system had kept control of itself and all the outside factors influencing it, legal and otherwise."

Blake Shaffer expounded further, "The reason I initially associated myself with Global was that I recognized this prospect for physicians and hospitals to retake the reins of medical care. We need to keep the feds and liberal democrats out of it. Naturally, free healthcare for all can be a no-lose campaign promise."

"Of course, and who's going to pay for it?" Piazza chimed in rhetorically while sounding almost indignant.

"We all are," Shaffer responded. "The momentum for increasing responsibilities and decreasing reimbursements for physicians and hospitals won't slow until the U.S. government suddenly finds itself the manager of the entire healthcare system."

Piazza added, "After all, look at what a mess the government has made of the Medicare and Medicaid systems, not to mention the flu vaccine shortage."

"But big business itself has stepped in where the feds have left off, making healthcare even more cumbersome for patients. Treatment obstacles for physicians and hospitals get worse daily," Shaffer explained as Cullen glanced down at his drink and twirled the ice cubes.

"Actually, most of my peers see your organization as one of those big businesses." Cullen looked directly at Dr. Shaffer, almost interrupting the surprised medical director. "They have been reluctant to release control of the management of their medical and surgical practices to anyone ...or anything, for that matter."

"Cullen, we at Global believe that our unique company has a better formula for physicians, hospitals, and management organizations to work together financially, as well as legally. Over the weekend, we want to share with you the impressive specifics and progress toward mutual improvement of quality healthcare. This, we believe, will result in higher profits." Raising his scotch as though to toast, "Much higher profits for everybody."

The retired orthopedist turned to the waiter who had come to summon the group to their table. "But let us enjoy the rest of our evening with a fabulous dinner. Save the particulars of our business proposal for the golf course tomorrow."

Dr. Shaffer had already instructed their server to bring him the check. The platinum card in the name of Global Healthcare, Inc., satisfied the almost $4,000 tab and tip without hesitation. The fixed price, multi-course dinner was lavish and supplemented by multiple bottles of seven-hundred dollar wine. Unlike the men who devoured each presentation, Madelyn politely accepted but did not complete each beautifully prepared and sumptuous course. Someone even joked at the dining table about the social mores that prevent women in public, even if they have appetites, from eating as much food as men.

The dinner and festive conversation were meant to entertain and impress Dr. and Mrs. Cullen Gwinn. Although Madelyn thought the dinner was nice, she and her husband had dined at numerous exquisite restaurants. Tonight she had felt stuffed as the men began their desserts, some prepared from flaming fresh ingredients at tableside and labeled with names like *Death by 'This or That'*. Her satiety was beginning to overpower her, when Cullen mercifully rose from the table and initiated the appreciative and good evening wishes. As he helped his wife from her seat, Madelyn was amazed that her husband had started the goodbyes without her usual silent prodding.

"I'll be out at the driving range by 6:30 in the morning. That ought to give me enough time to hit a bucket of balls before we get started," Cullen announced to the other members of the planned foursome as he and his wife walked from the table toward the exit.

"Sounds great. Looking forward to it. We all are," responded the hospital administrator. "I confirmed our seven o'clock tee time at check in," he reassured everyone as he looked around the table. Practically in unison, Piazza and Shaffer then also announced their goodnights to the departing honorees.

"Six forty-five sounds awfully early, Cullen," his wife whispered as the two walked from the restaurant. The outside temperature had dropped significantly during the evening, and Madelyn's tailored jacket did not seem as warm as it had earlier. Pulling closer to her husband as they continued along the stone path to their room, she offered, "I think a nice warm water massage would be perfect on a cool night like this one."

"Funny you should say that. My mind was drifting in that direction, too. You know, the two of us really do think alike," he chuckled as he reached toward Madelyn to put his arm around her waist, moving her tightly against his side.

Deciding that this section of the resort had great potential for romance, Madelyn was happy that she and her husband were walking alone. After strolling past the canoe pond, the couple reached their room. Thoroughly exhausted and with stiff, achy muscles, Madelyn longed for the warm Jacuzzi in their bathroom suite. When Cullen unlocked the door and pushed it open, she quickly walked ahead of him while reaching back for his hand. Pulling Cullen into their room behind her, she eagerly undressed; he followed her lead without hesitation. The two gently slipped into the Jacuzzi as soon as it filled.

As Madelyn began to savor the massaging warmth from the whirling hot water, she could sense that her usually attentive husband had his mind elsewhere. She assumed that he was thinking about his medical practice and was sorting out the general business discussions of the evening. Even Cullen had admitted during a few of their other trips together that his mind required a day or two to unwind. He had found it difficult to forget quickly about his medical practice, particularly if there was a patient about whom he was especially concerned.

When Madelyn was first introduced to Doctor Cullen Gwinn almost twenty-three years before, he had in two years of solo practice already built a successful obstetrics and gynecology clinic. After she graduated from the University of Mississippi Law School and took a position in a Montclair legal firm, several women whom she knew through work recommended that she choose him as her doctor. However, once she met Cullen at a charity fundraiser, she wanted more than medical care from him.

Within a few weeks they were dating, and in eight months they were married. She did not practice law much after that (much to her father and mother's disappointment) but instead assumed the role of a Montclair physician's wife. Madelyn felt that she had filled that role extremely well.

Remaining devoted to his work even after they wed, Cullen did his best to preserve a loving relationship by spending ample time with Madelyn. There had been no children to distract him although they had tried to have some. Naturally, the couple utilized all of the available infertility treatments, but none were successful. Even though a few chances to adopt a newborn had presented themselves through the years, there were too many unknowns, too many variables about racial paternity or birth mother health issues that they wished to avoid.

"I hope this new guy we brought into our practice will eventually work out." Cullen interrupted Madelyn's thoughts about families and continued as though the two had been engaged in a thorough conversation about Dr. Knox Chamblee. "Elizabeth doesn't seem to think much of his abilities or believe he will or ever could be a successful doctor. She has also made some rather unprofessional remarks about his looks and physique," he added half-jokingly. Being well acquainted with Elizabeth Hawes and her antics, Madelyn was not surprised that Cullen's longtime partner in medical practice would be opinionated.

"I know that he wasn't the head senior resident at the Med Center in Jackson or anything like that," Cullen continued, "but the guy was well-liked and respected by all the OB/GYN professors I talked with. He seems to want to work hard, and I have no doubt that he will stick it out for the long haul. You know, be a breadwinner for himself and some cute girl." "What about that doctor you hired right before him?" Madelyn asked as she started to rub Cullen's back gently, using a sponge.

Concentrating on his now relaxing muscles, he shook his head. "That girl is already out on maternity leave. She went into advanced pre-term labor and developed pulmonary edema — had to have the baby early. Erin was a high-risk patient, just like most pregnant doctors and nurses, but all along Aslyn has been doing a great job taking care of her. Fortunately, both mother and baby are now doing well." Cullen recognized that, despite her personal medical complications, Erin Dixon had proven herself to be a competent, productive physician. He was reconciled to the fact that adding more female doctors to his practice would continue to be worthwhile financially.

"Is Erin coming back to work after the baby is older?"

"Pretty sure she'll be back," he nodded, " 'cause I don't think her husband works. He was already staying home with their two year-old when Erin got pregnant this time." Laughing somewhat, as he took the sponge from Madelyn and reciprocated, "In my next life I want to be a house husband like Mr. Dixon."

While some considered Cullen Gwinn old school, he had tried from the moment he started his medical practice to think progressively about where medicine was going, both patient care and business-wise. Researchers once announced that there would be a 20 % excess of physicians in some specialties, but the forecasts had not rung true, particularly in obstetrics and gynecology. The reasons for the present shortages were manifold. One serious issue had been that the medical liability crisis had affected both the number and caliber of men and women entering medical schools and certain specialty residencies. Partly because of this perceived and growing OB/GYN physician shortage, the Montclair Medical and Surgical Center for Women was being forced to guarantee increasingly large salaries for its newly hired MDs. This trend was particularly loathsome to Cullen because of his frugal, demanding work ethic.

As he rotated the soft sponge with caressing strokes all around his wife's torso, he reflected further on these issues. What irritated him most, however, was that he had established his practice from scratch, with only a meager initial one-year salary guaranteed by the now defunct Caring Physicians Hospital of Greater Montclair. Those wages enabled him to work long hours to develop what was now considered the premier OB/GYN group in the Montclair-area. Not only did Cullen desire to protect his investment and guarantee his retirement fund through the practice, but he also wanted the group to survive as a viable entity after he retired. Then again, he did not plan to retire anytime soon.

Moreover, to add to his frustration about the general status of medical practice and the direction it was taking, the increasing percentage of female physicians entering the medical workforce had also complicated staffing. Since additional female obstetrician-gynecologists were sought after by other established practices and hospitals, they were difficult to come by. Naturally, the women physicians then demanded and received higher salaries than their male counterparts.

"Maybe this new guy, Chamblee, can absorb some of Erin's patient load while she's out," contributed Madelyn. "I bet when she comes back to the office, particularly with a new baby at home, she'll want a fairly light patient load. Don't you think?"

"You're right, Mad. Maybe we should hire you as a consultant. Erin Dixon can't possibly continue to see 60 or 80 patients daily and maintain her own health, much less high quality patient care. After all, Elizabeth — I mean Aslyn — herself has never consistently worked that hard, although she cornered the market as the first female gynecologist in Montclair." Cullen drifted from the conversation, realizing that he might not have given Dr. Hawes enough credit through the years. While the two senior members of their group did not always agree, he did have a basic respect for her. After all, he remembered that during her obstetrics and gynecology residency Elizabeth drove herself from her home to the hospital when she went into labor and could not locate her golf-playing husband. Her overly strong work ethic, or perhaps her grief coping mechanism, returned the resilient Elizabeth to work twelve days later after giving birth to a stillborn baby girl.

Becoming a busy obstetrician-gynecologist had not been the former Elizabeth Aslyn Bryant's primary intention. She had attended medical school at her father's insistence and finished in the middle of her class. Since female physicians competing for OB/GYN residency training spots were more of a rarity then than now, she easily won a spot in a prestigious medical training facility in New England. Both Bryant and her father thus believed that she had positioned herself well in both a professional and social standpoint.

Fulfilling the duties of an OB/GYN resident was physically and emotionally easy for her, partly because she had no financial concerns. While her father was still footing most of her bills and supplementing her skimpy resident's salary, she discovered a new source of income during the third year of her residency. That source was Stan Hawes.

Stan was an entrepreneur, and a good one. He had made a fortune in the oil industry and related endeavors. Thought by many of his friends and colleagues to be a true example of a self-made man, he knew how to shift pecuniary gears whenever economic conditions dictated a change. In fact, it was the downfall of the oil empire in the United States during the late eighties that led Stan Hawes and his childless physician wife to relocate after she completed her residency training.

During that era in the South, and in Mississippi particularly, the cellular and discount long-distance telephone industry was becoming a major economic force. Several start-up companies needed CEOs and CFOs. With the aid of his accounting and marketing degrees, Stan found himself employed by, and later owning, one of the most successful cellular and paging companies in the southern United States. His company actually grew to national and then international prominence because of its innovative equipment and service.

Elizabeth Hawes grew socially as her husband and his company grew in stature. She had attended medical school only to please her father, choosing obstetrics and gynecology as a field because she liked the patients and was good at it. After her marriage, Stan Hawes and his successes eventually made that choice unimportant. Practicing medicine was simply not a financial necessity for the couple. What's more, instead of Elizabeth's being stuck in a hospital, Stan desired her to be near him. Truly, this was the life his wife had always dreamed of as a young girl. Having affluent friends and associates all over the world, she and Stan traveled extensively, usually at company expense. Even though his Piper Malibu came with a personal pilot, Stan quickly acquired his own license, enabling the exciting Stanford Hawes to spirit his wife away on spontaneous luxurious getaways.

There was never another pregnancy to interrupt this glamorous life style.

Tragically, the weather over the Mississippi River one weekend was more than Stan Hawes could handle. Pieces of the Piper were discovered washed up near the sand dunes along Rosedale, but only the alligators found his body. This change of circumstances placed Dr. Hawes back in the medical workforce. Despite the fact she had not practiced medicine for several years, she had wisely kept her New England medical license current and was fortunately able to get a Mississippi license by reciprocity. Furthermore, when her formal residency training had ended, she was granted lifetime board certification in the obstetrics and gynecology specialty. For that reason Cullen saw few obstacles to her joining his practice when Elizabeth Aslyn Hawes showed interest. Actually, there was no hurdle to jump from a business standpoint once Dr. Gwinn saw the profitability in Hawes.

"Cullen, let's think and talk about something different," Madelyn interjected into what she correctly assumed was her husband's ongoing, mind drifting thoughts about his medical practice situation. They had covered all the problems facing the new doctors in his practice, and she decided that there was no telling what else Cullen was silently worrying about.

"We haven't been away together in a while, a long while." Madelyn tried to interrupt Cullen's train of thought by taking her turn as masseuse, thoroughly covering his neck and shoulders. She could see and feel the stress building up inside him as his face got tauter. She was a professional at soothing her husband with her well-bred metropolitan southern accent. "A lot of your patients may want to see a younger doctor, so let this new guy... what's his first name... Knox?...take some of your workload, too, in addition to some of Erin's patients. His practice will get busier; I'm sure of it. By the way, you need to slow down, particularly with all of this 'business of medicine' you all keep worrying about."

"I know. I realize that I've worked pretty steadily all my life, almost obsessively for as long as I can remember," he said softly to her as he thought about the products of that labor: their primary residence in Montclair, the place at Seaside, the new Jag, and the Benz.

"We do get to take some nice trips even if we haven't been away for a while, 'cept for this little jaunt," Cullen continued. "My stress level would lower if I got involved in some more activities, non-work related activities." He lay back in the Jacuzzi, enjoying the intimacy of his massage, and continued to think out loud. "Devote more time to my golf game, for sure. No doubt my handicap is higher than all three of those guys added together," he lamented, referring to the game planned for tomorrow. "I'm particularly lousy at tennis," he added, almost as a joke, since he had not picked up a tennis racket in fifteen years. "I guess I should have stuck with those piano lessons my parents tried to make me take."

"Cullen, you really could take more time off, even a day here and there," she suggested as they lifted themselves from the bubbles and began to dry with plush towels.

"You're right, as always, my Dear," Cullen decided as he reached for his complimentary robe hanging nearby. "Think I may take Jay Rutledge up on his offer to go to his hunting camp soon. He mentioned at the hospital a few weeks ago that an opening in his club might become available. Some of the hospital radiologists and plastic surgeons hunt there also."

"More outdoor activities would really be a stress reliever, and then maybe you wouldn't have to wrinkle your forehead like that," Madelyn commented as she reached to touch his face gently. "I hope you'll follow through with these ideas. After all, Cullen, all you do is practice medicine and go to meetings. And, another thing, Cullen, you don't need that robe. I don't need one either."

"You may regret encouraging me with this hunting thing. There are probably more hunting widows out there than golf widows, particularly during certain times of the year. I'll need to hit the hunting equipment store in the mall, but I can order some of the stuff over the Internet and from various catalogues."

Madelyn could see his mind at work, planning, almost transforming a future hobby into a quest.

"In a few days I can probably come up with all the outdoors hunting paraphernalia anyone could ever need. And who knows? I might even turn out to be a pretty good marksman," he said with great anticipation.

"But, Darling, I'm not worried about what kind of hunter or marksman you could be," she offered as they walked toward their bed. "You have always been good with your hands. They are what have made you ... have made us ... so successful, along with your personality and your brain ... your brain inside that handsome, sometimes thick skull of yours," she chuckled as she moved closer toward her husband across the king-sized bed. "Anyway, just how can a fifty-six year-old guy remain this cute?"

Cullen shrugged his shoulders as though it had been easy.

"You've got all of your hair, and it's still so thick," she pronounced, lacing some of it between her fingers. "Also your belly and the underside of your chin don't sag like a lot of other guys'," she added as she followed the contour of his chest and abdomen, reaching down firmly between his thighs. "And everything about you works and works so well."

Madelyn turned out the light and stopped talking.

Chapter

5

...

THE PURSUIT

Another homicide was not what the Montclair chief of police needed. While the grisly murder was horrifying enough for the victim and her family, another brutal crime under Chevelle Agee's watch was just one more step toward the loss of his almost four-year old job. Promoted from the lower ranks of the Montclair Police Department, Chief Agee had been given a firm directive by the then new mayor. He was to make good on the mayor's campaign promise: a major reduction in violent crime.

Inscribed in bronze lettering across a shiny wooden plaque were the words: *A strong mayor has a strong police chief.* This message propped on his desk was an incessant reminder to Chevelle Agee. Montclair Mayor Netz firmly believed that he had been elected to his first term because his predecessor had failed miserably in improving the city's crime statistics. Unfortunately for Mayor Netz and Chief Agee, Montclair's major and minor crime rates in all categories had not decreased. Instead, as the city had prospered financially during the past several years, the numbers had actually begun to rise steadily. Chevelle's theory for this increase was that, as the users and sellers of illegal drugs in Montclair flourished, they made excellent criminal targets themselves, particularly since they could not get along with each other. Likewise, from the numbers and types of crimes he was seeing, he was not sure that even the legally prosperous citizens lived together all that harmoniously.

Unfortunately for the chief, he had no immediate leads on this latest murder: a white nurse named Taylor Richards, young, divorced, living alone, found submerged in her bloody bathtub. Chevelle Agee was enduring yet another tortuous phone call from the mayor, who clearly was incensed that one more homicide had occurred on his watch.

"And to make matters worse, Agee, the victim is white," the mayor emphasized. "Yes, white. As it is, a large proportion of our Caucasian citizens already feel unsafe in our fair city. Another killing will just increase the white flight into the suburbs. Do you realize, Agee, what happens when all those people move out of my city's limits? Well, do you?"

Chief Agee really did not believe he was supposed to answer. He was just supposed to sit there, listen, and take it.

"When all those scared doctors, lawyers, bankers, and housewives move out to Slattery and Carsonville, they can't vote for me any more. Don't you see? I need those white people out there to stay in Montclair as registered voters and return me to office. My God, Chevelle, the next election will be here before we know it!"

"Sir, we are right on top of the murder investigation..."

The mayor interrupted the chief's lying. "Not to mention what happens to my, the city's, tax base when the census is down. Remember, Chevelle, if I go, you go right out the door with me, fella." The mayor's yelling was to such a decibel that Chief Agee was forced to hold the receiver away from his ear.

"I expect you to handle this case personally, Agee, and solve it real quick. I want an expedient arrest that leads to a swift trial with certain conviction. I want Montclair to know that we, that I, will no longer tolerate this, this, terrorism. Yes, that's what it is, local terrorism." He hesitated slightly. "'Violent, criminal acts of the worst kind.' That'll be a great quote for the paper." Mayor Netz emphasized as he hung up with a bang. Luckily for Chevelle, he was still holding the receiver at a distance.

The chief's investigation of the slaughter of Taylor Richards thus far had not uncovered any strong leads. Although Chevelle had engaged the assistance of Lamar Boston, one of his best detectives, he was following the mayor's directive by handling all of the major details himself. Thus far he had learned that the body had apparently been discovered only a few hours after the murder.

The young woman's mother had gone to her daughter's house fairly late that night to pick up a jacket she needed for the next day. There was no answer to the front doorbell or to her knocking. Next, the unsuspecting mother entered with her own key, thinking that her daughter was not at home. She remembered that Taylor had called her earlier about plans to work overtime; nonetheless, the mother could not remember the specifics.

When Richards's mother noticed some of her belongings scattered around the living area and kitchen, she realized that her daughter had3 already returned home. Puzzled that there was no answer from Richards after she called for her, the mother began to walk to the back of the house. As she turned from the living room into the carpeted hall, she found it soaking wet and stained. Now nervously shouting Taylor's name, she cautiously continued down the hall toward the bathroom. Horrified, she found her dead daughter floating in bloody tub water. The faucet was still slowly running, and the tub was overflowing.

The police and ambulance responded quickly to the screaming call from the hysterical, grief-stricken woman. The first officers on the scene had appropriately cordoned off the crime scene and handled the initial evidence gathering. Chief Agee had questioned the victim's mother himself, following the dissipation of the sedatives her doctor had administered. He planned to interview the employer and co-workers of the dead nurse in addition to her ex-husband, who he had been told now lived out of state.

Thankfully, the next day's room service was punctual, because she needed to take her daily medication with breakfast. Since Cullen had already left for the golf course, Madelyn answered the door and signed the service ticket, adding a generous tip. Even though it was early in the morning, she felt rested and satisfied. The time spent last evening with Cullen in the Jacuzzi had been relaxing and the physical nightcap in their bed, sensual. All of those intimate moments with him had overshadowed the dreary dinner with the hospital-types and the commiseration over medical practice problems.

Remaining mindful of Cullen's instructions never to take the drug on an empty stomach, Madelyn had ordered the single continental breakfast, which included juice, some fresh fruit, bagels with cream cheese, and coffee. The appointments of the serving cart were elegant enough to appear extravagant, even to Mrs. Cullen Gwinn. Unsnapping the petite container from her makeup bag to retrieve one of the red and blue-colored capsules, she immediately noticed that only four or five remained. "I need to get some more of these when I get home," Madelyn mumbled as she popped a capsule under her tongue and swallowed it with freshly squeezed orange juice.

Chasing the orange juice with black coffee, Madelyn remained conscious of her calorie reduction plan that had gone beyond low-carb. To this end, she picked up only half a wheat bagel and left off the cream cheese. Ignoring the newspaper lying folded on the cart next to the loaded bud vase, she delved into her own copy of the latest *People*. Likewise, she paid no attention to the television playing at low volume in the sitting room of their suite and missed the story of the brutal slaying of a nurse in Montclair, Mississippi.

Madelyn's light breakfast blended into an enjoyable and busy day around Point Clear and vicinity while Cullen played golf. With another generous tip, the concierge secured a rental car to take her to the varied antiques shops and clothing boutiques. Skipping lunch except for some frozen yogurt purchased from a tiny café, Madelyn began to feel guilty about the calories she had consumed during the last twenty-four hours: drinks and snacks on the jet, cocktails before dinner, wine with dinner, and then all that rich restaurant food.

After trying on what would be her last purchase of the shopping jaunt, Madelyn stood staring at her reflection in the mirrored dressing room of the boutique. Suddenly she envisioned last night's dinner table covered with heavy food and glasses of wine. "I won't be able to squeeze into this skirt two or three days from now," she almost berated herself loudly enough for the store clerk to hear. However, bolstered by the security of the pill container back in the hotel room, she immediately purchased the garment with great satisfaction.

While Madelyn and the delighted merchants were successful during her outing, Cullen was mediocre on the golf course. The number of unique finds for both her body and home measured achievement for Mrs. Gwinn, but staying out of the sand traps was enough of a triumph for Dr. Gwinn. Luckily, Cullen avoided the beach when swinging his five iron on number nine even though the resident alligator ambled out in front of him.

Mitch Piazza had followed one of the golf pros recommendations and scheduled the foursome on what he was told would be the most enjoyable of the two courses at Lakewood Country Club, located adjacent to the Grand Hotel. Unfortunately, their tee time on the Dogwood course led to more challenging play than would have been met on Azalea. Since Piazza's goal was to ingratiate this Dr. Gwinn with Global Healthcare, Incorporated, he had hoped to make the outing pleasant for the prized doctor. What Piazza did not expect was the difficulty of the confrontational course interrupted by lagoons and their natural inhabitants.

"I hope he slices better with a surgical knife than with that three iron," Piazza whispered to Dr. Shaffer as Cullen attempted to gain yards down the fairway but instead propelled his ball into a thicket of palmetto grass. "Rutledge says that Gwinn will be the make or break of any financial deal we make in Montclair. Supposedly, he carries a lot of influence with the other docs. Could be a hard sell."

"Definitely seemed skeptical last night during dinner."

"Jay also mentioned that Gwinn doesn't play that much golf. Surprise, surprise," Piazza joked as Cullen drove his ball from the palmetto grass completely past the upcoming green. "Works at the hospital all the time, though."

"Hope he continues to do so. Work, I mean," Shaffer commented before he walked over to his ball and chipped it smoothly onto the green. He missed the cup by only a few inches.

"Typical," Cullen remarked to Jay Rutledge, who had made his way over to the rough to help him locate his ball. "I bet those guys do nothing but play golf. Entertaining doctors all the time. Just look at their tans. And it's winter."

"You're probably right." Retrieving Cullen's fairly scarred ball buried among some leaves, Jay handed it to him. "Look, here it is. Go ahead and toss it up on the fringe. Give yourself a fair shot."

Cullen accepted the generous offer of the hospital administrator. Even though he threw the ball the best he could to line it up with the cup, he remained several strokes away.

"Try your wedge." Blake Shaffer walked over, having already sunk his ball during Cullen's meandering trip to number twelve. "A little loft, that's all you need."

Suddenly Cullen felt as though he were the focus of attention, like winding up on the pitcher's mound, or on the basketball court making a free throw, or at a meeting giving a speech — everyone watching him, rooting him on. He followed Dr. Shaffer's advice as though the retired orthopedist had recommended a certain surgical instrument. Trying to recall every single facet of his recent Montclair golf pro lesson, Gwinn adjusted his grip and popped the repositioned ball onto the green, a few inches from the cup.

"Nice shot!" Piazza announced from his position farther down the fairway.

"Hold the applause, please," Cullen responded, feeling more confident.

By the time the foursome had reached number fourteen, Cullen was playing slightly above average and finished the round with 106. His group had been forced to let only one other foursome play through, but the hospital executives would not let him take all of the blame for their slow round.

Chewing the final juicy bite of the last grapefruit section, Madelyn thought about going ahead and waking Cullen Sunday morning but decided instead he should sleep in. Again regretting the culinary overindulgences of the last day and a half and the expected increased thickness of her hips and thighs, Madelyn remembered the workout facility. Their plane was not supposed to leave Mobile until four thirty for the short return to Montclair, and there were no planned group activities before departure. Assuming that Cullen would probably be up by the time she arrived back at the room after exercising, Madelyn decided that the two of them could have an intimate low-carb lunch today at Lakewood Restaurant on the golf course before leaving the Grand Hotel. Someone had told her to try the Cobb salad there.

His letting out a slight grunt at that moment as he turned over in bed made her think Cullen was waking. When his breathing remained steady and his eyes shut, she chose to let him rest and simply leave a note about her exercise plans and lunch idea. Looking around for something to write with, she once again admired the antique French writing desk standing against the wall across from their bed. Complete with a leather top, the piece was placed appropriately near the French doors that led out to their private courtyard area. Madelyn had thought it attractive when they first checked in and had already decided that it would fit handsomely in their own library at home. She reached for its drawer pull, looking for a note pad or some stationery. Oddly, the writing desk contained no writing supplies.

Searching the room for another way to leave Cullen a message, she noticed his briefcase near the closet. As she grasped the handle to check inside for writing materials, the snap popped open, startling her. The first article Madelyn spotted was a piece of lightly scented, masculine note stationery tucked over out of the way. Apparently torn from the matching envelope lying near it and written in longhand, the note was headed with *Jay* embossed in bold blue, almost round, letters. Madelyn reasoned the correspondence was from the hospital administrator on the trip with them and almost absentmindedly picked it up to read. All of a sudden she felt guilty about going through her husband's briefcase. In fact, she could not remember another occasion when she had even looked into Cullen's briefcase, much less rummaged through it as she was doing now.

Madelyn knew from Cullen's remarks that Jay Rutledge was persistent in approaching the medical staff for service projects to promote the hospital. As she pushed the note aside unread, she decided that this was probably a thank-you to Cullen for his part in some sort of public information seminar.

"Here's something." From another compartment of the opened case Madelyn lifted a pad of self-stick notes with the name *Peyton-Rose Pharmaceuticals* inscribed at the top. She tore one sheet off for the message to her husband, then immediately closed the briefcase and set it back down in its position near the closet.

An hour and a half later Madelyn returned to their room, sweaty and feeling slightly thinner. She discovered her husband out of bed and the bathroom door closed. The water was running, indicating another long, hot shower, one of Cullen's trademarks. The sticky note she had left for him on the dresser mirror had been taken down.

Unexpectedly from near the closet, a chirpy, muted version of Dixie played. Madelyn soon understood that Cullen's cell phone was ringing from inside his briefcase. "Good for you, my Boy," she said proudly as she realized that he had left the device unused since they had boarded the jet in Montclair. Once again she walked toward the briefcase, concerned that maybe the call was urgent. Nevertheless, the ringing stopped before she reached the phone. Somewhat concerned that it might have been a call from their house sitter (she knew the hospital would not dare call Cullen when he was not on call), Madelyn reached again for the briefcase.

Mrs. Gwinn hurriedly retrieved the last received call and its maker. *J Rutledge 662-555-1234*. Assuming that Mr. Rutledge was simply touching base about the departure plans, she figured that they had missed his earlier call to the room. Madelyn decided not to respond to Jay Rutledge at this time for fear that he might interfere with the couple's private lunch plans. Instead she would let Cullen check his cell messages later. After all, if the call was important, the hospital administrator would try again.

Madelyn's wondering eyes drifted back down to the reopened briefcase and to Jay Rutledge's note. This time she took a closer look at the handwritten piece and read it:

Dear Cullen,

I appreciate your help last week with the corporate executives regarding the renovation of the hospital's Critical Care Unit.

Your meeting with the vice-president of development was vital in getting the project approved for adequate funding. Sometime in the near future, I hope you will let me show you my appreciation over dinner.

With sincerest regards,
Jay Rutledge

The sound of the running shower ceased, startling Madelyn and accentuating her feeling of awkwardness, as though opening the briefcase had signified prying into her husband's affairs. Hurriedly, she snapped the case shut after replacing the note in its exact location. She repositioned the briefcase in its precise, former spot near the closet, taking extreme care to match the slight impressions its corners had made in the carpet. As she swiftly sat on the couch to greet Cullen emerging from the bathroom, Madelyn chose not to mention Rutledge's cell phone call or note.

Chapter

6

◆◆◆

THE HUNT

Fortunately for him, Cullen's Monday morning surgical case rescheduled at the last minute, letting him sleep in with Madelyn. They both needed the rest because the return trip from the Alabama coast had not been as smooth as the trip there. Instead of departing Mobile Regional Airport at four-thirty Sunday afternoon as scheduled, mechanical trouble delayed the party until nine o'clock. The passengers' relief that the jet malfunction surfaced on the tarmac rather than somewhere over the southern pine forests did not soothe their aggravation. However, the Gwinns and their hosts drowned the delay with wine, scotch, bourbon, and green apple martinis, consumed when they returned to wait at the Grand Hotel bar. Since the diagnostics of the aircraft mechanical crew were never successful in correcting the problem with the original plane, the transportation service flew another one over from New Orleans. This courteous gesture thwarted Dr. Shaffer's threat of a lawsuit.

After departing the jet at Montclair Regional, thanking the Global Healthcare executives and easily retrieving their luggage, the Gwinns did not arrive home by limo until long after midnight. Exhausted and still inebriated, they went straight to sleep.

Madelyn and Cullen took turns pressing the snooze button until Cullen first pried himself out of their king size bed. While following her husband slowly to the kitchen, Madelyn braced against the railing of the stairs and then stumbled slightly entering the kitchen as she moved toward the coffee maker. As the two reached into the pantry for the Advil, the painful, mutual understanding about their terrific hangovers became evident. Cullen doubted if the ibuprofen would be strong enough for him. He wished that he could skip work today and squash the throbbing with a few narcotic drug samples stored in the cabinet below his bathroom towels.

"Is it OK to mix this with that medicine I'm taking?" Madelyn inquired as she poured two of the dark orange pills unto her cupped left hand.

"Yes, but I wouldn't take all of it at the same time. One of the capsules with that Advil could make you nauseated," Cullen advised.

"Then I'll take the other later and swallow these for my headache now. Oh, and I believe I'm running low. Can you get me some more?"

"Sure, Mad, I'll look at the office tomorrow if I don't have some around here someplace," Cullen answered as he stepped cautiously outside to retrieve the newspaper, trying to keep his head motionless. Finding that the temperature that morning had dropped closer to wintertime, he wished he had a robe over his pajamas.

Because of routinely tipping the newspaper delivery boy, Cullen received almost doorstep delivery of the *Montclair Journal* and did not have to go far. As he reached for the paper, it slipped to the ground from its plastic wrapper, exposing the front page. *NURSE MURDER UNSOLVED, NEIGHBORHOOD STILL SHOCKED* was the main headline appearing over a color photo of a compact but comfortable-looking home, surrounded by yellow police tape. Walking painstakingly back through the side entrance to the house, Cullen became so engrossed in the newspaper feature that he almost tripped over the Gwinn cat as she followed him inside.

After pouring two cups of coffee, Madelyn set the breakfast table with place mats and silver utensils but this morning chose to omit the linen napkins. She added filled crystal orange juice glasses and put out Wedgwood china cereal bowls. "What's all that fascinating?" she asked, as her husband continued carefully into the kitchen while staring down at the daily.

"Madelyn, get this. A nurse who used to work at my office was murdered in her home while we were gone. They think it happened sometime Friday night."

"Who was she?"

"Taylor Richards. We phased out her job at the office awhile back. Didn't have a place for her anymore. But the hospital was short a nurse and needed someone with some experience in maternity care. Wisely, they picked her up. Taylor was one of the best nurses, for sure." Shaking his aching head in disgust and sorry that he had agreed to her lay-off from the Center, he sighed, "Her death is a real shame."

Cullen handed the *Journal* to Madelyn, who would be interested in the midtown Montclair atrocity. Police Chief Chevelle Agee was quoted numerous times in the article as personally investigating the case. Although the chief was convinced that the heinous perpetrator would be promptly identified and brought to justice, it was plain to the reader that little concrete information had been collected about the crime. No motive was apparent. The slain nurse was divorced and lived alone. Her mother had discovered the body. There were no suspicious fingerprints. The death had been by stabbing, but no murder weapon had been recovered thus far.

The Montclair police had begun their investigation with questioning Mrs. Richards's hospital co-workers. A few of the nurse's friends at work were quoted in the piece, extolling her virtues and expressing their horror over the pointless murder. Even though the girl was slain in a markedly different Montclair neighborhood than hers, Madelyn felt uneasy about her own overall safety and protection from criminals. Her chilly concern was not relieved by the authorities' assurance that the killing would be solved, and soon.

"It sure will be interesting at work later today," Cullen said between spoonfuls of Smart Start. The Advil was beginning to dull the pounding in his temples. "The office and the hospital will be abuzz about this. Probably won't be much work done. The hospital nurses ... they'll have all the scuttlebutt about the murder."

"There'll be several theories, don't you think?" Madelyn replied.

"Oh, I expect the gossips will be in full force. There was a lot of trouble with her husband; I remember hearing someone say. He was rumored to be into drugs — cocaine, I think. She divorced him shortly before we had to let her go."

"That was sort of cruel to let her go right after a divorce, Cullen," Madelyn countered rather loudly before she remembered that her head was still throbbing.

"It was Aslyn's idea. I never really thought that Taylor and Hawes meshed well. Maybe it was because Taylor was intelligent enough to have gone to medical school and should have. Her reasoning was as good as that of a physician, maybe better than some. She easily learned how to handle a lot of patients' problems hands-on."

"Cullen, this newspaper article about Taylor's death makes me feel really sad for her family, particularly after hearing from you about how wonderful she was," Madelyn interrupted.

"Taylor was without a doubt bright and attractive."

"Ummm, maybe the 'attractive' part is why you never mentioned her before."

"Oh, please..."

"Is she the one you rescued that time after work with your jumper cables? Made you late for dinner?"

"Yeah, you're right." Cullen hesitated for a moment. "I'm surprised you remembered that. Anyway, it's really crazy to think this, but several times I thought that Aslyn seemed to feel threatened by Taylor, almost jealous of her."

"Cullen, you mentioned before that Elizabeth — oops, I can't keep from calling her that — Aslyn has such a booming practice. The notion that she would be jealous of a nurse is really absurd."

"I agree," he continued. "However, Aslyn may have taken advantage of our money concerns in pushing to get rid of Taylor. Even though Taylor Richards brought us many years of nursing experience, she was low on the seniority totem pole of our Center's own nursing staff. Because she was such a highly compensated employee, it just made sense to let her go and distribute her duties to the others. "

"Cullen, after all, you have always liked to save money."

"Well, the girl seemed to take it well. I was relieved to find out later that she was able to get a higher paying fulltime job at our hospital where she already had some seniority as a part time employee. Therefore, my conscience was clear."

Driving home from the airport, Jay Rutledge was thankful that no one had bothered him in Point Clear about the hospital employee's murder — no page, no cell call, no email. The assistant hospital administrator had clearly understood how important that business trip was to be for his boss and boss's superiors, especially since the costly weekend excursion had been planned for months. Shaffer and Piazza were key people in their healthcare organization and had expected the trip to be enjoyable, productive, and uninterrupted. They also understood, as did Rutledge and his assistant, that hospital *administrator* and *administrator's assistant* are never tenured titles.

Because his assistant well understood the mind of Jay Rutledge, he knew how to filter information to his boss in a timely manner. He simply notified Jay of the Friday night stabbing by leaving a detailed message on his home answering machine, which Rutledge accessed on the way home from the airport. Moreover, he had competently dealt with the media in covering for the absent administrator.

When queried by a snooping newspaper reporter about how the hospital was dealing with the tragedy, the assistant administrator went on an on about the tightly-knit, extended family composed of Grace Community Hospital employees. Naturally, he and all the personnel were grief-stricken over Ms. Richards's passing but knew that she would want them to carry on in her absence, providing the highest quality healthcare available to the people of the Montclair metropolitan area.

However, like any ambitious underling, he stressed to the reporter that his superior, Jay Rutledge, was regrettably out-of-town but would want to be contacted upon his return. On hearing the last part of the recorded telephone message, Jay liked the way his importance sounded. The chief decided that his assistant had done a good job for him during this tragic situation and needed more than just a cost of living raise next year.

Realizing that the recent murder would cause the beginning of the workweek to be more than a Monday from Hell, Rutledge decided to go to the office early that morning. As he expected, the light on his desk phone was actively blinking *you have messages*. He first waded through the multiple requests for other interviews from the local television stations, as well as from the *Montclair Journal*. Finally, the one recording he was searching for played, "Jay, this is Cullen Gwinn. I was calling you back to take you up on your offer."

When Cullen went by the hospital late Monday morning, Nurse Baker was standing in L&D, as though waiting there specifically for him to return from out of town. "Dr. Gwinn, I think you should know what happened last Friday. There was this unreferred patient. She died!"

Pressed for more details, Margina revealed the heroics of Dr. Chamblee in saving Zoe's newborn. Cullen Gwinn was not surprised to hear the expert blow-by-blow of Knox's handling of the emergency surgery and its aftermath. Talkative Margina Baker added information about the other patient care situations as well. She detailed that last Friday, without assistance from any other doctors, the newest physician ably handled all of his assigned patients.

Cullen scrutinized the Delivery Record Book, which was an artifact from the pre-computer age, and noted that Knox had delivered several babies during his day on call. Fortunately, most were considered a lot more routine than the case of the maternal death. As Dr. Gwinn looked over the documentation compiled while he was away, he determined that he was the primary physician of record for the majority of the established patients whom Knox had delivered. Through her favorable report, Margina had reinforced Gwinn's confidence in Dr. Knox Chamblee. Despite Aslyn's contradictions, Cullen felt good about his recruitment of Knox Chamblee. He fully expected that Chamblee's reputation as an extremely competent physician could only grow.

The workweek progressed smoothly at the Montclair Center for Women's Services despite the occupation of a uniformed police detective and his chief, who thoroughly interviewed Taylor Richards's former co-workers. After respectfully going through the proper channels by way of the office manager, the police had twice questioned Cullen during the early part of the week. Both episodes had unfortunately taken Dr. Gwinn's time away from patient rounds or medical record dictation, causing him to stay late to catch up at the hospital and office. Cullen felt obligated, however, to assist in the investigation into what everyone including himself felt was a heinous act on an innocent, outstanding young woman.

"Everybody at the office here considered Taylor friendly, outgoing, helpful," he had told the investigators without much thought. "I suspect that she would have still been employed here had we not phased out her position," he explained further. To the questions about her personal life he had answered, "I remember hearing some of the other employees mention that Taylor continued to seem happy and in a great mood even though she was having marital difficulties. Naturally, I did not discuss that issue with her because she was fulfilling her work duties admirably and did not seem to be distracted by her personal life."

When the Chief of Police and his detective investigator came to realize that there was no other contributory information to be gathered from Dr. Gwinn at this time, they declined his offer to make the other doctors available for questioning. Ending this discovery phase of his investigation, Chevelle Agee appeared to be content with the rather nebulous information about Taylor Richardsthat was gathered from the Center's physicians, nurses, and secretaries.

"Please contact me or my office manager if we may be of any other help," Cullen had said at the time of the final meeting with Chief Agee and his detective.

Even without the meddling of the police that week, Cullen found that each day seemed to be more demanding than the preceding one, the usual scenario for him and his office assistant whenever he had been absent from the office schedule for even a few days. Cullen was relieved that the patients who had received treatment from Dr. Chamblee while he was away were doing well and seemed pleasedwith their care.

Cullen's custom at the end of the workday was to pull up the following day's office schedule on his computer. After an exhausting day in surgery and in L&D, he noticed Wednesday mid-afternoon that his Thursday office schedule was much too overbooked. Several new patients were assigned to see him in addition to the multiple gynecology annual check-up visits and return obstetrical patients.

"Nell, I need to see you. Could you walk back to my work station?" Cullen called over the speakerphone to his office manager. Nell was accustomed to receiving calls during the day from her most senior physician, the one who had hired her as the original office manager. Since then she had watched the Center expand from a solo organization to a multiple physician, single-specialty group. Nell Lowery valued what she considered to be a prestigious position. Although she could not know for sure, Lowery believed that she was one of the highest paid medical office managers in the state, particularly among those who were female.

"Yes, Dr. Gwinn," Nell reported without delay, finding Cullen studying the computer screen at his desk. He had saved the information on his schedule and then had accessed Knox's office patient schedule for that same day, now comparing them side-by-side on the same screen.

"Why is my tomorrow's schedule that packed? I compared it to Dr. Chamblee's and found that he was easily able to see some of those new patients that were put on my schedule instead."

While she leaned her head over sideways to look at the same information on the computer screen, she seemed perplexed. Pushing some additional buttons on the keyboard, she was able to review some of the history of the appointment scheduling.

"Well, Dr. Gwinn, the appointment secretaries' comments indicate that these new patients specifically requested to see you and on this specific day."

"Nell, I assumed that," he countered, placing his hands firmly on the desk. "When we hire these new doctors, we expect them to get busy. We expect them to have their appointment slots filled. This is why we pay those girls in the scheduling department as much as we do."

"But, Dr. Gwinn, the patients asked to see you."

"I know that, Nell. I'm glad that they want to see me and have me take care of them. But there is no way that I can see everyone. Like I've said many times before, 'That's what the new associates are for!' " His voice was beginning to have a definite edge to it. "Dr. Chamblee, for instance. The appointment clerks could have easily shifted some of this overflow to his list. We have given those girls up in the front thorough information about the new doctors, all sorts of facts about their background and qualifications. That should help in directing some of these patients to the new doctors."

Nell could sense Dr. Gwinn's growing aggravation, worsened by his fatigue from the recent trip and other interruptions of the last few days. "I will talk with them immediately. I would think that the appointment clerks have already encouraged many of the patients to see Dr. Chamblee. The problem is that many of these new patients were referred specifically to you by friends who are your established patients. Also, you do agree that you have an extremely high satisfaction rate among your established patients, don't you? Then why would your patients ever dream of leaving you for another doctor?"

"I realize all that, Nell. I'm just asking you to make sure that we as a medical group strive to make the new doctors productive. Unfortunately, there is no overflow from Langley's slow practice that would benefit Knox. My real concern is that Dr. Chamblee in particular receives help in building his own practice here. The female doctors don't need any help. They seem to sprout patients from thin air."

"Clearly, that's part of the problem," Nell responded with a renewed air of authority. "Many of the new patients who don't insist on seeing you simply want to have a female OB/GYN as their doctor. Unless they have a preference for Dr. Hawes, they'll settle for any of the female physicians. They just want to see a woman."

"Nell, of course, there are patients out there who prefer a female OB/GYN over a male. And, I suppose, that the reverse situation also exists. But there are a lot of patients who could care less about their physician's gender; they just want a kind someone who will listen to their problems and be a good doctor."

"But if you talk to the appointment secretaries, they'll tell you that the patients request ..."

"We both know that despite our success in hiring these women doctors, keeping them around to work a full schedule has been a challenge. They're young and, naturally, they desire a family. No one can blame female physicians for wanting to have some normalcy. After all, they've worked hard and want to enjoy what life has to offer. Men are the same way, I guess, unless you're talking about workaholics."

Nell Lowery listened intently to Dr. Gwinn's views and summations, all the while thinking that he was an example of a professional who worked too hard and worried too much.

Cullen Gwinn continued, "I may be old-fashioned, but I'm not a sexist. If the doctor's husband or significant other cooperates, then these girls can come back to work after maternity leave, but if he won't cooperate or if he considers himself the breadwinner

or even the potential breadwinner, then we have a problem."
During the years Cullen had personally interviewed every
physician associate hired by
his practice and never had any doubts about the integrity
or abilities of any one of them, regardless of gender. "The other
issue is that premature labor happens to pregnant physicians
just as it affects the rest of the population, and
if some medical or surgical complication is going to happen,
then it is going to happen to them. Doctors, like nurses,
spell *high risk*."

Nell decided that perhaps she should follow Dr. Gwinn's line
of thinking for now. "And how can we forget about our
wonderful Dr. Dedwylder. Remember that she retired a few
months after hooking up with that rich plastic surgeon down
in Jackson? You know, the older one."

"Right, she left after three years with our practice. I guess it
was my fault," Cullen confessed. "Phillip was in my medical
school class, and I introduced them one night at a party."

They both laughed quietly over this history, the chuckles
relieving the tense conversation. "They just don't make women
physicians like Elizabeth Hawes anymore — I mean **Aslyn**,"
Cullen concluded, waving Nell away with his right hand. His
office manager easily understood that he was referring to the
unwavering work ethic of the most senior female physician in
the group. From the appearance of her home, cars, and clothes,
the long-time widowed physician was doing a splendid job of
supporting herself financially.

The remainder of the week was punishing from a manpower
standpoint with the pressures of patient care fast-paced and
tiring. As luck would have it for Dr. Chamblee, he filled in
several times for the overbooked Dr. Gwinn. Because Knox
handled the more demanding load with such confidence and
patient satisfaction, Cullen was even more reassured about the
young doctor's abilities.

Unluckily for Dr. Gwinn, Wednesday of that week was
again his night to be on call. As the day's activities blended into
the night, he was required to stay at the hospital until nearly

3:30 a.m. Thursday. The whirlwind of hospital dilemmas included an unstable gyn patient with pyelonephritis who threatened ARDS, two early obstetrical patients who required emergency D & C's for spontaneous miscarriages, and a fifty-five year old who was hemorrhaging from the uterine fibroids she had wanted to keep.

This chain of events prevented Cullen again from completing another board meeting of the Center's physicians. While those meetings were routinely held monthly, the volume of business from the night before his trip to Point Clear had required the group to reconvene sooner for a special follow-up. One of the physicians always had to be on call; unfortunately, it was his turn again. Patient care could not stop just because of a business meeting. Leaving the conference still in progress to attend to the sick hospital patients, he was unable to return before the meeting adjourned.

The next morning, as soon as the Center's secretaries had clocked in, Dr. Gwinn had one of the hospital operating room nurses call over to update them on his whereabouts. When his secretaries heard, "Dr. Gwinn is still tied up in surgery and will be late to the office," they knew that his hectic hospital schedule would make the day's now delayed office agenda even more of a circus, at least until he caught up probably by early afternoon.

Initiating the fifty-minute major surgical procedure at the scheduled 7:00 a.m. time had not been the reason for Cullen's delay. Rather, the holdup resulted when the abdominal hysterectomy evolved from a routine case into a three and a half hour nightmare. Fortunately, the operation ended well with a healthy patient, although Drs. Gwinn and Langley would have benefited from back and neck rubs.

Once he escaped from the hospital to begin his delayed office day, Cullen could not disguise his advanced fatigue from his office nurse. In contrast, as he pushed through his packed office schedule, the patients ranging in ages between fourteen and eighty were oblivious to his weary condition. To them, Dr. Gwinn appeared to be his characteristically charming but thorough self.

When Cullen's noon surgical case for that day cancelled

unexpectedly during the early hours of the morning clinic, his office nurse jumped at the chance to end her day early. "Dr. Gwinn, why don't I reschedule the afternoon appointments so that we see patients through lunch? We'll be through by mid-afternoon; then you can go home early and get some rest."

"Are you really looking after me, or do they have a great sale at the mall this afternoon? Besides, aren't there several shopping centers on your way home?" he teased but understood her dual motive for the schedule revision.

When Dr. Gwinn did not veto her idea, his nurse grabbed the phone and computer keyboard to reschedule the rest of the day. In trying to see all of the patients and finish the day at an earlier hour, their pace was relentless. Only a quick sandwich gulped down with iced tea at their work desk broke the routine of patient interview, examination, consultation, and prescription writing.

As he worked through the final patient list, Cullen remained focused on providing meticulous care for his patients, while wasting no time. The afternoon's patients were typical:

- A newlywed couple was excited about the pregnancy Cullen had diagnosed for them that day, even though the baby was expected before the anniversary of their eighth month of marriage. Evidently the birth control patch unknowingly came unstuck while they were skinny-dipping in Destin.
- A forty-four-year-old housewife was having pelvic discomfort. When asked by Dr. Gwinn if she was having pain during intercourse and orgasm, she answered, "No, but it hurts when I have sex with my husband."
- The next patient was a seventy-five-year-old woman who was suffering from unbearable vaginal itching. She said that the discomfort had lead her to claw her private area to the point that she knew she would go to heaven because she already knew what Hell was like.
- Cullen's patience was wearing thin by the time he saw the patient with the tongue ring. Her partner, who himself boasted a nasal ring, accompanied Cullen's multi-tattooed patient to the examination room. To the shock of the

doctor and nurse, the boyfriend requested with the patient's easy approval that he look at her cervix during the Pap smear collection.

- The schedule had fortunately ended when the last patient took the practically new tube of K-Y Jelly left on the exam room counter. Apparently, as Cullen and his nurse later laughed, the woman either wanted a souvenir of her experience with Dr. Gwinn or believed that the pelvic examination lubricant possessed some type of magical powers.

During that frenzied afternoon, Cullen was too drained and pushed to think about his missing the conclusion of last night's meeting. Assuming that no crucial decisions had been reached in his absence, he anticipated a copy of the minutes to be distributed in a few days.

However, in Cullen's absence Nell Lowery had been anxiously called away before the special meeting's finale because of her sixteen-year-old's severely broken ankle. The break was suffered during nighttime drill team lessons when the teenager tripped and lost her balance from an over-zealous, above the horizon dance kick. Naturally, Nell's duty as mother and now self-taught trauma nurse kept the office manager and meeting recording secretary at home for the rest of the week, unaware that Dr. Gwinn had not returned for the final discussions.

Montclair Police Chief Chevelle Agee preferred to ignore the newspaper, but he could not. He dreaded the latest editorial or letter to the editor as well as the many other commentaries published continually in the *Montclair Journal* about the number of violent crimes in the area. All of this fury was ignited by the gruesome murder of Taylor Richards. For several days Chief Agee had been forced to hold a daily news conference about his investigation into the case which the media had now termed *The Bathtub Nurse Murder*. He felt certain that the reporters were able to see through his upbeat smoke screen of rapid progress toward solving the crime. To add to his daily strain was the mayor's constant scowl resulting from the lack of an arrest.

"But, Mr. Mayor, I am directing all of my resources toward this case, including the great majority of my own time," was his standard reply.

The disappointing truth was that limited new evidence had been gathered subsequent to last Friday's murder. Since Taylor's death, Chevelle had interviewed in vain nearly everyone who had worked with her during the last several years and had retraced the victim's known movements during recent weeks.

After driving to Atlanta to question Taylor's ex-husband, Agee and Detective Lamar Boston thoroughly interrogated Chip Richards, failing to uncover any evidence that could nail the jerk to the vicinity of the crime scene. His poker buddies provided a solid alibi supported by his pregnant girlfriend. In contrast, Chip Richards's declaration, "That damned bitch threw me out of our house for no good reason," could not be corroborated by others. Likewise, his accusation, "Taylor dreamed of having an affair with one of those rich, asshole doctors she worked with," was believed unfounded. Following the fruitless out-of-state, face-to-face query of Taylor's ex, Chief Agee had more leads pointing to Richards as a classic son-of-a-bitch than as a cold-blooded murderer. He was of the same opinion as Taylor's mother: the guy was worthless, and the poor girl had definite reason to divorce him. Furthermore, Chip's overly critical description of his dead, ex-wife was typically out of character for someone who would have murdered her.

Other evidence worked in Richards's favor. No liftable fingerprints from the victim's body belonged to him or did any of those found in or around the Booker Street home, a reflection of Taylor and her mom's detailed post-divorce fumigation and cleaning. As expected, various spots around the home yielded her mother's prints.

There were few other discoveries of interest in Taylor's house except for a dirty, unopened newspaper discovered later by

Detective Boston. The folded, evidently unread periodical was found crushed as though run over by a tire. Analysis of the tread, fairly well preserved by the black stain smeared across a portion of the front page, did not match that of the victim's car nor that of her mother or ex-husband.

In pursuing the significance of this new evidence, Chief Agee received consistent denials from the newspaper carrier that he had run over the *Journal* that day with his delivery vehicle. This refutation was supported by police examination of the teenager's tread-worn tires. When quizzed extensively, the apprehensive kid explained that he would hurriedly toss Miss Richards's newspaper into the middle of her short driveway near the house. Because delivery that particular day had been delayed by problems with the printing presses, the investigators determined that Taylor had left for work before the newspaper arrived.

Several retired neighbors in adjacent houses assured Chief Agee that no one had been to Taylor's home after she left for work that morning. They confirmed the newspaper boy's story about the delayed delivery. The elderly neighbor directly across the street was particularly annoyed about her own tardy newspaper.

Located at the edge of the neighborhood, Taylor Richards's house had no others to its immediate rear because low elevation in that sector had prevented residential development. A wide four-wheeler path wound through the vacant area that was dotted by electrical power poles, scrubby pine trees, and native brush. Neighborhood kids with their ATVs kept the trail well cleared and firmly embedded in the hard clay soil, preventing flash flood waters from washing away the path.

"I grilled some chicken outside, and some baked potatoes are coming out of the oven."

"Sounds great," Cullen responded drowsily as Madelyn woke him from the late Thursday afternoon nap, a seldom-claimed luxury of making it home early from the medical office and hospital.

"I let you sleep until eight o'clock. I hope you'll be able to go to sleep later tonight," his wife whispered as she licked his left ear playfully.

"That's OK. I was really tired. In any case, I may need to stay up late tonight, getting my stuff together for the weekend hunting trip." Madelyn detected a definite air of excitement in his voice. "Are you going to leave right after work tomorrow?"

On Monday when Cullen broke the news of the hospital administrator's hunting invitation, Madelyn assumed that Rutledge had invited him while they were in Point Clear. Since Cullen had mentioned several times before that he wanted to get out in the woods and become an experienced hunter, she encouraged him to accept the offer. Madelyn reassured herself that her support of this new hobby was not merely a ruse to draw her husband's attention away from her own costly plans. Hers was going to be a last minute idea, as long as Minor was available to go with her.

"Madelyn, I've got a minor surgery case reposted for noon tomorrow after it cancelled today," Cullen answered. "The procedure won't take long, and since we don't see patients on Friday afternoon, I should be out of there by around two." Cullen noticed that his wife did not seem at all concerned about his leaving for the weekend.

"Besides," he continued, "that'll give me plenty of time to make it to Pecan Grove before dark to meet up with Jay Rutledge. He's been at the deer camp since Wednesday."

"I'm sure all of the investigation into that nurse's murder has just worn him out," commented Madelyn, as though she were really concerned about the hospital administrator.

"Jay left the workings of the hospital to his administrative assistant for a few days so he could get away from the police and the reporters. Taking for granted that the answer was 'Yes,' Cullen inquired, "You've made some weekend plans already, haven't you, Mad?"

"Funny you should ask," she answered with light humor. "I'm going to take that direct Southwest flight to Chicago Midway tomorrow afternoon and come back Sunday around five. Get some shopping done." Madelyn did not mention Minor.

"I should be home from Jay's place before you get back from the airport. Rutledge said he would show me around the area first when I get there tomorrow afternoon. We'll hunt Saturday morning and afternoon. Sunday, too, if we haven't seen much or haven't shot anything by then. Since it's late in the season, he doesn't expect the camp to be overly crowded with other hunters."

"Does he think that you'll have a good chance to catch a deer?"

Even though a novice hunter himself, Cullen remained amazed over how little his wife understood about the sport. "You don't 'catch' a deer, Madelyn; you shoot one. Hunters hope to shoot the animal precisely to keep from having to track it far out into the woods and brush."

"Well, I hope you do catch one."

After a little sigh, Cullen continued to detail her about his hunting trip. "Jay believes from the signs in the woods that there are still plenty of deer even though the rut is over. In any case, he thinks it will be a good hunt."

"What is the rut?" Madelyn sounded intrigued.

"That's the deer mating season. Bucks with their thick necks start chasing the does around after having been lured from the deep woods. Then they're easier targets. I found a hunting magazine on the coffee table in the doctors' lounge that featured hunters' tales from the rut a few seasons ago. Some guy in Arkansas found a large, fully developed buck toward the end of its rut. The deer looked healthy, except that he was dead. There were no signs of injury by a hunter, natural disease, or another animal. The game biologists attributed the buck's death to the rut itself."

"So the women eventually got to him, huh? They did him in once and for all," Madelyn slyly joked as she moved closer to her husband. "The rut, huh?" She looked up at him as she pushed him suggestively back toward their bed.

The channel 8 television weatherman, the one who refers to himself as the chief meteorologist, predicted that the hills bordering the Mississippi Delta would receive a hard freeze that night. The pregnant girl on the satellite weather channel issued this same forecast. The members of White Tail Point Hunting Camp preferred to watch a lot of television between hunts, demanding a wide variety of program outlets. To keep up with the weather and televised sporting events, the living room of the hunting lodge was equipped with a 56-inch LCD monitor powered by every available satellite service. There was even a sensitive antenna for picking up nearby television stations for ordinary cable service was not available in Peace County, Mississippi.

The architect had structurally reorganized the interior of the former farmhouse into twelve separate apartments. Each member was then owner of a private bedroom, sitting area, walk in closet, and kitchenette that opened to a wide corridor leading to the spacious, communal area. A Wyoming designer had been flown down to decorate this living area of the lodge, keeping the décor compatible with Mississippi wildlife themes.

A well-appointed room resulted, made comfortable with deep, crushed leather couches that were substantially constructed but distressed to appear old. Likewise, promoting the ultimate in relaxation were the nearby over-stuffed chairs, covered in rich custom fabric incorporating a design of deer and turkey figures. The fabric looked as though it would not hold up to the wear and tear of a hunting camp, but somehow it had. Mounts of deer heads, entire turkeys, and an occasional bobcat occupied the walls, which were papered to look like castle stone. The members all cherished this motif, because those who had wives or live-in girl friends were restricted from having such furnishings in their own homes.

An intriguing aspect about White Tail Point Hunting Camp was the lodge structure itself. Built circa 1905 as the private residence for a prosperous farming family, the J. W. Spencers, it would be considered a large farmhouse for a single family by today's or any other day's standard. Since completion, the dwelling had remained the Spencers' property despite the Great Depression, a fire that destroyed the second story, and several dry farming years. When the last Spencer heir died a childless widower, no family member was left in Peace County to occupy the mansion. The executor of the estate was a disinterested California relative, who promptly put it up for sale by auction.

While reading the *Mississippi Business Journal* one day in his office, Jay Rutledge noticed the ad for the upcoming liquidation of the Spencer estate. The absolute auction was to include the family house, accurately pictured as a fairly rustic mansion, as well as all working farm equipment and the expansive, surrounding acreage. The choice property included fertile Mississippi Delta farmland to supplement the surrounding timbered, rolling hills known for their abundant deer and other wildlife.

Growing up in a family of modest means, Jay Rutledge had a lifelong ambition to be a member of an exclusive, well-managed hunting preserve complete with all the amenities. Regrettably, even as an adult, his salaried positions in lower-level hospital administration made such a membership unaffordable. However, after he was promptly promoted to administrator of Grace Community Hospital, Rutledge put together a consortium of mostly doctors and a few defense lawyers in the form of White Tail Point, LLC. The organization was successful in obtaining the advertised farmhouse and the adjacent eight thousand acre wooded plantation. Since the flat economy in the South was no different from the rest of the nation at the time, the bidding at the absolute auction was low; and the bidders, few. The administrator's fee for putting together the deal was a free, equal ownership share in the club and its facilities.

Not only did Jay now possess the same hunting privileges as all the paying members, but he was also gifted with identical private quarters within the mansion-like farmhouse. Also incorporated into the business arrangement was a provision for waiving Rutledge's five thousand dollar a year membership dues during the first six years of the organization's existence. Since he was a hospital administrator associating with numerous physician members in the club, Jay reasoned that he could eventually swing the pricey yearly dues by claiming them a business expense.

Appreciating the value of their investment, most of the members tried hard to get their money's worth out of the hunting facility. A skeet range, dove field, bass-stocked lake, and target range complete with deer decoys had been installed. Hours of consultation from outdoor wildlife and conservationist experts were solicited to develop the deer and turkey populations to the maximum. Most of the members who had families often included them on hunts and used the site and its facilities as a retreat for other outdoor mini-vacations. Being single, Jay usually avoided the weekends when there were large numbers of families occupying *White Tail Lodge*, the name given to the former Spencer home by the LLC members. Jay was immensely proud of this century old estate and its transformation into a relaxing, plush, entertainment facility surrounded by ample wildlife.

The lock-on tree stand arrived in a Cabela's box by UPS next-day delivery. It was camouflage-colored and the latest model. Mississippi hunters pride themselves on their deer hunting equipment, much of which is manufactured by now wealthy Southerners who hold the patents.

Being proud of his as well, Cullen had ordered the Uncle Buck Deer Stand only after doing thorough research into the makes and models of what are commonly referred to as climbing stands. His extensive inquiry consisted solely of discussing the issue with other doctors in the doctors' lounge. Every deer hunter he queried voiced an opinion. Most suggested that he purchase this particularly superior, but easy to use, model made of lightweight metal. Six hundred twenty-five dollars plus shipping charged to his American Express put it on his doorstep.

One reason Cullen felt it important to own and use a mobile climbing stand was that his doctors' lounge advisors had emphasized its vital importance: *If all you do is hunt out of a camp's permanent shooting houses and tree stands, you'll miss the spots in the deep woods — where the really big, big deer are. You need the flexibility to move around the terrain, to follow the signs.* Hence with much anticipation, Cullen practiced intensely with his very own Uncle Buck.

After watching the included instructional video, he used a slender oak tree in his backyard to practice climbing. That's what the teenage kid next door had suggested he do after he spotted Cullen's struggling with the assembly of the deer stand. The fourteen-year-old received a grateful one hundred dollar tip for helping Dr. Gwinn put the tree stand together and learn how to use it.

About six miles from White Tail Point Hunting Lodge was Pecan Grove, Mississippi, nestled in a rolling landscape that long ago had seen the death of the last pecan tree. Its lofty designation as the seat of Peace County guaranteed only that Pecan Grove's courthouse was maintained with heating and air-conditioning, a luxury provided despite the void of productive county business.

Actually, the exchange of federal food stamps at convenience food stores and gasoline stations was the predominant legal industry in the decaying town, although even that facet of commerce was tainted. The drug trade in the area was the even more illicit industry but nevertheless seemed to go unnoticed by the law enforcement. There were, of course, several licensed late night entertainment stops where many paychecks intended for food and housing were spent on liquor, cheaply prepared food, and companionship. One such establishment was the Silver Fox, which drew patrons from as far away as Montclair and Batesville.

As Cullen followed the penciled map from the interstate through the downtown square of Pecan Grove, he cautiously tried to maintain anonymity, although his current model extended cab truck was a standout in the economically depressed community. Considering all the reported shootings and knifings in Pecan Grove, Dr. Gwinn nevertheless admired the town's picturesque courthouse. Tall, whitewashed, symmetrically designed, it had been constructed under the typical blueprint of any now aged southern town, demanding attention on a perfectly square piece of land encircled by brick paved streets. Following Jay Rutledge's directions, Cullen entered the practically deserted highway leading from the square to White Tail Lodge, but not before he reached down to pat the nine-millimeter Smith & Wesson lying next to him.

Cullen's arrival at the camp was fairly late that Friday afternoon, yet enough daylight remained for Jay Rutledge to drive him around to potential spots for Saturday morning's hunt. The first official use of the Uncle Buck was to be affixed to a tall, smooth oak overlooking a creek bottom near Stand 72. Rutledge pinned this location for his guest on the camp's centralized map mounted in the main hall of the lodge.

Pointing to the map, the hospital administrator promised his important physician, "We have seen a lot of big deer coming up through this creek bottom." Tracing the trail with a finger, he illustrated, "The deer follow the creek bank as it leads up through the clearing to what's left of a planted cornfield, over here on the other side of this strip of woods." He gestured to the line of trees shown on the map as diminutive green balls.

The following morning was frigid outside the cozy confines of the lodge — the air made even colder by their riding a four-wheeler to reach the walking path. Then by foot, Jay Rutledge and his guest approached the hunting area pinned the previous afternoon. Neither man was surprised to find the nearby stagnant creek covered with a thin layer of ice.

With an air of authority, Rutledge pointed toward the site. "Cullen, why don't you just go ahead and hunt here on 72 itself and not go to the trouble of using your climbing stand." The inexperienced hunter surveyed the towering metal stand, already secured to what was judged as a fine, sturdy tree.

"This is your first time to hunt at White Tail so why not save the effort? We put this permanent stand up before last season, and this area really has not been hunted much since." Jay figured that Cullen Gwinn had minuscule experience in using the fancy hunting apparatus that he had lugged all the way from the four-wheeler, still parked back at the main road.

"After breakfast we'll go to another place in the woods that hasn't been shot up. It'll be perfect for your Uncle Buck. We'll leave it assembled there and put you back at that spot for a hunt this afternoon or maybe in the morning," the administrator promised.

This plan sounded reasonable to Cullen, at six o'clock the thick woods remained icy and pitch black dark. "That's OK with me," Cullen responded, as his breath rose like a frozen cloud through the opening of his facemask. Hiding his true disappointment at not using his own stand, he yielded to the host's reasoning and experience.

Motioning to a nearby thicket of cane and wild berries, Jay directed, "Just lay your stand out of the way in that brush, and we'll pick it up after this morning's hunt."

As Rutledge turned quietly away to walk back to the four-wheeler, Cullen spanned his flashlight beam up the soaring ladder tree stand, proving to himself that metal chains permanently affixed it to the oak. Yesterday afternoon he noted that some of the other metal stands had been in place long enough to appear to have grown into the trees themselves.

When he illuminated the bottom of the ladder and found it a few rungs short of the ground, Cullen quietly shook it to confirm stability. He recalled Rutledge's hunting camp history lesson. *This is a new stand. We put it up last season.* Between shaking the tree stand and shining his flashlight all around to get his bearings, Gwinn wondered if he had driven away all the living creatures in hearing range.

Leaning his head back one last time to look up toward the awaiting platform, Dr. Gwinn began to ascend the frosty ladder. Forced to lift his right foot a fair distance to reach the bottom rung, Cullen found that his bulky, insulated boots made this no simple feat. To add to the tricky exploit, the thick rubber soles would barely fit between the rungs of the ladder. As Cullen climbed slowly up the stand, his gun felt awkward, not only because of its weight but also because the strap was not tight enough. While he climbed, the loose semi-automatic rifle swung almost freely, frequently bumping into his camouflaged backpack.

Pausing about two-thirds of the way up, the doctor sought security in running his hands over the solid tree trunk bark. Even though he was wearing insulated gloves, he could appreciate the slippery texture of the frozen dew covering, a result of last night's eighteen-degree low. As he continued the ascent in the bitter cold, Gwinn decided he would later thank his host for discouraging the use of the new Uncle Buck.

Cullen's boots, 30.06 rifle, and backpack became much heavier as he finally neared the top of the deer stand. "It is so... damn... cold," Cullen mumbled slowly, watching his breath freeze. "What am I torturing myself for? I probably won't see a blessed thing here at the North Pole," he whispered, remembering Rutledge's remark that this particular morning was the coldest of the season.

"This camp stand is in as good a location as the one we had selected for your climbing stand." Jay emphasized as he walked toward the ATV, leaving Cullen alone. Dr. Gwinn assumed that Jay's aim was to provide a great hunt for him because he was one of the top-producing doctors at the hospital, and, as a rule, hospital administrators like to keep their staff members happy. Reassured by this universal philosophy, Cullen began to feel more confident about a rewarding morning deer hunt as he approached the top platform.

Although finally feeling secure in this assigned spot, Cullen was losing sensation in his booted feet despite the thermal insulation. Beginning to doubt the sensibility of this freezing weather sport, he wondered again why he was here at all, here in the dark. Not only would an afternoon hunt have been illuminated but it also would have been merely wintry, not frozen. Remembering what he had read in a hunting manual, he took solace in the fact that deer move around more and become better targets when it's cold.

"At least, in the daylight I would have been able to see where I was," he again whispered to himself, almost intentionally to break the eerie, deafening silence. Jay's cranking of the monstrous four-wheeler left parked back on the main road had not yet broken Cullen's stillness, especially since the vehicle was parked a considerable distance away.

Approaching the platform at the top of the stand, Cullen judged it was barely wide enough for one person, much less one person with all this gear. He realized the challenge faced in stealthily maneuvering his gun, backpack, and clumsy body onto the ledge. First, he planned to slip his 30.06 from around his back, move the strap off his shoulder and then over his head. Next, he would then set the rifle on the bench beside him. This action would enable him to take the backpack off and lay it beside the gun. He reminded himself to move extremely slowly to avoid the noise of bumping the stand or the tall lean oak tree. Cullen was surprised how winded he felt after the long climb up the ladder with the heavy gear and was certain that the deer circling around him could hear his deep, heavy breathing.

"This is almost as much trouble as goin' snow skiing," he determined.

As planned, Cullen methodically started to raise his gun to the platform bench. As he hoisted the weapon over his head, he realized that he needed more space to prevent the tip of the rifle from striking the frozen metal seat. To avoid waking the quiet woods with the thunderous echo of metal-to-metal contact, Cullen stepped to the rear onto the thick limb he had noticed adjacent to the top of the ladder. What he did not consider was that, like the rest of the tree beneath him, the bark on this substantial limb was covered with frozen dew and an undercoating of slippery green moss. At the same time, Cullen forgot about the fully stocked backpack still attached to his shoulders.

Despite the grids on his fine rubber hunting boots, he unexpectedly slid on the slick wide limb. Attempting to right himself, Cullen calmly reached for the edge of the metal stand's platform. This surprise miss caused him to jerk and turn suddenly, searching for stabilizing support. He then immediately lunged for a higher, sturdy-looking limb but unfortunately misjudged its proximity. The snap that followed from grabbing the thinner end of the branch was sickening and echoed throughout the calm of the surrounding woods.

Realizing his mistake, Cullen stepped reflexively on a lower limb spotted in the corner of his eye. The sound of more wood splitting bounced off each twig and pine needle, reverberating throughout the entire surrounding forest, returning to whirl around Cullen's head.

So startled that he was unable to even curse as he fell, Cullen unconsciously clutched another branch a few feet below. However, its moss and ice covering equally prevented a secure grasp. The twenty-foot plunge to a landing on his back took only a few seconds, maybe even less than a second. The crutch of a fall-restraint strap had not been recommended or considered by Dr. Gwinn.

Unsure if he had lain there unconscious after the drop, Cullen began to survey his own injuries, finding that he could painlessly move his legs slightly and also wiggle his toes. But the throbbing in his back and neck was intolerable. Next, a piercing sensation through his chest and a shallow cough cut short an attempted full breath. Not surprised, he assumed that some of the ribs on the left side of his chest were cracked. Cullen could sense swelling in his upper back and figured he had broken a vertebra or two as well. Barely able to move his head or neck to the side, he was unable to reach for his cell phone. Then he remembered that when they got to White Tail Point yesterday, the display pad on his Motorola had announced smugly, "No service." Jay had not mentioned using walkie-talkies as an alternative.

Lying supine on the soft, leaf-strewn forest floor, Cullen understood that the fall would have been a lot worse had his landing been on packed earth and not cushioned somewhat by his backpack. The pain seemed to be dulling as he found pleasant the smell of decaying leaves mixed with the clean aroma of rich forest humus.

Now able to move his legs and right arm more purposefully, Cullen used the tree close by for leverage as he pushed his boot against a protruding root. This feat to turn over to a crawling position met extreme obstacles not only in the thick, still strapped-on backpack but also in an electrifying, shooting sensation deep within his ribs. Resting motionless for a few minutes until the pain subsided, Cullen reassessed the situation before attempting to do anything else that might cause paralysis. Although he could breathe and move his extremities better, he knew that his condition could deteriorate with any spinal cord swelling; nevertheless he resumed his task. Enduring considerable agony, he finally rotated onto his stomach, then chose to just rest and wait to be rescued. He decided that crawling would only be more excruciating and a further neurological risk.

After all, he was not hunting alone in the woods because Jay knew where he was. They had both ridden out to this area yesterday afternoon to scout it and had placed his location pin on the camp's hunting area map posted in the main hall for everyone to note. Even if something also happened to Jay, Cullen figured that no one would assume that a novice hunter such as he would stay out in the woods longer than necessary. Surely he would be missed after a few hours, particularly if he did not show up back at the lodge by lunch.

As sunlight began to filter through the pine trees and leafless hardwoods, Cullen realized that he had landed near the icy creek. Able to lift his head enough to trace his descent from the top of the deer stand, through the tree limbs, and down the side of the steep creek bank, he felt fortunate not to have landed directly in the stream itself. Although his face barely missed the edge of the thin ice, the impact and vibration of his fall had shattered the periphery of the frozen water.

Despite the good luck of not landing in the middle of the ice itself, he still felt the stream's piercing, bitter cold. Trying to recover any strength, he attempted to push again with his boot while using his arms to slide away from the frozen water. His injured body would no longer respond to his conscious commands, not because of pain or penetrating chill, but because of sudden fatigue and overwhelming desire for sleep.

Cullen initially thought he was hallucinating as he was jolted awake by what sounded like careful footsteps — layers of leaves being compressed unhurriedly as though someone or something were approaching — calmly, secretly. However, by the time the crushing of twigs and leaves amplified, the sound ceased as abruptly as it had started. Now once again lucid, Dr. Cullen Gwinn tried vainly to call out for help. But opening his lips only let the freezing water rush in, gagging him. He managed to spit, believing that he must have slid deeper toward the icy creek as he dozed, further breaking the edge of what had become his abyss. An almost pleasant sense of warmth next overcame him, followed by dizziness.

The lift and twist of his head was not imaginary, neither was its being pressed back down, immersed into the water. However, by then Cullen could not at all be certain of what was happening: what was real, what was fantasy. He could not move any part of his body except his facial muscles. His arms and legs remained frozen, much like the surrounding landscape. As he opened his mouth to scream, the arctic liquid completely filled his mouth and nose, working down rapidly to seal the air passageways.

Chapter

7

•••

THE VISIT

The 911 call was ultimately routed from the police department to the Peace County Medical Center, a fifty-bed hospital providing ample sleeping arrangements for the ill and injured because the structure was never more than ten percent occupied. After all, most cognizant patients went to the hospitals in Montclair or Jackson. While the overall financial system of the shrinking town was floundering and the majority of the population was elderly, emergency medical care remained readily available even on a freezing day in January. However, the county's tiny fleet of medically equipped vehicles usually functioned more as hearses than ambulances.

Despite the county supervisor's efforts to engage a marketing firm to boost the hospital's image, business remained poor. The suggestion to change the name of the hospital to the Peace County Medical Center had done nothing to help admissions. Likewise, the gigantic bronze capital letters *PCMC* emblazoned on the front of the facility's main building had not drawn many patients. To compound its decline, the hospital had meager success in attracting and keeping qualified physicians on staff, mostly because of the medical liability crisis in Mississippi. A small and nowhere near full-service facility, PCMC was caught many times short of the necessary equipment or medical personnel to handle emergencies — emergencies that should never have found their way there in the first place.

Intense followers of television and newspaper ads, the generous jurors in Peace County believed that a medical center should perform just as advertised. The plaintiffs' lawyers as well had drilled that mentality into the citizens of the area to the extent that several big money medical liability and punitive damage judgments had been handed down against Peace County Medical Center and its few remaining doctors. Because of that poor track record in the courts, the hospital and its staff were on the brink of losing their medical liability insurance coverage.

Because he had started working there in junior high school as a male orderly, Jimmy Perry was one of the few remaining employees at PCMC with any longevity. That longevity assured his continued employment, putting him on ambulance duty that morning in the emergency room. When receiving the distress call relayed from the police dispatcher, Jimmy was without an assistant due to the hospital's lack of funds for twenty-four hour double coverage.

His job as an ambulance driver and paramedic required that he know where everything in the county was located. As he jumped quickly into the ambulance van to head to White Tail Point Hunting Lodge and Camp, he turned on the siren and flashing lights and thought about his unforgettable first trip there. As opposed to today's summons, his first invitation did not arrive through an emergency call.

Emergency medical technician, or EMT, is a title that carries considerable prestige in a place like Pecan Grove. Various grants added to the extra money picked up here and there had afforded Jimmy Perry the training. As in the case of most ancillary healthcare fields, much of that instruction was hands-on. Shortly after starting his two-year stint at Hinds Junior College down in Raymond, Jimmy Perry was assisting veteran, licensed technicians on ambulance rides to and from hospitals. All the while Perry predominantly kept to himself, not mixing with the other students, male or female. Instead, Jimmy worked out at the college's fully equipped gym during his free moments, bulking up his six foot frame while slimming and firming his waist.

Even before this physical transformation, his peers at Pecan Grove High School considered Jimmy Perry good-looking. Later, judging him handsome with a nice build, a few of the female EMT students and women instructors had tried to hit on him. To their surprise Jimmy resisted their invitations to party. Likewise, he usually had some kind of an excuse not to join the guys during their nights out. Jimmy was amused one afternoon when he overheard some of the girl students whispering in the break room about whether Jimmy Perry was straight or not.

One of his most memorable ambulance training sessions landed him at Grace Community Hospital in Montclair. The more senior EMT had pulled rank on him and required Jimmy to ride in the back with their transport, a screaming fifteen-year-old in labor. Apprehensive as he sat with the thrashing patient and her boyfriend, Jimmy Perry had never delivered a baby but had read about the process in his textbook and seen one extracted breech. Fortunately for all the cargo in the back of the ambulance, they made it in plenty of time to the nearest hospital in Montclair.

While the driver of the ambulance filled out the paper work with the Grace Community Hospital Labor and Delivery nurses, he offered to the shell-shocked appearing EMT student, "Hey, pal, go ahead and take a break. You look kinda pale. Fast and furious, bumpy ride down, waddunt it? These forms gonna take a while. Neither the girl nor the dude have any of her Medicaid stuff with them."

Feeling hungry more than queasy after that harrowing experience, Jimmy accepted the gesture and wandered around the hospital until he reached the door leading to the public cafeteria. After scanning the display in the food service line, he opted for the more appetizing vending machines. Buying a sandwich and a cup of coffee, he took a seat at a table near the arrangement of plastic plants meant to brighten the sterile décor of the quiet eatery.

Unexpectedly, a nearby door swung open, admitting a man in his late thirties who walked briskly by his table. Chewing his cold chicken club, Jimmy noticed that the impeccably dressed fellow did not stop to pay for his *caffe latte* at the coffee bar. Instead, Jimmy realized that the gentleman was suddenly standing at his table, watching him take another bite of the dry chicken sandwich, "Hello, I am Jay Rutledge, the hospital administrator," the guy introduced himself. The manner in which the hospital administrator extended his hand reminded Jimmy of a salesman.

Coming to attention, Jimmy shook the man's hand. Jay Rutledge noticed that the individual was taller than he appeared sitting at the table. Believing him to be one of the ambulance personnel by the way he was outfitted, Jay was impressed that this young man seemed of higher caliber than most other medical personnel types. "Are you here with Tri-County?" Rutledge went on to ask.

"Yes, sort of, Sir. I am an emergency medical technician student at Hinds out on a practice run with my supervisor. I thought I was going to get more experience than I expected when I almost had to deliver a baby in transport," he added, feeling relaxed although he thought he probably should act respectful to a hospital administrator. "But we got here in plenty of time. I'm taking a little break while Tom gets the paper work done in the ER," Jimmy explained as looked down hungrily at his half-eaten sandwich.

"Then you are a student ambulance driver?"

"Well, actually I'm being trained to do more than drive an ambulance. We have to learn a lot of fairly advanced acute medical care techniques. Anyway, they now call us emergency medical technicians or para-medics, not ambulance drivers."

"Oh, I knew that, "Rutledge chuckled with a touch of embarrassment. "If you have a moment, I can show you around the hospital."

After meeting the hospital administrator, Jimmy was awed by his friendliness — like maybe Mr. Rutledge was trying to recruit him to work for the hospital. The EMT student had not really worried much about finding a job once he finished his training and was licensed, but he decided that maybe he would later need this contact. He reasoned that he had a few more minutes to take before his superior would be ready to leave.

"Let's start with the administration department," Jay suggested, motioning toward the door through which he had entered the cafeteria. He next walked Jimmy down a short hall, pointing to a fairly spacious carpeted office. As they entered the room, Jimmy noticed the overpowering mahogany desk ruling an area near a large picture window obscured by tightly closed blinds. A couch completed the furnishings, and what appeared to be a miniature bar was recessed in the middle of another wall. Not that he had ever given it much thought, but Jimmy felt at the time that it seemed odd for a hospital office to be complete with a stocked bar. That would seem to be a fixture more likely found in the office of a lawyer or a businessman, he reasoned.

"Would you like something to drink, young man?" Mr. Rutledge asked Jimmy as he opened the cabinet above the sink and icemaker. Jimmy noticed that it was also filled with soft drinks, bottled water, and fruit juice.

"No, no, thank you. I just had that stuff in the cafeteria."

"Oh, that's right." Jay Rutledge followed with an edge of disappointment.

Eyeing the trophy buck mounted on the wall adjacent to the bar, Jimmy changed the subject, "Do you hunt?"

"Sure do. I belong to a hunting camp with several of the hospital's doctors. It's near Pecan Grove and called White Tail Point. Since I'm not married, there's plenty of time to go up there on the weekends and sometimes during the week. Heck, I'll even go when it's not hunting season!" Mr. Rutledge continued in greater detail than Jimmy had expected. "The lodge is extremely nice, and each guy's got his own space. It was an old house that we renovated."

Rutledge paused and Jimmy interjected, "Uh, I grew up in Pecan Grove. I've ridden by your camp and have hunted with my cousin on some land close to it."

Jimmy had already been told that a bunch of rich doctors from Montclair owned that hunting camp. He figured that this hospital administrator felt lucky to socialize with a group like that. Just as Mr. Rutledge was reaching for the breast pocket of his tailored jacket, Jimmy's hip pager went off. Prior to checking the digital readout, Perry already knew the message.

"I'm sorry, Mr. Rutledge," he responded as he looked on Jay's desk at the gold-engraved nameplate to make sure of the administrator's name. "But I've got to go. That's Tom, my boss, paging me. It's time for us to leave."

"Let me give you my card," he said in an understanding tone, while pulling one from his jacket pocket. Jimmy glanced down at the business card embossed with raised black letters. *Jay Rutledge, Chief Administrator, Grace Community Hospital* was proudly displayed in three distinguished lines above his business and home addresses with a listing of various phone numbers: cellular, pager, fax, business, and residence. His e-mail address was also included, printed in lighter blue italics. Jimmy accepted the card, sliding it into a section of his wallet.

"You and your cousin are welcome up at our camp sometime when you have time off." Jay made a mental note of Jimmy's first and last names embossed on the front pocket of his shirt uniform. The muscular teenager then thanked Mr. Rutledge as he darted out the door, following his own directional instincts toward the now impatient Tom waiting in the ER.

As the weeks ensued, Jimmy found himself employed fulltime, not down in Montclair but in his hometown instead. In spite of being a neophyte emergency medical technician, he was immediately elevated to head of the tiny Peace County Medical Center EMT Department. While working in his modest, dingy office finishing a report, the formal invitation came by way of a page to call the hospital operator. Dialing that extension, Jimmy was told that she had a Mr. Jay Rutledge on hold for him. As he asked the operator to direct the caller to the nearby employee lounge, Jimmy searched to remember that name.

Recalling a smidgen of the young fellow's family history, Rutledge gambled correctly that Jimmy would be working at PCMC. When dialing the hospital's number, he could not remember Jimmy's last name but reasoned correctly that the switchboard operator of a small town facility could figure it out.

"Hello, this is Jimmy Perry," he answered as he gulped a Mountain Dew just purchased from the vending machine.

"Jimmy, this is Jay Rutledge. I met you awhile back when you were here in Montclair transporting a patient to us."

As Rutledge spoke, Jimmy recalled that Rutledge was the hospital administrator at Grace Community in Montclair and assumed that the contact was a job offer. Even though the Sunday newspaper from Montclair routinely had an entire section of advertisements from hospitals, outpatient surgical facilities, and medical clinics seeking bodies to fill employee vacancies, Jimmy was content with this position at PCMC. All he had wanted was to be near home.

"Hey, uh, yes, Sir. I met you in the cafeteria. You showed me your office." A vivid picture came to mind of the trophy deer and duck mounts on Rutledge's office wall. He remembered the heavily stuffed, comfortable-looking furniture with its elaborate fabric. Scattered all around the room were lots of pillows, ones with fringe on the edges. Simultaneously he envisioned the built-in bar and was mystified that he could reconstruct the man's office in such great detail.

"You mentioned that you liked to hunt with your cousin," Jay continued, "and that you had ridden by White Tail Point. I'm going to be up there this weekend, checking some stands before the season opens in November and thought that you might like a tour. It helps for a potential guest to get a feel for the area, you know, before hunting there."

Jimmy chuckled to himself, imagining the surprised looks on the faces of the rich doctor members. They would have paid thousands of dollars in membership fees to belong to that swanky place, but suddenly he, Jimmy Perry, lowly emergency medical technician and ambulance driver, would be with them hunting for free. "Yeah, yes, Sir, I'd really like to do that," Jimmy jumped. "I'll check with my cousin Abe and see if he is off this Saturday, too."

"Oh, well, you see, Jimmy, we have certain new restrictions on the number of guests that a member can have at one time to our camp. I'm sorry, but your cousin won't be able to join us this time. But I hope you can make it. Anyway, I think I will be able to show you around better if you came by yourself."

"Sure, I understand." Jimmy paused briefly, thinking that a snobby rich man's club like this one probably did have some silly rules, even before hunting season started. "You snobs try to make a person practically beg to hunt at or even just visit your joint," he wanted to elaborate.

"Well, I guess poor Abraham will just have to miss out," Jimmy remarked to Mr. Rutledge. "I won't even tell him about my going out there," knowing full well that his older cousin would be highly envious when learning of his good fortune.

The conversation ended with Rutledge's instructions to Jimmy about where and when to meet him that upcoming Saturday afternoon. Thinking that Jimmy might consider four o'clock a bit late, Rutledge explained that he was in charge of a hospital director's seminar at the Peabody Hotel in Memphis that day and would not be able to leave before the meeting concluded. Jay reassured the eager hunter that using the club's fine ATVs would make a complete tour of the grounds and facilities possible before a 5:30 sunset. The well-kept roads through the woods and fields of White Tail Point would give easy access to the deer stands and food plots by four-wheeler.

The schedule sounded reasonable to Jimmy, and, besides, he did not have any other plans for that Saturday afternoon. Considering that White Tail Point was fewer than twenty minutes from his mother's duplex, he believed that if he could just get his bearings around the fields and paths, then he and Abe could slip over there during the workweek and hunt. Consequently, he and his close cousin would have full use of

White Tail's vast acreage while the membership was back in Montclair being doctors or doctors' friends. In Jimmy's mind, easing over to the hunting property of someone you knew, particularly after a prior invitation to visit there, was not really trespassing nor poaching. Since Peace County was reported to have the largest deer population in Mississippi, the great White Tail Point Hunting Club would never miss a couple of does or even a small buck or two, he reassured himself.

A few minutes before 4:00 p.m., Jimmy arrived as instructed at the front gate to the main drive of White Tail Point Lodge. The sign welded to the front of the barrier resembled the emblem of a country club instead of a deer camp. The main difference was the words *NO TRESPASSING* emblazoned across the bottom of the marker, which was further engraved with figures of deer, ducks, turkeys, and dove. Jimmy had been told that if he found the gate unlocked, it meant that the caretaker was on duty that afternoon and had opened the gate for him. Otherwise, he was to wait there for Rutledge to arrive and unlock it.

The gate was indeed locked. Four-thirty passed, and no Mr. Rutledge. Given that Jimmy kept his beeper activated even when not on duty, he thought that Mr. Rutledge would have paged him if something had come up. Ten minutes later he was getting ready to crank his truck and turn around to leave when a dark green Ford F-250 pick-up drove up behind him. He recognized Jay Rutledge as he sprang from the truck. Direct from the Memphis Peabody, his host was still dressed in a dark suit and printed silk tie.

"Sorry I'm late, Jimmy. I would have paged you from my truck, but my cell phone went out. Must need a new battery. This one suddenly won't recharge anymore," he complained lifting the sleek phone from inside his suit jacket. "My darn secretary was supposed to have ordered a spare battery for me. Anyway, rather than stop and use a pay phone to page you, I thought I'd better just try to come on and get here as soon as I could. Let's run inside the house, so I can get out of this suit. There's still daylight left to show you around the property."

Mr. Rutledge unlocked the entrance gate and motioned for Jimmy to drive on through. Passing his truck through the gate onto the main road, Jimmy Perry could not miss the prominent and elaborate hunting lodge rising before him. Rutledge drove around to his left, waving to Jimmy, as he led the awestruck guest to the back parking area. Pulling his dwarfed Toyota pickup next to where Rutledge had parked his large Ford, Jimmy followed the steps to the rear deck of the lodge. An impressive veranda wrapped completely around the house, making it look to Jimmy more like one of those grand homes pictured in hospital waiting room architectural magazines than a hunting lodge. Painted white and constructed of wood, Jimmy wondered how often it needed painting or replacement of rotten boards.

"Come on in." Mr. Rutledge unlocked the back door, releasing a faint aroma of lingering cigar smoke mixed with that of dry oak logs burned in a fireplace. From this entrance they passed through a lengthy and rather wide foyer lined with hunters' boots, orange vests, and a variety of caps.

"We keep a few extra things here, mostly stuff that has been left accidentally and never claimed. All the members have private lockers in their own quarters where they keep their gear," Jay explained, motioning about the passageway with his hands as though giving a tour.

The foyer led into a large room encompassing the tremendous stone-encased fireplace positioned on the far wall. The opening of the fireplace was tall enough for an average-sized man to stand erect. To the left was an expansive bar with a brass footrest following the entire length of it, reminding Jimmy of reruns of *Cheers*. Rutledge explained that the glass shelves in front of the mirror behind the bar were empty because the club kept the liquor under lock and key when no one was there. He clarified that the members did not want the cook and caretaker, who had the day off today, to get into the bar's supplies when no members were around.

Walking behind the bar, Mr. Rutledge removed another set of keys from his pocket and accessed a cabinet underneath the shiny walnut surface. "Can I fix you a cocktail, or maybe you would rather have a beer? I see some cold ones down here in the refrigerator. A beer might be easier since we'll be riding around on four wheelers," he said as he took out a Michelob Ultra longneck and twisted off the cap. He handed Jimmy the bottle wrapped in a camouflage-colored napkin with the name *White Tail Point* printed on it. "Here, Jimmy, have some of these while I go back and get out of this Corneliani suit," Rutledge added as he opened a bag of pretzels.

As he looked down at his beer wishing it were a full strength one, Jimmy glanced at his watch. It was nearly 5:15, almost sunset, with limited time left for the cruise around the hunting camp. He almost said something to Mr. Rutledge about the late hour as he walked off, but the administrator had already turned the corner, disappearing down the hall. Jimmy sat down to wait in one of the nearby stuffed leather chairs and picked up a *Mississippi Outdoors* magazine from a side table. It was a current edition, unlike the magazines around the Peace County Medical Center. He found the lead article about a small herd of albino deer that had been spotted last season along the Big Black River north of Canton interesting.

Half an hour later Jimmy had guzzled his beer, as well as a second one retrieved from the bar refrigerator Rutledge had left unlocked. All the interesting articles containing tall hunting tales had been read, and the ads featuring used pick-up trucks and modified four-wheelers almost memorized. Dumbfounded, Jimmy looked at the time again and wondered how long it could take for a man to change out of a fancy suit.

Through the large window at the end of the bar, it was obvious that darkness had fallen. Jimmy supposed that the polite action was to locate Rutledge and offer to come back another time. Retracing the route of his host, Jimmy found himself in a dimly lit hall, which led to a series of six-paneled, darkly stained wooden doors. The whole lodge structure seemed overly quiet to Jimmy as he realized that he and Rutledge were the only two people in it, a fact also supported by the lack of other vehicles in the back parking area.

Continuing to examine the immense corridor, he could not miss the vast display of trophy game mounts. Mixed among the antler spreads were several long-bearded gobblers in various positions of flight and an occasional massive freshwater bass. To complete the exhibit was an unfortunate bobcat, frozen in an angry pose by his taxidermist and now resting on a table near the staircase.

As Jimmy stopped to look at the life-like cat and its jagged fangs, he was startled by Mr. Rutledge's voice behind him.

"I'm sorry, I received an urgent call from the hospital on my cell phone while I was changing clothes. The baby-snatch security system alarm had gone off at the back door to the nursery."

"Oh, ah, that's OK. I was just going to say that I would come back another..." Jimmy offered politely but was interrupted as the explanation continued.

"The nursing supervisor panicked when he had an incorrect count of the babies on the afternoon patient census. He was worried that a suspicious-looking female visitor seen earlier might have had something to do with it. Fortunately, while we were discussing what to do, the security guard discovered that a faulty latch on the door had triggered the alarm." Trying to sound almost more perturbed than relieved, Rutledge added, "When the unit secretary rechecked her own records, she realized that the counts were off because a doctor had discharged the twins earlier in the day."

"Oh, that's good. A relief, I'm sure," Jimmy responded appropriately, moving past Rutledge through the opened door into what appeared to be a fully furnished hotel suite. Just as he noticed a colorful abstract of a semi-nude male figure hanging above the fireplace, he remembered that the administrator's cell phone had not been working.

From Jimmy's eye movements Rutledge judged that the boy had shown interest in his private quarters. "I'm extremely sorry that the afternoon has turned out this way," Rutledge continued. "My schedule was just not as free as I thought it would be. Of course, now it's too late to show you around our stands and fields."

"Sure, that's OK; I can come back some other time. I appreciate the invitation, though. It's been real interesting seein' the inside of this house. Were all these deer killed at White Tail?" Jimmy asked as he motioned back toward the walls of the hallway.

"Most of them, except for a few harvested by our members at other clubs. But, of all things, their wives forbade the display of the mounts in their own homes," he laughed as Jimmy forced a chuckle along with him.

"I'm not married," he reminded Jimmy. "That lets me do pretty much what I like," he explained, stepping a tad closer.

Feeling a little uncomfortable, but not really knowing why, Jimmy stepped back an equal distance and continued, "Thanks also for the beer and pretzels. But I sort of need to use the restroom before I go."

"Oh, OK," Rutledge paused. "Then why don't you go ahead and use the one inside my suite," he offered with a gesture toward the opened door behind him. "It's the closest one."

Looking around and not seeing an alternate men's room off the hall, Jimmy accepted. With only minor hesitation he walked into the hospital administrator's personal suite and headed to the bathroom, which he was told was located through the opening to the far right. After relieving himself of the two bottles of Michelob Ultra, Jimmy emerged to find Jay deep in one of his overstuffed chairs, his left leg hanging over the side arm. The top two buttons of his shirt were at present undone, casually exposing a pale, hairless chest. Another change to the atmosphere was the flickering gas log fireplace now warming the area near the bed.

"Why don't you sit and visit for a while longer, Jimmy," Rutledge suggested while motioning to the adjacent upholstered chair. "I'll get you another beer or a mixed drink this time, if you like, and we'll just talk. I might even be able to find something better than pretzels to snack on."

"Oh, no, thank you, I really gotta go, " Jimmy replied, beginning to feel awkward as he stared at the totally relaxed Jay Rutledge, whose body almost melted into the chair's lush fabric.

"I thought you would like it here, Jimmy. How often would a guy like you get an invitation to come to a fabulous hunting camp like this one?" he asked almost rhetorically, as he waved his right and then left hand around the room as though it were on display. "I wish you would stay a while," he continued with an edge of hurt to his voice. Jimmy's uneasiness grew. "We could drive over to Larkspur and eat at the Rexford. We could even spend the night there if you want. That miniature resort is as beautiful as the Peabody, and its restaurant is exquisite. All my treat, of course."

As Rutledge rambled endlessly, Jimmy began to rock slightly from front to back on his heels as though he were a cat preparing to spring.

"Their seafood is even flown in fresh daily, something pretty unusual for a restaurant around here. They also have the best hot tamales. You can even get a steak if you like. I had the crabmeat there fixed like..."

"Mr. Rutledge, thank you, but I really should be going," Jimmy interrupted. "I may have to fill in for Seymour tomorrow as the ambulance driver because... he is supposed to go to his father's wedding," he offered as the only excuse he could think of on the spot.

Reacting to the flimsy fib, Jay jumped from the cushions and hurriedly stepped toward handsome Jimmy. Reaching out as though he were going to take the boy's hands in his, he pleaded, "Jimmy, you seem to be such a nice young man. Let me help you with your career and further training if you like. You've got to need some financial help; all younger guys do. With me, you could become more than just an ambulance driver."

Then Rutledge actually took Jimmy's left hand in his right. "I really would like us to become friends." Adding with a gentle squeeze, "Good friends."

Resisting the reflex to slug the gentleman out of pure revulsion, Jimmy backed away and started immediately for the door leading from Rutledge's suite. "Shit, I've got to go now! Man, have you got major problems! And the wrong idea about me. I just came here to scout out the hunting camp. You're really screwed up, you know."

"I don't understand. What are you referring to? I was just trying to help you," Jay Rutledge countered with surprise and sincere rejection.

"I'll let myself out." Jimmy bolted out of Rutledge's room and flew down the hall, almost crashing into the bar as he rounded the corner. Despising what he thought to be true about Jay Rutledge, he hated to almost run away but he wanted out of there quickly. As he cranked his Toyota and sped down the drive to the gate, Jimmy Perry asked himself, "Why did that pervert pick me in the first place?"

Not only was the exit gate to the road shut, it was locked. Disgusted, Jimmy shook his head at the thought of having to confront the deviant back inside about unlocking it. He even considered just plowing through the obstacle with his truck. "That sure would serve the ol' homo right," Jimmy ruminated.

With mounting anger surpassing his bewilderment over the twisted evening, Jimmy thought about the metal cutters and what they could do to the gate lock. The borrowed cutters stowed inside his truck bed toolbox actually belonged to the Peace County Medical Center and were part of its sparse emergency medical equipment. As he expected, the metal lock was no match for the tool's more substantial blades.

The departing guest then popped the gate open, leaped into his vehicle, and anxiously sped though the exit — leaving a mushroom-shaped cloud of dust to settle back down on White Tail Point Drive.

Chapter

8

•••

THE RETURN

From the time that he made that expedient exit from his initial visit, the sign on the gate had not changed. The insignia for White Tail Point Hunting Lodge still looked just as Jimmy Perry remembered, more typical of a ritzy resort than a hunting camp. The gate was fully opened and the ambulance moved uninhibited through the two posts that supported and marked the entrance. Jimmy wondered how long it had taken Rutledge to replace the lock he had destroyed during his previous visit.

The driveway inside the gated entrance to the lodge was also as he had recalled. This time the EMT noticed a woman in a mid-length winter coat with a clashing wool cap, standing by the first curve waving her arms frantically. Spotting the edge of the white apron barely visible below the bottom of her coat, Jimmy assumed that she must be the camp's cook or maid. She signaled for him to continue to the back parking area of the camp house, the same space where Jimmy had parked his truck before.

Several men were standing near an idling gray Suburban whose exhaust cloud seemed to part the freezing air. "We weren't sure how long we should wait for you, so we moved him into the back of my Suburban. There was plenty of room in the back to stretch him out after I removed the rear seat," one of the men standing around reported to the ambulance driver through Jimmy's lowered window. Responding to the unemotional, businesslike gentleman dressed in the well-coordinated camouflage, Jimmy emerged hastily from his vehicle, leaving the flashing emergency lights to drape the rescuers.

As the EMT opened the back of the Suburban to assess the injured's condition, the group turned briefly toward the distant sound of an approaching police siren. The man inside the makeshift trauma unit appeared to be in his early fifties and was likewise dressed in thick, high-priced hunting attire. Jimmy wondered how much damage the good Samaritans had done by moving the motionless, unresponsive victim into the SUV.

Because a faint carotid pulse was barely palpable through the man's ice-cold skin, he did not initiate cardiac massage. Instead, Jimmy immediately retrieved the cervical collar, portable oxygen equipment, and thermal blankets from the ambulance. After stabilizing the man's neck with the cervical collar, he strapped the oxygen mask securely in place. Immediately, Jimmy removed the stretcher from the back of the ambulance, unfolding the equipment as he carried it to the rear of the Suburban. While requesting lifting assistance from the owner of the vehicle as well from the other two gentlemen onlookers, he instructed them not to jar the man's head or neck.

"We thought this guy was dead when Jay called us about finding him," one of Jimmy Perry's assistants commented as they all worked vigilantly to position Cullen Gwinn onto the stretcher.

"Yep, the situation sounded pretty hopeless when we first got the call," added another man, much smaller in stature but nevertheless an outdoorsman-type as judged from his thick beard and leathered skin. Jimmy noticed that this guy's outfit was not as well coordinated as the others. "We were back here at the house beginning to clean the ten-point I shot this morning. Thurmond and I here had just strung him up when Rutledge called on his radio, all panicky-like. You could just hear his voice shaking. He said that he had found this fellow floating face down, almost completely underwater in Custer's Creek." The story of Jay Rutledge's guest falling out of his deer stand and landing near the frozen stream was already undergoing embellishment.

Thurmond, the owner of the Suburban, continued the blow-by-blow, but more factually. "We then pulled a trailer behind my Honda ATV over to where this guy had fallen out of his stand and loaded him in the back. I tried to drive as careful as I could, but the path was pretty rough. I'm afraid he hasn't shown much life from the time we first saw him lying there at the creek."

Jimmy looked up at Thurmond, also searching the other faces gathered around him and this victim of a terrible fall and near drowning. While he was glad that he did not recognize Jay Rutledge among them, he realized that this would have been a second chance to belt the homo for the come on. As hoped, Jimmy had received no more contact from the Montclair hospital administrator since their last meeting however, unknown to Rutledge, Jimmy had since spotted him at a local club.

Returning his attention to the patient after wheeling him to the rear of the ambulance, Jimmy regretted his lack of any detailed medical or other helpful information about the injured man. All he had was the sketchy report of the other hunters. However, in his initial assessment of the trauma victim, he had detected no gunshot wound or medical condition ID bracelet. The self-appointed para-medic assistants helped Jimmy lift the weight into the ambulance as he connected the stretcher's portable oxygen delivery system to that on the vehicle's rear instrument panel. Next, after stripping away the hunting coat which covered his shirt, Jimmy attached the cardiac monitor leads to Cullen Gwinn's bare chest and checked the monitor screen....... *Flat line*. Starting resuscitation measures just as he had been taught, Jimmy began his first solo CODE, regretting that there had been no one free to accompany and assist him on this call. The high number of weekend winter flu cases had compounded the seriousness of the hospital understaffing.

Continuing the systematic but rather frantic set of emergency maneuvers to revive the man, he recalled that Rutledge bragged about all the doctors who were members of this hunting club. "Hey, I need some assistance! Get one of the doctors up in here to give me a hand. This guy is in cardiac arrest!" Jimmy shouted above the police siren, which was growing much closer.

"There aren't any doctors here!" one of the men yelled back. "The closest you could come to a doctor is the guy inside who is a hospital administrator. The fellow on the stretcher is a doctor. But it doesn't look like he would be much help to you, does it?"

Jimmy turned to stare coldly at the speaker but resisted giving a hand gesture.

The smart aleck continued, "That individual you're workin' on is the guest of the member waiting inside. Rutledge was really freaked about his friend's accident. We told him he should just stay out of the way in the lodge, at least until the ambulance came. But if you want, we can go get him now and bring him out to help."

"No, that's all right. I don't think he would be much help anyway," Jimmy answered, not wanting to come face-to-face again with Jay Rutledge any time soon.

While juggling his efforts at assisted breathing and chest thrusts, Jimmy pushed various IV medications but noted no improvement in the patient's cardiac status or breathing efforts. Each of the chest compressions produced only a modest rise in the flat baseline of the heart monitor. No spontaneous activity was ever detected by the electrodes on Cullen's chest — not even an abnormal cardiac rhythm to try to convert to a regular pattern.

One of Jimmy's camouflaged assistants — the one who had not said much until just recently — yelled inside the ambulance to Jimmy, "Why don't you just shock him, like they do on *ER*?" Jimmy reconsidered giving him the finger but thought better of it. Despite every chemical, electrical, and mechanical measure available to Jimmy, the outcome for the unfortunate patient was dismal. The hunting accident had been fatal.

Making the decision to stop the unsuccessful resuscitation effort, Jimmy believed that either a major neurological injury had occurred during the doctor's fall or that he had suffered other devastating internal organ injuries. The water from the creek had without a doubt worsened the man's morbid condition. Anyway, that's what he planned to document. He felt confident that even a more field-tested EMT would not have achieved a better outcome in this case.

Jimmy radioed back to the Peace County Medical Center Emergency Room that he would be bringing in a DOA. In addition, he gave a status report to the police officers who arrived too late to help. The officers told Perry that they would check with him later when completing a report about the hunting accident. Thurmond complied with Jimmy's request to sign an ambulance release form. With the paperwork completed, Jimmy Perry closed the back doors of the ambulance and started back to the ER. There was no longer any need for flashing lights, a siren, or much speed.

The Answer Quik! computer rerouted the call, bypassing the Gwinn home, and assigning it to the next available operator. Whenever planning to be out of town, Cullen arranged for phone calls to his published residential number to be forwarded to the answering service, which would then contact him as necessary. For years this telephone arrangement had run smoothly, preventing Madelyn from getting involved with any persistent patient trying to reach Dr. Gwinn at home.

"Montclair Center for Women's Medical and Surgical Services, your home for a woman's total healthcare needs," the operator responded into her headset. The keyboard beneath her wrinkled hands accessed her Answer Quik! computer screen, her modern switchboard. From the caller identification feature she saw the name *White Tail Point Hunting Lodge*.

As he heard the formal, elderly voice, Jay realized immediately that he had been transferred to an answering service. Irritated at the inconvenience, he explained, "This is an emergency. I am the administrator at Grace Community Hospital. Dr. Gwinn has been involved in a terrible accident, and I need to reach his wife immediately. I dialed the Gwinn's residence and have apparently, and unfortunately I might add, reached you instead." He pushed forcibly, now sounding thoroughly exasperated.

"I apologize, Mister, but I guess they have call-forwarded their residential line to the service. There is nothing I can do but page Dr. Gwinn," she offered per protocol.

"Why would I want you to page Dr. Gwinn? As I just told you, Miss, he has been in an accident, a terrible one. As we speak, I'm watching through a window while he's being loaded into an ambulance. Of course, his wife will want to know about this. Please, for heaven's sake, ask your supervisor or someone else if you have any method of reaching Mrs. Gwinn ... maybe through a cell phone or something." Jay Rutledge had assumed that Madelyn Gwinn's cellular number would have been in the memory or speed dial of her husband's own cell phone. However, a search of Cullen's pockets found the phone too damaged by the fall to be of any immediate use.

"Oh, no, no." She sounded horrified. "We wouldn't have anything like that. No, not for the doctors' spouses," the operator replied almost automatically, even though she was not absolutely certain that Answer Quik! really did not have access to that information. "But we do have the physicians' cell phone numbers and electronic mail addresses."

"Miss, please listen to me. Dr. Gwinn is lying unconscious, or maybe even dying, outside in an ambulance. His cell phone is with him, not his wife. And besides, the phone is broken," Jay sighed audibly. "Furthermore, Miss Whoeveryouare, why would his email address be of any use to me? I need to reach Mrs. Gwinn. Don't you understand? This is urgent!"

"Sir, let me put you on hold, and I will check with my supervisor," she countered, trying to avoid becoming outdone with the insistent, abrasive caller.

After observing the older woman's hand gestures and tight facial expressions, all of which signified a difficult customer on the other end, the Answer Quik! supervisor intuitively walked by. Relieved, the operator leaned over to share the predicament with her superior, who suggested that the operator check for an alternate, second residential line. This telephone number was typically unlisted, never to be released to a caller but utilized only by the answering service to reach physicians in emergencies.

The operator then retrieved the number for the back line, as it was sometimes described by the service, by pulling up the Gwinns' private home phone number. Six rings after hitting "Enter," she heard what she assumed was Mrs. Gwinn in a cheery, pleasant recorded voice expressing appreciation for the call but regretting that no one was available at the time. The gracious greeting promised that any message left at the beep would be returned as soon as possible. The Answer Quik! agent was quite charmed and responded appropriately.

"Sir, there was no answer on their other home line either," she then informed the rude caller after she released the hold on his call. "I left a message for someone to call Answer Quik! as soon as possible. Now who did you say you were?"

Realizing the futility of his efforts, Rutledge forced himself to thank the operator and hung up.

Chief Agee followed the hospital corridor signs to the morgue, wondering how many times the innocent, unsuspecting nurse had walked these same halls. "May I help you?" A gray-haired, pasty-complexioned woman looked up from behind a computer, which displayed the digital photos of the previous autopsy case. Her black plastic eyeglass frames featured Coke-bottle thick lens, each side rising from a crescent-shaped mound of facial skin as though the spectacles were congenital. Deep crows' feet caked with make-up erupted from the outside corner of each eye. The sign on the wall several feet above her head read:

Welcome Desk. The friendly inscription did little to offset the eeriness Chevelle felt. Somehow massacres at crime scenes were less creepy to him than a sterile-looking, austere science lab, particularly one that dealt with death after death.

"Yes, Miss, I am Chevelle Agee, Chief of Police, City of Montclair. I am investigating the murder of Taylor Richards," Agee responded as he proudly popped opened his badge case, directing her to it.

"Oh, I see. Yes, I assumed someone from your department would eventually come. Well, I'm **Dr.** Grimes." The pathologist sought to correct the policeman's inaccurate salutation, erroneous despite the name badge prominently clipped to her long white lab jacket as a supplement to
the front pocket monogramming *Helen Grimes, MD*. If a snobby put-down was directed at the policeman, it was lost on him anyway.

"I need to talk with the doctor about the autopsy findings in the Richards case," the Chief continued, unaware that he had made any professional faux pas.

"I just finished the study and was categorizing my summation but actually need to verify a few of the findings. Follow me into the dissection lab," she motioned while rising from the desk.

"No, Mam, that's not necessary. I just wanted to get a few questions answered about the..."

"Sorry, but I'm a little pushed for time and need to get this report out. That's why I'm here working on a Saturday. The family is already upset that our department has kept the body so long, delaying the funeral. But it really could not be helped. You see, things have been rather slow around here since the other pathologist has been out sick from a herniorrhaphy." Seeing Agee's suddenly changed facial expression, she clarified, "Oh, ah, he's out from an operation to fix his hernia." The pathologist mistakenly assumed that his look
of puzzlement was the result of her use of specific medical terminology. Instead, his expression was one of alarm over the potential of seeing Taylor's corpse splayed beyond her killer's work.

Chevelle had no choice but to tag along through a pair of swinging metal doors into the next room. With remarkable speed the stooped-shouldered, seemingly frail woman whisked open the second bin from the left. From within what resembled rows of neatly arranged stainless steel ovens, she extracted case number 2565 — Richards, Taylor. Before the chief could offer the alternative of simply obtaining some written comments regarding the doctor's findings, she had positioned the nurse's corpse face-up on an adjacent smooth, gleaming table. Agee noticed that the ghastly purplish-white glow radiating from Taylor's face under the overhead lights resembled that of the pale pathologist.

"The chest wounds were primary ... inflicted first ... as shown by the greater amount of bleeding from that area versus that from the neck trauma, which nearly decapitated the victim. According to the quantity of blood recorded in your department's crime scene reports, the stabbing apparently preceded the drowning." To illustrate the findings, Dr. Grimes had lowered the sheet to expose Taylor's chest, breasts, and abdomen, including her pubic area; however, Agee forced only a professional look.

"The location of the drowning was placed to the bathtub itself, based on finding no material in the bronchiole spaces foreign to that expected in a woman's bathtub — that is, no plant life, large quantities of clay dirt or sand, etc. And another interesting discovery was that, since water existed in the bronchioles, the tiny spaces of the lung tissue, she was still alive and trying to breathe when the trachea was severed." Chevelle remained silent during this dissertation, forcing his feet to remain firm against the tiled floor.

"Except those to the neck, you can see that there are no head area wounds other than some broken scalp hair. The killer most likely grabbed the victim by the hair to pull her head at such an angle to facilitate severing the carotid arteries and trachea. When we opened the scalp and cranium to study the brain and dural spaces, we detected no hemorrhage or significant bruising there, basically ruling out direct trauma to the head itself."

As Dr. Grimes reached for a scalpel from a tray close by and motioned toward the surgically sutured scalp of Taylor Richards, Chevelle envisioned her lifting out the girl's pickled brain to show him its pristine condition. With that thought, he choked back the burning fluid rising in his throat, tossed one of his business cards on a nearby counter, and pretended not to run from the pathologist's lair. Fortunately, there was a men's room in the hall immediately outside.

"Fabulous, just fabulous, Miz Madelyn. That gown is so, so wonderful on you that Dr. Gwinn won't be able to keep his hands off!" Minor Leblanc blurted when she emerged from the private dressing room in the designer department. "I know now why he sometimes calls you Mad, because he'll be absolutely mad about you, especially with that scrumptious thing on!" he burst out while clapping his hands together.

"That's what I am afraid of. When Cullen gets the Neiman's bill and sees how much this dress costs, his hands will go straight for my neck," she acknowledged in mock horror mixed with laughter. Madelyn Gwinn well understood that because her husband had been able to afford such luxury, he had preferred that she look good. No, not simply good; he desired her to look exquisite, particularly when they were out together as a couple.

She arranged this shopping trip to Chicago quickly, taking advantage of her husband's plans to be out of town for the weekend. When that hospital administrator had invited Cullen up to his deer camp, Madelyn knew that he could not decline again. Cullen had explained to her that the regular gun season for deer was soon ending in Mississippi for the year, and he needed to go ahead and accept this latest invitation.

Anyway, Madelyn had pushed Cullen's interest in hunting, resulting in her husband's parting with a considerable amount of money on hunting clothes, supplies, and equipment. Even though Madelyn thought it almost humorous that her husband had gone to the extreme of buying a camouflage-colored four-wheeler and ordering a special edition extended cab pick-up, she was glad he had developed another interest beyond practicing medicine. After all, the husbands of most of the other women in the Montclair social circles were avid wild game hunters. On occasion, cooking game in various ways, even experimenting with exotic-sounding recipes, was a topic at bridge club.

"That elegant thing will look great under your mink!" Minor asserted, bringing Mrs. Gwinn's attention back to the dress and the importance of completing this wardrobe addition.

Madelyn was thrilled when Minor Leblanc had agreed to make this short weekend trip with her. She and Minor had departed Montclair yesterday on the only late afternoon Southwest flight, leaving approximately an hour after Cullen left for Pecan Grove. They had flown directly from Montclair into Chicago Midway, an airport much closer than O'Hare to the exquisite shops and hotels of the Miracle Mile. The short travel time and low fares had compensated Madelyn not only for the inconvenience of no first class seats but also for the passenger herd mentality that comes from the total lack of assigned seating.

The money saved on those plane tickets softened Madelyn's guilt over splurging on the Ritz Carlton. She had requested separate, nearby rooms, non-smoking a must. Minor was delighted to learn that they would be staying at the Ritz. On other occasions with different clients, he had actually suggested that location. "The view of the Navy Pier from the higher floors is fine, so fine," he would tell them. Extolling other virtues of the hotel, he would mention all the stars and other lovely people he had seen relaxing there, having drinks in the Greenhouse.

Madelyn had employed Mr. Leblanc's services several times in the past, but this was their first out-of-town excursion. The gifted as well as outlandish fellow was extremely sought after by many of Madelyn's peers. Apparently self-taught, his talents ranged from personal clothes and accessories shopping, to complete wardrobe revamping, and to selecting jewelry for affluent husbands to present to their wives. He began his evaluation of a new client by inspecting her closet and preparing an inventory of what he termed *her things*. Then he would proceed with rearranging the closet, designating much of its pre-Leblanc contents as Salvation Army donations.

"Oh, Miz Madelyn, this selection here has got to go!" He once declared, while waving flamboyantly at an entire rack of spring clothes, some of which still had purchase tags. When Madelyn first engaged his services a year ago, he confided some of his clientele history with her. "After one of our state governors was sworn in to begin his first term, I had to dispose of most of the clothing and accessories belonging to the first lady," he had confided to Madelyn. "The Governor was so pleased with his wife's transformation that he had me do the same for his girlfriend, even help her select maternity outfits," he added, obviously pleased with himself.

Likewise, Minor had even been known to cast out much of the wardrobe of a new client's husband, if his attire was not worthy of hers. His ultimate goal was to blend a couple's hair, skin tones, clothes, and shoes as much as possible to achieve a look not only striking but also overpowering. In a pinch, Mr. Leblanc could even arrange or cut a client's hair himself although for special occasions he preferred to bring a professional hairstylist directly to the client's home.

Leblanc made the majority of his income through commission arrangement with most of the upscale stores in Montclair but had progressed to contacts in larger cities, such as San Francisco and New York. One reason he raced to accept Madelyn's invitation to accompany her to Chicago was that more recently he had cultivated many such arrangements with several merchants there. He was to receive a percentage of his clients' purchases when he accompanied them as a consultant on buying trips. The funds paid to him by the business establishments were on top of either the hourly or daily consultation rate that he charged the client directly.

Most of the women he accompanied during out-of-town shopping trips also paid for his separate hotel room as well as his meals. He provided supportive, emotional companionship to the ladies with whom he shopped and traveled and consistently did an outstanding job making them feel and look beautiful. And all the while, their husbands had no worry about any romantic or sexual advances.

Completely ignoring the Neiman's sales associate who had materialized nearby, Madelyn glanced back over to Minor from the full-length mirror, agreeing that the gown would be splendid under at least two of her furs, particularly the sable. Once Leblanc and Madelyn had entered the expensive designer dresses section of the store, her personal shopper had become the sole director of the selection process. "We'll call you when we have finished," he abruptly announced to the Neiman's employee, who then obediently walked away.

"Kill for this necklace; yes, that's what most women would do," Minor called over to Madelyn from the adjacent jewelry boutique without looking up. He was fingering an eighteen-inch double-stranded diamond and pearl necklace just removed from the secure glass case. Since a clerk with a key was necessary to access these expensive items, the establishment's enthusiastic jewelry consultant had been summoned to assist. "It would look perf' with that gown we just picked out, particularly if you put your dark crocodile-skin shoes with it. The aura we want to achieve here is drama, drama, and drama!" he underscored with his finely manicured hands thrown up in the air, almost waving the necklace around like a small flag.

"I don't think I can push Cullen that far, Minor. The last time I went on a shopping excursion with you back home he couldn't sleep for a week!" she screamed almost giddily. Moreover, she considered the necklace splendid, a must have. "Cullen won't let me have another piece of jewelry for years if I splurge on this," she elaborated, taking the piece from Minor and began to display it around her neck. As Minor helped her with the difficult clasp, he hoped she was joking about Dr. Gwinn not letting her have any more jewelry.

"Now, Miz Gwinn, you know that the doctor has exquisite taste. When you wear this grand thing home, he'll be crushed that he didn't first find it for you."

"I think we better stop with this 'grand thing,' Minor. Oh, but, I simply have to have it!" she squealed like a schoolgirl and then grimaced as though embarrassed about her outburst. Feeling certain that her usually generous husband would approve of the extravagant but gorgeous purchase, she rambled on with uninhibited excitement, "Even though I absolutely know that Cullen will love it, I'm still going to put it up for a while before I surprise him with it." While continuing to covet the piece gracefully adorning her neck, she planned to herself, "If I write a check to pay for this out of that separate emergency account, the money market one that he doesn't look at often, I'll be able to shock him."

Madelyn knew that within reason her husband never objected to purchases for herself and their home. She crushed the twinge of guilt over this necklace with the excuse that Cullen had even encouraged her to join her friends in engaging the services of Minor Leblanc. That was part of his remedy for her recent down-in-the-dumps attitude about her looks and wardrobe.

Minor's successful revamping of Madelyn Gwinn had bolstered her self-image and naturally made her husband's life a lot more pleasant. The one drawback to following her consultant's assistance toward a trendier, closer-fitting wardrobe was that she had become dissatisfied with her figure. Madelyn wanted to be thinner, svelter, and she had persuaded her usually conservative physician husband to help her reach that goal.

While Madelyn signed the check and the credit card receipts, Minor Leblanc provided the store salesperson with their local address at the Ritz Carlton, so that some of the packages could be delivered while others were to be mailed back to Montclair, saving sales tax on part of the out-of-state purchases.

Noting that it was nearly seven thirty, the two shoppers decided to call it a day and explore another shopping district tomorrow afternoon. Inasmuch as their Sunday flight back to Montclair was not until early evening and because the airport was less than forty-five minutes away by car, there would be ample time tomorrow to accumulate more treasures. Minor assured Madelyn that his connections with the various merchants around Chicago would save them precious shopping time tomorrow afternoon, and Madelyn believed him as she always did. With the paperwork for today's final purchase completed, he suggested that they relax with cocktails at the Whiskey Bar, taking for granted that Madelyn would treat.

By nine thirty the cocktails had progressed into a dinner of appetizers at a table for two. Madelyn started with a flavorful chardonnay but promptly progressed to several lower-calorie scotches on the rocks before the night was over. Minor ordered a variety of martinis with one Cosmopolitan thrown in. As the alcohol lightened her mood, Madelyn turned the tables and mentally critiqued her companion's appearance. Laughing to herself that his only exercise must be moving fine clothes on and off hangers or fastening the clasps of precious necklaces or priceless bracelets, Madelyn questioned how he kept such a trim, polished physique.

The longer she sat with Minor gossiping over cocktails, the more in depth she studied his clothes and hairstyle: black, slim fit jeans; dark leather boots with strong heel; opened collar white linen shirt; closely cropped hair. "Metrosexual. That's it. Metrosexual," she decided. He maintained immaculately groomed fingernails, kept trimmed at a relatively long length for a man. His slender, almost glamorous fingers accentuated the martini and cosmo glasses in elegant fashion.

Around 11:30 Madelyn was over-powered by either fatigue or intoxication. She was not sure which but suspected the alcohol. Hoping to circumvent tomorrow's hangover, she suggested that they call it a night and taxi back to the Ritz. Getting off the elevator on their floor, Madelyn and Minor agreed to meet in the hotel coffee shop for breakfast, then store the luggage and packages with the bellman at checkout. The markets and fashion were waiting; there was no time to waste.

Blinking red lights from both telephones attempted to illuminate the darkened hotel room. As she entered, Madelyn noted the message-waiting indicators and assumed that Cullen had called to check on the success of her shopping trip. She also wondered if he wanted to brag about his deer hunt, honestly hoping that his trip had been as productive. Taking a few moments to hang up her coat, use the toilet, and take off her shoes, Madelyn's head started swimming as she reached for the bedside phone.

"I should have ordered an entrée," Madelyn decided as she sat on the bed to steady herself and struggled with the telephone prompts. After depressing the message retrieval button, she learned that she had one unheard message. Mistakenly, she first punched the wrong number choice and inadvertently stopped the playback. Fearing that she had erased the message, Madelyn was relieved that the automated system was more forgiving than some of the electrical conveniences in her own home.

Finally, Mrs. Gwinn was able to focus on the appropriate prompts and push the correct buttons on the telephone keypad. Returning to the main menu of the system, she then worked back through the instructions until she accessed her message. Another technical convenience mess-up, she surmised as she heard Cullen's recorded voice that was apparently left last night but not delivered to her room phone until sometime today. "Mad, it's Friday afternoon late. I've made it to the hunting camp here in Pecan Grove. The hotel operator told me that you might not have made it up to your room yet, and I guess you haven't. Anyway, I really wouldn't call this place your average hunting camp. The lodge itself is really plush, probably too comfortable for a bunch of hunters. I've never seen anything like it." By the excitement in his voice, Madelyn knew that her husband was truly thrilled to be there.

"Especially that Jay Rutledge. His private quarters are elaborate. You would positively approve of his furnishings. Some strange artwork, though... Anyway, I didn't know our hospital administrators received such high salaries!" he laughed slyly. Continuing with his message, "I was kind of late getting here because I had a few add-on surgery cases this afternoon but still made it up to White Tail before dark. You could call me back, but the cell phones around this place don't seem to work consistently. Maybe it's the terrain. I don't know the actual phone number to the hunting lodge, but anyway you really can't refer to this Taj Mahal as a lodge. It's a mansion!"

Before disconnecting he added, "I'll try you again tomorrow from this line. There was a big crazy mix-up over some office stuff that I want to tell you about. See you Sunday. Oh, and I have a great idea. Let's plan another little getaway. This time, just us. — Love you.

As sleep overcame her, Madelyn pressed the *Erase All Messages* feature shortly before buzzing the front desk for a wake-up call.

Chapter

9

•••

THE RAINY DAY

The Montclair Center for Women's Medical and Surgical Services had never been closed on a regular business day, until now, that is. In fact, since its inception as a physician's clinic originally manned only by Cullen Gwinn, MD, the facility's doors had remained open Monday through Friday except on weekends and holidays. If on the extremely rare occasion that Gwinn was too ill to practice or stole a short vacation, the Center was staffed at the minimum by a nurse and secretary. If there were problems with patients that Cullen's assistants could not handle, they called Dr. Gwinn for advice from his sick bed or from the beach.

Before the benefit of physician partners and associates, Cullen bartered with other nearby clinics to provide temporary coverage for his hospitalized or emergency patients when he was unavailable. However, in the early years of the practice this was seldom necessary because Dr. Gwinn never missed more than two consecutive days of work. Nevertheless, this system worked more smoothly as the Center expanded to include more physician members, providing the luxury of built-in substitutes.

Despite the growth of the women's center in both size and prestige, it remained symbolic with the name *Cullen Gwinn, MD*. Accordingly, the news of his unexpected death was devastating although no one was more distraught than the office manager, Nell Lowery.

With forced composure, Nell carried out her emergency duties in canceling Monday and Tuesday's office schedule. She coerced two of the appointment secretaries into working that Sunday evening, the day after the accident, to reschedule all of the appointments. Despite her intense grief, Nell Lowery could not help finding weak humor in the closing of the Center due to Dr. Gwinn's death. From a financial aspect, he himself would have argued against it.

The problems the appointment secretaries encountered in the rescheduling efforts often revolved around some of Dr. Aslyn Hawes' clientele. Most of her patients had never seen Dr. Cullen Gwinn as a physician and surprisingly were unfamiliar with his name. Despite the explanation that one of the senior physicians had died suddenly, several patients seemed irritated by the inconvenience of having their appointment with Dr. Hawes delayed. Many were quick to point out that they had already endured a nine-month to a year wait for their turn to see Dr. Aslyn Hawes.

Much to their delight, some of the perturbed had their demands met when Dr. Hawes interrupted Nell during the rescheduling session. Aslyn did not agree with the office manager's unilateral decision to close the Center for two full days. Instead, the senior female physician insisted upon honoring her Tuesday morning schedule before the late afternoon funeral ceremony.

As would be expected, devastation overcame the majority of Dr. Gwinn's patients as they learned of the tragedy, then tearfully begged for details about the cause of death and burial arrangements. A few screamed uncontrollably over the news. Attempting to comfort these distraught, worried women and retain them within the overall practice, the unlucky callers fought back their own tears to reassure these orphaned patients that another Center physician would be there for them when needed.

Inasmuch as Madelyn and Cullen were themselves childless and both sets of their parents deceased, there were few immediate relatives to be notified. It was not necessary, therefore, to delay the funeral services awaiting throngs of out-of-town relatives. Hoards of patients and their families, as well as numerous doctors and nurses, attended Monday evening's wake, filling the void of family members. Davis-Daughton Memorial Home had never before seen a visitation line extend from a casket in its quiet alcove, down the stairs, and through the funeral home lobby as it spilled out into the parking lot.

As 9:30 p.m. approached, there were still many waiting to pay their respects. Carson Daughton, the funeral home director, was forced into direction. "Mrs. Gwinn, I know you are exhausted." At least he knew that he and his staff were. "May I suggest that we end the reception tactfully at 10:00 p.m., which is an hour later than you had planned? I'm sure all of the grieved will understand."

This proposal relieved Madelyn and her younger sister, who had flown in hurriedly from Dallas to stand next to her only sibling. The sister could not stay for the funeral itself because of her daughter's upcoming junior high cheerleader try-outs. A first cousin of Cullen, who had taken a break from his Jaguar dealership in Memphis with a drive down in a new XJ8, completed the undersized family entourage that preceded the casket in line.

Despite having been left back at the hospital to provide call coverage, Dr. Knox Chamblee pried himself away long enough to pay his respects, arriving late to the funeral home and joining the rear of the well-wishers' and grievers' line. The funeral home director followed through with his plan to end the visitation by 10:00 p.m., turning away everyone after a certain point in the procession. This cut-off was four individuals ahead of Knox. Not wanting to miss the opportunity to pay his respects to the sparse family members, Knox respectfully pulled Carson Daughton to the side, identifying himself as one of the late Dr. Gwinn's partners.

"Oh, yes, Dr. Chamblee, I am sure Mrs. Gwinn will want to see you," the funeral home director responded with emphasis to his typically sympathetic monotone. On the other hand, he announced his assumption loud enough for the others in line to understand why a more important individual was being moved ahead, bumping them. Daughton was not about to offend this doctor, who he hoped would eventually purchase a comprehensive funeral and burial plan. As the potential doctor client was pulled from the string of rejected visitors, the instant celebrity tried not to appear embarrassed by the special attention.

Knox had always felt awkward at funeral homes but fortunately had visited few. He could never completely come up with effective soothing or comforting things to say to the bereaved, a skill not taught in med school but instead acquired.

Rehearsing his condolences as he approached the family, Knox watched Madelyn Gwinn live through one of her saddest moments. Despite hours of being comforted, she still appeared fresh. Even in mourning, her dress was impeccable — a posh dark suit accented with a long strand of flawless pearls. Knox did not know a great deal about women's shoes, but hers had to be expensive. There was also no way to miss the large glittering diamond earrings displayed on pierced ear lobes above a taut, wrinkle-free neck. Completing the attire was a jeweled pin in the design of a bird, affixed to the feminine lapel of Mrs. Gwinn's suit and resting just above her left breast.

The funeral home director had repositioned Knox directly behind a portly, well-heeled woman who had actually been the last "legitimate" person in line before the cut off. As he watched the visitor adorned in heavy jewelry and snug clothes display a diligent effort at commiseration, the incongruous comparison was not lost on Knox. Beyond the talkative, weighty woman was a prominent doctor's wife, now a widow, tastefully dressed and nicely preserved because of her late husband's hard work and success. Madelyn Gwinn's much younger, healthier appearance was a marked contrast to the unattractive, old money standing before her and talking her head off. The old money had long ago lost the opportunity to be as polished and beautiful as Madelyn Gwinn was now.

Not certain of either Madelyn's or Cullen's ages, Knox had assumed him to have been in his mid-fifties at the time of his death. Remembering that he had heard Cullen mention that he had first met his wife in college, he decided that would put Madelyn also in her early fifties. No one could argue that her face and mannerisms concealed that probable age. Moving closer to the widow, Knox embarrassed himself by wondering how much plastic surgery she had undergone. He also found that there were almost no wrinkles on her forehead or around her eyes and wondered if he was witnessing the successful results of repeated cosmetic toxin injections.

Extending his hand as the portly women moved on, he reintroduced himself to Madelyn. "Mrs. Gwinn, I'm Knox Chamblee. I met you at the dinner the hospital hosted when I joined your husband's group." After that time, Madelyn and Cullen had never privately entertained Knox. Apparently, everyone stayed just too busy. "I'm deeply sorry about the accident," he sincerely offered.

"Yes, I understand that you were the first to be notified through the answering service. I do appreciate that you tried to locate me. Unfortunately, I was out of town," she replied in what struck Knox as an extremely refined speech, polished with an aristocratic light southern drawl.

"When the hospital administrator could not reach you, he called me because I was on call for all the Center's doctors. The only phone numbers that I had stored for Dr. Gwinn in my palm pilot were his beeper and cell phone as well as your residence number. That's why I left a message for you to simply call me."

"My traveling companion checked the messages for me when I got home. There was just a great deal going on, so much shock and disbelief. I already knew about my dear Cullen by then, found out right before we left Chicago." At that moment Madelyn felt a burning pain in the side of her head that she fought to ignore.

"I really do appreciate your thoughtfulness, Dr. Chamblee," Mrs. Gwinn's dry eyes produced a new crop of tears. The younger woman standing beside her handed Madelyn a fresh Kleenex, which she swiftly drenched. "If only Cullen hadn't insisted on taking up hunting in the first place." Her voice broke abruptly, and for a moment Knox thought that this genteel lady might blow her nose right in front of him. Regaining composure, she continued, "I'm not sure what happened. Somebody said something about a tree limb that broke... when he put weight on it. No one's given me many details, not even that hospital administrator who took him up there."

Thinking it odd that Mrs. Gwinn had not already discussed her husband's accident with his host, Knox decided that the grief-stricken widow was only confused. "Your husband was an outstanding physician who was truly kind to me. I will miss him; we all will." Knox replied in parting as he eyed the funeral home director staring impatiently at him.

Extending her hand once again as Knox was saying good-bye, Madelyn looked as carefully as she could at the young doctor standing before her, without seeming to stare. As he turned slightly to move down the short receiving line, Madelyn found his manner and looks attractive.

After meeting Mrs. Gwinn's sister from Dallas, Knox glanced sadly toward the casket, noting the absence of any young relatives or children to mourn this premature passing. Before approaching the body, Knox was first forced into an untimely conversation with Dr. Gwinn's cousin. Upon learning that Dr. Chamblee had been in practice with his dear late relative, the distraught relative from Memphis offered his services as a luxury car dealer.

Pulling away from the Jaguar aficionado, Knox stepped toward the illuminated casket, amassed with layers of fresh flowers. Noting Cullen's pale and swollen face, Knox could almost detect a bruise beneath the make-up on his mentor's cheek. He wondered if there were any autopsy incisions hidden under the tailored suit. Dr. Cullen Gwinn had been an important man in Knox's eyes and no doubt held in high esteem by most other physicians and community leaders. Surely, Knox decided, particulars regarding his deadly accident were being sought.

The next day was bleak, made all the worse by a funeral. Drizzling rain and overcast skies served as a miserable demonstration of unpredictable Mississippi winter weather. While the temperature the day of Cullen's death had been bitterly low, the ensuing days were moderately warm, thawing the ground. A resulting fog had settled over the funeral procession, which Knox joined almost as the caboose. Feeling rather isolated within the entourage as it traveled slowly from the church to the cemetery, Knox wished he had not come alone.

The procession mercifully picked up speed as it approached the gravesite. Parking his Audi next to the car in front of him as the parade ended, Knox noticed a freshly dug mound of dirt covered with a water-proof tarp next to an enormous green tent labeled *Davis-Daughton*. Cullen Gwinn's casket was now closed; its metal cover was shining brightly even though the tent blocked the rare sunshine. An abundance of seating remained among the slim white folding chairs arranged in six short rows. Knox spotted Dr. Hawes in the group gathering under the tent with the few family members, but she did not look in his direction. Aslyn stood clearly away from the person next to her, even though a nearby seat was empty.

On the opposite side of the temporary amphitheater, Jay Rutledge and a man whom Knox did not recognize sat stylishly dressed, much too conspicuously for a funeral. Several other grieving souls, who were also well-dressed but more conservatively, began to walk across the green artificial turf to fill in the vacant seats near the widow and the cousin. Despite being a business and professional associate of the deceased, Knox felt strangely removed from the rainy gathering.

The graveside service was appropriately short, considering the dreariness of the weather. Walking to his car, Knox spotted Dorothula Rivers, his matchmaker friend from Labor and

Delivery. She was standing at the fringe of the dispersing crowd, streaming from under and around the shelter of the funeral canopy. Knox greeted her sadness with a reassuring smile and a loose hug.

"I'm glad to see a familiar face. Why aren't there more hospital employees here?"

"Hi, Dr. Chamblee. I worked last night. That's why I could come. It was hard for a lot of people to get off work."

"Of course, the hospital can't close, can it? Like the Center did. Even for a sad day like this."

"Those people that run the hospital are just too stingy," Dorothula replied flatly, not her usual bubbly, sweet self. "All of us were warned not to take off today if we were scheduled to work," Rivers explained. "Also, this nasty weather may have kept some people away."

"I'm sure that Dr. Gwinn would be pleased to know that at least you came. He seemed very fond of you, Thula. I've seen him stop to talk and joke with you in the hall even when he was busy."

"Dr. Gwinn was one of the originals who hired me, back when the hospital was owned by doctors — back in the good ol' days. Those were the good ol' days, for sure. I've always felt at home at Grace 'cause the people at work are real nice, the patients and the most of the doctors — like you, Dr. Chamblee."

While Dorothula Rivers continued with welcomed accolades, Knox looked back toward the funeral tent.
Before the funeral director ushered Madelyn away toward the waiting limousine, she first touched her hand to her mouth and then to the lid of the casket as she placed a final flower on her husband's resting place. Knox noticed her designer sunglasses, which covered her eyes even though there was no sunshine.

"Through the years have you ever gotten to know Dr. Gwinn's wife?" he inquired of Dorothula as he turned his head back toward her, unintentionally interrupting her favorable comparisons of him to Dr. Gwinn.

Peeping back over toward Mrs. Gwinn, she whispered to Knox, "I've never had a chance to — never seen her at the hospital visiting like some of the other doctors' wives or husbands do. Some of my co-workers say they think she's sort of uppity. But a person just shouldn't say such bad things about a widow, especially a new one."

Knox issued his goodbyes to the unit secretary, promising to come by at work tomorrow to visit with her. The trek back to his car was sloppy through a heavier drizzle, making the occasion all the gloomier. Even with the slosh and the mud to tread through, several of the funeral attendees stopped to chat under umbrellas with other bereaved individuals. Unfortunately for Knox, those chatty individuals belonged to the cars blocking his exit from the cemetery.

While waiting for the traffic to move, Knox put in a CD and prepared for the duration. Staring out the front passenger window through the rain, he could see across the ridge toward another area of Davis-Daughton Memorial Park. A much smaller tent had been erected there in a treeless, apparently recently opened area of the cemetery where, instead of established landscaping, sloppy mud encircled the canopy. The Gwinn ceremony had drawn a significantly larger attendance than had this other event, which was still underway. Knox watched several older people praying over the casket. Remembering Dorothula's complaints about a rigid hospital employee time-off policy, he was surprised that the attendees seemed to be more youthful, many dressed in various medical attire.

"That must be Taylor's funeral." Knox could not recall her last name. The last time he had seen her was when she helped him with the delivery of the prima donna. From the newspaper accounts, Knox remembered that the bloodied body had been found in her bathtub and that the investigation was continuing. Someone had mentioned that Taylor's ex-husband was reported to be a suspect. The news of her horrific murder had been overshadowed around the hospital by Cullen Gwinn's likewise unexpected death. Knox decided that even though her death had occurred several days before Gwinn's, her burial must have been delayed by the criminal investigation. While studying the modest ceremony through the rain, Knox felt a twinge of physician guilt for not having attended the slain girl's burial. As he was about to open the car door to dignify the family with his condolences, Knox noted that the group for Taylor was also breaking up. Relieved that his dress shoes were now spared from battling the mud sliding toward his car, he decided to skip another potential mud bath and remain in his dry automobile.

The stream of cars began to move at last toward the exit of Davis-Daughton Memorial Estates, marking the finality of Cullen Gwinn's death. Dr. Gwinn's funeral had weighed heavily on Knox as did that of the young nurse. Nonetheless, human nature being what it is, he realized that Cullen Gwinn's demise was much more likely to affect him directly than the violent passing of a pretty hospital nurse. When signing his employment agreement with Gwinn's practice, it was the young doctor's supposition that he would work almost in the shadow of the industrious, over-worked older physician. Even during the interview process, Knox began to assume that he would inherit a large portion of Gwinn's practice as the senior doctor grew closer to retirement. Now that Dr. Gwinn was gone, Knox anticipated an earlier inheritance.

Every employee of the Montclair Center for Women's Medical and Surgical Services, including Dr. Knox Chamblee, expected it. The day following the Center's temporary closing was to be a killer. Knox feared such an overwhelmingly busy Wednesday because of Dr. Gwinn's absence that he had considered driving out to the office after the funeral to check his own patient appointment list. He even had difficulty sleeping the night of the funeral, practically dreading the next day's workload and the number of office patients he would have to see.

Startled by his obnoxious alarm clock Wednesday morning, Knox was thankful that he had gotten some sleep. He was going to need that rest to handle his day's double-booked patient appointment slots.

That morning Knox met Marshall Langley driving into the Center's physician parking lot. Inside the building the office staff was still buzzing with the arduous task of rescheduling Dr. Gwinn's appointments. As each secretary continued to work overtime, diligently reappointing a year's worth of patients, her imagination ran wild with the dollar amount of her next salary bonus.

"I saw you from a distance at the service yesterday," Knox said to Langley as the two emerged from their cars. Dr. Marshall Langley had served as the third most senior physician partner, having joined the practice a few years after Aslyn Hawes. Now he was second most senior. Not exactly sure of Langley's age, Knox assumed him to be around sixty. Pale, fairly short, thin, and bald, he resembled milk toast. Dr. Langley remained cavalier about his mediocre practice volume, especially for someone of his longevity. Even if Marshall Langley accepted an early retirement from the medical practice, his permanent absence from the Center would essentially go unnoticed. Since he rarely performed major surgery as the primary physician, no longer accepted new patients, and left the office before three o'clock every afternoon, his contribution to the business aspect of the practice was minimal.

"I wasn't able to make it through the crowd at the church to speak," Langley answered although he really had not tried that hard, "and I decided to skip the graveside service. Too rainy." As he gestured toward his faded blue dinosaur Cadillac, he added, "It doesn't take much climate change to put my baby under the weather, you might say," Even the Center's lowest level employees had transportation much newer than Marshall Langley's antique.

"The graveside service didn't last all that long but was really muddy and wet, Langley, a real shoe spoiler."

"Uh, OK, I'll see you around, Knox." Instead of pausing to chat further, Langley disappeared into the medical office building and immediately rounded the corner toward his section. Typically, Langley would have lingered with small talk as though he had no reason to be anywhere in particular.

"Oh, ah, of course. Sure, Marshall," Knox replied, thinking that the elder doctor seemed uncharacteristically curt.

Assuming that his own patient-care assistant would be in a real tizzy over the pair's first overbooked daily office schedule, Knox walked with determination to his separate work area. Surprised to find Lovejoy calmly browsing through a few charts at her nurse's station, he asked her with a certain degree of urgency, "How heavy is the schedule today?"

"Oh, not that bad," she answered, bringing up their scheduled patients on the LCD monitor. She saw the surprise on Knox's face as he reached over to the keypad and scrolled through the patient list, noting empty appointment slots where he expected to see double-bookings. *How can my schedule not be full? What happened to all of Dr. Gwinn's patients?* He almost cried aloud. The shocking fact was clearly visible in light yellow letters on a black computer screen background: *APPOINTMENT AVAILABLE, APPOINTMENT AVAILABLE, APPOINTMENT AVAILABLE.* Knox's patient schedule appeared no busier than usual.

"Did the secretaries understand that I could handle any and all patients that needed to be seen or worked in today?" he probed of his nurse assistant even before, as she noticed, he had said good morning. "There had to be a backlog of Dr. Gwinn's patients needing appointments. I'm sure his schedule today had been chocked as full as it always was," he continued in disbelief as he stared at his own spotty list. "And now that he is not here, I thought that you and I would be pulling up all the slack!"

"Nell told me when I got here this morning that Dr. Hawes herself came up here last night to work with her in straightening out all the patient assignments and pretty much told Nell how to schedule the patients. Puzzled, Lovejoy shrugged her shoulders. "Nell Lowery said that Dr. Hawes seemed to be really worried about the future of the group with Dr. Gwinn gone."

Trying to disguise further his astonishment over being excluded from the rearrangement of patient flow, Knox decided he would question the office manager later about how the situation was handled. Fortunately, a lone patient was ready for him, so he picked up his first patient chart for the day. Lovejoy had already made a short notation in the upper right hand area of the patient registration slip regarding the reason for the doctor's visit.

When Knox had accepted the offer to join this practice, his contract had specified that he would be provided a qualified individual to assist him in the office. This individual materialized from a five-person applicant pool in the form of a veteran employee of the practice, Lovejoy Montez. Married and with several children, Lovejoy enjoyed being around pregnant women and seeing their newborns. She was thrilled when patients brought their children, products of the women's center, back with them to routine doctor appointments.

Her proficiency at handling patient care issues came naturally, partly because she was genuinely concerned about the problems and needs of others. It was her previous experience within the practice working in several other capacities that overshadowed lack of an actual nursing degree. Knox was ever mindful of the fact that no physician's help could be any better than the much admired and beloved Lovejoy. Beginning to feel that he and Lovejoy Montez were truly working together as a team, Knox sensed her sincere loyalty to him and their mutual, scarce number of patients.

Even though her salary and benefits were paid from the overhead of the Center and not directly from Knox's back pocket, Lovejoy shared a mutual respect for Knox Chamblee. Instead of the office manager or one of the more senior doctors, she had begun to feel that Dr. Chamblee was her boss. Part of her dedication to him was to help the patients appreciate his talents. Toward that end, she made every effort to run the office schedule as smoothly as possible, even though its many empty time slots made that task unchallenging. At the top of the single-sheet form on the outside of each patient chart, Lovejoy consistently left Knox a "cheat sheet." Not only would she have listed the required facts regarding the patient's age, problem or reason for the doctor's visit, and her present medications, but Lovejoy would also have noted personal patient details. This personal information typically included the employment specifics or names of any known relatives who were also patients.

During the months she had worked assisting Knox, Lovejoy had never complained, been late to work, nor called in sick. Perhaps, even more importantly, she had never put him in the embarrassing situation of mixing up patients and their charts. Having total recall for more than just a few patients' names was a stretch for anyone, including a struggling, young physician like Dr. Knox Chamblee.

Knox put aside the bewildering disappointment of another meager schedule to survey the first patient's information. At Lovejoy's direction, the clerical secretary had printed a paper-based medical record for her since the Chamblee arm of the electronic system was non-functional. At the top of Velma Wingfield's chart just under her name was the following:

Age 72, New Patient, "Something's hanging out."
(She's Mitzi Park's grandmother)

Thumbing through the document, he noted no physician referral notes. In contrast, Knox spotted Lovejoy's written message to him and the usual insurance information, as well as the other obligatory patient personal statistics: patient mailing address, her insurance information, pertinent medical and social history, and the federal government's mandated patient signatures. He opened the door to the consultation room in which Mrs. Velma Wingfield was sitting with her husband. Both faces looked weathered.

"Hello, Mrs. Wingfield, I'm Dr. Chamblee, and you must be Mr. Wingfield," he said with soft authority as he shook George Wingfield's hand while smiling at both of them.

Before he could proceed in asking her if Mitzi was enjoying her new baby, she blurted out, "Doc, you got to do somethin'!" As she darted a glance toward her husband, she continued, "There is a big bulge down there, and it hurts." Mr. Wingfield nodded obediently in agreement.

Knox asked both of them a few additional questions and then led them down the hall to the examination room where Lovejoy waited. The short procession of young doctor and bent couple proceeded slowly. Looking wide-eyed at the exam table equipped with stirrups, Mr. George Wingfield excused himself and returned to the waiting room, trotting away at a fairly more rapid pace.

"Please put these drapes on, and Dr. Chamblee will be with you directly," Lovejoy gently instructed Mrs. Wingfield, pointing her to the examination table as she exited. The custom upholstery on the chairs in the room was lost on Velma. The pricey high-tech, fully adjustable exam table did not impress her either. She did not even look around the room to notice the attractively framed prints hanging on the walls. Unfortunately, all of the fluff meant nothing to the seventy-two year old. All she wished for was a blindfold and a shot of Jack Daniels to help her endure what was about to happen.

Over the last twenty years, Velma had not been to any physician who performed pelvic exams. While she figured that all of this activity was routine for a gynecologist's office, she still began to perspire heavily, almost disintegrating the paper vest covering her torso. By the time her new physician opened the door to the exam room, Velma was so tense that she would have jumped off the examination table had her sweaty buttocks not been glued to the paper covering.

Per convention, Lovejoy accompanied Knox into the room to aid with Mrs. Wingfield's physical. Her efforts to help Velma further into the position necessary to complete the evaluation of her pelvis prompted the patient's remark, "If I had known how much trouble that thing was going to get me in, I would have stayed a virgin." Knox glanced up at Lovejoy from his exam stool at the end of the table and bit his lip to keep from laughing. With a persistent, but gentle effort, the physical findings were documented.

After Knox counseled his new patient that surgery was indicated to correct her problems, Velma asked that the procedure be scheduled as soon as possible during the next month. The initial step to this process was a search of unfilled time slots in the hospital operating suite before beginning to cross-reference the physician's office schedule with that of the hospital and anesthesia services. Complying with Mrs. Wingfield's request, Lovejoy typed Knox's unique physician staff number into the computer software, selecting the next available date for the following month. Shaking her head she exhaled, "I hate this stupid thing," as the computer rejected her request:

Physician identification not recognized. Scheduling denied.

Perplexed by these words floating across the computer screen, Lovejoy blamed herself for striking an incorrect key by mistake. Reentering the same information was met with the identical greeting and even greater confusion. She then asked Mrs. Wingfield to wait for just a moment in the consultation room and sought help in Knox's office, where he was sitting at his desk, thinking about working a newspaper crossword puzzle.

"The computer won't let me schedule Mrs. Wingfield's surgery, Dr. Chamblee. I can't even enter the surgery-scheduling program to check for available time slots." Knox was surprised by this rare moment of confusion for Lovejoy. The pair had been momentarily handicapped by similar episodes of frozen screens and unresponsive software, but the earlier computer faults were usually a simple fix. Because permanent paper records were no longer maintained, only the files stored within the multifunctional half-a-million-dollar computer system harbored patient medical history, laboratory values, or radiological findings.

Knox valued Lovejoy's diligent efforts toward organization and the way she fought delays or inconveniences in getting her work done. "Lovejoy, this thing with the computer, it's probably just some simple screw-up," he determined, trying to appease his assistant. "We'll let Nell handle it. That's one of her jobs as office manager. I'll get her to call the support system this morning to get our computer back up. For now, just use the paper forms and the telephone to schedule Mrs. Wingfield's surgery."

Much to Knox's relief, this plan seemed to placate Lovejoy. While she began a search for the dusty paper forms, Knox decided to continue with his crossword puzzle since there was no other patient ready for him. Almost delighted that she could once again schedule surgical hospital procedures without the aid of cyberspace, Lovejoy found the printed documents she needed and headed to Velma Wingfield's room.

A six-letter word, a type of artwork. Knox looked up from the puzzle to re-check his sparse patient schedule display. Noting that the intra-office computer system remained operational, he grumbled, "Well, at least some part of the system still works." Since no other patient was checked in to see him, he decided to shift his attention toward talking with Nell about his mounting concerns.

Walking toward the office manager's suite, which anchored the front of the building complex, Knox passed by Dr. Aslyn Hawes' congested patient care arena and was not surprised at the marked contrast. Although identical in size and configuration to his area, her section was bustling with patients and activity. However, at this particular time, it seemed even more hectic than usual. Every chair in the assigned waiting area was occupied, leaving the overflow to stand and lean against the walls. A few visitors, probably expectant fathers, had removed some potted plants from a counter and had perched themselves on the hard surface. The patients and their support teams were gladly waiting to receive expert medical and surgical care from Dr. Aslyn Hawes, a physician highly respected by her patients and their families. They were not interested in the individual, human female dressed in a doctor's white jacket and scrub suit who possessed her own emotions, her own problems, and her own prejudices.

Aslyn was nowhere to be seen, no doubt buried in consultation with a patient solving hormone, infertility, or anatomical problems. Knox recalled the boastful statement of Aslyn's office nurse when she announced that "her doctor" could accomplish more with a patient in a shorter amount of time than any other physician she knew. Out of necessity, Dr. Hawes had perfected a skill whereby she could manage to spend precious little time with an individual patient yet accomplish a great degree of evaluation and treatment. In contrast to some other physicians, during even a brief office visit the talented Hawes could make her patient feel as though she were the most important person in the world.

As he looked over the herd awaiting audience with Dr. Aslyn Hawes, Knox was once again amazed at her seemingly successful practice. He had once decided that she must have an aura about her that caused patients to see her as godly. Once Lovejoy had shared with him what a friend, who was also a patient of Dr. Hawes, had told her. The friend had divulged that because most of Dr. Hawes' clientele feel lucky simply to be accepted by her as patients, they do not expect the pressured doctor to heap individual attention on them.

Knox did not feel guilty about his sarcastic, almost jealous, thoughts regarding Aslyn Hawes. He had heard Cullen Gwinn remark a few weeks ago that she insisted on getting an assistant in addition to her registered nurse so that she could see more volume faster. The partnership had quickly agreed with the mandate and hired the medical assistant for her, someone slightly less expensive to employ than a registered nurse but no less capable for most office patient work. Aslyn Hawes would not have accepted any substandard employee. Knox had heard from Lovejoy by way of the employee-lounge gossip that the doctor had personally interviewed more than sixteen candidates for the job before she approved one. Having not yet achieved the status of physician partner at the Montclair Center, Knox was not a part of the discussions surrounding the Center's employment issues.

As he stepped slightly back around a partition to conceal himself better from the flurry of patients and their families,

Knox wondered if the increased overhead expense of Aslyn's new employee would really be offset by increased work productivity. In fact, he had noticed that Dr. Hawes seemed to be leaving the office earlier each day, an advantage to having her increased office assistance. He wondered if she was really seeing more patients or just seeing the same number more quickly.

Chuckling to himself, Knox figured that regardless of her extra office help, Dr. Hawes would not be finishing the schedule early today. In contrast, the bountiful groveling subjects still waiting to be treated by the great Aslyn Hawes would no doubt force the doctor and her team into overtime.

Walking past that area of the office building and turning at the water dispensers, Knox entered the short hall leading to Nell Lowery's office. The sobbing stopped him. Peering through the half-opened door, he found the office manager apparently trying to cheer up an hysterical young pregnant woman. "I can't believe that he's — he's dead!" she cried even louder. "I loved Dr. Gwinn. He even delivered me eighteen years ago," the girl bemoaned.

She rambled further, holding a crumbled Kleenex that muffled her sniveling and nose blowing. "I was very comfortable with Dr. Gwinn as my doctor. I ain't never seen another doctor 'cept Dr. Gwinn since I was a little girl!" she snorted. "In fact, he's the only other man who has ever seen me — I mean REALLY SEEN me, except for my boyfriend, if you know what I mean! What am I goin' to do? Who will deliver my baby?" the now trembling girl demanded, almost gasping for air as she broke down into even louder panic.

Nell stood from her desk chair, moving closer to this immature patient of the Center, who was obviously in an advanced stage of pregnancy. "Let me reassure you, Miss Reynolds, that your medical care here will not be interrupted. Dr. Gwinn would never have wanted you to be worried or have any problems because of his unfortunate accident. One of our other doctors will be happy to see you ... and welcome you ... now that Dr. Gwinn is gone."

Observing Lowery's attempts to appease the mother-to-be, Knox began to think of himself as the new doctor of this distraught patient.

"Dr. Gwinn was wonderful. How can I ever find another doctor as good as him?" Portia Reynolds carried on with great drama.

All Nell could think to do at that point was just stand silently, holding the expectant girl's hand, and just let her ramble uncontrollably. There was no way to interrupt the incoherence.

"Why did he have to die, especially now with my baby comin' in just a few weeks? Maybe I should just go somewhere else, to another clinic, one that ain't so busy. There's no way that one of the other doctors here will want me."

Nell Lowery stepped even closer to Portia, trying to salvage the situation when the ranting abruptly turned into a scream. "Oh, my baby! Something's wrong!" Suddenly grasping the lower part of her swollen abdomen, Reynolds wailed, "The baby is moving, moving too much. She's hurting me!"

Understanding that she was dealing with immaturity, Nell doubted that the unborn baby was in distress. Her reassuring words futile, Lowery chose a different tactic: comfort the bereaved girl with a face-to-face new doctor-patient experience. This time more urgently, she interrupted the howling. "Miss Reynolds, let me take you real quick to meet your new doctor."

When Knox realized that they might catch him eavesdropping, he started to skirt backwards down the corridor away from the manager's office suite. He wanted to beat them to his own work area where he would appear busy but ready to welcome his new obstetrics patient. However, Nell had moved abruptly to get the distraught girl out of her office and down the hall, leaving Knox short time to dodge the two. Darting for refuge into the nearby visitor restroom, he practically stumbled into an adjacent alcove, almost knocking over an artificial weeping ficus. Fortunately for him, neither the office manager nor the patient detected any of this commotion.

After Nell and the pregnant teenager were clearly down the hall, Knox began to follow them nonchalantly at an unnoticeable distance. Much to his dismay, the office manager led Portia Reynolds not in the direction of his area of the building but instead directly to that of Dr. Hawes. Continuing to use the building's decorative plants as camouflage, Knox inconspicuously watched but angrily listened as Nell located Dr. Hawes' new medical assistant, introducing her to Portia.

Explaining that Portia Reynolds had been an established patient of the late Dr. Gwinn, the office manager declared that she would be now a new patient of Dr. Hawes. The still tearful Portia seemed relieved by this decision as her new mother figure, Nell Lowery, insisted that she would be the next patient seen today. After all, thought the pregnant teenager, Dr. Hawes' pretty medical assistant did seem to have a friendly, warm smile.

More dumbfounded than hurt and not wanting to admit his eavesdropping, Knox remained hidden behind a dense rubber plant until Nell left the patient waiting area. Walking slowly back toward his section of the building, he recalled that the upset patient had already demonstrated her comfort in seeing a male physician. The absurdity of Nell's placing the girl with Hawes was obvious to him when considering that Aslyn already had an overly full patient load.

After introducing the frenzied patient to her new medical team and relieving herself of the burden, Nell Lowery could not get back to her own office fast enough. With her head spinning from the last few days' events, she practically ran back to her section of the building. She also desperately missed Dr. Gwinn, who had personally hired her years ago from a meek pool of business college graduates. During her tenure, she had maintained her job security by following a strict protocol: follow doctors' orders. Likewise, she had kept her office administration degree by accumulating continuing education credits and attending various seminars, all fees for such paid by the medical practice Dr. Gwinn founded. She valued her job and loved what she did. Despite her less than college education, Lowery was certain that she was capable of administering as well as any MBA.

On the other hand, Nell Lowery recognized her limits. She reported to duty every day promptly at 8:00 a.m., understanding that she could be as easily replaced as she was hired. In fact, she feared that any substitute for her would be younger and better educated.

Yes, Nell Lowery was a Trojan, a survivor.

"Nell, I'd like to talk to you for just a minute."

Heavy in thought as she sat at her desk covered with a mountain of files, sticky notes, ledgers, and junk mail, Nell jumped slightly when Dr. Chamblee walked through her office door.

"Yes. Hi! Uh, come on in," Knox detected a hint of strain in her usually inviting voice, not unexpected since her senior boss had just died.

"How are you holding up?" he asked sincerely. He had been fond of Nell Lowery from the moment that Cullen Gwinn had introduced them. Considering her an extremely conscientious and diligent worker, he admired her for her productive but conservative approach to management. As office manager, her responsibility had been to explain his physician employment contract to him when he was hired by the practice. Since he had not wanted to spend his own money on outside legal advice in reviewing or understanding the document, he had relied on her explanation of the legal terminology in what she assured him was a standard physician employment agreement.

"I'm fine. Thanks for asking." She forced a smile, unmatched with her eyes. "There has really been a lot to do around here over the last few days. The Center cannot not just stop functioning because Dr. Gwinn was...," she hesitated momentarily, "because Dr. Gwinn died. Of all people, Dr. Gwinn would not have stood for the Center's productivity to slow down, for any reason."

"Speaking of productivity, Lovejoy and I are having difficulty getting the computer program to let us schedule surgical procedures. The problem started today," Knox explained as Nell dropped her eyes to the mounds of cluttered paper work hiding her desktop. When she failed to respond, he focused on his real concern. "And another thing, I was available to see some of Dr. Gwinn's patients today. Even though I had several empty appointment slots on my schedule, there were no add-ons of any of his patients onto my appointment list."

"Dr. Chamblee, this is a difficult time, difficult for all of us." She lifted her eyes meeting his — hers blurry, vague — his piercing, almost angry. "The partnership has been looking at some reorganization and long-range planning. We hired Perkins and Unger Medical Consultants to help us analyze the productivity of the practice. I'm sure you have seen some of those people from Atlanta hanging around the office. They boast complete access to extensive research regarding medical practices, particularly those that deal with OB/GYN and have asked for all sorts of financial data from me. I have stayed late after work for the last several weeks and have even worked on this at home. By analyzing how the Center's total productivity compares to that of the individual physicians, this consultant company has come up with certain determinations about our practice overhead costs. And they have made some recommendations..." Her voice seemed to trail off as she looked blankly past Knox, concentrating on the wall behind him.

"What kind of recommendations?"

"From the standpoint of cash flow, they have determined that female obstetricians and gynecologists are by-and-large more productive than males. Their evaluation is all about money on the books. When P & U looks at the financials of a medical practice, they also evaluate the amount of overhead a new physician costs a practice. With the skyrocketing malpractice rates and the escalating salaries that the supportive staff demands, it costs a tremendous amount to maintain a doctor in a viable practice."

Knox wasn't quite sure where this discussion was going, but he did not want to interrupt Nell, not just yet.

"The problem wouldn't be that serious if we could raise our patient fees across the board to offset these out-of-control overhead levels. But, as you know, with managed healthcare the medical insurance companies block us from utilizing the principles of American free trade. Through practically forced contractual arrangements, we cannot pass along our increased expenses to our customers, customers who are more demanding everyday. Anyway, the Perkins and Unger firm tells us that to survive in the medical market place, the Center must concentrate on physician productivity. Each physician has got to see as many patients an hour as possible, and to fill that hour, each physician must be able to attract patients to the appointments. P & U has determined from their surveys and research that the large majority of women patients want to see a female doctor. No, how did they put it? ... they **demand** to see a female OB/GYN."

"Nell, I disagree with that absolute generality. I have noticed that some patients in our area have a gender preference regarding doctors. However, all through my residency and in private practice, I have never knowingly had significant problems with patients rejecting my care because I am male. This has proven true despite situations where the primary attending physician is female."

"Yes, but those were most likely emergency, on-call situations; don't you think? The P & U opinions are based on what their research has shown. When shopping for a physician, the trend is that female patients more and more seem to prefer a female physician, or so the firm says. Those female ob-gyns will then produce much faster monetarily than their male peers. The important thing is to put more money on the books, overcome the overhead, and take the financial burdens off the rest of the practice."

Knox wondered if the consultant firm also brainwashed the office managers of the practices they evaluated, reprogrammed their brains like a computer hard drive. "You mentioned a recommendation from this Perkins and Unger firm," Knox doubted that he could win this gender debate with Nell, armed with all her statistics. "I initially came in here about the problems Lovejoy and I have been having with the computer software, but you have ignored those concerns. Also, I had planned to complain about all the thumb twiddling I have had to do today. While I was looking at a dumb crossword puzzle, the other doctors in the office had much more densely booked patient schedules than usual. Marshall Langley seemed more pressed for time today, of all things. Naturally, I didn't expect to benefit from Dr. Gwinn's death; however, I should have at least seen some of his patients today."

Silently Nell stared, letting him vent, although her gaze was as vacant as her draining pinkish-white complexion. She hated to admit to Knox that she had installed a firewall against his computer access along with an audit trail to track any of his attempts at on-line activity.

"But I'm here in the office today," Knox continued, "as I have been everyday since I was hired, available to work and take care of patients. Anyhow, I'm never going to get more productive as a physician unless I see a greater volume of patients. Part of the advantage of joining a larger group is that you get to benefit from a trickle down effect from the other more established physicians."

Knox took enough of a break from his frustrated oration that Nell interjected, "That's just it, Knox. The dilemma is as the surveyors have pointed out: male physician domination in the OB/GYN field is history, like the dinosaurs. A male OB/GYN physician is not as valuable an asset to a practice as is a female one." As though she were changing the subject, she lamented, "Oh, how I wish Dr. Gwinn had not died, for a lot of reasons."

"Well, we are all devastated by the loss of Dr. Gwinn, as I am sure his family is. Cullen Gwinn, his talents and knowledge, could never be replaced by any other physician," Knox summarized as he continued to pace around Nell's office.

"Knox, Dr. Gwinn pushed your employment here through the Center's Board of Directors. You were obviously qualified since you had completed the university's residency program in Jackson. And your recommendations from the university chairman and faculty were good." She hesitated. "This issue has been discussed again and again at the board meetings with Dr. Gwinn always there — on your side."

"What issue?"

"Regrettably, and you know this, your accounts receivable has been stagnant. Dr. Gwinn was beginning to run out of financial ammunition on your behalf."

"Ammunition?"

"Dr. Hawes told me earlier this morning that I should go ahead and let you know after work today, but I don't think I can put it off any longer."

"Let me know what? Can't put off what any longer? Nell, you can't be ... surely you're not telling me that ..."

"I'm telling you that you have sixty days severance pay coming to you, just as your contract provides, and that we will provide an outstanding recommendation for you. I'm sorry, but the Montclair Center for Women's Medical and Surgical Services no longer requires your services effective tomorrow." Nell struggled to keep her voice steady and unemotional. "This is very difficult for me because you are a very fine, well-educated young man, Knox," Nell Lowery continued as she lost the battle, and her voice broke, "but you're ..."

"Fired, fired for being a man." he quietly completed her sentence as he turned around and left her office.

"They dumped me! Can you believe it? They fired me because I have the wrong set of genitals," Knox declared to Lovejoy, found still at the workstation, pretending to be busier than reality required. "I'm a victim of my Y chromosome, Lovejoy... Might as well wear the letter in red around my neck or pin it on my lab coat." Trying to maintain a controlled demeanor, Knox somehow kept his voice at a professionally low decibel and octave. Nevertheless, his assistant was startled while filing away the completed surgery forms for Velma Wingfield's anterior and posterior vaginal repair procedure.

"Whaaaaaaat?" Bewildered, Lovejoy straightened up from peering down into the filing cabinet. "They can't do that. They just can't! Dr. Gwinn hired you."

"But Dr. Gwinn's not here anymore. I guess he didn't list my job guarantee in his will. Sweet Nell just dropped a bomb on me, explaining that the practice here plans to replace me with a female physician, someone more productive from a monetary standpoint. The discussions terminating my physician employee contract apparently started before Dr. Gwinn's death."

Lovejoy was devastated. First, the cornerstone of her overall job security, Dr. Cullen Gwinn, dies. Now, her promotion to nursing assistant for Dr. Chamblee is jeopardized by the loss of his position. She wanted to scream and cry at this turn of events but could not admit to Knox that her sorrow was more for her plight than for his. "How long do you, do we, have to draw a paycheck?" she asked him.

"Nell did not mention anything to me about letting you go. Actually, your name did not come up in the conversation," Knox answered, feeling slightly awkward that he had not questioned Lovejoy's job security. "I think that you probably will always be welcome here at the Center, Lovejoy. Good, experienced medical office assistant nurses are hard to find. They're not a dime a dozen like male ob/gyns," he explained sarcastically.

Feeling somewhat better now about her own job security, Lovejoy tried to think of anything she could say to cheer Knox up. She searched for something that would sound positive, but there was just nothing there that Dr. Chamblee did not already understand. The indisputable fact was that Dr. Chamblee was a great doctor. Although he was not her personal physician, she could sense his genuine interest in his patients. Whereas his patient numbers were presently low in comparison to the other doctors, she had never questioned that his career would blossom as his highly technical surgical skills and gentle bedside manner were more greatly appreciated.

Over the last several months, Lovejoy had arrived for work enthusiastic in the belief that Knox Chamblee, MD, would soon become one of the most sought after doctors in the Montclair area. Never had she witnessed another physician like him as she admired his persistent attitude — calling his post-op surgical patients after their hospital discharge to check on their continued recovery and similarly contacting his small number of post-partum maternity patients to see how new mom and baby were doing. During the many empty time slots on his schedule, she had watched Knox draft personal thank you notes to the pleased clients who had referred their friends to him as new patients. He would also spend idle office hours productively telephoning problem ones to further discuss their treatment options or their response to prescribed therapies. No one could argue that his practice was building more slowly when compared to other physicians in the past. But times were different; everybody knows that, Lovejoy assumed. There were many more obstetricians and gynecologists for patients to choose from, both male and female.

During her medical career, Lovejoy had worked with many physicians in multiple capacities. Some positions had been menial, but now that she had ascended to the status of a physician's *right hand man*, she did not want to lose that valued although unofficial title. Even though Dr. Chamblee had tried to reassure her that her job itself was not threatened, Lovejoy did not feel content whatsoever in her future employment status at the Center. She believed, however, that if Dr. Gwinn were still alive, he would make sure that she was taken care of.

Becoming teary, Lovejoy knew that for the moment she had to put concerns about herself and her family's financial welfare aside and counsel this poor doctor through this difficulty. Lovejoy truthfully affirmed, "You are a wonderful physician, Dr. Chamblee." She thought her words sounded all too ordinary. "Your patients love you. The other doctors here are making a mistake." A thin tear erupted in her left eye, rolled down her cheek, and was promptly followed by a fatter one. "What are you going to do now?"

"I'm going to finish the minute amount of chart dictation I have to do, make rounds, and go home early. Thank you, my sweet Lovejoy, for everything you have done for me," he managed to say without letting his voice break, hugging her in such a way that she could not see his own wet eyes.

Chapter

10

• • •

THE SEARCH

"Madelyn, let's move over to the car," Carson Daughton directed in hushed sympathetic tones, as he gently led the grieving widow by the left elbow toward the black Cadillac. The long-time friend and patriarch of the local funeral services empire, he had handled all of the arrangements for her, assuming that cost was of no concern. And it wasn't.

Several years ago Cullen and Madelyn subscribed to a funeral insurance plan with Davis-Daughton Memorial Services that provided for both of them separately or, heaven forbid, as a couple. The arrangements included all of the funeral service details, from a double gravesite with a tasteful marble marker designed specifically for Dr. and Mrs. Gwinn to the music and number of eulogies. Located among the thick tall oaks and ivy-covered brick walls toward the back of the cemetery, the tranquil location was in the "old" section of Davis-Daughton Memorial Estates, where long ago the choicest spots had been either occupied or reserved. All Madelyn had to do was sign the formal paper work, activating the provisions of their burial policy, and Carson Daughton went to work.

The church service had started with the procession of Dr. Gwinn's polished upscale mahogany casket draped with fresh flowers. Coming to rest at the front of the church, the adorned casket joined the more massive floral arrangements that almost completely obscured the altar. Because of her consuming grief, Madelyn had noticed none of that spectacle or the one following at the cemetery. She had barely heard the preacher's eulogy or the one from Mayor Netz or the one given by the president of the Chamber of Commerce.

Those sitting in the pews near the widow watched her with sad interest during the service, assuming that Madelyn's flowing tears were in reaction to the other testimonies lauding her outstanding husband: a compassionate doctor, one long-time patient said in eulogy; always an unselfish professional, a fellow hospital physician called him; truly a valuable friend to the underserved community, another volunteer at the homeless shelter announced. In reality, Madelyn's tears were not for the life cut short but for the future with Cullen that she had lost forever.

As the limousine departed those lingering after the graveside ceremony, soft tears continued to stream down her cheeks. Riding toward home, Madelyn remembered concentrating not on what the minister and the others were saying but instead upon the life that she and Cullen had shared. Those times had seemed empty on occasion, particularly during holidays, because they were without children or any nearby nieces or nephews. They had desperately tried to have their own family. She had seen Cullen's fertility specialist friends, even driving to Memphis and New Orleans when the doctors in Jackson had been disappointingly unsuccessful with her case. Her late husband had indeed found an acceptable baby or two for them to adopt, but in both situations there was a last minute change of heart on the part of the birth mother. No options to expand their family beyond a happily married, financially secure couple ever seemed to work out.

Looking forward to the next several years with her husband, she had hoped that they would be able to relax together, travel extensively, and enjoy what they already owned. For instance, their home in Montclair was paid for long ago, and the last payment on the vacation house at Seaside had been made recently. Madelyn had fulfilled the obligatory charity and volunteer work expected of a doctor's wife in Montclair, leaving her with fewer day-to-day responsibilities. Along those lines, she had hoped that Cullen would lesson his workload.

Cullen's own work ethic had been simple: work all the time. With her late husband's renewed interest in golf, Madelyn had also hoped that their lifestyle would become more leisurely, more completely devoted to each other. Because Madelyn had participated in several ladies' charity golf tournaments, she had actually played more of the game in recent years than he had. However, with his newfound interest in game hunting, she sensed that Cullen was beginning to develop a broader prospective of life. As the tears fell with greater force, she realized that her husband would be alive if he had not been interested in going to that hunting camp.

As the limousine traveled south on the interstate toward her section of Montclair, Madelyn's compunction was almost paralyzing, made all the worse by the twinge of a developing headache. "Why was I out-of-town at the time of Cullen's death?" she cried almost loud enough for the driver to hear. Nonetheless, Madelyn sought solace in understanding that her absence would not have prevented, as the editor of the local newspaper had published, her husband's "tragic, untimely, shocking and mournful demise."

Embarrassed about the extravagance of her weekend shopping trip and the unheard critical comments of others (Can you believe she was running all over Chicago, throwing money around while her husband lay out there, dying in the freezing cold?), the widow reminded herself that she had not planned her excursion until Cullen had planned his. Furthermore, she felt sorry that her leaving town was so rushed that no one except Cullen, not even her house staff, was aware of her whereabouts.

Contributing to the delay in finding Madelyn in Chicago and informing her about her husband's death was that the tragic news was not circulated around Montclair until late Saturday. But once Tricia Pennington became involved in that dissemination, the information spread like wildfire. The first link in a chain of any reliable gossip, Tricia Pennington remained drenched in knowledge about newsworthy persons in the Montclair area. Eventually and indirectly, Madelyn was located and informed Sunday morning through the efforts of Tricia Pennington.

The source of Tricia's information was inadvertently her own husband. Paul Pennington had himself been hunting that Saturday afternoon near Pecan Grove and had heard something on the local radio about an area hunting accident in the area. The particulars had been sketchy, but his attention was caught by the mention of a doctor from Montclair killed earlier that day at nearby White Tail Hunting Camp.

On the way home from his own disappointing hunt, Paul Pennington called his wife to check on the evening's supper plans. He casually mentioned to Tricia the radio news item about the hunting death of a Montclair doctor. "Oh, Paul, that might be Madelyn Gwinn's husband. She mentioned something at bridge earlier in the week that her husband might accept an invitation to hunt in Pecan Grove this weekend. Some employee at his hospital had already invited him several times. I don't remember the name of the hunting camp, and I'm not sure that Madelyn even knew the name herself," she replied to Paul's news, nearly squealing.

"Well, there are several hunting camps up this way," he informed Tricia, "but White Tail sounds suited for a rich doctor like him."

"Did they say if he had been shot?" she inquired, more out of sensationalism than real concern.

"No, the radio just described it as a hunting accident. Something about the police having been called to the scene, though. Don't remember any more details."

"This is just awful, Paul. Surely it wasn't Cullen Gwinn. No one around here has said a thing. It's strange that I haven't seen Madelyn since bridge earlier this week. She wasn't up there with him, do you think?"

Paul's cell phone was beginning to break up. "That hunting camp .... swanky, I understand .... plenty of room for people to .... might have been with him because I've heard .... take guests .... up there with .... "

"Poor Madelyn. She has little family and nobody in Montclair.

"We .... to switch to Cellular Certain, Trish. I .... barely hear you now."

Priding herself in knowing this sort of first hand tragic-type information, Tricia began to formulate a plan to verify it and then disseminate it. Not really sure that her husband could actually hear her, she continued nevertheless. "I need to call Madelyn. I'll try her house first and then her cell if there is no answer," she told her husband.

As he ended the call, Paul Pennington let out a sigh that was inaudible to his wife. While the cellular drops prevented him from hearing all that was said, he had learned to accept that Tricia relished involvement in these types of things, the morbid ones. However, he hoped that her motives were genuine.

Receiving no answer on the Gwinn private telephone line, Tricia tried Madelyn's cell phone. The recorded message from the cellular provider indicated that the number was out of the service area. There was no option to leave a message. This obstacle was not going to stop Tricia Pennington. She was going to find Madelyn Gwinn.

Even though one client on a project had engaged him, Minor Leblanc had great talent in being able to maintain mental files of the needs, preferences, sizes, and tastes of many other patrons. While assisting one client and devoting his complete attention toward her, he was still able to shop for and set aside apparel and jewelry for others. This ability was practiced skillfully during the Chicago trip. While Madelyn was trying on one prized outfit after the other in the fitting room, Minor was reserving jewelry and clothes for other customers, including Mrs. Paul Pennington. Ultimately, it would be his association with Tricia Pennington that would break the word of Cullen's death to Madelyn Gwinn.

Sunday morning before his planned breakfast with Miss Madelyn, Leblanc reached Pennington without difficulty through his cellular service. He was anxious to tell her about several perfect spring outfits that would not last long in the stores. Answering while dressing for church, Tricia groaned when she saw the caller identified only as *M Leblanc*. Sometimes she was interested in talking with Minor, but during distressing times like these, she was not. While as a rule she found him entertaining and could not discount his talent for putting together good-looking outfits, Tricia had never let her husband know that she had ever engaged Minor's services.

She decided to answer the call rather than let the answering machine get it. "Minor, how are you?" she responded in the shrill, sweet voice that was typical Tricia.

"Tricia Pennington, I have got some really great stuff for you!" He went on and on about the unique ensembles, shoes, and jewelry he had spotted especially for her in Chicago. He wanted to have some of it shipped to her on approval if she thought anything sounded appetizing; however, he assured his client that all of the things were stunning and irresistible.

In the middle of becoming enthralled with his description of a must-have Escada outfit, Tricia was squeezed by justified guilt and then pity over her vision of a distraught Madelyn Gwinn. She knew that Madelyn was also one of Minor Leblanc's clients. There had never been any competition between the two for Minor's finds because she and Madelyn were not the same size, were of different ages, and had tastes that were fairly dissimilar. Disrupting the experienced personal shopper as he was describing the coordinating shoes, she blurted into the mouthpiece, "Oh, Minor, you're out-of-town, so you may not know. Madelyn Gwinn's husband was killed yesterday in a hunting accident."

Tricia did not hear Leblanc's high-pitched gasp because his cell phone was now on the carpeted floor beside his feet.

In addition to being flamboyant, humorous, and talented in wardrobe design, Minor Leblanc was kind. Now shackled with the responsibility of delivering this terrible news to one of his most his loyal clients, he had decided that it was best to break Tricia's disturbing information to Madelyn in person. While a progressive, persistent businessman, he also had great respect for his clients and their feelings.

After retrieving his cell phone from the floor, Minor was overjoyed that it still worked because the rug had cushioned the impact. Allowing Madelyn adequate time to dress for the planned but ill-fated breakfast that Sunday morning, he then knocked on the door of her hotel room and told her as compassionately as he could that her husband was dead. Leblanc cried with Madelyn over the devastating news, Madelyn feeling fortunate that she was not alone at this time. Minor then helped her pack and made all the travel arrangements for them to return to Montclair as soon as possible. He refused to accept any of his usual fees and, as was not his custom, paid for his own hotel and airline ticket.

Sitting there at the funeral and mulling through the last few days, Madelyn felt certain that her escapade in Chicago had been and still was fodder for the town's gossips. Many of those gossips were her supposed friends. "Madelyn was in Chicago with her fashion consultant, maxing out her husband's charge cards. And no one knew where she was when he was killed!" she could imagine the bridge club members recounting among themselves. It would be these same genuinely interested individuals she would have to face when she arrived home after the funeral.

"Madelyn, Paul and I feel such a terrible loss. The whole community does, I'm sure." Madelyn nodded almost automatically to Tricia Pennington as a gesture of acceptance for the sympathy. Tricia was the first to greet Madelyn as Carson Daughton led the widow through the side entrance of her home. After the driver had dropped Madelyn and his boss off, he followed advertising protocol and parked the limousine prominently out front in the circular drive.

Naturally, Tricia was the earliest person to greet Madelyn at the post-graveside feast. The rising Montclair community-service mogul was in her element at this type of activity. Considering this function a vital part of her service to local society, Tricia felt it her duty to organize the trappings of home visitation before and after a funeral, particularly for a good friend.

Patricia Montrose Pennington was of the opinion that some funeral activities deserved more pomp and circumstance than others. One example would be the present one. Tricia had never used Cullen Gwinn as her gynecologist because she thought it mattered that she knew him personally. However, she possessed great respect and admiration for him as a talented physician and had several times tapped him to present community service programs on various women's health-related issues. Marching toward the goal of becoming the next president of the Montclair Humanitarian Alliance, she had served on the governing boards of numerous local charity organizations. Tricia consistently put herself in the middle of the current social scene, whether joyous or remorseful.

Madelyn had not invited anyone in particular to join her back home after the funeral, assuming correctly that an entourage of grieving people would be there regardless, anxious to greet her. She was correct in that Tricia had done another wonderfully organized job. All of Madelyn's Montclair loved ones were there in full force: her entire bridge club, every one of her Alliance committee chairpersons, the twelve members of her country club tennis team, the complete women's circle from the church, and every adult who lived or who had ever lived in her neighborhood. Inconspicuously absent were the members of medical spouses' auxiliary.

Not only had Tricia summoned multitudes of guests to fill the public spaces of the Gwinn home, but she had also arranged for mountains of beautiful food to feed them. Madelyn's expansive mahogany dining room table was weighted with elegant, delicious-looking hors d'oeuvres. Sterling silver hollowware overflowed with casseroles, sliced ham and roast beef, and home-baked bread. The antique sideboard on the adjacent wall was burdened with pastry desserts and sliced fresh fruit.

Tricia's team of volunteer assistants had completed the feast with a wine, juice, and coffee bar on the French enfilade in the breakfast room nearby. After scanning the spread and all the noisy, festive people, Madelyn wondered sardonically why the revelers had not turned on the stereo system.

Carson Daughton was relieved that today's booking was nearly complete because dealing with the funeral of a more prominent client was always draining. Now that he had delivered the widow home, all that was left was to have his runner deliver the funeral sprays to the house before sending Mrs. Gwinn her final bill for any overages. Happy to transfer the care of the widow to Mrs. Pennington, he made a quick exit.

As Tricia greeted her with a loose hug, Madelyn's manners snapped back into joint, although forced. "Thank you, Tricia; it is dear of you to be here and for you to have put this all together. Is Paul out in the living room?"

"No, uh, he's at home, feeling under the weather," she hesitated as she lied. Her husband did not know Cullen well since veterinary medicine and human obstetrics and gynecology do not often intermingle professionally. Quietly, Dr. Pennington was offended that the Gwinns had never brought any of their pets to him. After emphatically declining to accompany his wife to the funeral services, Paul Pennington even questioned why his wife was going to all the fuss for someone not even considered a good friend.

"Madelyn, someone told me that your sister had to leave before the funeral. Would you like for some of us to spend the night with you so you won't be all alone in this house?" Tricia asked, while walking with Madelyn through the dining room and motioning to the other self-taught caterers.

"Tricia, that's really kind of you to offer. But I've spent many a night and weekend all alone in this house when Cullen was on call a lot. I know the circumstances are different this time, but I'll be fine," her words breaking.

Giving Madelyn this time a more thoughtful hug, Tricia suggested that she call later if she needed anyone to come over. "Let's join the others in the living room," she tendered, while leading Madelyn from the banquet table through the long front hall.

Tiring of the long hours of condolences, Madelyn wished that every brokenhearted patient, sympathetic doctor, anguished nurse, and long-faced hospital employee would leave. Many who had never seen the late Dr. Gwinn's house or met his now widowed wife came to pay their respects as much out of curiosity as out of the need to express commiseration. Once the last well-wisher, who happened to be Minor Leblanc, had filed through the Gwinn home and left, a dull throbbing sensation in the left temple reminded Madelyn that she had not taken her morning medication.

Walking around the formal foyer, back into the living room and through to the library, she paused to examine each wall painting and each piece of art that she and Cullen had chosen together for their collection. Customarily, they would mark a vacation or medical-business trip with such a memento.

Coming across the most recent purchase from an antiques shop in Point Clear, a rack of leather books now displayed in a Georgian period breakfront, she slid out the first volume and gingerly opened the treasure. Realizing that she had never even read any of the other antique books in the entire collection, she gently replaced the new acquisition back on its shelf. As she exercised caution not to inadvertently damage the brittle leather covering of the novel, she noted that the bindings of the shelved rarities needed waxing.

A fresh tear appeared as she remembered Cullen's comments about their excursion to Point Clear: that he had hoped that the business surrounding that trip would be profitable and favorable so that he might be able to retire early. She further recalled how relaxed Cullen seemed to be as the weekend progressed. They had even shared renewed intimacy at a thrilling level, something that she had not experienced with

Cullen in quite some time. He also seemed to be genuinely excited to be alone with her, wanting to please her emotionally as well as physically. Despite her present grief, Madelyn found it easy to remember their last night together in Point Clear. The memory of his caresses caused his touch to seem even more vivid now than when he was alive.

Screaming, "Cullen! Cullen!" she fell onto the library sofa, sobbing uncontrollably. Madelyn was not afraid anyone would hear her because she was alone, completely alone.

Prone on the sofa, she began to wail in shrill octaves as she soaked the pillows. Her despondency regressed to the barren state of her marriage, a childless marriage; and her weeping then progressed to near wailing. Self-pity had completely consumed the exhausted Madelyn Gwinn. Despite the nagging, pounding headache, she slept.

Madelyn awoke a few hours later to find mascara stains smeared across the silk-covered pillows of her antique library couch. While wiping the fog from her blood-shot eyes, she noticed her late husband's leather briefcase lying closed on the nearby English mahogany Pembroke table. Recalling that she had last seen the case in Point Clear, Madelyn reasoned that Cullen had likely not used it since. She touched the handle and lifted Cullen's briefcase to her breast, holding it as though it were one of his most cherished possessions. As she cradled it in her arms in the manner she might have held her dying husband, she shocked herself into laughing at such affection for an inanimate object.

At the same time as she held Cullen's briefcase, Madelyn remembered looking through its contents after finding it unlocked in Point Clear. As she pictured the correspondence found there, she realized that she had not noticed the hospital administrator at the funeral, nor had he come by the house after the funeral with condolences. Since the whole ceremony felt like a blur to her now, she decided that maybe she had just missed him. She felt no anger toward Jay Rutledge and had no reason to believe that the accident had been his fault despite the fact Cullen died on his watch. Madelyn knew enough about corporations and their profits to know that the hospital administrator and his bosses were undeniably going to miss her husband and the money that he brought to the hospital. Perhaps, she almost snickered, the administrator was overcome with such financial grief that he could not regain his composure long enough to attend the funeral of the hospital's primary admitting physician.

The more Madelyn thought about it, the stranger it seemed that Mr. Rutledge had not even telephoned his sympathy. Recalling his preponderance for writing notes, she assumed that he would at least send her an empathetic one as a substitute. As she rested the briefcase in her lap and discovered the snap unlocked, Madelyn popped the top loose, finding the message she had noticed earlier in Point Clear:

Dear Cullen,

I appreciate your help with the corporate executives regarding renovation of the Critical Care Unit. Your meeting with the vice-president of development was vital in getting the project approved for funding. Sometime in the very near future, I hope you will let me show you my appreciation over dinner.

With sincerest regards,
Jay Rutledge

Cullen had not often worn cologne; and the few times that he did, it was always out of the same several year-old bottle of Polo. Yet upon opening his briefcase, Madelyn detected another aroma, one of which she was unfamiliar. She realized that the strong, semi-sweet scent had come from Jay Rutledge's note stationery and had permeated the closed briefcase.

Even though no one from the hospital administration had visited or contacted her since she returned from Chicago, a parade of legal officials and grieving laymen had. One of these was the Montclair Chief of Police, whom she had never met. Striking Madelyn as a rather large but agile man, he explained that his involvement in the investigation of her husband's death was by invitation of the smaller Pecan Grove police force. The request also stemmed from Dr. Gwinn's official residency having been Montclair, not Pecan Grove. Chief Agee and his head police detective Lamar Boston had come to talk with Madelyn not only out of courtesy to her but also as a part of their own inquiry into Dr. Gwinn's death.

Later, two of the men who were at the hunting camp the day of Cullen's accident respectfully spoke to her at the funeral services, expressing regret over the incident. The hunters' account basically confirmed what Agee and Boston had already reported to her: Cullen had fallen out of the tree after putting weight on a limb that most experienced hunters would have avoided. The investigation had determined that the limb cracked before he fell, but that he might have slipped from the icy branch regardless. It was believed that before being found, Dr. Gwinn had lain unconscious for several hours, almost face down in an icy creek near the tree stand. Despite appropriate procedures, the ambulance driver had been unable to revive him; and the emergency response records seemed in order.

An autopsy was performed as part of the police investigation. Madelyn had not objected to the procedure and received the forensic pathologist's report the day before the funeral. The pathologist had known her late husband and came by personally to deliver his written findings. She appreciated his kindness and was struck by a bedside manner not expected from a physician whose patients are all dead.

Other than his kindness, she found no comfort in the pathologist's verbal information. "Drugs and/or alcohol were not involved. If Cullen had survived, he probably would have been left paralyzed or at least mentally disabled from severe brain injury." Madelyn knew that Cullen would not have been able to cope with being physically nor mentally incapacitated. Instead, she firmly believed that her husband would have rather been dead.

Madelyn thought again about the pathologist's written statement regarding the cause of death:

Even though the vertebrae in the lumbosacral region were shattered by blunt trauma from an apparent fall, the lethal event resulted from a combination of cervical neck injury to the spinal cord and drowning.

Now that Cullen was buried, Madelyn was able to recall all of these visits, reports, and conversations, meshing the information and condolences with Minor Leblanc's burden of initially breaking the news to her.

Her husband really was dead.

Chapter

11

◆◆◆

THE CLOSET

The sun piercing through the library picture window woke Madelyn about nine o'clock the next day. As she rubbed her burning, swollen eyes, she realized that she had cried herself to sleep on the library couch. Cullen's still opened briefcase rested nearby on the Pembroke table with Jay Rutledge's note lying on the top of the other papers in the case. The throbbing in her temples from the day before had mercifully remained dormant while she slept but now had returned as a generalized burning pain, encircling the top of her scalp.

Finally understanding that it was this severe headache and not necessarily the sun that awoke her, Madelyn was reminded that she needed to locate some more of her medicine. Each pill bottle and container, including the one in her purse, was now empty. She began to thumb through Cullen's briefcase, again not finding the key. The last time she had looked for it was when the Pecan Grove police returned her late husband's key chain.

The doorbell chime startled Madelyn, interrupting her desperate search and causing her to slam shut the briefcase as though someone were secretly watching. Tricia Pennington was the source of the noise coming from the front door. Pursuing her self-appointed duty as Madelyn's primary community support, she had returned to check on the bereaved widow. Tricia possessed the rare quality of unshakable self-confidence. She assumed that unless she touched an unfortunate situation with her pleasing physical presence, there would be no recovery for the unfortunate. The former University of Mississippi co-ed, Patricia Alexis Montrose, had been chosen Most Beautiful at Ole Miss in the late 1980's and had never gotten over it. *Tricia*, the name she had used for the last ten years, sounded younger than *Patricia*.

Tricia planned her trip to Madelyn's this morning on the premise that she make certain that the widow had breakfast. While Madelyn stumbled to the door, the echoing ring hit her in the back of the head like a sledgehammer, the force impacting the inside of her eyes. As she answered the door, the ringing mercifully stopped. The widow forced a "thank you for checking on me smile," as she stood in the foyer talking to Tricia and reassuring her that she was going to be all right. She resisted Tricia's offer to come in, cook her breakfast, and straighten the house.

"Madelyn, didn't your regular housekeeper quit last week?" Tricia questioned, as she prodded her way through the front entrance into the foyer. Slyly scanning the state of the richly decorated interior residence, Tricia could barely stomach the fact that the house remained in order. She felt immense disappointment after insisting on walking through into the kitchen. Inside the refrigerator and freezer she discovered enough stored food to feed a family of ten for a month.

Even Tricia could not ignore the obvious; the Gwinn residence clearly did not need her touch at this time. Trying as hard as she could, Tricia could not think of any significant assistance that she could offer Madelyn, nothing interesting or challenging. As Madelyn expected, Tricia failed to offer help with any menial duties such as picking up the dry cleaning or going to the grocery store for personal hygiene or other non-food items.

"Thanks for coming by, Tricia. I'm really OK. I think I'll just lie back down for a while. Everything from the last few days is just catching up with me." The recurring, splitting headache and not fatigue was the main reason Madelyn desired to lie down. Each episode seemed to be getting worse and lasting longer. This particular hurting seemed to have reached a pinnacle of almost blindness during the course of Tricia's latest interference. It was more of a piercing throb at the temples rather than a general headache.

Inquiring again in a most sincere-sounding voice, Tricia decided to give the poor widow one more chance. "Madelyn, are you sure there is nothing else I can do for you? I don't have anything pressing today; my other luncheon club was cancelled, and I can call off today's tennis lesson if I call the Club right now."

"Please go ahead and take your damn tennis lesson," Madelyn wanted to say through her headache. *"Please just leave me alone to rest."*

But, instead, she forced a cordial thank you. "I really appreciate everything you have done." Realizing that someone had needed to make the after funeral arrangements for her, she added with strained unaffectedness, "I don't know what I would have done without your friendship, Tricia. You really have done too, too much already. I'll be fine, but I'll be sure to call if I need anything."

Madelyn had worked Tricia back through the house to the front door and had it opened before the do-gooder could insist on staying any longer. Refusing to give up, Tricia almost pleaded that Madelyn call her any time she needed anything or if she simply needed to talk. Madelyn had never called Tricia 'just to talk' and likely would not start now.

As Tricia walked though the front door and down the wide steps, she snarled, "Madelyn looks horrible, terrible. Hair hasn't been brushed, make-up smeared, last evening's clothes. And all wrinkled." Snubbed and ruffled, Tricia snapped her car unlocked with the keyless entry. As she stepped into the Lexus, Tricia grabbed the cell phone from her unfastened purse left in full view on the front seat. Jerking the 360 out into the street without first looking for oncoming cars (after all, she was Patricia Pennington), she hit the speed dial buttons in rapid succession, calling several of her friends with an update. Regardless of whether they were interested or not, Tricia was anxious to report to the rest of the Montclair social order. She wanted be the first to comment on Madelyn Gwinn's deteriorating appearance and the woman's peculiar resistance to accepting companionship. Within minutes, this future Alliance president had declared to the rest of Montclair society that they should just leave Cullen Gwinn's widow alone.

Much relieved that Pennington was gone, Madelyn went to the master bathroom, showered, and dressed for the day. Deciding what would be appropriate widow's attire for the day after a funeral, she did not sacrifice expense in choosing a conservative ensemble from her collection. Black was avoided; that was for funeral day. A diamond and gold bracelet, a gift from Cullen at their last anniversary, completed her outfit as the dominant ornament.

Madelyn stood before the full-length mirror in her dressing room and thought that she looked amazingly rested, even after accidentally sleeping all night on the couch. Her hair was presentable, she believed, particularly after the benefit of a few hot rollers. In a compassionate but professional manner, the Gwinn attorney had suggested to her at the funeral that she give him a call or come to his office when she felt like it. Maybe she should do that today and drive downtown to see the attorney. Since Madelyn was not concerned about money or how she would be treated financially by Cullen's medical partnership, she saw no urgency in contacting her lawyer. Her husband had told her that he routinely forwarded copies of the Center's medical partnership documents and agreements to their attorney for his files. As the widow of the founder of the practice, Madelyn assumed that the remaining doctors would treat her fairly.

Having endured the funeral crowds, Madelyn wanted a slower pace, but not isolation. She missed her husband, realizing that a drive down to Cullen's office might recreate her closeness to him, maybe provide an element of serenity. She tried to disguise from herself the true reason for wanting to visit the Center: she needed some Vasapene. Hoping to find some in Cullen's personal office or at least locate the key to the samples closet, she grabbed her purse and her coat and rushed down to the garage.

Reaching her deceased husband's office in an easy fifteen minutes, Madelyn parked the BMW convertible in his spot. Located immediately beside the private doctors' entrance to the office building, the space had been marked by a funeral wreath above where *Dr. Cullen Gwinn* was painted. The private entrance afforded her direct access to Cullen's office without having to enter the main part of the one story building.

Finding that his office appeared untouched since his last day there, she noticed the usual pile of unopened mail in the "in" tray on the side of his desk. She picked it up and thumbed through the pieces. All of it looked like junk mail to her: medical equipment and pharmaceutical advertisements as well as a few brochures for medical education seminars and cruises. Cullen had all of his mail sorted by the secretaries, who sent the important personal mail directly to the house.

After sitting at his antique leather partner's desk, she looked through the window into the garden and courtyard, remembering the few other times she had been to this workplace. Searching the drawers for the key to the sample medication closet, it was impossible to miss the framed photo on the edge of the desk. It was of the two of them, smiling at last winter's Arts Museum Charity Ball. Madelyn stopped to admire her evening gown, accented by an anniversary gift of double-stranded black pearls. In getting the pricey outfit together, she had cheated on Minor by having a Memphis boutique send her a collection on approval. Subsequent to modeling all of the dresses for Cullen, they both agreed on this Vera Wang. Madelyn held the frame lovingly and ran her fingers across the glass. Everything she was wearing in the photo looked outstanding, she thought.

"He told me several times that night that I looked gorgeous and that he wanted to keep me that way," she blurted out. " 'Mad, I want you to get even thinner and keep that figure', Cullen whispered right before the photographer snapped this," Madelyn said alone as she raised her head to check her facial reflection in the glass of the frame. Studying the color photograph more closely, Madelyn decided that even her husband appeared younger, thinner, and overall healthier.

As she reminisced further about that magical night at the country club, Mrs. Gwinn started to weep once more. However, after refocusing on the amount of cellulite lost from her hips and buttocks during the preceding fourteen months, she came to her senses and resumed the search. Between tears, she even checked inside the paper clip holder on the desk and under a small planter, but still no key.

When Lovejoy tapped on the door to Cullen's office and opened it slowly, Madelyn suspected that her sobbing must have been louder than she realized. "Mrs. Gwinn, are you all right?" she inquired, walking into the office and hugging her. Although having always been fond of Lovejoy, Madelyn had developed few other close relationships with Cullen's employees. Even though their lives revolved around entirely different social circles, she would occasionally telephone Lovejoy at home to chat. Madelyn had even given senior high school graduation parties for four of Lovejoy's children and would make plans for the fifth.

"I heard some noise in here and thought I should check," Lovejoy continued as she attempted to console Madelyn with squeezes. "I know you miss him so much. I loved him, too. Such a nice, sweet man," she added, while wiping away Madelyn's largest tears with a fresh tissue pulled from her pocket. "Made sure I got a raise every year and a nice Christmas bonus, too. He sure did, every time. You know, me and my family owe a lot to you and Dr. Gwinn."

"Thank you, Lovejoy. You're a dear," Madelyn replied to the genuine comments, her voice quivering. "Those sentiments mean much to me." Lovejoy was not surprised that Madelyn had been crying; the woman's spent emotion was obvious from the reddened, swollen eyes. "Dr. Gwinn told me that you had started working with the new doctor. Chamblee, isn't it?" Lovejoy nodded as she dabbed Madelyn's left cheek. "Cullen was very pleased because the change meant a real promotion for you. How's it working out?" Madelyn asked, taking a tissue from Lovejoy and dabbed her eyes herself.

"Oh, it's a real mess! They fired Dr. Chamblee earlier today."

"Really? That's awful! I've never heard of a doctor being fired." The change of subject away from her husband's death halted the tears. "What was the reason?"

"The office manager told him that he wasn't busy enough. Dr. Chamblee thinks the other doctors want to replace him with a woman. They think a female OB/GYN is what the patients are askin' for. Guess they think the practice wasn't makin' enough money out of Dr. Chamblee."

"That's odd. Cullen hadn't mentioned anything to me, even in generalities, about getting rid of the new doctor," the tone in Madelyn's voice verified her shock at Lovejoy's unexpected news. "Naturally, Cullen didn't discuss all of the Center's plans or decisions with me. But I'm really surprised. What with all the favorable things he shared about Dr. Chamblee, I know he would have confided that in me. I met the young doctor shortly after he was hired, and he spoke to me at the funeral yesterday."

Madelyn paused a few seconds and then continued, "As I said, Cullen never told me all of the practice's secrets." She said the word *secrets* in a sarcastic manner. "However, I am absolutely sure that my husband would have shared something that drastic with me ...like the firing of a doctor!"

"It's just awful, Mrs. Gwinn. When Dr. Chamblee left the office, I cried. I think he wanted to cry. He kind of shook a little bit when he hugged me good bye."

"Maybe I should call the poor boy. Does he have any family here?"

"I think that his mother died a few years ago. His parents were divorced, and he never mentioned his father to me."

"Does he date anyone? What about a girlfriend?" Madelyn remembered Knox from the funeral as attractive; physically fit; taller than average height; dark, short, thick hair; masculine, but not burly, by any means. As a woman, Madelyn had always believed that being sexually attractive could be a detriment to the success of a male OB/GYN physician. This opinion confirmed what she had picked up during bridge club chatter. But her first impression of Knox Chamblee was that he was nice-looking but not too handsome. If he was "hot," he did not exude it to the fifty-year old Mrs. Gwinn.

Fairly perplexed with Madelyn's engrossed concern over the plight of the young doctor and his social life, Lovejoy answered, "He mentioned one of the social workers the other day, but I don't think he has struck up no big time romance with her or anything."

To change the subject so that she could appear busy and avoid the same plight as Dr. Chamblee, she added, "Miz Gwinn, is there anything I can do to help you? I'm really going to miss Doctor Gwinn. All of his patients are really upset about his passing."

"I am going to miss him, too," Madelyn replied with a return of the faltering voice.

Her shaking speech matched the subtle tremor in Mrs. Gwinn's hands that Lovejoy had never noticed before. First attributing this tremor to grief and stress after the awful death of Dr. Gwinn, Lovejoy compared the shaking of Madelyn's fingers to that of an old man with some sort of neurological disease.

As the physician's assistant reached out to give her friend Mrs. Gwinn a goodbye embrace, Madelyn caught her forearms first, pulling Lovejoy into whisper range. "I had mentioned to Cullen a few days ago that I needed some more of my medicine. You know he always brought samples home for me, but I usually had to remind him several times. Do you think you could help me with that?" she kept her pleading to a hushed tone. Madelyn was aware that most of the local representatives of the major pharmaceutical companies supplied promotional samples of their products to doctors' offices. These drug reps kept the pharmaceutical closet overflowing with their wares, providing the various capsules, pills, and elixirs for physician use in initiating routine patient treatments. One exception to the usual flow of these prescription drugs was that of Peyton-Rose Pharmaceuticals, the makers of Vasapene, which provided supplemental dosages to the practice for other reasons.

Feeling awkward about having to break the news, Lovejoy informed Mrs. Gwinn about a weeks-old policy restricting access to the stored samples. Lovejoy apologized. "I wish I could help you, but there is this new rule about getting meds from the sample closet. I don't have a key to it no more. Only the doctors do, and I think they're all gone for the day."

Madelyn tried to act surprised. However, Cullen had recently mentioned the Center's decision, explaining that much of the sample medication had gone unaccounted for. The physicians had raised concern that their employees or those of the outside cleaning service were taking the samples without proper authorization. To ease Madelyn's concern about this change in the availability of the Vasapene, Cullen had reassured her that each physician had a key to the sample storage closet, granting unlimited access to the shelves of sample prescription drugs. The problem Madelyn faced was locating the Vasapene he was to have brought home to her before his accident.

Despite a thorough home search of all the typical places, Madelyn had found no Vasapene. An inspection of the large compartmentalized plastic box in Cullen's bathroom, the drawer in the bedroom chest, and the revolving shelf in a kitchen cabinet had come up empty. Apparently, before he died, her dear husband did not manage to bring home any of the needed medication. But Madelyn did not want to share all of these details with Lovejoy or mention her dependency.

By looking through her late husband's office, Madelyn had hoped to find Cullen's personal key to the sample closet, thereby bypassing this new policy of physician-only access. Located on the central back hall of the building, this designated storage closet was in close proximity to Cullen's office. During recent after-hours trips with Cullen to the Center to pick up some capsules, she had waited for him in his office while he went to the sample storage closet for her. On their last excursion, Madelyn had not actually seen him with the key to the medicine closet. Consequently, she had not found it on his key chain, in his briefcase, in his office, or among any of his other personal effects.

Lovejoy sensed that Madelyn was perturbed over the inconvenience of the locked medicine closet. Having no idea as to the type of pharmaceutical that Mrs. Gwinn needed, Lovejoy figured that she was probably too old to require birth control, which was the majority of the medications stored in the closet. Besides, her husband was now dead, and Mrs. Gwinn should not need contraception anyway, she reasoned slyly before feeling ashamed of herself. If it were diet pills she wanted, that would explain her being secretive about the samples rather than asking for a prescription. Nevertheless, appetite suppressants had never been kept around the office.

Then she remembered that Dr. Gwinn never prescribed diet pills anyway. Not believing in their safety, he used to say that giving diet pills to a patient was an almost guaranteed way to get dragged into a malpractice suit. Scanning Madelyn from head-to-toe, Lovejoy could see the weight loss in Madelyn's trim figure and agreed with someone else's recent comment that Mrs. Gwinn had lost significant weight. Since the decreasing poundage preceded Dr. Gwinn's death, Lovejoy reasoned that his widow's new, svelte figure was not the result of stress and grief but must have come from multiple trips to the gym. Hence, if it were not appetite suppressants that Madelyn Gwinn desired, then perhaps it was an anti-hypertensive drug or one of the hormone replacement medications.

The usually accommodating and thoughtful Lovejoy was not about to jeopardize her employment by deviating from the policies of the practice. She would not remove items from the sample closet without authorization ... not even to please Dr. Gwinn's widow. Surprised but relieved to see Dr. Chamblee approaching, she planned to defer this problem to him.

Hearing the approaching subtle footsteps on the carpeted floor, Madelyn turned to face Knox for a quick reintroduction. "Oh, yes, I know you, Dr. Chamblee," Madelyn announced reassuringly.

"Mrs. Gwinn, I am sorry about Dr. Gwinn. I am going to miss him greatly," Knox uttered in monotone. He, of course, understood that if the senior male partner of the practice had not died this past weekend, then possibly he would not have been thrown out on the street. Politely he continued. "I spoke to you at the memorial service yesterday. It was such a moving experience for everyone." Knox remained uncomfortable at handling the bereaved on a personallevel although he decided he was coming along fairly well in this instance.

"Oh, I wish you had come by the house after the graveside service. Our friends had prepared such a spread, a real feast. I think it would have impressed even Cullen!" she replied with a hint of levity to her gentle but precise voice. "Lovejoy, you should have come by, too." Thinking it inappropriate to bring up Knox's change in employment status until it was made public, Madelyn tried desperately to come up with more small talk.

Anxious to shift Mrs. Gwinn's request to someone else, Lovejoy interjected, "Dr. Chamblee, Mrs. Gwinn needs some of her medicine. She told me that Dr. Gwinn had forgotten to bring some home from the sample closet. You know there's a new policy, so I don't have a key no more."

"You're in luck. They haven't taken mine yet," Knox realized that he sounded sarcastic. "What is it you're looking for?" he asked Madelyn but then felt embarrassed over appearing blunt. Not really meaning to invade her medical health privacy, he quickly recovered, "I tell you what. Let me just unlock the closet, and you get whatever you need." He motioned toward the end of the hall, indicating that Madelyn should walk with him toward the locked doors. As he accompanied her toward the closet, he reached into his right front pants pocket for his keys.

Madelyn was awash with relief to see the door open wide, revealing the interior of the closet that was more like a small room. "You know, I guess I have always been the proverbial naive doctor's wife, never paying any attention to the names of my medicine," she remarked as she twisted the truth. "Whenever I'm sick, I simply swallow whatever Cullen brings me — I mean brought me." Anxiously scanning the shelves of diminutive, brightly colored boxes and packages searching for that typical Vasapene carton, Madelyn added, "I know I'll recognize my medication when I see it."

Knox looked away as he stepped back from the opening of the closet to give Madelyn some privacy. He then turned around to look for Lovejoy; but she was no longer standing there, having slipped away to wash speculums and dispose of used paper examination drapes. Madelyn soon emerged from the closet feeling slightly disappointed that she had found only one small package of three capsules but realized that she could have struck out totally. She was grateful that bending down to retrieve the medication from a lower shelf had not made her head swim, particularly with her emerging headache.

Unknown to Madelyn, missing a single daily dose could initiate withdrawal symptoms, depending on an individual's metabolism. Because of the drug's short half-life of 18 hours, the effectiveness of one dose of Vasapene wore off rapidly because of poor accumulation in the body's tissues. For the typical person, the withdrawal symptoms should have been minor, even with a miss of two dosages. However, Madelyn was not typical.

"Thank you, Dr. Chamblee, this has helped me tremendously. There's no telling what I would have done without you," stated the relieved Mrs. Gwinn. As the headache that emerged just a short while ago began to blind her, Madelyn discreetly slid the blister card containing the treasured capsules in a side pocket of her tailored jacket. Shaking hands goodbye with Knox, she tried to avoid appearing frantic in her escape down the hall to the parking lot.

Remembering the partially filled bottle of spring water stored in a side pocket of her car, Madelyn gulped down a capsule as soon as she was inside the vehicle. Although the days were starting to run together, she believed that up to that point she had been without the drug for three days. When the over-powering pain began to subside within a few minutes, Madelyn was now sure of the cause of her physical torture. These headaches had nothing to do with hangovers or sleep deprivation. What Madelyn did not know was that Vasapene's primary action on the body was to alter the constriction of the brain's blood vessels. What she did understand was her private reason for using it.

Cullen had explained to her that the pharmaceutical company had submitted impressive study data comparing the improvement in depressed patients who were managed with Vasapene over those treated with a placebo. Even though the FDA accepted Peyton-Rose Pharmaceutical's impressive, unbiased research proving the medication's effectiveness in the treatment of depression, the exact mechanism of the drug and its blood vessel constriction effect in the treatment of depression was unknown.

Madelyn was not using Vasapene to treat depression. Instead, she had started taking it a few months ago when Cullen informed her about a non-publicized, secondary effect of Vasapene. Cullen had received this information verbally from a Peyton-Rose Pharmaceutical Company representative during a sales pitch for the newly released compound.

When developing the chemical formula of the medication, the P-R research team discovered that a certain number of women taking the actual compound lost approximately six percent of their body fat. The women taking the placebo did not experience this weight loss. Nevertheless, the company did not seek FDA approval of Vasapene for the treatment of obesity. This weight loss, which involved mostly cellulite from the hips, thighs, and buttocks, became buried in the study as an uncommon side effect of the drug and was not published in the pharmaceutical literature.

Always proud that Madelyn worked to keep a pleasing figure through productive dieting and exercise, Cullen had hoped to dissuade his wife from resorting to plastic surgery. In a non-surgical effort to help her further to reshape her body, he chanced that she would fall into the six percent: the percentage of women benefiting from Vasapene's cellulite shrinking properties. Since the anti-depressant had not been shown to affect the mood or psyche of a non-depressed person, Cullen had been unconcerned about altering Madelyn's mental state with the drug.

Over the last few months the medication granules in the red and blue capsules had served as a successful and pleasing alternative to surgery for Madelyn, eliminating the need for liposuction or a tummy tuck procedure. Undeniably, the results of her surgery-free cellulite reduction had been pleasing for Cullen as well. Since her secret use of Vasapene for eliminating weighty cellulite had died with him, her vanity would not allow her now to reveal the truth. Never would Madelyn Gwinn embarrass herself by admitting, not even to another doctor, that she was still pursuing this non-conventional treatment.

The phone was ringing with one of many condolence phone calls as Madelyn returned home from the medical office. Thankfully, the headache had eased and had not returned. Nevertheless, she wanted to rest but was continually disturbed by the phone until about eight-thirty that evening. Hating to turn the ringer off or to have the communication forwarded to her voice mail, the widow politely took each call from every distant relative or professional acquaintance of her late husband who felt obliged to call. Their excuses for not attending the memorial services were variations of living too far away to travel to the unexpected funeral or having other commitments to deal with.

Some callers who had been out-of-town and had just heard about her tragic loss shared sentiments such as ... "A loss to the whole community ... I know there were hundreds of his patients there at the funeral grieving over him ... He was such a kind, dear man ... We all loved him in medical school and residency ... I would come over now to see you, but I know you are exhausted." These statements were just a sampling of the valiant, but unsuccessful, efforts to comfort Madelyn over her loss.

Though she undressed for bed and knew she should rest, Madelyn's racing thoughts were nowhere near sleep. Grateful to be free of a headache, she realized that a night's painless sleep was her only escape from grief and emptiness. Reaching to her nightstand for the plasma remote, Madeline selected a repeat of a recent edition of *America's Most Idle*. As the rerun ended, she decided that had she instead been viewing the live broadcast, she would have voted for the skinny singer over the fat one who had ultimately garnered enough audience votes to win the contest.

By 2:30 a.m. Madelyn had not dozed off despite watching several programs. Even after searching all eighty-six of the available stations, she could not find anything interesting. Madelyn regretted that there had been no relative or genuine friend to spend the night in the guest room. Not that she would have expected the guest to talk or visit with her at this hour, but it would have been comforting just to have someone else in the house. Madelyn's spacious home now seemed outsized to her. With Cullen dead, Madelyn was overwhelmed by the space, the hollowness around and inside of her.

Chapter

12

•••

THE BOXES

Completed in the early 1920's, the Gwinn home was unlike other houses in the Montclair area in that its structure included a basement. Actually an afterthought by the Baton Rouge architect, the subterranean space was the result of erecting the 7800 square foot structure on the side of a hill. The basement became an extension of the storage space adjoining the under-house garage and had never been utilized.

Remembering that she had not eaten much during the last twenty-four hours, Madelyn Gwinn thought about some of the untouched leftover desserts from yesterday's condolence spread. Because watching television had not made her drowsy, she decided to get out of bed despite the early hour and get a snack from the kitchen. Upon opening the Sub-Zero and looking over the ham, fried chicken, cheese-stuffed rolls, pecan pie, and congealed salads resting heavily on the shelves, she envisioned previous widows who gained substantial weight after the death of a husband. Immediately, she became concerned about preserving her improved, shrunken waistline.

Suddenly, the tray of leftover cheesecake and sugar-dusted lemon squares staring at her through clear plastic wrap did not seem so appetizing after all.

Madelyn was not only concerned about gaining weight from the carbs flagrantly beckoning her, but she also worried about another impending headache. Despite the fact that it had been fewer than twelve hours since she had taken one of her two available capsules, Madelyn hoped that drinking some coffee would prevent a returning headache. Finding none in the pantry and not recalling the last time she had included any on her grocery order list, Madelyn did not even come across some miniature gourmet packages. Many times Cullen would receive such gifts of coffee from appreciative patients. Apparently, the gratefulness over the last few weeks had been sparse, she thought.

Since there was no coffee and deciding against a Diet Coke at this hour, Madelyn reached for the bottle of Advil. Swallowing three of the orange pills without water, she thought again about how alone she really felt, given that her married life was over. She had devoted almost all of her adult life to her marriage — a marriage that was built not only around her husband but also his career. Considering that really good friends were actually in short supply — *you certainly could not count Tricia as a true friend* — Madelyn had no clue about what to do now or how to live. She was not worried about money because the estate attorney had reassured her that there was plenty. Instead, she was concerned about how to exist on a simple and daily basis without the anchor she lost in the death of her husband.

Madelyn wanted to be away ... away from her life ... distanced from their house, her house. She decided to drive somewhere in the Jag, to nowhere in particular. Since the car was parked in the garage underneath the kitchen, she could leave unseen out the back staircase dressed only in her robe, pajamas, and simple house shoes. As she walked from the main section of the kitchen into the corridor leading to the back steps, Madelyn passed the dumbwaiter. Now a dinosaur of another era when she personally did her own grocery shopping, it had been installed to lift groceries from the garage directly into the kitchen area. This convenience was to squelch both Gwinns' hatred of hauling bags of groceries up the steep garage stairs.

Over the last many years Cullen had splurged by engaging the neighborhood grocery delivery service, turning the once essential dumbwaiter into a seldom-used device. Almost absentmindedly, Madelyn reached for the on/off button of the dumbwaiter and pushed it. Curious as to why the cables strained loudly while pulling the shelf up from the garage, she opened the door of the dumbwaiter to check inside. Instead of discovering an empty, musty-smelling cabinet filled with spiders, Madelyn found a sealed, sturdy-looking cardboard box labeled Peyton-Rose Pharmaceuticals.

Hoping that the container held her much needed Vasapene, she grabbed it and struggled to pull it from the dumbwaiter. Because the box was much heavier than expected, she lost her grip, letting it fall to the floor. The crate's top then popped off, exposing the contents, which surprisingly were not pharmaceutical samples at all. Instead of packages of medication, dark yellow-colored folders were packed standing, labels up into the container. Thumbing through the contents of the box and picking up the thickest of the folders, Madelyn immediately recognized these documents as patient medical records.

Earlier the night before Knox turned into his condo garage after pushing the door remote on the visor. Montclair Professional Bank had loaned him the $225,000 to buy the 1900 square foot condo, a debt guaranteed by his employee contract with the Montclair Center for Women's Medical and Surgical Services. Like most other doctors, Knox had found that banks will lend a physician just about as much money as he or she needs or wants. However, suddenly with no certain employment or monthly income, he wondered how long it would take for his personal bank officer to call him out of "genuine" concern. Knox also wondered if patients ever realize that physicians, being human, look forward to getting their own paychecks as do all other red-blooded Americans.

Knox was grateful for the severance pay guaranteed by his former employee contract in cases of termination. That contract rested comfortably and securely in his safety deposit box at the local branch of MPB, where his private bank executive enjoyed a well decorated, spacious third-floor office. The fired physician decided he would retrieve his contract tomorrow from the bank and for the first time read it through completely.

He heard the phone as he walked into the marbled foyer of his condo. With the monthly mortgage at a locked-in interest rate, the place would have been paid for in thirty years. Naturally, neither he nor his private banker assumed that he would live in the smart, but small-for-a-physician, dwelling for three full decades. When Knox chose this fairly upscale section of Montclair, he figured that he would qualify for a more substantial neighborhood as his practice prospered. Unfortunately, he had not yet lived in this condo long enough to realize anything financially from its upcoming sale.

The call was Sibley Paige. "Knox, I heard this afternoon from one of the nurses at the hospital about your...," hesitated the attractive hospital social worker.

"Being fired?" Knox helped her.

"Gee, I didn't exactly know how to put it. The nurse said that one of the Center's doctors casually leaked the news that you had decided to relocate, on your own, that is."

"That's a real stretch."

"But she also let it slip that one of her friends who works at your clinic, I mean your old clinic ..." Pausing again out of embarrassment over discussing this situation with Knox, she cleared her throat and continued, "... told a different version of the story."

Knox did not mind sharing his plight with Sibley. In fact, he was relieved that someone would be interested in his disastrous circumstances. He gladly filled in the details.

"The office manager told me that I was not as productive a physician, dollar-wise, as the practice wanted. She broke the news that the board of directors planned to replace me with a female obstetrician-gynecologist. You know, put some chick in there that would be in greater demand by patients. A real money machine."

"Knox, that sounds ridiculous. I've heard lots of compliments on you from the hospital staff. A few of my friends have seen you as patients at your office... I mean at your former office...and have had some nice things to say. They told me that you made them feel completely comfortable and seemed genuinely concerned about their problems. In fact, one of them had been using a female physician but changed to you." Sibley paused, as though in summation of the situation. "Knox, I don't think those doctors had any real basis to terminate your contract. This is flagrant sexual discrimination!"

"I remember skimming over a clause in my employment agreement that provides for termination of a physician if he or she is not financially productive enough. I'm sure it's in there because of the increasing practice overhead from medical malpractice insurance. I do know that it is expensive for a medical practice to pay all of that for a salaried physician, particularly one not up to full working capacity and not bringing in a big cash flow."

Beginning to feel that she was championing Knox's plight more than he, Sibley continued, "Knox, it just doesn't seem like you have been treated fairly. I would think that when the group hired you they did so with a realistic expectation of your potential. They probably already knew how long it would take you to build up to heavy patient load. Also, by hiring you, those doctors kept you from looking into other opportunities that might have turned out better."

"Well, I guess you're right," Knox inserted half-heartedly.

"You told me earlier that the office manager dropped the bomb on you. Isn't there one of those doctors who would be sympathetic toward your predicament? One you could talk to about this?"

"Dr. Gwinn would have been that person. He was the doctor in the practice who recruited me. Of course, he's gone now," Knox added in a tone as sorrowful for the deceased as for his seemingly hopeless predicament. "Anyway, the office manager implied that the managing partners decided to give me the axe before Gwinn died. I just can't believe it, but that would mean Cullen Gwinn was aware that I was going to be fired."

"Knox, you just can't let them treat you like this! You're too well-trained and educated."

As he pulled the receiver away to prevent a ruptured eardrum, the despondent, unemployed soul replied the best he could. "OK. I'll go to the bank tomorrow, get my signed contract out of the safety deposit box, and look it over."

"You need to do more than just look over that piece of paper, Knox. If you haven't already gotten some legal advice about your employment situation, you need to do so immediately. I normally don't encourage litigation, but you must retain a lawyer before this goes any further!"

Knowing that his new friend was correct, he asked the social worker, "And in your line of work I'm sure you have some contacts in the legal profession. Don't you sometimes get involved with adoptions or child-custody cases and have to testify in court?"

"Even though I've worked here for only about three years, I've been thrown into some pitiful situations. Right before you came to Montclair, this little bitty guy came up to the delivery unit and almost beat his wife to death. He believed the baby was his brother's, not his. I got involved in sorting out the paternity testing, and it turned out that neither guy fathered it. She was a prostitute on the side."

"Gosh, all that garbage makes my problems seem minor."

"No, Knox, your situation is major. But it's beyond the reaches of a social worker. Let me think about this. Who would be a good lawyer for you?"

Knox was drained just thinking about having to work through a complicated, costly legal dispute. He wanted to thank Sibley for her interest and simply toss in the towel but decided instead to hear her out. She seemed so intense.

"When testifying in court, I have come across some pretty savvy attorneys, ones that have impressed me as both smart and good communicators as well as compassionate with their clients. Of course, there have been some lawyers that have struck me as totally inconsiderate and incompetent, to put it nicely, particularly when handling sensitive personal medical history."

As the unemployed doctor listened to Sibley Paige's telephone summation of her legal profession contacts, his mind drifted, wondering if she wore her hair in the courtroom in the same style as she did in the hospital. He was now in his kitchen, preparing an extremely simple salad and getting ready to cook a steak outside on his gas grill. Surveying the kitchen while she rambled on, Knox wondered how long his savings would hold up and enable him to keep living this way.

From the first time that he toured this home with his real estate agent, he ascertained that the kitchen was designed more for a gourmet cook than a bachelor doctor. Since moving in, Knox had never even turned on the stainless steel Dacor oven located across the room from his multi-functional kitchen phone or touched the oven clock as it was already set to the correct time. Admiring again what he understood to be an expensive dishwasher housed under the counter by the sink, he decided that he would need to go ahead and tell his weekly housekeeper that he would no longer need her. Unfortunately, she was the only person who knew how to run the dishwasher. His realtor had stressed with great enthusiasm that all of the kitchen appliances were top of the line, not really a selling point for Knox. Of extreme importance, however, was whether or not the microwave in this state-of-the-art kitchen would turn on and off.

Fortunately for Knox, Sibley was running out of examples detailing her frustration with the Mississippi legal system. As she was telling him about the latest, nasty family situation that she was called upon to untangle, he began to consider ways of getting to know her more on a social level than on a professional one. If she were to go out with him, it would add another to his few dates since arriving on the Montclair social scene.

About a month after he had completed his residency at the University of Mississippi Medical Center in Jackson and had moved up to Montclair to practice, one of the older hospital nurses had paired him with a newly divorced girl who worked in medical records. During their date at a restaurant, the attractive secretarial type had tried to impress him with the fact her fallopian tubes were tied. She also worked into the conversation that her mother, who also lived in Montclair, could take care of the three kids, leaving her plenty of time for him. He declined to accept her offers at the end of their initial and final date, although she had some creative ideas and the obvious physical shape to make them a reality.

Jumping back into the phone conversation with Sibley, he interrupted, "Sibley, today has been a lousy day for me and my medical career. Do you think maybe we could meet somewhere and continue this conversation in person?" Upon her immediate acceptance, he then returned the lettuce, tomatoes, and rib eye to the refrigerator.

Staring at the group of medical record files in the thick cardboard box, Madelyn decided that tomorrow she should call the office manager of Cullen's practice and tell her about her find. Discovering these medical files was puzzling, because Madelyn had never known Cullen to have patient charts at home. In fact, she had heard Cullen mention a few months ago that the Center was in the process of converting to a paperless, computerized record system.

Her late husband had complained on several occasions at dinner about how much the conversion to electronic data was costing the practice. "Too technical, too much trouble, and too expensive," he had said. Not only had he worried about the major capital expenditure to purchase the hardware and software, but he was also upset over the cost of employee overtime generated by the switch. The remaining bulk of more than twenty thousand paper medical records required manual shredding once conversion to computerized storage was completed. Federal government regulations required that duplicated patient records not be casually discarded but instead destroyed to preserve patient confidentiality.

The new computerized "Point and Treat" system, he had called it, was set to save the Center future expense. Cullen had voiced concern that this was just one more blow to physician "hands-on" treatment of patients. The new computer system was also intended to justify the appropriateness of doctors' fees in comparison to different levels of patient services. This documentation of the complexity of surgical and medical care had become more cumbersome in recent years by the requirements of the federal government and private health insurance companies. On many occasions Cullen had fussed that doctors had just become "machines — machines controlled by the Feds and the Blues."

As she recalled her husband's repeated exposés regarding the dismal future of medical practice, a dull throb originated in the base of Madelyn's skull, not at her temple, as was usual. Typically, she was warned of an impending headache with a foreboding aura of generalized uneasiness. This time the headache seemed to spring unannounced and spread like a wave of hot water across the top of her head.

The tiny light shining from inside the dumbwaiter magnified into the intensity of a high-powered beam, blinding her. Unknown to Madelyn, this photophobia was another manifestation of the shrinking levels of Vasapene in her system. She turned swiftly away from the piercing ray as a searing, burning pain moved from the back of her head down the middle of her neck, settling in the pit of her back. Madelyn Gwinn immediately felt an overwhelming desire for relief, associating that reprieve with an immense craving for another dose of Vasapene. Remembering in desperation that she had only two more dosages, she reached into her pocket and punched the center of the blister card packet, freeing the second capsule. She could not save it for later; she needed it now. With paralyzing panic she swallowed the medication whole, wondering where she would find more.

As Madelyn fought back the pain, waiting for the medication to dissolve and reach her head, she retraced her Vasapene search: Cullen's briefcase, his private office at the women's center, the cabinet drawers in her deceased husband's bathroom, and, most recently, the kitchen cupboard. Her efforts had been fruitless. She considered calling that young Dr. Chamblee, confessing her problem to him, and requesting a prescription for Vasapene. However, Madelyn came to what she considered her senses and did not call him, fearing that she would be humiliated. At all costs she would not divulge her reasons for using the drug.

Conversely, she decided that she would just have to be more diligent, that she could not give up on her search for the capsules. Madelyn convinced herself that there must be some hidden storage site in the house that she had forgotten about, that she had missed. Then she pictured her husband's Jag and the inside of the trunk.

Hoping that Cullen had packed some samples in his car but had not unloaded them, she reached for the concealed set of car keys hanging around the side of the door leading to the downstairs garage. Finding the ones belonging to Cullen's Jag, she felt dizzy as she descended the garage steps, which seemed unusually steep. There was Cullen's navy blue Jaguar reigning in its usual spot, reminding Madelyn about his new truck still parked at the hunting camp. He had driven the pick-up to his doom, and she needed to verify the arrangements for getting it delivered home.

Almost leaping over to his garaged car, she peered anxiously through the raised windows. Extremely disappointed, she saw no boxes or containers suspicious for sample medication. Barely able to hold her vision focused due to the pounding in her brain, Madelyn shuffled around to the trunk of the Jaguar.

Because the duplicate key she was holding did not have a remote feature to pop the trunk, she tried to fit the key manually into the lock mechanism. No matter how hard Madelyn concentrated, the developing tremor of her fingers made purposeful movement a strain. Struggling to open the trunk, she burst into tears of relief as the lid snapped open, certain that she had finally located some Vasapene. However, Madelyn collapsed into unconsciousness at the rear of the Jaguar, shortly after her shock that the trunk was empty, except for a spare tire and an old raincoat.

Madelyn regained consciousness about twenty minutes later, realizing that she had fallen onto the garage floor. Her headache was gone, as was the tremor. Lying on the damp cement trying to get her bearings, her eyes found the door to the nearby storage room. Though this space had been a carpentry workshop for the previous owner, it was now used only to house a few idle garden tools. Uncertain why light would be penetrating from the space under this door, her attention was drawn to her neck and shoulder's ache from the fall. Having to push up from the cement made the tight, sore muscles in her arms throb only more. While attempting to steady herself against the nearby brick pillar, Madelyn refused to believe that Cullen kept medication supplies in the dank, dirty garage storage room. However, her curiosity and sense of hope drew her toward the closed door and shimmer of light, chancing that maybe he had squirreled away some Vasapene there.

As she reached to turn the doorknob, Madelyn expected it to be stuck shut because of the dampness. To her surprise, the door was not only unlocked but also simple to unlatch. Madelyn instinctively reached for the light switch, even though the room was already lit, revealing not empty shelves lining the wall off to the right but stacked, sturdy-appearing cardboard boxes. Because her vision was distorted as though she were peering through an old Coke bottle, she cautiously entered the musty space and walked toward the nearest container. Madelyn was intrigued about her find, although her mental perception remained foggy after the collapse.

The box was similar to the one discovered in the dumbwaiter, containing charts arranged as files in alphabetical order and standing upright with the patients' names printed in easy view. One of the first files had an index tab label complete with the name: *Gwinn, Madelyn B.*

When she bent over to make the shot, the tattoo had been as impossible to miss as the curve of the crest of her hips. Knox had noticed that a great majority of his youngest patients had similar, colorful tattoos, the kind that distort with aging, sagging skin. He assumed that most of them would regret the branding later, particularly since colored ink is more difficult to remove than traditional dark blue or black inscriptions.

Most of the tattoos of Knox's patients were in the lower right or left quadrant of the abdomen and were usually renderings of a butterfly, rose, or occasionally some boyfriend's name. He had noted a few on the backs of patients, usually near the panty line. When documenting the physical exam findings in their medical records, Knox tried to remember to mention the tattoos with an appropriate description, some of which were almost humorous. His custom of accurately depicting this part of the examination started while a resident at the University Medical Center. During his four-year tenure there, he had treated a woman several times in the continuity clinic who was abducted while using an ATM and subsequently murdered. Once the victim's family named him as her physician, a homicide detective called requesting forensics information about any unusual body markings.

For now Knox was focusing on the body markings of the present. To propel the striped ball into the front corner pocket, Sibley bent over just enough for her light blue, low-rise jeans to fall in unison with the rise of her tight tank top. This clothing adjustment exposed a narrow two-inch high cross figure staining the skin above her right hip. Entwined with the cross was a vine adorned with tiny red roses, the plant crawling up the cross as though it had been planted in the ground supporting the base. The dark red color of the petals blended nicely with Sibley's slightly below-shoulder length auburn hair that was streaked with a lighter version of her primary color.

As she knocked a second striped ball toward a side pocket, it was obvious that, like Knox, Sibley was thinking about more than just billiards. "This just all sounds so crazy to me. You were fired not for incompetence, obviously, but because the practice wanted to replace you with a female. Even if that were the intention in dissolving your employment agreement, I can't believe that the office manager actually told you the real reason why they were terminating you!" Sibley proclaimed as though she was in fact systematically reassessing Knox's predicament. Her lack of concentration on her shot resulted in an unsuccessful attempt to bank the ball into the lower left pocket, and she almost scratched.

"I was hoping that I might have a chance at this game with you, and I'm glad to see that I might," Knox responded slyly, the pun intentional. Her interest in the unfortunate plight of a lowly, unemployed physician was a positive for him from a romantic standpoint. "Tomorrow, I'm going to explore my legal rights with an attorney," he added with air of self-empowerment as he took his turn and prematurely knocked the eight ball into the far right pocket, ending and losing the contest. "Let's let someone else have the table since you've beaten me. At least you could have let me win to sort of cheer me up!" he joked.

Moving toward Knox, his billiards partner turned the corner of the pool table slowly, extending her arms to reach for him. As she delivered the tight hug that followed, Knox was able to appreciate her unsupported but ample chest. He was promptly getting the sense that Sibley Paige was a party girl at heart. Clearly, he could use and appreciate a party girl right now.

Most moldy, seldom used basement storerooms are draped with dusty cobwebs hanging from the support joists of the floor above. The certainty that Madelyn's housekeeper skipped this area made the cleanliness of the spot seem an enigma. The heavy-looking, corrugated cardboard boxes, which were all labeled in large handwritten letters of the alphabet, filled half the wall to the right of the room where they were neatly stacked. Madelyn was likewise amazed that these boxes were also free of insects and other debris, suggesting that these containers had been a recent addition.

Puzzled, she reached again for the box labeled *F – J*. Madelyn then guardedly removed it from the shelf, noting it weightier than the similar one first found on the dumbwaiter. Bending at the waist to position the container on the floor, she felt a foreboding as her head throbbed. By dropping her head to put the box down, she unknowingly forced excessive blood into the vessels of her brain. Although only a slight increase of pulse pressure resulted from this head down position, there was enough elevation to distend temporarily her tiny, secret cerebral aneurysm.

With Madelyn's modest efforts the lid of box marked *F - J* popped off. *Faulkner, Fitzgerald, Forrest, Garry, Goldberg, Graves, Gwinn, Harris, Hopper, Ivory, Jabour.* After thumbing through the tops of the alphabetized files standing upright in the carton, she realized they were all marked as assigned to *Dr. Gwinn*. Feeling overwhelmingly inquisitive, she almost jerked from the group the record she had first spotted, the one branded *Madelyn Gwinn*.

Characteristic of most doctors' wives and most other family members, Madelyn had not been consistent with her annual physical check-ups with the gynecologist or any other doctor, for that matter. The cost of the medical care was not a concern to her, but like most normal women, Madelyn hated to have a pelvic examination. What she dreaded most about the exam, and she had repeatedly shared this opinion with her husband, was the insertion of what she called 'that cold, metal vise.' Madelyn had almost convinced herself that having an OB/GYN for a husband essentially protected her from health problems involving that and other areas of her body.

"Madelyn, it's ridiculous for you not to come in for a check-up. If all women were like you, I'd be out of business in a heartbeat!" Cullen used to say to her in joking admonishment. Like many other human females, additional factors had made her morbidly dread the annual gynecological exam fanfare. Besides the speculum itself, Madelyn wanted to avoid the nurse in the lab whose morbid delight was to weigh each patient. In any case, major weight gain was fairly obvious to all but the blind, Madelyn had always reasoned, even without the advantage of the digital scales in her husband's office.

Long ago, Madelyn had decided that having to wait to see one of Cullen's partners and be submitted to the torture in the laboratory was a waste of her coveted time - a waste of time even though her professional husband had lectured her that lives could have been saved or made much less miserable if patients had only followed their doctor's advice. Cullen had shared several anecdotal stories with his wife about cervical, ovarian, or breast cancer cases that might have been prevented by routine exams and testing.

Eventually succumbing to his sad stories about the nameless patients who had ignored their health, Madelyn persuaded her late husband himself to do her Pap smears and physical exams. At the yearly convenient-for-Madelyn after hours' trip to the office, he routinely suggested that she weigh herself and even come by extra times to do so. Madelyn could not deny that she had begun to rather enjoy that reinforcing activity, reinforcing and rewarding to her only after she had begun to lose inches while taking Vasapene.

Running her hands over the folder marked *Gwinn, Madelyn B.*, she was astonished that her husband had compiled a medical record on her. Perhaps more unexpected was the printed table attached to the inside front cover of the file, listing her decreasing weight measurements. Since she had never noticed Cullen's taking notes during her physicals, she was further amazed that the record in kilograms was written in her late husband's own handwriting.

The medical file of Madelyn Gwinn did not appear as thick to her as those of the other patients in the box. Of course, she had not been a frequent flyer of the Center as she assumed had most of the others. Mystified as to why all of these files were in her storeroom, Mrs. Gwinn skimmed through her own medical record information. She noted her blood pressure readings and found it almost repulsive to read her husband's formal description of her gynecological anatomy. Madelyn scanned the few pages of her entire record again, surprised that despite the other written details her doctor husband had not documented her treatment with Vasapene, except for the weights listed on the inside front cover.

Babs Reppeto, Tipper Simmons, Marcie Woodfield. Even though the electric garage doors were tightly closed and impossible to raise from the outside without a remote, Madelyn was worried that her little covert operation would be uncovered. How horrified would anyone be to know that here she was thumbing through these cardboard crates containing confidential medical information. Bewildering as it seemed, at her fingertips were the complete medical records of many people she knew. Before her were the secrets of other doctors' wives as well as those of a few lawyers' wives, female attorneys, and other fascinating individuals.

With a pang of guilt she opened the next file, finding intrigue as she peered into these private aspects of several friends and acquaintances. As she reached for Tipper's chart and removed it from the adjacent file container, she reassured herself that this collection could not actually be the legitimate, legal medical records of these patients. She was not certain what the documents truly represented but refused to accept their authenticity. Nevertheless, the papers were absorbing and demanded perusal. She scanned down to the last entry in the record of Tipper Simmons, which was not professionally transcribed like the rest of her chart. Instead, her late husband had handwritten this information:

The patient confides that she wishes to be screened for sexually transmitted diseases. I have informed her of the tests typically used in screening for STDs and have answered her

*questions regarding test sensitivity and patient
confidentiality, particularly concerning this issue. I am
complying with her request to avoid any outside knowledge of
her concerns by personally handwriting this section of her
medical record rather than utilizing the outside medical
transcription service. I will personally notify her of the results
of the following tests: HIV, RPR, and Hepatitis B as well as
cervical gonorrhea and chlamydia antigen screens. In this
instance her identity will be reported to the outside lab using
only her social security number.*

Wondering why the wife of the Methodist Church minister
would be worried about sexually transmitted diseases, Madelyn
started to replace the file in its alphabetized position. Before
she fully closed the chart, she spotted the record of weights of
the minister's wife, likewise posted in neat columns on the
inside front cover. In the lower right hand corner of this
tabulation sheet, clearly separate from any chart numbering
system, was the following notation manually printed in small
figures using purple ink: *R-50*. Questioning, she went back to
her chart and found a similar notation on its tabulation sheet;
however, the number was different: *R-25*.

With growing fascination, Madelyn continued to look
through the private patient files in her possession —
information that must be authentic. She found it chilling that
she would never have considered rummaging through similar
charts in Cullen's office. Why these medical record charts were
here she had no clue, although she had to assume that her late
husband was responsible. Madelyn recalled again Cullen's
concern over the conversion of his patient records to a
paperless, electronic charting system.

*Earline Applebee, Constance Bridgewater, Mary Neal
Dearborne.* Madelyn selected this collection next for
investigation, lifting off the box top to reveal the charts of
several women physicians from varied medical and surgical
specialties who also had been treated by Cullen. Also
knowing these women personally, she overcame her guilt in
reading the documents.

First, Madelyn began to absorb the information about Earline Applebee, MD... *had an affair with her brother-in-law, has broken it off, and is now depressed but does not want to be treated with any drug to which she might become addicted* ... Madelyn's husband had recorded this sticky situation for poor Earline to document her need for an antidepressant.

After next reading Cullen's recommendation that Earline herself seek in-depth psychiatric counseling, Madelyn remarked aloud, her voice hollow but echoing through the storage area, "Ha, I seriously doubt that Earline Applebee would ever see a psychiatrist since she and her husband are themselves thought to be the best ones in town. I guarantee that Marvin Applebee would find it remarkable that his wife has been sleeping with his brother!" Between the grief and headaches, this humorous thought brought a stream of laughter that served as a welcomed relief.

Aware of Cullen's interest in managing the psychiatric aspects of gynecology, Madelyn noted the record of the Vasapene prescription for poor Earline. "I wonder if it helped her depression," Madelyn wondered aloud as she looked disgustingly at a large roach crawling high across the opposite wall of the small room. Completing her read of this chart, Madelyn noted a table of apparent weights in the front of the record as well. There at the bottom of the page printed in purple was *R-75.*

Suppressing any ounce of guilt over reading this information found on her own private property, Madelyn could not resist continuing this diversion that was helping her temporarily forget her loss.

As she continued looking through the medical records, she discovered with shock that Constance Bridgewater had an elective abortion out of concern for her advancing legal career and unsympathetic partner. By slipping up to Memphis for the procedure, her goal was to keep the news of her pregnancy from the conservative community gossips. Requesting a follow-up exam during the recorded office visit, Constance also wanted an IUD. Before closing the medical record and returning it to the file box, Madelyn checked for the patient's purple letter and number combination. "*R-25*... Just like mine," Madelyn remarked.

Dr. Mary Neal Dearborne, the town's busiest pediatrician, sought another prescription for Valium in addition to medicinal management of her hormonal hot flashes. In recording the indication for the anxiolytic, Cullen had justified its use based on the patient's overwhelming anxiety from her own treating of, as she described to him, "screaming, sick children and their neurotic mothers all day." As Madelyn continued to read the medical assessment of and management plans for Dr. Dearborne's problems, her late husband alluded to his suspicion of the pediatrician's own abuse of anti-anxiety medication. He planned not to refill the Valium again. Madelyn found that Mary Neal's purple designation was *R-75*.

In the next container she recognized the names of some women golfers who had long ago foregone bridge and now were consumed with the links at the country club. Although she did not know them personally, she still perused their files but this time with minimal guilt. Once more, she was astonished over the significant dilemmas faced by these women and that they voiced them at a routine doctor's check-up. Such problems as marital affairs, medical illnesses beyond the OB/GYN realm, and drug dependency were mentioned in the text.

Flabbergasted that some of these patients seemed to live such miserable lives, Madelyn wondered how Cullen had been able to treat all of these sad, unfortunate souls without becoming depressed himself. Surely, she reasoned, some of his patient office visits consisted of happy, pleasant individuals with only minor problems. Fascinated, she continued to look through the other stored patient files as though skimming a paperback and discovered that each was marked with a purple *R-*, followed by some numeric multiple of the number *25*.

While delving into the private lives of several women that she knew and of many that she did not, Madelyn's enthrallment simply overpowered any guilt over the intrusion. Despite the improbability of such, she was fearful that someone would discover this invasion of privacy here in her locked garage. This weak but expanding conscience had forced her into a rapid read of the charts, an immediate consequence of which was to trigger an even more brutal headache than previously. Plus, the glare from the bare bulb of the overhead storeroom light served to amplify the pain.

With her head again pounding unmercifully, Madelyn's attention was redirected to her primary reason for entering the storeroom. Her fears of not finding any additional, precious Vasapene were now becoming almost unbearable. For some unknown reason, the most recent dosage had not lasted as long as others. Unsuccessfully, Madelyn fought the urge to take the last dose from the prized blister pack still safely stored in her pocket. She had no method of rationing that one remaining capsule and did not want to chance splitting the drug into sections. Her fear was that a lower milligram dosage would have no effect at all in alleviating and preventing the agony.

Had Madelyn been able to continue a regular daily dose, her particular painful side effect could have been prevented. What Madelyn did not know was that no subject in the Peyton-Rose Pharmaceutical Vasapene Study had been exactly like Mrs. Gwinn. In fact, the wife of Cullen Gwinn, MD, had never been made aware of the study's existence. Her problem now was that what had been initiated as a simple but effective method of reducing her thigh and buttocks cellulite had suddenly become the only way to keep her head from feeling like a hot water heater.

The maintenance of a therapeutic blood level of Vaspene in Madelyn Gwinn's tissues, especially her brain tissues, was doing more than merely preventing a recurrent, explosive headache. In her unusual medical case, the pharmaceutical was beneficially affecting the vasoconstriction and vasodilatation mechanisms associated with the blood vessels in her brain. Unknown to Madelyn, her body sculpting medication was delaying her death from the impending rupture of an undiagnosed congenital cerebral aneurysm.

In a slightly less fashionable area of Montclair, Jay Rutledge was likewise alone and also having difficulty sleeping. Embarrassed over the death of Dr. Cullen Gwinn at his invitation, Jay had quietly attended the Gwinn funeral services with a friend. While he assumed that there had been a funeral condolence get-together afterward, he had not felt up to facing the widow directly. No, not yet. Though he was almost relieved at the time that Mrs. Gwinn had not answered his call to her home about the accident, Jay knew that he could not avoid the inevitable. He would have to confront her eventually because she would want specifics about her husband's last day.

Rutledge believed that the entire medical community associated him with Dr. Gwinn's demise, and many would out right blame him for it — the primary accuser, of course, being Cullen's wife. Jay Rutledge was certain he had detected whispering from a funeral gossip that Cullen Gwinn's accident would not have happened had the physician been a more experienced hunter. When the person speaking realized that Jay was nearby, the comments abruptly ceased.

Rutledge's problems resulting from Dr. Gwinn's death extended beyond the Montclair area. Reluctantly, he had called his company president to break the news that one of Global Healthcare's major money producers was now dead. Of course, he knew that Mitchell Piazza would learn the distressing financial news eventually, but he wanted to be the first to inform him.

While Piazza detailed a conflict that would prevent his attending the wake or the funeral, he did plan for his secretary to send Dr. Gwinn's widow a sympathy note on his behalf. "Of course, Jay, the local customers must not go underserved regarding their medical and surgical patient needs," the president stated in an almost stilted reaction to the news of Cullen's death. Jay had thought that he detected a slight quiver in Piazza's voice. What he did not directly say to Jay, but what the administrator knew Piazza meant, was that the hospital corporation had better not suffer fiscally from the physician's deadly and untimely accident.

Before hanging up, Piazza added, "This will only temporarily delay our plans. Anyway, Jay, I'm not sure that the good doctor was in favor of our proposals. The pecuniary restructuring we were pushing during our discussions in Point Clear may eventually go smoother without him."

The business department of Grace Community Hospital was operational with a software program allowing Jay access from his office or home computer. This afforded the administrator prompt monetary performance updates on a whim. As he was talking with Piazza, Rutledge was relieved that the system's firewall would prevent any other outside access of Grace's financial network.

Revenue totals from patient services could be called forth only by Jay Rutledge and a few of his underlings granted security clearance. The daily funds in the hospital's coffers as posted by the account clerks were dependent on the mercy of health insurance companies and a paucity of cash-paying patients. This accounting system enabled projections of the hospital's future cash flow, basing monthly or yearly profit estimations on historical trends. Jay Rutledge knew more than any other that this detailed, secure financial information must remain favorable to keep the doors of the hospital open and its employees, especially higher-ups like him, employed. These meticulous actuarial tabulations of the surgical cases and patient admissions credited to the individual physician staff members drove the hospital and its economic success.

Lounging with his laptop, Rutledge maximized the image. Filling the screen were colorful pie graphs of surgery and patient admission totals attributed during the last twelve months to Cullen Gwinn, MD. "My God!" Rutledge screamed, almost rattling the liquor bottles in the study bar near his chaise. "Cullen consistently produced more than 25 % of the entire patient volume of my hospital!" he shrieked. To learn more, he typed in *Gwinn, C* to bring up the physician staff web page singularly devoted to Cullen Gwinn, MD. A fairly current picture was exhibited in the upper left hand corner to introduce Dr. Gwinn's current continuing medical education credits and practice location.

Reading through Cullen's additional personal information, including his wife's name and the fact they had no children, Jay looked closer at Cullen's photograph. As he studied the image of this attractive, youthful-looking man, Jay Rutledge wondered if Cullen had been happy in his marriage to a woman. He speculated further about his chances in forging a more personal, physical relationship with Cullen Gwinn had he lived, although the physician had never given him any encouragement along those lines. Thinking that Cullen was pleasingly pictured, looking eight to ten years younger than his published age, Jay lamented the lost opportunity at the hunting camp.

Returning to work at his office the following morning, Rutledge opened the computer site he had studied intently at home the night before. As he sat mesmerized, gazing at Cullen Gwinn's handsome professional photo, now enlarged to fill the entire monitor screen, his secretary walked through the half-opened side door into his office. "Mr. Rutledge, sorry to interrupt you, but the nursery supervisor needs to talk with you as soon as you're available." Because of the proximity of his desk to the office side door entrance, Jay wondered how long she had been standing there watching him.

Chapter

13

•••

THE SOAK

"How soon can you have her here?" the cellular connection over the speakerphone was unusually clear.

"Dr. Hawes, she fulfills her current contract at the end of this month and has wanted to return to the southern United States for some time now," the rep for Professional Physician Placements responded in Brahmin.

"Unfortunately, our latest associate is leaving. You know, the physician we hired instead of her," she complained to the headhunter. "Undoubtedly, if we had had a crystal ball, we would have offered her the position rather than that guy we regrettably hired." Without releasing further details surrounding the departure of Dr. Knox Chamblee, Aslyn Hawes continued, "And surely no one expected our senior partner Dr. Gwinn to die, leaving us more shorthanded." The PPP representative detected only minute personal sorrow from Dr. Hawes, mostly aggravation. "Suddenly, we're so understaffed that I didn't finish seeing office patients until 6:30 tonight!"

"Yes, I see," Mrs. Patel, the Center's agent with Professional Physician Placements answered, also detecting self-satisfaction in Aslyn's boisterous objection to being overworked.

Even with the clarity of the cellular service, Aslyn continued to have difficulty in understanding Patel's accent. Dr. Hawes was hostage to the increasing use of foreign outsourcing by such service companies, utilized to fill their own employee needs. Aslyn stopped herself short of requesting help from someone who spoke plainer English. "Our group is extremely sought after by patients in the Montclair area, and we really need another physician as soon as possible," she stressed.

"I do not think that Dr. Tinsley really wanted to take that position in Arizona, Dr. Hawes. While the job did meet her desires to practice in a female-only OB/GYN group, she has remained in contact with our firm regarding monitoring other employment opportunities. I got the impression from her that she was disappointed when the original negotiations with your group did not result in a contract," the PPP negotiator responded from an office somewhere near Calcutta.

Listening intently to the extremely cordial but still hard to understand example of outsourcing, Dr. Hawes made a turn to the right off the narrow asphalt road, entering her winding Bradford Pear-lined driveway. All of a sudden Aslyn began to worry that she was portraying a desperate physician manpower shortage for her woman's center. "I will call Dr. Tinsley tonight and let her know of the renewed opportunity with your group, Dr. Hawes, and that you want to reopen negotiations," Ms. Patel reassured Aslyn as she made a note to inflate Tinsley's salary offer.

The thought of laborious discussions surrounding a physician employee contract helped Aslyn remember the hot tub. She put the headhunter on hold briefly as she dialed a separate cell number to activate the remote control. This early evening ritual, thirty minutes at one hundred degrees in her outdoor Jacuzzi, was vital for her to unwind. Once she received the confirmatory beep that her instructions had been received, she returned to the waiting lady from India.

"Surely we can pickup where we left off in working out her contract without having extensive renegotiations," Aslyn countered, realizing that the higher the salary that the prospective female obstetrician and gynecologist received, the more commission the headhunter would pocket. Dr. Aslyn Hawes, the physician who had now inherited the most senior status of her medical firm, cared as much about her own purse as did any other doctor. New, highly paid physician associates starting a practice from scratch added significantly to a medical practice's overhead. "I bet the little bitch will want a hefty increase over what we offered her the first time before that bastard insisted we take the male instead," Aslyn said to herself in the car with the mute button pressed.

Advancing up the lengthy driveway, Aslyn raised the garage door by punching some other numbers on her cell phone keypad. As the first door of the four available parking spots lifted, Patel offered more certain plans to secure the new female associate. Relocating this physician to Hawes' practice would reap for her and Professional Physician Placements double fees and salary commissions from the same medical group and candidate, all in less than two years.

"I will contact your office manager in the morning to arrange another interview, Dr. Hawes." Mrs. Patel planned with enthusiasm. "Of course," she added, "as an alternative there is that American-trained lady from Connecticut whom I e-mailed you about a few months ago. Both of her parents are originally from Nigeria. She is still available for immediate relocation into an OB/GYN practice."

Aslyn bristled. "I've told you already that I ... that we ... do not wish to make any ethnic strides in these physician expansion or replacement matters, Mrs. Patel."

"Oh, yes, ... I see ... Of course, I will immediately remove Dr. Buhari from your possibility list."

"Great! Anyway, Nell remains our office manager, and her office phone number has not changed. I will tell her to expect your call. Thank you, Ms. Patel," she forced politeness as they disconnected. After some contemplation, Aslyn reassured herself that even if the practice were forced to pay Dr. Tinsley a revised, pricey sum to join them, the group would quickly recover monetarily. The Center might even squeeze a profit out of her because a new female associate would rapidly become busy with office patients and surgery. On the downside, Aslyn considered the possibility that the hiring of Gretchen Tinsley might not materialize at all.

Dr. Hawes' cell phone lit up once again, and the caller ID flashed *Nell*. "How did he take it?" Aslyn greeted Nell Lowery as she hurriedly accepted the call from her office manager.

"He was upset, but not at all belligerent. Actually, Dr. Chamblee seemed puzzled."

"Puzzled? That's stupid. He shouldn't have been at all surprised."

"He was sure that our practice had not given him enough time to build up his patient and surgical load. In fact, I broke the news to Knox after Dr. Gwinn's funeral when he cornered me in my office about his slim schedule. He was upset because some of Dr. Gwinn's former patients had not been reassigned to him."

"How forward! How ridiculous for him to assume that Cullen's patients would become his or even want to go to him in the first place."

Nell purposely avoided reaction to Dr. Hawes' remarks. "That's when I went ahead and told him that his contract was being terminated. Knox did ask me if Dr. Gwinn had known about the plans for his termination, and I told him, yes."

"Look, I definitely owe you one for this. How about a manicure and pedicure? Nell, you pick the salon and I'll pay for it."

The office manager forced an appreciative response to what she considered a ridiculously meager reward for such a dirty assignment. "Oh, that would be nice." In any case, Nell knew that a well-trained young man's professional employment and early career had ended with her serving as the doomsday herald. When Dr. Hawes gave her the firm directive to fire Knox Chamblee, she had said under her breath, "Lucky me, at least I'll know how to fire a doctor the next time."

Returning to this pitiful act of generosity on the part of Dr. Hawes, the office manager reminded herself that in this era she should be thankful to have her own job. "Skin Works in the mall would be nice," she resolved.

"All right, go ahead and call Skin Works in the morning and make yourself an appointment. Just charge it to the corporate Visa. Oh, and by the way, that Patel woman from the physician recruitment company will be e-mailing or calling you. We need to set up an interview with that girl the practice talked with before, ... Gretchen ... Something-or-Other. The placement company thinks she would still be interested. However, I could hear between the lines that ... I think her last name is Tinsley ... will want even more money to come here. We need to watch this one. She shouldn't expect that much more just because of the little bit of practice experience she has gotten since we last dealt with her. That's my humble opinion." Raising her eyebrows in hidden astonishment, Nell could not remember any situation in which Aslyn Hawes had been humble.

"Dr. Hawes, you may recall that the Montclair Center for Women carries a practice-overhead insurance policy." Aslyn wanted some good news and listened intently hoping to get some. "The insurance provides funds that can be used to offset increases in practice expenses when there is death or disability. We can use the insurance proceeds from Dr. Gwinn's death to help with our overhead expenses from hiring a new doctor."

Even though Nell had not concurred with terminating Dr. Chamblee's employment at this or any other time, she knew that her livelihood as a self-supporting widow depended on Dr. Hawes and the rest of the Montclair Center for Women's Medical and Surgical Services, Inc. Her pension and profit plans were there, and she doubted that she could duplicate her salary elsewhere. Maintaining a professional tone with Dr. Hawes during this entire contact, Nell promised to be on the watch tomorrow for Ms. Patel's communication.

Ending her call with Nell, Aslyn wasted no time in unlocking the garage door leading into her house. Reigning over ten secluded acres, yet just twenty-five minutes from Montclair's central business district, her home and its surrounding spread was referred to by many as a country estate. She prided herself on its new custom construction despite its heavy mortgage. The home had been crafted in such a way that the approximately nine thousand square foot stately mansion appeared completely vintage in its surroundings. Gentle Blossoms, as she called it, seemed to rise out of the magnolia covered crescent of land on which it stood.

Carefully selecting the property after a comprehensive search, Aslyn took immense pride in its beauty and reputation as pristine acreage. While she did select a local architectural and construction firm to design and erect her new home, by the time the house was completed, she had grown tired of working with someone locally. For the interior design of her baby, as she referred to her house, she refused to settle for any of the local proposals. Reaching beyond Jackson, Memphis, Atlanta, or anywhere else in the southeast, she secured a Manhattan interior decorator.

The interior design results for Gentle Blossoms did not surprise anyone who knew her because the house was decorated to Aslyn's total satisfaction. Her chosen New York designer had flown down to Montclair via Memphis several times during the planning and construction stages after the doctor initially interviewed and commissioned him at his Madison Avenue studio. During the ongoing, evolving, always changing, and never ceasing effort at pleasing Aslyn Hawes, MD, the lucky fellow made available to his client a wide range of materials procured throughout the United States, Europe, and Asia. There were rumors among design circles that the decorator planned to retire after the Hawes compound was finished, either out of exhaustion or an overflowing bank account.

After walking from the garage area through to her breakfast room, Aslyn stopped briefly to admire her new Jane Shelton wallpaper recently installed as a finishing touch to the room's decor. Looking in the opposite direction across to her expansive garden room, she was tempted to forgo the hot tub and instead sprawl across her new daybed there. Located near the fireplace and covered in a two hundred fifty dollar a yard Brunschwig & Fils stripe, it unquestionably invited an after-work nap.

Alternately the Jacuzzi beckoned her with its hot jets of water and bubbles of warmth. She next proceeded through the kitchen, pausing at the attached bar to select a bottle of Toasted Head from the wine cooler along with a wine glass from the cabinet above. Throughout the planning phase of this structure, Dr. Hawes had pushed the architect to create something that her late husband had not been able to do for her. She had given herself a magnificent home, which incorporated every detail she could have ever imagined. One of these amenities was this hot tub that she now stood beside, holding the chardonnay and wine glass. Shrouded in privacy by a ten-foot wall constructed of old New Orleans brick, the pool area and Jacuzzi were located just off her back yard patio and invisible from the main house. One facet of this elaborate, private water feature was that the tense, exhausted Aslyn could enjoy it in the nude.

Peeling off her clothes and laying them on a nearby deck chair, she turned on the soft lighting strategically illuminating the patio and pool areas. Next, Aslyn slid into the hot water of the bubbling tub and promptly checked the thermometer bobbing in the foam of clear water — one hundred degrees, as expected. "So satisfying," she whispered, her voice barely rising above the steam. The outdoor remote to the centralized stereo system was within easy reach, allowing John Mayer to warble from the garden speakers, hidden among the surrounding plantings and statuary. Because heated, dilated blood vessels absorb and circulate the effects of alcohol quickly, Aslyn looked forward to the rapid numbing of the chardonnay. She planned for the hasty consumption of two glasses of wine to make her skin super-absorb the water's warmth. By then she hoped that the tension in her tired neck, back, and feet would have eased.

Because of the heavy drizzle yesterday that persisted after the funeral, she had skipped her ritual. That release was sorely missed in that Aslyn found the funeral services to be extremely strenuous and exhausting. Greeting one bereaved Dr. Cullen Gwinn patient after the other had been emotionally draining for her. She had tried to slip into the church through a side entrance to avoid as many people as possible but was nevertheless thrown into the throngs of the grieving. Likewise, keeping a low profile at the graveside service afterward was fruitless.

Now nearing completion of her second glass of wine, Aslyn fought back a twinge of guilt over Knox Chamblee and his situation. During the funeral she had purposely steered cleared of him. Certain that ending the boy's employment was the right move, Aslyn immediately reminded herself that from the start she had doubted his skills and ability. After all, he had been working at the Center for nearly two years without reaching a profitable, successful practice load. Sinking deeper into the soothing current, she repeated to herself that Knox Chamblee's patient and surgical volume was nowhere near what it should be by now; she could think of no reason to feel any remorse over the handling of the situation. As the last drop of that second glass slipped down her throat, her conscience was clear.

"Cullen should have listened to me and offered Chamblee's position to that other candidate!" she blurted out, while kicking the bubbles and splashing some of the steaming water over into the adjacent pool. "The practice should have hired that Gretchen Tinsley from the start. She would have fit right into the medical community and immediately established a lucrative patient base," she stressed in nearly slurred speech to the lion's head statue mounted on the wall beside her. "My own patients would have felt more comfortable with a female associate in my absence than with a male. Yes, I'm sure of it," she informed the aged concrete animal, then hoisted the wine bottle in salute to the figure and poured a third glass of chardonnay.

"Can I have a taste?" the low voice unnerved her, causing a little Toasted Head to jostle into the endless bubbles coming from the hot tub's jets. The penetrating lyrics of Sting had masked the sound of footsteps along the flagstone path leading from the back gate to the pool area.

"I didn't bring another glass from the bar since I wasn't expecting you," Aslyn answered, trying not to appear startled.

"Why don't I just drink from the bottle as I did last time?"

In a childlike voice she replied, "I might get some of your germs."

"You've already had plenty of chances to get everyone of my germs, Doctor," he whispered in her ear, mocking the playful speech. As he bent down to her body, he simultaneously unbuckled his belt and caressed her neck. With Aslyn's back still to him, he hurriedly removed his shirt and pants and slid down bare into the hot tub, landing tight against her hips.

"Where's your momma?" she asked as he put his right arm around her chest and felt her full breast.

"Playing bingo," he answered.

Police Have No New Leads, screamed the headline. After barging unannounced into the police central office, the mayor tossed the newspaper and its front-page headline in front of the startled chief. The *Montclair Journal* landed on top of Agee's desk but not before reducing his full cup of hot coffee into a splatter over the reports and files he was reviewing.

Fortunately, Detective Boston interrupted just as Chevelle jumped up to defend himself. Trying to lessen the heat on his boss and defuse the situation, Lamar stretched, "Mr. Mayor, about the Taylor Richards case, we still have several parties of interest to interview."

"The media is destroying me on this issue, Chevelle," the intruder shouted. "I don't have to remind you, Agee, that if I am not re-elected because of Montclair's increasing crime rate, then you won't have a job either. Judging from the group lining up to run against me in the primary and general elections, I doubt if my successor will keep a guy like you around."

"Mr. Mayor, I promise you that we are right on top of it," Chief Agee responded unconvincingly as he blotted the coffee stains off Taylor Richards's file photograph that had been reproduced from her nursing school yearbook. "We have an appointment in thirty minutes with another one of the doctors she worked with at the hospital," he continued to lie.

Jumping abruptly from his chair, which flew back against
the wall behind the desk, Chevelle hastily grabbed his coat from
the nearby wall hook and gestured to his assistant to follow him.
"Come on, we'll be late for our appointment with Dr. Hawes,"
Police Chief Agee demanded as his investigating assistant
obediently trailed him out the door. Chevelle was determined to
solve this case and shut the mayor up as they left his boss,
mouth gaping open. Too insulted from the blow off to produce
any further caustic, critical remarks, the Mayor of Montclair
watched begrudgingly as his underlings ran out on him.

"Chief, since when do we have an appointment with Dr.
Hawes? I just made that up about 'parties of interest to
interview'," Lamar questioned while opening the passenger door
of Agee's cruiser.

"What made you think we had an appointment, Lamar? For
days I have been trying to get Dr. Aslyn Hawes' secretary to put
me through on the phone or allow me to see her between office
patients. I was supposed to talk with Dr. Hawes earlier today in
her office, but when I got there, the assistant told me that the
lady had just been called away to deliver a baby. She was lying
because I saw the doctor lady duck into her private quarters
when I walked up."

"So where are we going?"

"We're going to try to catch her at home. Even doctors
eventually go home to rest, don't they?" he looked over to his
investigator as they turned onto the interstate headed toward
the country estate of Elizabeth Aslyn Hawes, MD.

"You're really too young to drink that, aren't you?" Aslyn
asked him as he returned from the pool house bar holding a
cold longneck.

"The drinkin' age in Mississippi shouldn't be twenty-one,
anyway," he answered. "I've been polishin' off a cold one or
two ever since I was twelve when an older cousin bought me
my first six pack."

This lack of viral male modesty never ceased to shock or please Aslyn as she watched him approach the Jacuzzi with anticipation, this time with a frontal view. Jimmy Perry settled slowly back down into the hot bubbles as he kissed and fondled his mature partner without losing the steady grip on the Budweiser. Between the deep wet kisses, he was still able to guzzle the drink before the hot tub had a chance to warm it.

"Maybe we should continue this inside," Aslyn whispered to her lover as he pulled her closer. Typically the aggressor in most of relationships, she found his firm, youthful, forthright touch particularly exciting. From the other side, Jimmy enjoyed the practiced experience she brought into each encounter.

From the first time that she approached him at the hospital in Montclair and asked him to meet her later, he had discovered something that he craved. From the way Aslyn responded to him when they were together, he truly believed that she craved him, too. As Jimmy satisfied the doctor's growing desire right there among the Jacuzzi's bubbles, the police cruiser turned up the long drive silently approaching Gentle Blossoms.

Finishing with her for the second time, Jimmy pulled away from Aslyn, although she wanted him again. "I'm supposed to pick her up at the bingo parlor at eight tonight and drive her back to Pecan Grove. Mom gets real nervous if I don't pick her up on time. My aunt promised to give me a break next week and bring her down here instead of me doing it. But then, I wouldn't get to see you, would I, Baby?"

"Why don't you meet me up at The Fox this weekend?" Aslyn proposed to Jimmy as though she did not know his answer.

"Do you think you can wait that long?" he winked, pulling himself up out of the hot water.

The Silver Fox was a misplaced eclectic drinking hole located midway between Montclair and Pecan Grove. Often patronized by Montclair professionals and Pecan Grove blue-collars alike, the profitable establishment never seemed to close. Confident that bumping into a patient at The Silver Fox was unlikely, Aslyn enjoyed the nearby getaway where she could blend into frivolity.

The dimly lit bar, complete with rocking, high-decibel music, had become a regular rendezvous site for Aslyn and Jimmy. Their meetings began weeks ago after she eyed the athletic-looking specimen hurriedly leave the cafeteria and administration area of Grace Community. The never shy Aslyn Hawes immediately left patient rounds to track him to the emergency room. She then introduced herself to Jimmy Perry as suggestively as possible and scheduled their first social meeting at The Fox for a few days later.

Much to Aslyn's relief that initial tryst occurred as planned. At first, she was concerned that the somewhat shy boy would be a no-show. Her delight was that his shyness was not evident that night neither at the bar, nor later in the backseat of her BMW, nor at anytime thereafter.

The physical pleasure remained mutual, and today had been no different. Feeling totally expended after being with his lover in her Jacuzzi, Jimmy thought highly of himself. Although older, his rich sexual companion was remarkably well preserved. When he held her close that first time at The Fox, appreciating her firm and ample bust, Jimmy was unaware that she had breast implants. Likewise, he was oblivious to her eyebrow lift and liposuction procedures expertly performed by a Memphis plastic surgeon during a vacation. The end product of Aslyn's total body cosmetic improvements was what intoxicated nineteen-year-old Jimmy Perry. Whether her body or their relationship was natural or artificial did not seem to matter.

Jimmy relished that neither his cousin Abe nor his mother knew anything of the fiery relationship with Dr. Aslyn Hawes. Keeping her an ongoing secret increased the sensual excitement and importance of his treasure. While previous propositions from less mature women had been an emotional and sexual turn off to young Jimmy, he had begun to crave Aslyn's smooth, almost authoritative manner.

Admittedly, Jimmy had felt somewhat ill at ease when first meeting her by chance on the ambulance run to Grace Community Hospital. After his cousin Abe Perry agreed to shadow him to the initial rendezvous with Aslyn, Jimmy's uneasiness about the invitation from the good-looking, perhaps more-experienced woman doctor lessened. "Sure, I'll meet the gal for a drink," he soon decided.

Despite the reluctance of The Silver Fox bartenders to ID drinkers, Jimmy's twenty-one-year-old cousin had routinely served as his security blanket — a backup to overcome any hurdle of a nineteen-year-old consuming alcohol. By the time Aslyn walked into the establishment that night, Jimmy had totally erased his inhibitions by polishing off three longnecks and starting a fourth.

For that first date with Aslyn, Jimmy and his one-man support team had arrived about an hour and a half early. Just as he and Abe were walking through The Fox's lime-green lit entrance foyer, Jimmy was taken aback to find the infamous hospital administrator frequenting an establishment of the Perry league.

As Rutledge and another man later left together, Jimmy had not realized that Jay had spotted him as well. "There's that head guy who runs the hospital in Montclair," Jimmy had whispered loudly to his cousin as he elbowed him. "I met him in the cafeteria one day on an ambulance run. After we talked about hunting, he invited us to his hunting camp over by the river. Remember, I told you that he's a member at White Tail Hunting Camp."

"Yes, I see him," Abe had responded, suspiciously eyeing Jay and his friend as they exited the front door, wondering where their dates were. Thinking at that time that he could continue to find his way around White Tail without any guidance or charitable invitation, Jimmy's cousin added with forced interest, "Yeah, we do need to go up there and, you know, scope the place out. Anyway, I've ridden down Peace Road on the border of their camp before. Big ass bucks have jumped out on me several times from the camp's side." Through the deafening music, Jimmy listened intently as Abe continued. "I nearly wrecked my truck a couple of weeks ago because of a nice, fast ten point that darted out from a thicket there. What a hoss! He almost made it across the road before I hit him on his right backside. It's a fuckin' miracle my bumper got only a small dent!"

Somewhat taken aback by this tale, Jimmy had not recalled seeing any recent damage to his cousin's twelve-year-old truck; however, he realized that new damage to Abe's junk heap would be easy to miss. "I wasn't gonna waste a rack like that, uh, particularly since the collision didn't hurt the head none when the buck landed in the ditch. Yeah, it's at the taxidermist over in Cleveland now. That rack is gonna look good in my trailer above my bed," Abe had bragged.

Hoping that he could shoot a deer of that caliber, or better, Jimmy determined then, "There's got to be of a lot of other bucks like that out on that land. I hope he calls us to go hunting over there before the season is over."

Jimmy or Abe had not realized that evening that the hospital administrator not only spotted Jimmy but recognized him as well, and with renewed admiration. However, since Jay Rutledge was also interested in the guy he had already met that night, he decided it best not to complicate matters by stopping to acknowledge or speak to the memorable ambulance driver. Briefly Jay had wondered who the fellow was accompanying the young meat, whose last name he struggled to remember with eventual success. The administrator easily blocked out the slightly older guy with Perry as not at all polished, or nearly as handsome.

As Jay and his new friend got into the car, Jay immediately made a mental note to pull up his computer records pertaining to that first meeting at the hospital with Perry — Jimmy Perry, he finally fully recalled. Redirecting his attention to matters at hand, he and his guest then departed The Fox and waved goodbye to the weighty bouncer still guarding the front door of the festive establishment.

In addition to the music system and outdoor lighting, if Aslyn had activated the video security monitor mounted to the outside wall of the pool house, she might have noticed the visitors approaching the front entrance of Gentle Blossoms. Instead, she was likewise thinking about their first date at The Fox as she admired Jimmy's smooth but chiseled looks. The glasses of chardonnay and the sex had easily washed away any guilt or worldly concerns. She did not want her energetic, thrilling lover to leave. He had never stayed overnight with her, but she desired that tonight be the first.

"I'm surprised a house like this one doesn't have restricted access, you know, like an electric entrance gate down by the road," Chief Agee remarked to Boston as he rang the doorbell. Fully expecting a snooty, white-tied butler in tails to answer the door, the investigators instead found themselves standing ignored under the porte-cochere.

Agee again rang the doorbell that went unanswered for the fourth time. His younger assistant with more acute hearing suddenly pointed to the right of the building and said excitedly, "Chief, I think I hear some tunes coming from around the back. Somebody must be here after all!" A closed gate stood in that direction, nestled in a brick wall that apparently encircled the back acreage of the doctor's estate.

His torso hot with uneasiness even though it was January, Agee felt uncharacteristically nervous, standing there before this elaborate home. The mayor's demands to uncover the young nurse's murderer were creating desperation for the Montclair chief, putting his entire livelihood at stake. Still frustrated that no one had come to the door, he refused to end this investigative attempt empty-handed.

Following Lamar's discovery of the music, Chevelle assumed that the doctor might actually be home, and he could not lose this opportunity to talk with Hawes about Taylor Richards. His department had no search warrant regarding the questioning of another potential witness, but he had not and did not plan to search anything. Opening a closed gate to someone's backyard to complete police business did not, in Chief Agee's opinion, define a search.

"Aslyn, I really do have to go, Baby. My mom is expecting me," Jimmy said as he grabbed the towel retrieved from the pool house on a beer run. In full view of Aslyn, Jimmy thoroughly dried and dressed himself, then bent down to kiss her as he left her alone in the Jacuzzi just as he had found her.

Jimmy exited Aslyn's backyard by opening the rear gate where his truck remained parked in the accessory driveway. This additional entrance and driveway were not considered public, being utilized regularly by only Aslyn's maid and yardman who worked only certain days of the week. As she and Jimmy had made love tonight in her hot tub, Aslyn had been thankful that this had been her staff's day off. She was also thrilled that Jimmy had discovered the private back entrance to her estate, surprising her with what she needed.

As Jimmy departed Aslyn's aquatic resort, swinging shut the gate behind him, the front gate through the solid New Orleans brick fence crept opened, admitting Chief Agee and Detective Boston. Proceeding as delicately and silently as possible, the duo of Montclair's finest moved through the vine-encased arbor that marked the entrance into Dr. Hawes' backyard. The closer they got to the pool area, the louder the music sounded. Because of the noise, Chevelle and Lamar both wondered if a party was in progress but remembered that they had seen no extra cars out front. Not familiar at all with the facility's layout, they turned toward the warbling of Celine Dion just in time to catch a glimpse of a tall, well-proportioned nude woman stepping up out of a steaming outdoor hot tub. She was drying herself slowly, but pensively, with a thick white towel. Chevelle was the first to drop his jaw in disbelief at the erotic scene, regretting immensely his impromptu decision to intrude on this lady doctor's privacy.

Frantic to formulate a defense of his reasons for barging over tonight to interview Dr. Hawes, Chevelle started a mental list that turned out entirely void. In spite of everything, she was not at this time under investigation for murder, not even close to it. As the January sweat soaked his neck and flowed down his back, Chief Agee kept reminding himself that he was simply trying to do his job, although his timing for this interview was disastrous.

Despite his 245 pounds, Chevelle Agee's image of himself was much smaller. Likewise, he predicted that as soon as Dr. Hawes reported this invasion to the mayor, he would become even more diminutive. He could vividly hear the mayor once Netz got hold of him. "You idiot, the white voters will think we now have a Nazi state here in Montclair. They'll believe that as long as I remain their mayor they will be subject to routine, unprovoked raids of their property."

Lamar, who had extended his head around Chevelle's swollen trunk to take a peak, interrupted his boss's vivid first image of Aslyn Hawes with her towel as well as Agee's self-destructing image of his own future in law enforcement.

"Who in the world is that good looker, Chief?" he whispered as Aslyn instinctively began to turn in their direction. Chevelle chose not to answer his assistant but as an alternative roughly pushed him behind the holly and arborvitae lining the lengthy path from the arbor to the pool and Jacuzzi area. Jumping behind him to use the thick, tall vegetation as a visual screen, Chevelle was certain that they had been quick enough to avoid detection.

"I wonder if she has got any guard dogs, Chief." Lamar muttered, pushing a cluster of red berries away from his mouth. Chevelle was too embarrassed to admit he had not considered that possibility, just as he had not thought about any security cameras.

Fortunately for these high level members of the Montclair police department, Dr. Hawes had no guard dogs, and her security camera system was not extensive enough to catch the two officers buried under the landscape vegetation. "Let's just lie here real still and quiet, and maybe she'll go inside," Chevelle suggested, forcing an authoritative and reassuring tone as best he could while whispering.

"Do you think that's the doctor?"

"I guess so, Lamar. But I don't think this is the best time to find out," the boss replied as he peered around a holly branch, almost catching a thorn in his left eye. While also trying to keep the plump berries out of his mouth, he was able to see that the presumed Doctor Elizabeth Aslyn Hawes had finished toweling off. Chief Agee closely eyed her as she juggled a wine glass and bottle along with beer empties and walked au naturel from the steaming hot tub. Apparently returning to the main area of the house, she was also dragging two plush towels behind her.

"Let's get out of here," Chevelle commanded.

As they pulled out of the shrubs and hastily moved through the gate to the front of the massive house, Lamar witnessed rapid moves by the Chief not seen since his days in police academy. While they scrambled out of the back yard, Aslyn revolved toward the backyard video monitor. Had she checked the auto-activated monitor screen sooner, she would have witnessed a total of four hundred and five pounds of Montclair's finest, panicked and running from her sight. Instead, she saw nothing of the spectacle and walked back to the Jacuzzi to silence the music and darken the video monitor.

"You want me to ring the doorbell now, Chief?" Boston proposed as they ran to the police car.

Looking down at their rumpled suits and grass-stained trousers and sensing the massive perspiration roll down his belly from his underarms, Chevelle gasped, "Let's get the heck out of here and come back later!" So out of breath that he could barely talk, Chief Agee's main concern now was to drive away undetected from this fiasco-ridden segment of the Richards murder investigation. As silently as possible, Agee and Boston eased down the other side of the public circular driveway in the unmarked police cruiser, remaining unnoticed since no one was watching the scene caught by the security cameras.

After leaving the get-together in the hot tub, Jimmy was only a few minutes late picking up his mother from the Montclair Community Bingo Center. Millie Perry had won top prize that evening, scoring a thirty-five dollar gift certificate for a pedicure at the mall spa. Announcing her prize as she climbed into the passenger seat, Millie wished it had instead been thirty-five dollars in cigarettes. Seriously doubting that his mother had ever been to a spa and sure she would not start indulging herself now, Jimmy responded to her almost jokingly, "Do you want me to bring you back down here next weekend to the mall so you can get your toenails beautified?

"Maybe you should give it to your girlfriend down here in Montclair," Millie Perry offered, handing the printed sheet over to her only son. Mrs. Perry could not have missed her son's recent fondness for excuses to drive down to Montclair from Pecan Grove.

Jimmy almost ignored the comment and gesture but instead countered, "I don't have a girlfriend."

As they passed the city limits of Montclair and drove up the interstate toward Pecan Grove, both were quiet. Nearing the exit to his hometown, Jimmy looked out over a field toward his cousin's singlewide trailer. "I see that Abe's out again," he finally said to his mother, breaking the ice. His observation was based on the absence of his cousin's truck, an impossible to miss eyesore that consisted mostly of discarded exterior body parts meshed together in various colors.

"Darlene told me that Abe was going huntin' again this afternoon," she informed Jimmy. Millie kept up with her nephew's activities through her elder sister. "Darlene says that she's gonna have to buy another freezer to hold all the deer meat her son keeps bringin' over. She's got enough venison sausage to give it away for birthday presents!"

Not paying all that much attention to his mother's rambling, Jimmy thought again about her earlier reference to his love life. Wondering if maybe his cousin had already told his mother about Aslyn, he decided to remain secretive.

"Mom, I already told you. I don't have a girlfriend."

Chapter
14
•••
THE WATCH

Unattached and living alone in a trailer on the outskirts of Pecan Grove, this experienced poacher had no deterrent from leaving work at the service station to slip over for a last minute wild game harvest. Parking his truck in an obscure clearing in the woods immediately outside the gate, Abe Perry accessed his private, and better yet, free game preserve, using his own key on the replacement padlock. While cruising around the perimeter of the elite hunting camp several months ago, Jimmy Perry's cousin had spotted this seldom-used road to the property. The metal gate barrier to the entrance had been transformed into a trellis by a thick wisteria vine, which he stripped away to uncover an ancient, rusted padlock. No match for a pair of his pliers, the fragile mechanism was immediately replaced with one of his own. Apparently escaping detection because of its location in the far eastern section of the club's property, this way into the hunting paradise was known to few, if any, of the regular members of White Tail Point, LLC. With little effort it had now been transformed into Abe Perry's private entrance.

After illicit exploration of his outdoor wonderland found well stocked with turkey, deer, and large-mouth bass, Abe had made an additional discovery. Tucked among a group of mature, full-bodied magnolias and rolling hilled terrain was Abe Perry's bonus, an abandoned sharecropper shack.

Moldy and dank, but unexpectedly equipped with a leak-free roof, the diminutive building completely served the needs of a pilferer. Even though the wooden and tin structure had no utility service, Abe continued to enjoy the convenience of bedding down on site in a dry, cozy sleeping bag, anxiously awaiting his next morning's hunt. After cleaning out the cobwebs, hornet nests, and rat waste, he was able to transform the shack into a dwelling fit for any overnight stay or a nap. Fit enough, at least, for him. By the time deer season had officially opened for all the law-abiding hunters, Abe Perry had comfortably ensconced himself in his new hunting ground complete with private lodge.

During one of his first secret hunts at White Tail, Abe nailed the big buck that was soon to become a work of art by the Cleveland taxidermist. That conquest resulted in the hunter's complete addiction to this complimentary wild game preserve. Four points, six points, button bucks, small does, big does. Since his hunts were not controlled by rules or any minimum size requirements, Abe enjoyed shooting whatever he wanted, whenever he wanted.

"I'm really goin' to kick ass here during turkey season," he had said to himself several times after killing one of several deer.

As he began this particular late morning hunt toward the end of the legitimate season, Abe Perry trekked to a section of the camp that he had scouted a few days ago. Reaching the selected hill, he climbed a large oak. This perch afforded Abe an unobstructed view of the wide path below, long-since cleared by loggers. The members of the hunting club, according to the detailed wooden sign marking the passageway, had named the site Major General John Magruder's Path. Abe considered the naming of hunting areas in this way stupid, something silly that only rich doctors and lawyers would do.

Another privilege of Abe Perry's complimentary hunting club membership was the freedom to ignore established times for morning and afternoon hunts. There was no sign-up list or map location for him to pin. Abe had little concern for the one drawback to this convenience; he was not aware of the day's plans of the legitimate hunters. Since most of the members were busy, productive, out-of-town professionals, there was rarely any weekday hunting to interfere with Abe's trespassing. He was uninhibited in his quest to explore and ravage the beautiful property covered with spreading hardwoods and towering pines. Nevertheless, in this instance, as he was nestled securely among the thick tree branches towering above Magruder's Path, the silence of White Tail Point was broken by the rumble of an approaching four wheeler.

After the disastrous, draining events of the last several days, Jay Rutledge had decided that a short out-of-town trip would be calming. That morning he notified his administrative assistant that he would be out for the rest of the day, not bothering to explain that his "errand" was a diversion to his fancy hunting place. Rutledge believed that this short excursion would be just the change of scenery he needed to clear his mind. Not bothering to invite a friend this time, Jay arrived alone at White Tail and parked his truck in its usual location behind the large hunting lodge.

Given that the non-primitive gun season for deer hunting in Mississippi is usually over by Martin Luther King Day or Robert E. Lee Day, if one prefers, most of the club's members by now had already packed their freezers full of venison. Naturally, Jay assumed that he would be alone on the grounds for the entire day. Retrieving his four-wheeler from the storage shed, he decided to check out some areas over by Magruder's. After Cullen Gwinn's death, Jay had sworn to himself that he would never hunt solo again, but he now looked forward to this leisurely gun-free excursion around the trails and hunting sites of the manor he had created.

Having changed from his business suit into a pair of tight, slightly faded jeans and a semi-rugged Lands End shirt, Jay needed only to supplement his outfit with a camouflage windbreaker plucked from his clubhouse closet. He skipped protective orange.

The dark-rimmed designer sunglasses added to top off his ensemble were not so much needed to shield away the bright day as they were to block the crisp wind meeting the speeding ATV. Before cranking his Polaris 350, Jay decided at the last minute to strap on his rifle to the back mount. Though not planning purposefully to hunt, Rutledge wanted to be prepared for the unexpected shootable deer jumping out on the grounds of the heavily populated White Tail.

"What the fuck!" the poacher cursed under his breath. Even though Abe had not been privy to or previously interested in the official rules of the camp, the four-wheeler yet stunned him. He assumed that like most established hunting camps this one had rules prohibiting joyriding during hunting season, except on main paths between scheduled hunt times. Abe's astonishment at the disturbance unexpectedly changed from aggravation to a feeling of luck. Considering the other several thousand acres of hunting land surrounding them, how could he catch this guy here at this particular site, at this particular moment? Sitting motionless in the deer stand, he magnified the driver's face with a Leopold riflescope recently picked up at the pawnshop. Watching the pervert's every motion, Abe had no difficulty matching his looks with the cologne-scented letter, the words of which he could effortlessly remember.

It was not rare for the postmaster of Peace County to confuse delivery of mail between the Perry residences in Pecan Grove. Instead of being delivered to Jimmy's address at his mother's house, the note written on sissy-looking stationery had mistakenly arrived at Abe's trailer. The next day Abe drove it over to Millie Perry's house and caught Jimmy there after work. His younger cousin then nonchalantly opened the envelope, sharing it aloud with Abe:

Dear Jimmy,

I am so sorry that you left my place that abruptly. If you would like to reconsider getting together again at White Tail or perhaps somewhere else, please call me.

Fondly,
Jay Rutledge

At the bottom of the message were listed several phone numbers and even an e-mail address. When Jimmy finished the note, he refolded it and stuck it back in the envelope as he stepped toward an awaiting garbage can.

"Let me see that," Abe snapped as he practically yanked it from Jimmy's hand. Rereading the message aloud, he blurted, "What's this all about?"

"That's the hospital administrator I told you about. He was going to have both you and me out to White Tail Point; but as it turned out, he invited only me. He wanted only me there."

"What happened? You didn't mention that you'd ever hunted over there." Abe studied the blank, almost embarrassed look on Jimmy's face.

"The only thing the guy cared about huntin' was me, it seems. The fag came onto me! It was weird. At first, he didn't seem to be strange or act queer at all. In the beginning I wasn't sure what was going on, but I figured it out pretty quick!"

Hearing about deviants like this turned Abe's stomach 360 degrees. "That sonnavabitch! Did you slug him?"

"No, I didn't. I just left in a real hurry. I told him somethin' like he had the wrong impression of me."

Remembering a similar incident he had once experienced with a now deceased great-uncle, Abe charged, "Jim Boy, you should have punched that homo's eyes out!"

"I was afraid to. He might've had me arrested, you know, like for breakin' and enterin' or assault or somethin' like that. I decided at the time that it was best for me to just bust out of there; so I left in a hurry. A real hurry! It's amazing that he didn't try to stop me."

"Did the asshole bastard try to call you later?" Abe became more incensed as he could tell in Jimmy's tone how disturbing the incident had actually been.

"Shit, no! This is the first time I've heard from him since then. I guess he got my address from the hospital. Makes me feel kinda spooky that he knows where I live."

Since learning of that incident between Jimmy and the hospital administrator, Abe had been troubled that the closest thing he had to a brother was queer bait. In his opinion there was nothing about Jimmy Perry that looked, sounded, smelled, or otherwise appeared homosexual in any way. Always easy to anger, Abe's emotions turned villainous in that oak tree as he replayed Jimmy's emotional assault.

As Abe continued to stalk with his scope the hospital administrator as he approached on the four-wheeler, he said, "You fuckin' deviant," loud enough to startle the plump squirrel on a nearby branch. Abe's stomach boiled with revulsion as he envisioned the scene where this lecher had sexually propositioned his beloved, normal cousin. Abe's imagination was racing for fear that Jimmy had omitted some of the actual sordid details of the encounter. He believed that since Jimmy had witnessed the temper of Abe Perry in its finest hours, he might have withheld some of the truth to keep him from truly going ballistic.

"I'm not worried about that guy, Abe. Go on, and just forget about it, please, Man. I mean it!" Jimmy had begged, trying to calm Abe's growing fury. Abe underestimated Jimmy's sense of masculinity, refusing to accept that his cousin's self-confidence was never threatened by Jay Rutledge's proposition. Unknown to the elder Perry, Jimmy's masculine persona was now impenetrable as a result of Aslyn's amorous attention to all the physical details of their growing relationship.

For a while, cousin Abe honored Jimmy's request and did forget. However, his resentment for Jay Rutledge's unnatural advances toward his cousin resurfaced during the party that night at The Silver Fox. Seeing Jay Rutledge in person, even in the dim light of that bar, amplified his hatred of him.

At the time that Jimmy pointed Rutledge out to him in the dim neon lights of The Silver Fox, Abe was quick to notice that the guy was in the company of a man, not a woman. To Abe, the vision of the two men leaving together was a nauseating example of twisted filth. Rekindling his hatred for that kind of person and bringing to life a reminder of his own demeaning experience, Abe then vowed silently that he wanted, even needed, vengeance for Jimmy. This retribution was fundamental to Abe, even if Jimmy was ignorant to his own need for it.

Looming over Mr. Jay Rutledge with microscopic scrutiny as the ATV slowed, Abe watched him lean over the right side of the four-wheeler. While checking a buck's rub on the bark of a large pine, the driver's face was a solid match for the fagot at The Fox. Abe was certain of it. Even from his invisible location at high elevation, Abe Perry was able to plan a clear shot.

As he targeted the head with his rifle and pulled the trigger with fervent rage, the mechanism unexpectedly jammed. "Damn!" he exclaimed under his breath. While removing the faulty shell and reloading the cylinder, Abe fought to calm the scorching, chemical anger pulsing through his body.

Subsequent to the aborted shot, the now moving target reached down to silence his one-way text pager, an urgent summons from an office assistant. With aggravation Rutledge realized that he would have to interrupt his four-wheeler excursion to drive back to his truck where he had left his cell phone. As Jay depressed the automatic starter button of his Polaris with his left hand, the shooter effortlessly aimed the reloaded rifle at the right temple.

Abe's hunting skill overpowered his temper as he refocused on his mark, pulling his trigger just a fraction of a second after Jay squeezed his. Rutledge's trigger was the accelerating gas lever of the ATV that propelled the hospital administrator down the trail, just ahead of a Federal Premium 165 Grain rifle cartridge. The revving of the four-wheeler could not completely mask the sound of the gunshot, even though Abe thought that the miss had gone undetected by his target. Bewildered and shocked that someone was apparently shooting at him, Jay continued to speed down the trail toward the camp house. He heard and escaped a second shot shortly before he rounded the first curve in the path, almost flipping the screaming vehicle and himself over into a cavernous ravine.

"What the Hell!" The fleeing ATV muffled Abe's shout into the encircling woods. Following this second unsuccessful shot at the lucky four-wheeler driver, Abe was disgusted with his usually reliable weapon and aim. His annoyance with himself was heightened because he believed he had killed Jay Rutledge a few days before.

Rutledge never expected to serve as human game, particularly since he thought he was alone that day at White Tail. As his mind raced nonstop at near-maximum four-wheeler speed, Jay realized that his cavalier omission of a protective orange vest could have led to one accidental shot. The second shot, however, could have been no accident.

Flying into the camp house parking area in a storm of dust and gravel particles, Jay encountered no other vehicles there except his truck. He sprang off the moving ATV, leaving it to slow to an idle as it ran into the stack of nearby firewood. Nervously unlocking the back door, the hunted ran through the equipment storage hall, by the oak bar area, across the great hall decorated with dead animals, and burst into his private quarters, bolting the door behind him. Rutledge jerked open the drawer beside his bed, gripping his semi-automatic pistol while grabbing his cell phone to call the police.

Until last night, Knox had avoided the temptation to have a date stay over at his condo. Deciding that the bank would likely not afford him the opportunity to entertain in his home much longer, he had suggested to Sibley that they stop at his place when they left the restaurant. His original intent in asking her out was not necessarily to have her sleep with him; however, as the outing continued affectionately, his plans for the evening changed.

Knox's error was in continuing the alcohol once they arrived at his condo. Sibley had followed his lead of two beers during the pool game; but as Knox now realized, she should have skipped the third and sleep-inducing fourth. Finding Sibley's pulse and respiratory efforts stable, Knox plucked the limp girl from the couch and settled her fully clothed on top of the guestroom bedspread. As he covered her with a blanket from the room's closet, Knox flashed back to his meetings with the real estate agent who had pushed him into buying and completely furnishing this place, ownership of which was slipping away.

Admiring the peaceful, sleeping Sibley, Knox felt certain that without a job it would be impossible to keep an attractive girlfriend like her. As she dozed, her delicate facial features covered with smooth healthy skin moved subtly, almost suggestively, in unison with her every breath. An example of ultimate contentment, he decided. However, Knox's gratification was not in someone's finally utilizing the guestroom and its furniture bought on credit. Instead, he wished that his guest's satisfaction tonight had resulted from a roll in his bedroom across the hall.

The buzzing of the alarm clock was especially cruel. Knox silenced it the following morning before walking across to the guestroom in his boxers and tee shirt to check on Sibley. Sadly, her bed was vacant and the blanket neatly folded at the foot. In the living room he found her note:

> *Knox, thanks for the evening. I'm sorry I was such*
> *a sleepy head. Somehow I woke early enough*
> *to make it to work. I had a great time with you.*
> *See you later.*

> *Sibley*

Knox then turned his attention from the lost opportunity to the day's appointment with Cable Tate. Courtesy of Sibley's premature departure, he was left with ample time to shave,

shower, and grab some breakfast before his ten o'clock
appointment in downtown Montclair.

With the advent of fax machines and e-mail, many lawyers
had relocated their offices away from the city's courthouse
area to more luxurious buildings in the suburbs. Separate
from the norm, Cable Tate maintained his law practice
downtown and kept the operation simple. His appointment
secretary-typist was only a part-time employee, and the
telephone answering machine filled in for the other parts.
Mr. Tate purposely chose to keep his legal practice low-key,
low stress, and low in profits. After all, law practice profits were
not an absolute necessity for Cable Tate, Esquire. He had been
wise enough to liquidate his ambitious stock portfolio at the
market's peak before the turn of the century correction and was
now seriously into semi-retirement.

Once he took the business district exit off the interstate, Knox
followed the secretary's directions until he eventually found the
renovated 1930's art deco building, Home to the offices of Cable
J. Tate and equipped with several eclectic first floor breakfast
and sandwich shops, the four story building stood on one of the
few remaining brick-paved streets in Montclair. Somehow
Blueberry Street had escaped the concrete or asphalt burial of
the city's other pre-Civil War roads. The dingy white letters
identifying the building's occupants hung askew in the directory
case, which rested on the wall just to the right of the front
entrance. Its smoky glass front had been neglected for eons by
the building's janitorial service.

Knox touched the dust coated panel as he found the name and
title of *Cable J. Tate, Attorney- at-Law* across from suite
number 401. Wiping his now greasy forefinger on the back of
his right pants leg, he turned to find the elevator.

After a brief search of the building's foyer, Knox found no
elevator. Fortunately, the structure had been centrally
ventilated sometime during the 1970's; thus, the walk up the

four flights was bearable. Even during a Mississippi January, air conditioning is useful, particularly in the upper levels of a building. Finding a wall directory specific to the fourth floor, he stopped a moment to catch his breath and then followed the numbered doors until he reached the one labeled *Cable Tate and Associates Legal Services*. Knox suspected that the only associate was the part time secretary with whom he had conversed earlier on the phone.

There was no glass front to the office door nor to the exterior hall wall, not even a smoky glass window. He tried the locked doorknob twice before he noticed the instructions to push the electric call button posted to the left. The lingering reverberation of the bell remained as a gentleman who looked to be in his late fifties opened the door.

"Yes, please come in. Dr. Chamblee, I presume," Cable Tate laughed as they shook hands. "I guess you're thankful your name's not Livingston!" Knox totally ignored the anemic joke. "Tabitha has the day off. That's why the front door was locked. I don't want any solicitors in here, Dr. Chamblee. Oh, by the way, I prefer to start things off on a personal basis with a new client. May I call you by your first name?"

"Sure, Mr. Tate."

"Ummm, let's see. What is your first name? Darn it, Tabitha didn't write the appointment down on today's schedule." Knox watched as Lawyer Tate was staring down at the scheduling book, lying opened on Tabitha's desk and loaded with blank spaces. Apparently, thought Knox, the secretary had failed not only to write down his name but omitted those of Tate's other clients as well.

"It's Knox, Knox Chamblee," he answered to fill in his blank.

"Knox," Tate repeated with a slight devilish grin. "Then you're having some hard knocks, Knox?"

As Tate burst into uncontrollable laughter after another weak inquiry, Knox reminded himself of the urgent reason he needed an attorney and why he had chosen this one. First, he had been fired unjustly, and second, Cable Tate was cheap. Rather than the typical local rate for legal services ranging from $150 to $200 per hour, Tate charged $95. Since Knox was no longer employed and owned a meager portfolio, he bit on the lower quoted rate of all the firms he polled.

"Mr. Tate," Knox interrupted his attorney's laughter during a brief lapse.

"Oh, please call me Cable," he replied, while wiping his eyes with a handkerchief produced from his back pocket. "I guess we should get to the point. I was just trying to lighten things up a bit."

"OK, Cable, this is my former employment agreement with the Montclair Center for Women's Medical and Surgical Services." As the potential client was being led by the arm into the inner office sanctum of Cable Tate and Associates Legal Services, he briefly took in the décor of Tate's private office — furniture, drapes, and carpet obviously installed about the same time as the building's air conditioning. At Tate's invitation Knox took a seat in the vintage leather chair directly across from the lawyer's desk.

"My assistant, Tabitha, told me that you called because you had been recently terminated as a physician employee of a medical clinic here in Montclair. First of all, young man, one doesn't hear too often about a doctor getting fired for any reason." Tate rested his fat forefinger on the edge of his mustache and tweaked it a bit. "No, no, I can't recall another time. Guess it could happen if they're into drugs or something like that," Tate added as he looked over at Knox somewhat suspiciously. Not really expecting a response, he continued to skim through the fifteen pages of Knox's former employment agreement.

"Ah, here it is," Tate focused again at his new client while keeping his right index finger as a marker on the page. "*Article Roman Numeral Six, Section Four*," he enunciated slowly, "*Sub-section A: Reason for Termination* This is the important part. Have you read this, young man?"

"Yes, recently I ..."

Again Cable Tate did not anticipate an interruption but instead persisted in reading the contract aloud. "*Failure of*

Allegiance to the Practice- Have you or did you start working for another doctors' group or begin taking care of patients outside of the confines of the established practice?"

"No, I..."

"I didn't think so. *Subsection B - Failure to Maintain a Mode of Transportation-* I'm sure you've got some kind of car and car insurance," once more not slowing for a reply.

"Subsection C-Failure to be covered for Medical Errors Insurance- That sounds like some expensive lawyer's term for malpractice insurance. You haven't screwed up some woman's hysterectomy or dropped a baby during a delivery, or anything like that, have you, young man?" This time dramatizing his performance with a smirk, as he still sought no reaction from Knox, he directed his attention to a tree branch brushing against his office window. "Someone once told me about this doctor who lost his balance while delivering a baby. The doc wound up butt first in a small garbage can down below the woman's spread out legs. But lucky for him, he had a good tight hold on the baby and just kept right on congratulating the..."

Knox interrupted the lawyer's waste of his time and money, "No, I have no litigation against me regarding patient care. None that I am aware of, that is. There was a patient who unavoidably died recently; but the Hospital Catastrophic Events Committee cleared me of any wrongdoing. They even called me *heroic.* Of course, there's the ridiculously long Mississippi Statute of Limitations but..."

"Please don't recite the law to me, Dr. Chamblee. That's what you're paying me $90 an hour for."

Knox decided not to inform Tate that he had been quoted $95.

"So from the malpractice standpoint, you're clean as a whistle, Knox." Cable decided that maybe he ought to seem more personable in addressing the young doctor. That leaves us with *Subsection D- Failure to Generate Revenues to Cover Practice Costs.* What do you know about this subsection?"

"The partnered physicians have never allowed me to have access to my particular practice financial data. Associate physicians have never been given computer clearance to check the Center's financial records. Likewise, I have never received any monthly or quarterly financial reports regarding just my part of the practice or even the practice as a whole."

"Nowhere in this document does your former employer state that you were to be provided with that financial information, Mr. Chamblee."

"I believe I would feel more comfortable if you called me *Knox*. Anyway, if we're going to keep it on a professional level, it would be ***Dr. Chamblee***. I may not have a job anymore, but I still have a valid Mississippi medical license."

"Ok, Dr. Chamblee, your contract merely guarantees your job as renewable on an annual basis for as long as you remain alive, stay under the age of 68, and fulfill your service obligations to the practice. It states right here in the next section that the women's center is to give you sixty days notice of your employment termination. The next clause gives them the right to void the sixty days notice as long as they pay you sixty days of severance pay."

"Yes, Nell, the office manager told me she would mail me the checks."

"Now then. Look at the bright side. You've got sixty days of paid leave to find a new job, Doctor."

"That might sound adequate and fair, Mr. Tate. But you're missing the point! The office manager let me know, rather matter-of-factly, that the physician executive board basically fired me to replace me with a woman physician. That sounds like sexual discrimination to me. Opportunities for male obstetricians and gynecologists don't just appear out of thin air. I'm not sure I can find another job in just sixty days, particularly after having been fired from another practice."

"Why don't you just set up your own practice?"

"That would be too expensive, and I'm not ready to take on the kind of debt required to start up a solo practice. Also, being in solo OB/GYN practice would mean being on call 24 - 7. No, that's not for me."

"Your accusation of being fired because of your gender would be hard to prove unless another valid reason for termination does not exist."

"They thought that I wasn't pulling my own weight, not billing enough medical and surgical procedures. In my own defense, I showed up for work on time everyday and felt like I was building up a practice slowly, but steadily."

"Since you say that you haven't had access to any of the Center's financial records, we would have to subpoena the documents if you want to push this being fired issue. If the financial records regarding your performance are in order, then the discrimination issue could be explored."

Knox felt at a total loss, overwhelmed and confused about which direction to take in solving his unfair dilemma. He was leery of Tate's advice because most likely the financial records of the practice would prove the consultants correct — that the senior doctors had truly thrown away money on him. However, he returned to focus on what he considered the reasonable truth: it is not unusual for a medical practice in the beginning to lose financially on a new associate physician. This unemployed physician gifted with approximately fifty-eight days of severance pay remaining and a mounting legal bill was not sure what to do at this point.

His attorney directed their discussion into a more serious tone. "Suing the Montclair Center is going to be expensive. If they reinstate you following a verdict on your behalf, I doubt that returning to work with those doctors would be pleasant. Of course, if you're interested in suing them for some sort of large pain and suffering award, then a court win or even a large out-of-court settlement would be worthwhile. Heck, maybe you wouldn't have to practice medicine at all," Tate proceeded to howl with laughter at this proposed resolution as he leaned back in his wooden, revolving desk chair.

"I'm not sure at all what to do. I..."

Judging from the contorted, sad response on his client's face, Cable Tate assumed a more sober tone and offered, "Let me do some legal research regarding similar cases, if there are any. In the meantime, why don't you take a vacation, for gosh sake? Besides you've got the time off. Fifty-eight days worth, in fact."

"Thanks for rubbin' it in."

"I just mean go grab some girl. Skip town. Find a nice spot and relax. You know — get some R & R."

Thinking that Tate's last comment might turn out to be the only worthwhile advice for his ninety-dollar hour, Knox popped up from the leather chair to terminate the meeting. The attorney shook hands empathetically with his young client and promised to contact him in one week for further case discussion. "Do us both a favor and do some soul-searching about where or how far you want to go with this, Knox," Cable Tate sincerely offered as he walked Chamblee back through the dated front office to the exit.

Pulling out of his parking place on Blueberry Street, Knox decided to drive by the Center and Grace Community on his way home. As long as his building keys still worked, he planned to get some of his personal things from his office and doctors' lounge locker.

Sometime during the night before, Madelyn Gwinn awoke on a slab of cold, damp concrete. Stunned that she had once more slept somewhere else than her bed, she rubbed her face and eyes while fighting the bitter glare of a bare light bulb. Eventually regaining her bearings, she understood that she remained in her garage storeroom but wondered why her neck, shoulders, legs, and arms were massively sore and stiff. Not associating these symptoms with the aftermath of a major seizure, she moved her shoulders and slowly turned her neck from side-to-side only to produce instant pain. Mrs. Gwinn reached up to touch her swollen left forehead, then opened and closed her mouth with considerable effort. Instinctively, she covered the bitten area of the inside of her cheek with a swollen, almost macerated tongue.

Madelyn struggled to prop herself up and finally reached the garage door opener, her only visible outlet for a call for help. The nearest garage door responded promptly to the depressed electric control button. The outdoor security light shone through the enlarging garage opening, gradually enveloping Madelyn, as she lay yet again unconscious, once more in a post-ictal state, the consequences of another seizure.

At the funeral he had surveyed his client thoroughly and admired his work. Believing that he had molded her well, the extremely satisfied Minor Leblanc felt that he was worth every penny he charged. Even in a time of overwhelming grief, Madelyn Gwinn had appeared poised as she was impeccably dressed in an outfit selected by him. Minor believed that fate had directed the selection of that elegant, but still uncomplicated, black dress, which coincidentally now served as the perfect funeral ensemble. He beamed over Madelyn's choice to adorn her mourning attire with the unpretentious, although pricey, jewelry recently selected in Chicago by fashion consultant, Minor Leblanc.

As Leblanc saw things, part of the ambiance of utilizing his services was his complete confidentiality as his patrons were molded into perfection, and their friends and acquaintances were enveloped in certain envy. He wanted the jealous to believe that his customers had put together their own personal looks without outside help. For that reason he personally delivered many of his clients' things to their homes at night and to the back door. To uphold his inconspicuous professional relationship with the distraught widow, he chose not to attend the wake before her husband's funeral or the gathering at her home afterward but alternatively paid his respects by briefly speaking to Madelyn at the funeral. After all, Minor's major contact with Dr. Cullen Gwinn had only been in seeing his signature on payment checks.

During the services Mrs. Gwinn had discretely pulled him to the side. "Minor, I know that it was awkward for you in Chicago to have to tell me about my husband's death. It was really prophetic that you were with me. I don't know when I would have learned about Cullen if it had not been for you."

Since the Gwinn funeral, Minor had concentrated on his next commission to produce a twenty-fifth anniversary present for Mayor Netz's wife. The city head had desired something unique but not too gaudy — still suitable for his planned re-election party. Minor grinned as he admired the rose cut multi-diamonded necklace set in platinum. After designing the piece himself, he had then turned assembly of the piece over to the most exclusive jewelry boutique in Montclair.

"Mr. Mayor, this necklace will be fabulous at an anniversary dinner dance, but I doubt if Mrs. Netz will find an occasion to strut it at any re-election gala," he chuckled aloud to himself as he pretended to be talking to the mayor.

Driving toward the Netz estate to make the expected jewelry delivery, Minor approached the intersection marking the block of the nearby Gwinn residence. Since he had not talked with her since the funeral, he reached for his cell phone to call Madelyn. However, he changed his mind and pushed the 'end call' button before she had a chance to answer, choosing instead to stop by unannounced for only a brief stay. In fact, he decided to break his own professional rule and give Madelyn Gwinn a peek at the mayor's necklace. Of course, he planned not to divulge the price or real owner to Mrs. Gwinn but believed that her viewing and touching this superb collection of precious gems and metal might actually cheer her up. He had to admit to himself, though, that he hoped she might want one for herself.

As was his custom when visiting the Gwinn mansion, Minor descended the back driveway toward the garage, planning to park his Land Rover out of street view. Perplexed, he noticed that one of the garage doors was opened and that a light was shining from an interior room.

"Hello, there!" Minor called out toward the garage, unanswered as he left his vehicle. During his many previous trips to Madelyn's, Minor had never noticed such a situation, assuming that the garage doors were left down when not in use for security reasons. Slowly approaching the opening, he yelled this time, "This is Minor Leblanc. Is anyone there?" The tinkle of Mrs. Netz's diamond and platinum necklace striking the bare garage concrete was more than muffled by the scream.

"Oh, my God!" Minor instinctively next dropped the leather and suede jewelry case to join the necklace on the concrete. Almost in unison, at least forty beads of sweat erupted on his tall forehead.

Knox walked from his previous employer's building over to the hospital, approaching Grace Community by way of the emergency room entrance. Marking its importance with silent, revolving roof lights, an ambulance sat parked at the unloading ramp. He noticed a gentleman dressed in a velvet shirt with black leather pants getting out of the front passenger seat. The obviously distraught fellow, perspiring profusely, had apparently accompanied an emergency patient.

Pausing briefly by the rear of the opened ambulance, Knox watched the paramedics as they removed an ashen Caucasian woman strapped to a stretcher. Although her face was partially obscured by a supplemental oxygen mask and distorted by massive bruising, he thought that she looked vaguely familiar. Britton Stewart ran through the opened double doors from her ER physician desk, brushing by Knox to greet the ambulance. Finding this immediate personal attention unusual even from such a conscientious emergency room physician, Knox jokingly shouted toward her, "Britton, who's the V.I.P.?"

She looked back quickly in his direction. "Madelyn Gwinn! That fellow over there," she was gesturing toward the hand-wringing Minor Leblanc, "found her unconscious in her garage. I think she has had a seizure or two." While receiving a hurried report from the paramedics, Knox noticed that Britton gestured a slight wave toward the nervous front seat passenger. He believed that he saw her mouth, "Hey, Minor, are you okay?"

Dr. Britton Stewart's daytime appearance seemed somewhat different to Knox, a little more feminine and appealing. Since he had last run into her, she had apparently undergone a metamorphosis of her professional appearance. Her hair was no longer pulled back with a colorful rubber band. She now boasted a more youthful hairstyle, still fairly easy to maintain even for a busy woman doctor. A more en vogue pair of soft-soled Merrells had also replaced her signature tennis shoes. Even her scrub suit looked somewhat more fashionably upscale.

Knox planned to check with some of the nurses to see if Britton was still dating that guy he had seen her with at the restaurant. If not, he planned to call her later and ask her out.

Chapter

15

•••

THE TRACE

Because of a cellular service technicality, the call from Pecan Grove was directed here: "Montclair Police Department. What is your emergency, please?"

"Someone has just shot at me... twice. Some maniac," the panicked, screaming voice of Jay Rutledge could be heard completely across the front office of the department. The 911 dispatcher was utilizing the hands free speakerphone option to answer her calls. It is easier to do one's nails that way.

"Sir, I must have your location."

"I'm, I'm," he was so distraught that he could barely remember where he was. As Jay continued to point his automatic handgun at the locked door of his private suite, he was able to get out, "I'm near Pecan Grove in Peace County, Mississippi, at my hunting camp. It's called White Tail Hunting Lodge. I've been intentionally shot at twice, at fairly close range."

"Sir, you have reached the Montclair Emergency District. I'll have to transfer you to your local Peace County 911 operator. Please stay on the line and try to remain calm," the operator insisted as she completed her press-on creation. A tiny, iridescent star now adorned the bright-red, elongated nail of her left forefinger.

"Wait a minute before you transfer that one, Shaqueta!" shouted the Chief of Police. Ambling into the front office to get some coffee, Chevelle Agee's attention was diverted as he overheard the man's screams. "Shaqueta, I heard that caller say his point of location was White Tail Lodge. That's where that doctor from Montclair died. You know, the one that was up there hunting. Let me go ahead and talk to this guy."

Agee reached down to pick up the receiver and switch off the speakerphone, wincing from his sore shoulder. The bruised joint still had not recovered from yesterday's tumbling into the Hawes flowerbed. "Sir, please calm down. This is Chief Chevelle Agee of the Montclair Police Department. Can I help you?"

After confirming the exact location of the incident, Chevelle advised the accuser to stay in his locked room. While assuring the caller that the nearby authorities would be immediately contacted, the chief told Rutledge to expect an officer from the Peace County Sheriff's Department within minutes. Proceeding as promised, he hung up with Rutledge and telephoned his sheriff friend to share the outlandish-sounding tale. Agee eagerly accepted Peace County's invitation to assist with this new investigation. It was not often that he could probe complaints of someone being used as target practice.

"Meet me at my car pronto," Chevelle instructed Lamar when he responded to the page. "We need to head back to that hunting camp near Pecan Grove where that doctor died. Something else strange has happened there." Trying to sound as professional as possible, Chief Agee did his best to disguise his excitement.

The Peace County Sheriff was well into his interview of the visibly shaken hospital administrator when Chevelle and Lamar arrived at White Tail. Insisting that he had been the victim of an attempted murder, Rutledge was certain that the assailant was someone not connected with the hunting camp.

As the questioning and interviewing of the dumbfounded Jay Rutledge pressed on, searching for suspects and motives, he denied any reason for a fellow hunting camp member to shoot at him. He countered as absurd one officer's suggestion that a disgruntled hospital patient or relative of a patient may have been responsible for the shots.

From the looks exchanged between the police chief and sheriff, it was clear they considered Jay Rutledge a real basket case. "It seems by the point, Mr. Rutledge, that we're at a dead end with this complaint — particularly if you can't even come up with a guess at why someone would take pot shots at you!" Agee declared, poorly disguising his growing concern that the whole incident had been prefabrication. As he winked inconspicuously at the sheriff, Agee continued, "However, Sir, if someone has deliberately shot at you, then the perpetrator most likely left discarded shell casings or other evidence in the area."

Nervously upset despite two cocktails during the short wait for the law enforcement officials, Jay remained tucked in his plush leather chair and focused on the large policeman staring down at him. Reacting as though he were the criminal being interrogated, Rutledge countered, "I can assure you, Officer... (Rutledge was so overly beside himself that he could not focus on Chevelle's identification tag, much less remember the introductions.)...Officer Whoever, that some asshole did honestly shoot at me, not once, but at least twice. I'll be glad to take you to the scene of the crime, and I would appreciate your taking me seriously."

The sheriff chimed in, "Mr. Rutledge, just show us where this happened and we'll take it from there."

After Rutledge led the law enforcement team to General Magruder's Path where he had just served as target practice, a lower level officer safely escorted him back to Montclair. The rest of the investigative team, composed of a combination of Montclair and Pecan Grove's finest, then fanned out to begin a thorough search of that section of the hunting camp.

Below a tall oak found missing a small number of thin, freshly cut branches, one of the officers discovered a not long spent rifle casing. As the group stood under the oak studying the area in more detail, they judged that the shooter was likely positioned high in the tree in some sort of climbing tree stand. Now bolstered with evidence corroborating the hysterical fellow's tale, the sheriff called for a few county locals to assist with the remaining investigation and search. Although this incident had occurred fairly early in the afternoon, combing the wooden canopy of White Tail's acreage began rapidly to consume the remaining daylight hours. Chief Agee agreed with his peer that they needed to pick up their pace to finish before dark.

Lamar was the one who first stumbled upon the dilapidated shack. As it appeared to have been recently inhabited, he excitedly covered it with his weapon and called for back up. A thorough ransacking of the filthy dwelling then ensued, first yielding an empty rifle cartridge box that matched the casing found at the tall oak. The box was then sealed in an evidence bag.

Lying near some rotting leaves in a recess of the shack, a pile of empty beer cans was next spotted by Lamar, who hoped for a source of fingerprints. Pumped up by this additional collection of potential evidence, the detective advanced his exploration to include the exterior of the little building. A few hundred feet away he came across a narrow road obscured by deteriorating leaves and fallen tree branches. Lamar, following the passageway with intense scrutiny as it led to a rusted gate, halted at the fresh tire tracks embedded in the soft forest mulch.

The Restful Inn was located on the Interstate 79 exit about midpoint between Montclair and Pecan Grove. In contrast to the motel's name, Jimmy's experience there that evening had been anything but restful. Aslyn had reached him late in the afternoon on his cell, suggesting that he get off work a little early and meet her at their frequented rendezvous spot.

After becoming physically entangled with Aslyn on a regular basis, Jimmy never needed much prodding to agree to meet her for more. However, in this instance, she still offered him an excuse for such a short notice call; she was overly tense due to the shortage of physicians in her practice. Her more mature almost insatiable appetite constantly amazed Jimmy, as she craved sex with him in a bed as much in her hot tub. Before he departed the Restful Inn that evening for his mother's house, Jimmy coaxed Aslyn into one last experience in the shower although she had not needed much encouragement. He was certain that Aslyn could no longer feel any tension caused by her doctor work, especially after all they had done together that afternoon in the motel room.

Today's meeting with her youthful, virile lover had been no different from any other — satisfying and addictive. While she had almost lost track of how long she had been seeing Jimmy, she had also lost count of their uninhibited sexual unions. From the moment she was first attracted to him that day in the hospital, she allowed no age barrier to interfere with her repeated physical pleasure. Equally, she had detected nothing in the nineteen-year-old that suggested anything unnatural about what they did together or to each other.

Aslyn rationalized that being with Jimmy was her way of coping with the same hormonal fluctuations that her patients constantly complained about. Suspecting that she was in the midst of her own early 40's perimenopausal experience, Aslyn believed that these changes in her cycles had led to rediscovering the pleasures of intimacy. She reassured herself that Jimmy must take great pleasure in being with her, too, or he wouldn't keep coming back for more.

For fear that the housekeeper would find traces of their clandestine unions, Aslyn always fought the temptation to invite Jimmy inside her house. Meeting him in the hot tub, in a car, or at a motel had afforded her plenty of opportunity to enjoy him. While Jimmy had never asked for any money, she always paid the bill at the Restful Inn, gave him modest gifts along the way, and covered any food or beverage expenses.

Neither partner, as well, had ever mentioned love. She believed that both were fully satisfied with only a physical relationship.

Jimmy had spent so much of that physical time with Aslyn that by now it was pitch-black dark outside. However, as he passed by Abe's trailer on the way home to his mother's, Jimmy could not miss his cousin's truck illuminated by a large, single light hanging on a nearby pole. As was his custom, he decided to stop and say hello.

Not bothering to knock, Jimmy merely walked into the unlocked trailer and, as expected, encountered his cousin sitting on the tatty couch watching the Hunting Channel. Discovering Abe alone in the dark, stale dwelling was not unusual; what was odd was finding him distracted and rudely moody. Feeling rebuffed, Jimmy left Abe undisturbed and drove off for home, planning to stop instead for a beer at a convenience store.

Abe remained deep in thought as he ignored Jimmy's departure. For several hours after Jimmy left, he continued sitting there in the dingy trailer, brooding over the events of his day at White Tail. He had already decided that he was not going to share any of this with anyone, not even his cousin. "How could I have missed? Why did my rifle jam at first? Why didn't I reload and try to chase that bastard down somehow?" he continually berated himself. There was one fact of which he was sure. Abe was certain that the Rutledge fellow had not been able to see the shooter or even his form perched high in that oak.

As the evening progressed and the hunting videos seemed repetitive, hunger struck. Finding a few slices of non-molded bread left in the cabinet, Abe made himself a cheese sandwich and poured a dented can of microwave-cooked soup into a stained ceramic bowl. Soup, sandwich, and five or six beers later, his mind remained cluttered with images of White Tail. He had been exploring the area for months, even before Jimmy mentioned that the hospital administrator had invited him there. Abe's frequent trespassing had afforded great familiarity with the property's trails, four wheeler paths, shooting houses, and metal hunting stands.

Now clouded in a drunken stupor, his recollection drifted to one Friday afternoon when he was scouting game at White Tail. On that occasion he was likewise surprised by a four-wheeler coming down a nearby path, this time prompting him to duck behind some brush. He watched as two guys of similar height and build were riding around the property as though on tour. They stopped briefly near his hiding spot, apparently checking out a potential hunting site. Remembering that night at The Silver Fox with Jimmy, he immediately recognized one of them as Rutledge, the queer hospital administrator.

After they drove away, Abe sauntered over to where they were inspecting the tree by the creek. High in the tall oak he spotted an attached metal ladder stand. Assuming that one of the hunters would be using this tree stand the following morning, Abe gambled that Rutledge would be situated there. He thought that Rutledge would consider the location ideal for bagging a big deer and that the greedy queer would grab it for himself. After closely studying the site, Abe quietly climbed the ladder stand, then used his hunter's saw to weaken the tree branches and the stand's support.

As he sat there in his trailer and relived the events of that particular weekend, Abe relished having watched the masked camouflaged figure approach the sabotaged stand the following freezing morning. Silently lying in wait in the same nearby brush used the afternoon before, he remained completely hidden from view. Watching with great hatred and then with great pleasure, Abe was overjoyed as the hunter eventually slipped from the site high in the tree, almost landing in the nearby creek. Initially, the trophy was perfectly still as his body lay at the edge of the frozen water. Just as Abe was planning to steal away by foot and return to his own private 'lodge' on the property, the man he assumed to be the homosexual Jay Rutledge unexpectedly tried to turn himself completely over.

Cursing under his breath, Abe then stepped toward the breathing mound of camouflage and orange, remaining behind and out of sight of the fallen hunter. Meeting no resistance, the stalker lifted the man's mask-covered head, turning his face toward the creek. The slight incline of the bank of the shallow creek practically forced freezing water into the mouth and nose. Finding the gurgling and gasping noises gratifying, Abe stood there motionless, waiting until the sounds stopped. He was relieved that the man he then assumed to be Rutledge never tried to lift his head away from the water or attempt to move his extremities further.

On that bitterly cold Saturday morning Abe left satisfied that the pervert who had tried to violate Jimmy was justifiably dead. Now disgusted at today's discovery that the man he murdered then was not Rutledge, he felt no remorse for the unknown man he had actually killed. In contrast, he reaped minimal gratification in believing that any deviant caught fraternizing with Jay Rutledge would be just as deserving to die.

After today's disappointing rifle misses, Abe retained his desperate desire to inflict final, deadly punishment upon Mr. Jay Rutledge.

"Hey, Your Honor, this is Minor Leblanc. I am calling from the emergency room."

"The emergency room? I thought you were making a delivery to my house today," Mayor Netz responded with a high degree of concern, not over the possibility that Minor was ill but that his wife had not received her anniversary necklace.

Minor explained his rescue of Madelyn Gwinn and promised a slightly later delivery time for Mrs. Netz's jewelry. Omitting a few details in his conversation with the mayor, Minor failed to mention that the work of art now needed a good bit of repair. He did elaborate on how he had spent his time patiently waiting in the hospital visitors' area while the neurologist evaluated Madelyn Gwinn and obtained a CT head scan. Appealing to the anxious Mayor Netz's sense of community, Minor hoped that this additional information about his ministering to the sick would help to buy enough time to get the necklace redone. "Of course, your honor, you know that Mrs. Gwinn is a recent widow and has no local family."

The mayor had no argument that his problem was worse than Mrs. Gwinn's misery, so he accepted his personal shopper's reassurance that the necklace would be delivered in plenty of time to celebrate.

The reality of Minor Leblanc's present situation at Grace Community Hospital was that he greatly enjoyed the notoriety connected with the rescue of his client, particularly, the ride in the ambulance. He was thrilled that he had known Britton Stewart, the emergency room physician, when he got out of the rescue vehicle. Dr. Stewart had made certain that the ER nursing staff kept him comfortable during Madelyn Gwinn's evaluation, and the result was that he felt like royalty. While Minor concluded that the waiting room magazines were stale and not comprehensive in the fashion genre, the soft drinks and doughnuts from the nurses' lounge were well received.

"Are you waiting for your wife or child?" a woman appearing to be in her early sixties had asked while he ate his third Krispy Kreme, this time chocolate-covered. Her husband was in the cardiology suite having a cardiac catheterization.

"No, Sugar, I'm here with a friend," he answered and then hesitated for a minute, "Mrs. Madelyn Gwinn." He then introduced himself to the lady, who appeared well-dressed but in need of some degree of fashion refinement.

"Oh, I know of her. Her husband was my gynecologist. He died recently and unexpectedly — and I'm still torn up about it," she added. "Cynthia Prescott," she proudly announced as she extended him a finely manicured hand. She found the young man to be as considerate as he was entertaining. "I trust that Mrs. Gwinn is doing well," Prescott continued out of polite concern.

"I do hope so. She has simply had a tiny accident, and the doctors are doing a few tests," Minor responded without elaborating further. Occasionally, he felt it appropriate to identify himself as a personal professional shopper and individual stylist. This was one of those instances. "Let me share one of my cards with you, Mrs. Prescott," he continued, handing her a masterpiece printed in gold embossed lettering. Simultaneously, Cynthia Prescott's daughter and sister joined her in the waiting area, taking a seat near the fashionably dressed man with whom Cynthia was seriously discussing changing her hair color. By the time Madelyn had completed her evaluation in radiology, Minor Leblanc had acquired three new clients and inconspicuously taken pre-Leblanc photos of them with his picture cell phone.

"What did ya'll find out about Mrs. Gwinn?" Knox asked Britton when he came back by the Emergency Room. He had completed a thorough clean out of his former private office at the Montclair Center. All of his personal items had been packed away, including his diplomas and medical licenses matted in their matching frames. Each of his former patient exam rooms had been adorned with a scantily filled bulletin board hanging on the wall. A collection of pictures of newborns was posted on each of these boards, gifts from the mothers and representative of the babies he had delivered. The display was now dismantled with the pictures stored safely in a few storage envelopes. Since the patient care equipment and the office furniture itself did not belong to Knox, the whole process had been swift. Fortunately, his former assistant Lovejoy had the day off, preventing much sentiment to his official departure.

"Let me show you what's been going on with Madelyn Gwinn," Britton answered as she led Knox just off the ER into the radiology viewing room. Pulling up Madelyn's findings on the digital viewing screen, she pointed to the right side of the image. "Look at this large cerebral aneurysm, suspected to be congenital. Even an OB/GYN can see it," Britton teased with a slight smirk while punching Knox affectionately in the gut.

Knox recoiled his abdominal muscles reflexively. "Hey, guess what? I do see it!" He played along as he pointed to the brain abnormality on the screen. "It's rather large, but I don't see any midline deviation." He recalled his medical school

neurosurgery rotation and hoped he could project a
degree of intelligence during the discussion. "Did the
neurologist have an opinion regarding how close she is
to rupture of the aneurysm?"

"Yes. Actually the neurologist is worried about an imminent
cerebral hemorrhage and has called in the neurosurgery team
for an urgent craniotomy. They are gravely concerned about
the size of the aneurysm and the degree of recent secondary
seizure activity."

"What kind of prognosis did Dr. Hesson give her?" Knox
asked Britton.

"Both the neurologist and the neurosurgeon believe that as
long as tonight's surgery goes well, she should fully recover.
That is, as long as there is not another underlying cause for the
seizures. Strangely, we don't have any medical history for Mrs.
Gwinn. She has never had a baby or any surgery here,
according to the hospital medical information department. I
called Dr. Langley for access to any files that the Woman's
Center might have on her, but that came up a bust. He told me
that there was no record in the electronic patient file system
that she had ever been seen there as a patient. Knox, don't you
think it odd that a gynecologist's wife would not have been
receiving regular medical care?"

Knox remembered the conversation that he, Lovejoy, and
Madelyn had that day in the back hall of the Center and how he
had unlocked the sample closet for Mrs. Gwinn. "I do know
that she was taking some sort of medication, but I'm not sure
what. She said that Dr. Gwinn had been giving it to her. Maybe
he was unofficially taking care of her and not keeping any
medical records."

"Once the results of her admission urine and blood
toxicology screens are released, we may be closer to putting
this all together. It's a good sign that she wasn't wearing any
medical alert bracelets when she was found. So we'll simply
have to hope for the best outcome possible," Britton said in
summary while shrugging her shoulders.

During Madelyn's uneventful craniotomy that night, her

talented neurosurgeon was able to clip the aneurysm, luckily finding no associated brain abnormalities. Regaining consciousness much sooner than expected during the post-operative period, Madelyn startled her Neuro ICU nurse into promptly paging the neurosurgeon. By the time he arrived at the ICU to reassess Madelyn's remarkable condition, she had begun to actively and symmetrically move all four extremities. The specialist proposed that Madelyn Gwinn's promising post surgical state pointed toward full recovery although she would require anti-convulsant therapy, at least temporarily.

"As we had hoped, the IV steroids apparently are preventing cerebral swelling, and Mrs. Gwinn's cardiac and respiratory functions have remained normal," the neurosurgeon remarked to the RN at bedside. "Let's go ahead and extubate her, although we'll still need to keep her fairly sedated. The post-operative narcotics should take care of that," he deduced while recording his assessment by touching areas of the nearby computer screen electronic record.

"The crime lab has lifted a set of prints off the casing we found under the tree, Chief, and they match a set pulled off one of the Mason Dixon Beer cans I picked up in that shack. I submitted them to the fingerprint bank to see it they match any others," Lamar broadcasted as he burst into the Chief's office. Lamar had taken great interest in continuing to help the Peace County Police Department in investigating the attempted shooting at the deer camp.

"Then we lifted more prints from the site than originally thought," Chief Agee responded, looking up nonchalantly from his review of an unrelated file. His mind was still preoccupied by the unsolved murder of the nurse from Montclair. Continuing to be frustrated over the lack of substantial leads in that case, Chevelle was relieved that the mayor had not hounded him recently about solving the mystery. The newspaper and local television stations had mercifully dropped the story as well. As is true of most crimes and heinous deeds, Chief Agee was slowly coming to the grim realization that often faces a criminal investigator: many of the facts surrounding the Richards murder would never be uncovered.

Chapter

16

◆◆◆

THE RETRIBUTION

Becoming spellbound with the girl standing in front of him at the convenience store, Abe Perry devised a method to check her out better. Stretching around and in front of her to grab a new can of Skoal from the counter display gave him ample opportunity to glance down her undone white blouse, seeing the tops of her elevated breasts. Judging from her uniform, he guessed she was a doctor or nurse. Then, hanging from the left side of her waist, he spotted a hospital identification badge displaying her picture and name *T. Richards*. Abe appreciated that her blonde hair had grown longer since the photograph.

As she left the convenience store with her twenty ounce plastic bottle of Diet Coke, Abe Perry followed the blonde with his truck until he lost his nerve at a red light. Deciding to pursue her later, he turned right when the light turned green and circled back to the convenience store. Surprisingly, the pay phone still had a Montclair phone book attached to it, and simple detective work was all that was required to find T. Richards' address.

Because Abe had worked for a housepainter one summer, he had assisted in beautifying several houses in the Booker Street neighborhood. Through that job he familiarized himself with the names and location of the neighborhood's tree lined boulevards and winding streets. His acclimation with the area went beyond the residential section. Within the several wooded acres serving as a natural barrier between the homes and the adjacent interstate, Abe's lunch break one day turned into a treasure hunt. The treasure was an enormous white tail buck spotted by his keen hunter's eye as the animal glided through the brush and pines. Needless to say, during the rest of the afternoon his concentration on paint rollers and brushes was minimal as he planned to return to bag the deer.

Later that afternoon after work, he proceeded to kill the animal, using the bow and arrow kept handy in the large toolbox mounted on his truck. The silence of the weapon made the out-of-season trophy snatching go unnoticed by the residents as well as the game warden. Abe hauled it out of the thicket with his four-wheeler also kept handy in the bed of his pick-up. During the retrieval of the 120-pound deer from the woods, he rode along the winding four-wheeler trail and noticed the houses whose backyards joined the area. Of the houses Abe Perry spotted, he recognized one later as belonging to T. Richards.

The morning after locating her address in the phone book, he readily pinpointed her house on Booker Street and pulled his truck up into the driveway. Checking his teeth and hair in the rearview and side mirrors of his vehicle, Abe decided that he was good-looking enough. Planning to walk up to her front door and introduce himself, he first noticed the newspaper lying on the driveway as he got out of the truck. Picking it up to take it to the front door with him, he once again lost his nerve in his pursuit of T. Richards. This time he was standing only a few steps from her front porch. Abe quickly turned around and took long steps back to his waiting get-away truck. As he opened the driver's door, Abe nonchalantly tossed the smeared newspaper back down to the drive, coincidentally in close proximity to his left rear tire.

"She's probably not home anyway," Abe reasoned, looking into the outside rearview mirror as he backed out of the driveway into the street. Turning his head forward as he pulled into the street, he once again spotted through his bug-covered windshield the patch of woods behind the houses on T.'s side of the street. Abe then remembered his four-wheeler trail from the summer before.

That evening he returned to the convenience store and parked to the side of the compact building near the racks of for-rent propane gas tanks. Gambling that he had crossed paths with T. Richards the night before during a routine on-the-way-home stop, Abe won his self-bet. The girl he desired yesterday, and still did, had returned to the Minute Stop but this time apparently to purchase gasoline. As he watched T. select a pump and pay with a credit card, the hunter studied her facial and body features more intently than before. Quickly he realized why he found her attractive and appealing. T. Richards resembled that girl in high school, the blonde who ruined his senior year.

"Sure, I was good enough to make out with her behind the fire station on Peace Street, but not good enough to be seen with her at the prom," he thought angrily to himself as he persisted in tracing Taylor's pleasing movements as though he were watching her through a rifle scope. "After all, she was the one who came on to me first, in study hall."

Abe remembered how the high school blonde had teased him unmercifully with sexual connotations during their secret after school meetings. It was not long before she let him touch her breasts and caress between her legs. At first she told him that she wanted to be his date to the dance. In fact, she practically begged him to take her, promising to have sex with him afterwards. Then Thursday before the prom on Saturday, she slipped him a text message during English class spelling out cruelly that her "daddy would kill her" if she went out with a "black boy."

Now as he glanced away from his human game toward his countenance in the rearview mirror, Abe still did not think of himself as a "black boy." Including Abe, practically all of the men in his generation of the family were light-skinned with predominantly Caucasian facial features. However, his cousin Jimmy looked the most white of any of the Perrys. Jimmy's hair did not appear kinky at all but was thick, dark, and only moderately curly.

The more he stared at T. Richards through his windshield, the more he remembered that white blonde from the twelfth grade and how much more he had grown to hate her since graduation. A few days after the prom was over, Abe learned that all along she had planned to go with one of the white high school football stars.

At this moment while watching T. Richards get back into her car and shut the door, he imagined that she had breasts and hips just like that whore in high school. He could also envision her laughing at him just like the other girl. Abe was certain that when T. Richards had been a high school student that she had looked and acted just like that other white bitch, the one he once knew and adored. He clinched his fist and pounded the steering wheel when he decided that T. would have treated him in the same humiliating way.

As Taylor Richards pulled away from the convenience store, Abe followed at a distance, making sure that she was traveling completely unaccompanied. Because of the traffic quagmire on the interstate resulting from the dramatic wreck of a sports car, Abe somehow got ahead of Taylor in the traffic flow and was the first on the scene. When she walked up to the spot where the car had flipped over the side of the overpass, he tried to talk to her, and she slighted him just as the girl in high school had.

Once the traffic cleared Abe continued to the house that he had scouted out previously. When he reached T.'s street, he checked the front seat central console of his truck to verify that he had his four-wheeler key. As Abe slowly approached her house, he parked his dirty pick-up an undetectable distance down the street from her house, hiding it curbside behind an electric utility vehicle.

Gazing through the bug-spattered windshield and the mud-smeared side windows of his truck, Abe was struck by the tranquility of the neighborhood. There was no movement associated with the houses around him. Practically all of the curtains and blinds were closed, and only a few homes were illuminated on the outside. Suddenly, a chill ascended his spine as a chord of apprehension attempted to thwart his plans to be close to this girl.

"What if she already lives with some guy?" Abe asked himself as he hit the steering column with a raging fist.

Certain that he was leaving his truck blocked from view by the utility vehicle, Abe slipped down and across the street, darting behind other parked cars and trees to approach her house. As he hid behind some overgrown shrubbery across the street, he observed her intently and with growing excitement as she drove into her garage. Abe's modest apprehension in hooking up with T. was erased when he saw that her garage was empty of another car.

Despite the darkness, he could still see her retrieve the newspaper that remained lying in the driveway where he had tossed it earlier in the day. Feeling a slight chill since it was getting colder and the wind was starting to stir, Abe thought about the jacket back in his truck. Wanting to appear as presentable to T. as possible as he went over to her house, he decided that the jacket would also hide the mechanic's grease stains soiling his blue denim shirt.

After he slipped back stealthily from retrieving his jacket, he reached first for the doorbell but changed his mind and instead knocked with his fist. T. kept him waiting too long at the front door he decided, as though she knew she was worth the wait. When she finally but barely opened the door, he could see only a glimpse of her shadow on the inside floor.

"What is it?" a cold, uninviting voice demanded in a tone that rekindled the boiling feel of high school rejection. "Yes, who is it? What do you want?" the voice pressed from behind the door, the voice hiding its face from Abe but seeing his through the peephole. Since Abe was forced to reconstruct the face to match the voice, the face he now envisioned was not that of the girl at the convenience store but that of the blonde from his senior year.

"Look, Joker, I don't know what you want or what you're selling, but I just got home from work, and I'm exhausted. So, bye!" Taylor shut the door rudely but with justification, almost stubbing Abe's right front toe in the process. "*My Daddy would just kill me if I went out with a black boy!*" Abe was sure he had heard her say as she slammed the door on him.

Abe jogged back to his truck humiliated. Once again, he wasn't going to get to go to his high school senior prom with the blonde chick, the same chick that had let him feel her up several times behind the fire station. He hated her when she dumped him then, and now he despised her even more. Slitting her tires after school the next day had only temporarily compensated him for the disappointment. A few years later, the stupid bitch had disappointed him again.

The blonde was a beautiful girl, though...well rounded in all the right places, blue eyes. No one in his family had blue eyes to go with their various shades of colored skin. If she had only given him a fair chance, then she would have even grown to love him. Abe was sure of it.

The stuck-up whore had missed still another opportunity to love him. Now she was inside her house, laughing her head off at him.

Abe recalled the dirt path through the patch of woods behind her house. He pulled his truck from behind the utility vehicle and drove almost silently back up the street, turning at the next corner. The street running perpendicular to Taylor's stopped at a dead end, meeting the forested barrier between the neighborhood and Interstate 79. Deciding that firing up the four-wheeler would be too noisy, he left it in the back of the truck. Next, he maneuvered the truck itself off the asphalt pavement and onto the narrow dirt road leading into the woods. Abe drove far enough into the thicket of cedars, oaks, short pines, and overgrown weeds to completely hide his small truck from anyone's view.

Looking back toward the neighborhood from the same undeveloped patch of land where he had nailed the summer deer, Abe Perry determined from this rear view which house was T's. Approaching her home this time from the rear, there was barely enough moon light and scattered artificial light to keep him from tripping on the live vegetation and fallen tree limbs. In addition, maneuvering around and over the partially rotten fallen trees was somewhat of a hindrance in reaching her backyard.

Abe considered this sort of trek a natural adventure for him, letting him practice his real talent of tracking, searching, and hunting. Luckily for Abe the logs, thicket, and dim light were now the only physical obstacles keeping her from him. Nevertheless, as he walked up the steps to the rear deck of the house, he was glad to hear no barking dog. Her locked back door was only a minor hindrance to their being together for Abe found the lock simple to pick with his pocketknife. As the door practically sprang loose when the mechanism released, he pushed it open with his foot, being careful not to touch anything with his hands. All of a sudden Abe shuddered when he realized that he had not considered a burglar alarm.

With great relief he still heard no alarm, dog barking, or human voices as he noiselessly moved unhindered through the width of the kitchen approaching a back hall. Her house stood silent except for the sound of the running water that he followed. The swishing of Taylor's filling bathtub and the shine of the bathroom light coming from under a door was irresistible. As he gradually, but without apprehension, opened the door opposite the tub, he found the blonde immersed waist high in her bathtub with her back to him.

Silently standing there, Abe jealously watched her massage sensitive areas of her body with a bath cloth. Abe's observation of T. was intense; her every move, particularly those using her fingers, excited him. He wanted to lurch forward and touch her wet hair and body.

Startling Abe, Taylor abruptly tossed her head back to sling some of her soapy wet blonde hair from her eyes. Because her eyes were partially closed and the room steamy, the gawking countenance standing in the opened bathroom door went undetected. However, this quick jerk of T's head reminded him of another time when she had thrown her head back in silent laughter: when she sent the message that she was breaking their prom date. All the disappointment, all the rejection, all the anger of that afternoon in English class resurfaced. He decided not to let her get away with degrading him again, not for something that he could not change.

She then began applying a solution to her hair in slow, methodical motions. He stared mesmerized while the steamy water poring in front of her gradually rinsed away more suds. As T. ducked her head under the faucet for the final time, Abe lunged forward. Grabbing the blonde's wet hair with his left hand, he then wrenched the head backward as he pulled his hunting knife from its belt sleeve. Then with his right hand he used the instrument on her in much the same way that he would on a dying deer.

Chapter

17

◆◆◆

THE RESULTS

"Oh, no, not yet!" a groggy Aslyn Hawes groaned as she rolled over to douse the alarm at the side of her bed. However, she ignored the time on her lighted digital clock until she woke up again approximately an hour later. "6:45?! Oh, damn! This is just great, just great! I'll be late to surgery!" Aslyn yelled out in her solitary bedroom as she tossed off the bedcovers and jumped to the floor.

Instantaneously, vertigo overcame her plans to rush to her shower. Explaining away the dizziness, she lamented, "I must have had more to drink last night with Jimmy than I thought." Slowing her pace, she progressed into her bathroom and turned on the miniature coffee maker kept on the marble counter by the sink. The normally pleasant aroma shifted her direction from the shower area to the toilet instead.

With great determination to make it to work reasonably on time, Dr. Aslyn Hawes fought back her hangover to make it through a brief, hot shower. Choosing to forego any makeup, at least for now, she threw on a scrub suit and pulled her hair back into a short bob.

Aslyn stumbled during the dash to the garage as she used her cell phone to notify the operating room of her late, extremely late, arrival. She knew the head nurse in OR would never dream of bumping her down the surgery list just because she was unexpectedly tardy. No, she wouldn't dare do that to her. Nevertheless, Dr. Hawes issued a curt apology to the nurse answering the phone at the OR control desk and also asked that her sentiments be passed along to her waiting patient.

After gaining access to the operating suite with her magnetic ID card, she hurried into the area, cursing the hassle caused by all the new security precautions. Rarely had Dr. Aslyn Hawes ever dreaded a planned surgical case like the challenge facing her today, and being behind schedule with a hangover had made the situation all the worse. The major surgery for this particular three hundred pound patient had been out of necessity rescheduled from last week, since the poor woman's asthma needed stabilization before general anesthesia. Not only were there respiratory problems, but also distortion of the pelvic anatomy was highly expected from prior bouts of pelvic inflammatory disease and a tubal pregnancy. There was no way around the necessity for this hysterectomy because of enormous, symptomatic uterine fibroids likely encased in concrete-dense abdominal adhesions.

"Where is Dr. Edmund?" Aslyn asked the scrub nurse as she entered OR room six.

"She called to say that she is stuck in with an unstable OB patient and won't be able to assist yet with your case. Rosie is going to scrub in to help you until Dr. Edmund can get free."

Aslyn cursed under her breath — another blow to an already miserable morning. Quickly reviewing all the major surgery cases she had performed during the last few months, Dr. Hawes felt strongly that this most complex one absolutely required the services of two physician surgeons. To aggravate matters, her substitute assistant Rosie, although very polite, was too timid in the operating room, as is sometimes typical of the less-experienced surgical nurses.

"Isn't there another one of my partners who can assist me with this case?" Aslyn asked almost rhetorically because she knew the answer was no. Cullen Gwinn was dead; the physician board had fired Knox Chamblee; one doctor was out on maternity leave; and Marshall Langley always took this day of the week off.

"Maybe we should have waited for Gretchen Tinsley to get here first before we fired him," Aslyn sighed in desperation as she stood over the patient with scalpel in hand. No one in the room, particularly the overwhelmed Rosie standing immediately across the surgical field from her, had any idea who or what Dr. Hawes was talking about.

As she meticulously entered the abdomen with precise surgical skill, Aslyn's predication that this patient would have a distorted anatomy was promptly confirmed. Numerous blood vessels, anxious to hemorrhage from the least little disturbance, were pumping in rhythm waiting for Aslyn to sever them inadvertently and obscure the surgical field. As a tidal wave of nausea overcame her without warning, Dr. Hawes blurted out to another nurse standing over in the corner of the operating room, "Would someone please turn down the thermostat in here and turn up the air circulation? Please do it now!"

With slow and deliberate breaths though her surgical mask, Aslyn desperately fought back the urge to vomit. Fortunately for her and everyone else in the room, she was initially victorious in keeping down the bagel and coffee she had gulped down while driving in to work on this turbulent morning. Unfortunately, as the challenging surgical case continued, her overpowering dizziness progressed to becoming intolerable. Luckily the patient's condition was now stable with all the pelvic bleeders either fulgurated or ligated and the innocent abdominal organs safe. By now Aslyn's nausea was so severe that she could hold back no longer. Her audience in this operating arena experienced a shocking first.

"I'm not feeling well, not well at all. I need to break scrub and lie down. I'm sorry," Hawes hurriedly announced as she covered the operative site with a sterile blue towel. Aslyn then immediately pulled away from the operating table and rushed out into the semi-sterile hall connecting the individual operating rooms. Upon reaching the nearest surgical scrub sink, she utilized it for an unintended purpose and then felt much better with a near empty stomach.

Chasing after Hawes from Operating Room 3, JoDonna Sherwood, the assistant circulating nurse assigned to that room, caught her with her head in the basin. Hesitating slightly out of awkwardness, she asked, "Dr. Hawes, are you all right?"

"Auuuggghhhhh, I'm not sure. I'm beginning to have terrific abdominal pain, more than just a stomachache. There's been a horrific strain of viral gastroenteritis going around here. Lately I've seen ... (Another uncontrollable eruption interrupted her explanation.) ... a lot of patients with the same problem. I guess I... (another interruption) ... caught it from one of my patients."

"Oh, Dr. Hawes, let's get you to the emergency room," JoDonna took control with an air of authority and frankly enjoyed it. The nurse led the pitifully sick doctor with the yellowish-green complexion by the arm to the welcome support of a waiting wheelchair and then rolled her swiftly to the elevator. The poor ventilation on the ride down four floors to the ER made the trip overwhelmingly unpleasant for both women. Britton Stewart remained on duty in the Emergency Department and promptly admitted Aslyn to an observation unit, attached her to an IV, and loaded her up with intravenous medication to manage her continued projectile vomiting.

The arrival of Dr. Aslyn Hawes was only the beginning of what would develop into an unusually swamped day for Dr. Stewart and her staff. As the day's activity mushroomed, one of the triage nurses remarked several times that this was developing into ER "celebrity day." The lively gossip in the nurses' break room revolved around those endless numbers of medical field-associated and pompous types who were being checked into the Emergency Department. Other than Dr. Hawes, one of the largest scenes of the drama involved the wife of the late Dr. Gwinn, transported in by ambulance after suffering an apparent seizure. Perhaps more exciting than that scenario was the hospital administrator's flamboyant admission for some sort of ongoing paranoid anxiety reaction. Of course, there was also the woman in her thirties brought in a neck brace after running her Lexus 360 into a building while talking on a cell phone. She kept ranting on and on about needing priority attention because she was missing some charity function where she was to serve as main hostess.

"Dr. Hawes, how are you feeling?" Dr. Stewart asked her a few hours after starting the treatment for severe nausea and vomiting with secondary dehydration. "If the Phenergan stops working, I'll order some Zofran." Having never been formally introduced to Dr. Aslyn Hawes, Britton had always felt uncomfortable professionally and socially around this female doctor with the abrupt reputation. Seeing her remain weak, somewhat green, and confined to a gurney cast a new light on the presumed personality of Aslyn Hawes. "We've given you a couple of liters of D5LR, and you're starting to get your color back."

Peering up through the Phenergan haze at the blurry-appearing female in a white lab coat, Aslyn assumed that this person talking to her was the ER doctor. She remembered her name to be *Britton Something- or- Other.* "This must be a terrific stomach virus," Aslyn slurred in response past thick medicated lips. Her own speech sounded distant to her. "I'm sure I shocked all of the operating room staff with my unexpected illness today. Do you have any idea if my surgery case turned out OK? It's *Stewart,* isn't it?" she asked.

"Oh, yes, that's right, Dr. Hawes. I'm Britton Stewart," she answered while offering a feminine right hand. Aslyn could not match the gesture because of the short IV tubing that pulled angrily against her right forearm vein. "I'm told that the OR scoured the hospital until they found someone to complete the case. Since Faye Edmund still could not leave L & D to replace you, Knox Chamblee came to the rescue. They paged him, and I believe he came to the hospital immediately. You might say that Knox served as the day's Good Samaritan."

"I see," Aslyn acknowledged as she looked away toward the privacy curtain hanging behind Britton. The hollow feeling now rising from the pit of her stomach was similar to what she had experienced earlier but now for a different reason. "I'll have to thank Knox later, when I run across him," she said with forced sincerity.

"Are you having any abdominal cramping at all now, or have you had any diarrhea in the last day or two, Dr. Hawes?"

"Oh, for God's sake, I'm not that much older than you, Britton. I'm only forty-four. Please call me Aslyn."

As Britton smiled politely at this friendly professional gesture, the laboratory technician handed her the printed lab results assigned to patient Aslyn B. Hawes. The value of Hawes' serum beta HCG titer was 8940. Smiling fairly more dramatically this time at Aslyn, Britton handed this clearly positive pregnancy test result to her unsuspecting patient.

After staring for a few seconds at the bold letters and numbers on the computer printout, Aslyn grabbed the nearby emesis basin off the bedside table and relieved herself again.

Oblivious to the whirlwind of events at the hospital next door, Marshall Langley, MD, was using this week's day off to catch up on his office mail. He found the letter from Peyton-Rose Pharmaceuticals about halfway down the stack. While the correspondence was addressed to both him and Dr. Cullen Gwinn, it was dated following the date of Cullen's accident. The gist of the correspondence was to announce that the president of Peyton Rose Pharmaceuticals had decided to close the Vasapene weight loss study.

The body of the letter was brief:

Dear Health Care Provider:

Peyton-Rose Pharmaceuticals has ceased its investigation of the weight loss indication for our product Vasapene (vasoporpholene). We wish to thank all of our physician researchers who provided valuable data regarding this

arm of the pharmaceutical study. Peyton-Rose
Pharmaceuticals plans to continue to market our product
Vasapene (vasoporpholene) for its valued indication in the
treatment of depression, as registered with the Federal Drug
Administration.

As he finished silently reading the announcement, Marshall
heard soft rapid steps coming down the carpeted hall toward
his office. Glancing away from the correspondence on his desk,
he spotted Nell Lowery walking by his door. Even though she
was busy delivering employee mid-month payroll, he asked her
to step into his office for a minute to discuss the study
termination notice. He knew that Nell would be familiar with
the research effort since she had been the initial contact
between Peyton-Rose Pharmaceuticals and their practice.
When the pharmaceutical company had e-mailed her two years
ago about its research plans, she had directed them to Drs.
Langley and Gwinn because they had been involved in similar
previous projects.

After Langley shared the letter with Nell, he wadded it up
and then landed it successfully in the trashcan by his desk.
"Cullen and I never compiled our data for those patients," he
told her. "Of course, it's too late now to send in our findings.
Darn, we blew collecting that participation honorarium!"

Marshall Langley reminded her that a couple of weeks ago
Cullen had planned to begin compiling all the patient weight
changes linked to their Vasapene dosages. During the patient
sessions when data was gathered, each doctor recorded the
body weight measurements and the corresponding medication
dosages on a simple supplementary sheet attached to inside
front of each patient's chart. Langley added, "It would not have
taken long to get all of the data together. Since Cullen never
mentioned starting on our research summation, I doubt if he
ever did."

As a proficient office manager Nell Lowery stressed, "The
patients who volunteered to be a part of that study group will
nevertheless need to be sent a thank you for participating. I'll
get the appointment secretaries to do that."

"Certainly, that would be a nice gesture, Nell."

"In the letter of appreciation we'll put in some flowery language but still stress our profound thanks for their 'invaluable contribution to the betterment of healthcare through research.' Something similar to what we did with the Zerapodare Study a few years ago."

"Regardless, I never thought that Vasapene was any good for losing weight. All that speculation: estrogen transformed into a fat metabolizing hormone after a few weeks of daily vasoporpholene, melting away cellulite while fighting depression in the brain. It seems we'll never know the truth."

"I'll just tell the study volunteers that there are no results to report because the research was terminated prematurely," Nell summarized.

Nell had assisted in organizing the Center's participation in the study. The preservation of the designated patient records in standard paper form was planned to be only temporary. This delay would allow the research team of Gwinn and Langley ample time to extract and compile the data for their Vasapene report before the forms were permanently scanned into the Center's new electronic medical record system. To prevent confusion, Nell had recommended that the charts containing the study's data be stored at a secure location away from the Center. Once the statistics regarding Vasapene and any other pertinent patient information had been compiled in a confidential manner, the report for Peyton-Rose would be drafted and the original paper charts shredded and destroyed.

"Dr. Langley, there has been one small glitch in the organization of our arm of the study, other than our not completing it. I guess it was doomed from the start."

Marshall turned and looked directly at the office manager as she continued, not actually positive that he wanted to hear the rest. "I had suggested to Dr. Gwinn that the practice rent a minor, separate office for a couple of months. The patient study records could be securely stored there and processed while the data was compiled. The pharmaceutical company was paying such a high honorarium for the results that I reasoned the extra rent would be negligible overhead. Dr. Gwinn cleared all of those decisions and plans. Since he was always tight with increasing expenses, I assumed that if he OK'ed the expenditure, you would agree as well.

"However, there was a little kink in my good intentions. The transport service mistakenly delivered all of the confidential paper charts from the Center to Dr. Gwinn's home instead of to the rented extra office."

"You're kidding, Nell! How could that happen?"

"I don't have any idea. When you're dealing with people who are paid minimum wage, I guess you never know what can happen. In the defense of the moving and transport company, though, other packages and mail meant for the Center have been mistakenly delivered on other occasions to Dr. Gwinn's private home. Perhaps it's because he founded the practice years ago. I don't know of any other explanation, except stupidity."

"Hell, where are the medical records now, Nell?" Dr. Langley was beginning to see this delivery error as a possible legal as well as ethical fiasco.

Detecting an unusual demonstration of concern on the part of her most nonchalant doctor, Nell calmly let the tale evolve. "Anyway," she continued, while laying her load of oversized envelopes on Marshall's desk and dropping into his plush office couch, "when the mistake was discovered by Dr. Gwinn as he arrived home late that Friday, you know, the day before his accident, the delivery service was already closed. When he called me immediately on my cell phone, poor Dr. Gwinn seemed horrified over the mix-up. To make matters worse, the housekeeper in his wife's absence had allowed the deliverymen to stack the boxes of patient medical records all over the living room and foyer. Dr. Gwinn was such a stickler for rules and patient confidentiality protocol, as you know. I wouldn't have been surprised if he stayed up all night worrying about that screw-up."

"What were Cullen's comments when he called you? I'm sure they were colorful."

"Actually, he tried to remain calm with me about the whole situation. So that Mrs. Gwinn wouldn't freak out over the whole mess when she got back in town, he did insist that we get all of the boxes moved and protected before his wife got home to find them strewn all around their entry. By offering them twenty-five dollars apiece, I was able to prod my two football player nephews, the ones who play at Peace County Junior College, and one of their PCJC friends to move the containers down to the Gwinn's basement storage room using the dumbwaiter by the kitchen.

"Telling me that he and Mrs. Gwinn seldom utilized their basement storage area, he chose to have the boxed documents placed there where they would be safe, dry, and undisturbed until transported to the correct site on Monday. Since all of this happened the day before Dr. Gwinn's accident, correcting the goof-up just slipped my mind. With the topsy-turvy state our medical practice is in, I just haven't had time to..."

Her last comment sparked Langley's interest even more. As he noticed the spreading stress wrinkles around her eyes, he interrupted, "Nell, what do you mean, 'topsy-turvy'?"

"The representative from our physician search service sent me an e-mail yesterday afternoon, informing us that our only new prospect, Dr. Tinsley, was not available to replace Drs. Chamblee and Gwinn. Therefore, regarding our physician coverage, we're going to stay short staffed for an indefinite period."

"Why isn't she coming? Does she want more money? More benefits, maybe?"

"No, I seriously doubt she will be concerned about those issues anymore. It turns out that while working in Nevada she met a neurosurgeon who's also a lawyer. Apparently he's nice looking, although a little older, has a well-established practice, no ex-wife, no children. Even has some family money to fall back on. I guess he popped the question to her when she threatened to move to Mississippi. She's taking the easy way out: marriage and retirement at the ripe age of 35. I can't say that I blame her."

Dr. Marshall Langley smarted with resentment over the news of the younger doctor's good fortune. Too bad there was no female neurosurgeon out there who desired someone like him. "Hell, I'd even settle for a prosperous veterinarian," he almost said aloud.

"By the way, the rep left a little addendum to her disappointing update. Because of the declining numbers of medical student graduates entering our field, she has no other interested and qualified prospects to recommend at this time."

The personal consequences of Dr. Gretchen Tinsley's decision to marry the neurosurgeon suddenly hit Marshall Langley hard. Since the practice had already fired Knox Chamblee and had no replacement for him or the deceased partner, Marshall would be working harder and longer hours. "I shouldn't have let Aslyn talk me into forcing Chamblee from his contract, Nell!" Thinking about any possible solution to getting out of this messy hole, Marshall continued to fire off. "How did Knox take the news that he was dumped? After all, that's what we did to him. We dumped him. Was he furious?"

"No, I would say that he was more hurt than angry."

"I wonder where he may be planning to go next. He might have already made a commitment to practice somewhere else, maybe with that group across town." Langley was squirming. "Have you heard from him since you fired him?"

Nell had always felt immensely comfortable around the easy-going Marshall Langley, having a great rapport with him because he was her age. "First of all, Dr. Langley, I'm not the one who fired him. You and the other doctors fired him. Please don't give me the credit for this fiasco."

"Hold on a minute, Nell. No one's blaming you." Nell Lowery remained the one firm rock of the practice, and all the doctors knew it, even Marshall Langley. No one could imagine the Montclair Center for Women's Medical and Surgical Services surviving without Nell Lowery.

"OK, now that we have that straight, I'll tell you the follow-up to the Chamblee story. I was in my office earlier when Dr. Chamblee came by to pick up his check, rather than have me mail it to him as we previously planned. He sarcastically told me that he wanted the Center to save a stamp since we had already lost so much money on him. We both sort of laughed at that. However, he didn't mention anything to me about his present or future plans. I know that he does own a condo in Montclair because I supplied his mortgage company with some of his financial information. I suppose that if he plans to leave the Montclair area, then he's already got it up for sale."

Marshall remained reclined in his desk chair, listening to Nell and fretting over having to hang around the Center and hospital more, cutting back on golf. As it was, he was already down to seventy-two holes a week.

"You know, Dr. Langley, Knox really wasn't doing that bad of a job around here. I'm not aware of problems he was having with any patients at the Center or over at Grace. He consistently came to work on time and all the employees liked him." Nell swallowed hard before she issued the next observation. "If we're terribly short of physician manpower around here, Dr. Langley, we might want to feel him out about coming back, before things get even more desperate."

Nell Lowery naturally assumed that proposing that bold solution to Dr. Hawes instead of Dr. Langley would have enraged the former. Nonetheless, through her years of multiple encounters with doctors and their multifaceted egos and personalities, she had learned to play upon the individual concerns and ideas of each one. Lowery completely understood that Marshall Langley's work ethic remained impeccable regarding patient welfare but was sorely lacking regarding productivity. She hated to admit to herself that he was just ... plain ... lazy.

Chapter
18
♦♦♦
THE TRIP

Just as Knox was completing the skin closure for Dr. Hawes' surgical patient, Faye Edmund, MD, darted into OR 3.

"I'm sorry. I wasn't able to break free to help you until now. My patient with triplets was in advanced premature labor and teetering on congestive heart failure. On top of that, I had to do a STAT section on another one who was breech."

Chamblee failed to take his attention from squeezing the skin staple gun.

"Geeze, if it makes you feel any better, Knox, a medicine nurse had to assist me with the Cesarean because there wasn't a spare physician around to help me either." Faye Edmond, seven or eight years Knox's senior, was originally from Wisconsin and had absorbed only a minute percentage of female Southernism since moving to Montclair with her physician husband. As a result, her authoritative, Yankee twang resonated across the operative room to be missed
by no one.

Believing that the surgical staff in OR 3 remained unaware of Dr. Chamblee's ex-employment status, Edmund continued with some degree of awkwardness, "Knox, thank you for saving the day. I know Dr. Hawes will be grateful for your relieving her." Faye admired him for understanding that the nurses were only trying to handle a difficult emergency when they paged him to take over the surgery.

"Sure, thrilled to fill in," he said with a semi-sarcastic tone that he planned only for Faye Edmund to appreciate. More truthfully he added, "Of course, I was shocked to get the call." As Knox hesitated slightly, Faye hoped he was not going to embarrass them both by now candidly discussing his termination. Instead, much to her relief, he continued as though his actions today had all been part of his contracted job. Forcing levity, he remarked, "I was floored to learn that Dr. Hawes had bolted from the case. Never heard of her being too sick to operate!"

Remaining in the doorway, Edmund added, "Knox, I checked with Britton, and she told me that Dr. Hawes was looking a lot better." Despite being on equal footing as managing partner of the same medical practice, thirty-nine year old Faye Edmund, MD, had never felt comfortable in referring to Aslyn Hawes by her first name, in person or otherwise. "She'll probably spend the night in observation and could be back at work tomorrow. Thanks again."

Nodding, "You're welcome," Knox dropped his head slightly; removed his surgical mask, gown, and gloves; and wordlessly exited the room. After all, he knew that Edmund had been one of the partners who fired him unjustly and had thereby radically altered his life and career. As he brushed by her through the doorway and started down the hall, she noticed again his smooth, yet masculine, youthful face atop his fairly muscular torso. Judging that he fit rather nicely into a scrub suit, Faye decided she would miss seeing him around. She was beginning to wonder if she and the other partnered physicians had acted in haste when they pushed him from his contract.

"Knox, thanks again. We'll see you later!" Edmund called out to him from OR 3 as she picked up the patient's chart to do the paper work. Knox turned partially back around without slowing his pace to return a cordial, but insincere, wave. Although he had found working with her to be tolerable, he had never thought the five-foot one-inch red-head to be the least bit physically attractive, particularly since her scrub suits always fit too tightly in the wrong places. In fact, Chamblee often wondered what her husband saw in her.

"What do you all think of Dr. Chamblee.... as a doctor, I mean?" Dr. Edmund asked inside the operating room to no one in particular as she started reviewing and signing the patient's pre-printed post-operative orders.

"I think he's a great surgeon," Rosie chimed in. "He jumped right into this case without being nervous or appearing under a lot of pressure. I like working with him because he's nice and seems to have his head on straight. Oh, and my friend-girl went to him as a patient the other day and was really impressed."

Faye kept her head down in the chart and made no comment while scribbling with greater haste and force.

The anesthesiologist in the room, Prescott Fellows, was coincidentally on duty the day that Knox was involved with Zoe's postmortem C-Section. "I agree. Knox handles situations really well, if you ask me," Fellows offered. Unfamiliar with the recent change of physician staffing events at the women's center, he contributed unabashedly, "Your group is lucky to have him, Faye."

Dr. Edmund finished the paper work in front of her, closed the surgical patient's chart with a snap, and silently slithered from the operating room.

In marked contrast, there was no silence in the police department across town, only great commotion. Chief Agee had just been on the phone with Mayor Netz about several issues although the mayor seemed preoccupied. Happily, his boss was outdone with someone besides him, mentioning twice during the conversation that there had been a delay in the delivery of his wife's anniversary gift. Actually the mayor would have been ballistic if he had seen the expensive piece crushed in the Gwinn driveway by the wheels of an ambulance gurney and the booted feet of hurried paramedics.

While saying goodbye to Mayor Netz and wishing him good luck with his anniversary, the chief was drawn away from his office desk to see Lamar almost jumping up and down in front of him. "Chief, we have a match with the set of tire prints lifted off that muddy road at the hunting camp. It fits the tire marks on the folded newspaper picked up from that nurse's driveway. You know, the girl that was cut-up in her bath tub over on Booker Street."

"Lamar, your sensitivity chokes me up," Chevelle chided.

"Sorry, Chief, I'm just wired. Let me tell you the real news from the crime lab. It was easy for the tech to think about comparing the two pieces of evidence since they don't get a lot of tire impressions submitted for cataloging. When they went back and re-examined that dirty newspaper for its tire mark, they found a fingerprint they hadn't seen before."

"And they don't think it's a contaminant?"

"No, Chief. Their analysis of the newspaper material aged the fingerprint to the same general time as the tire mark. Most likely, whoever was driving the vehicle that ran over that newspaper also picked it up." Then, in the same breath, Lamar continued with his theory, "And, Chief, since the fingerprint and tire mark found in the newspaper ink match the prints and tire impression lifted from that hunting camp, I think we've got a busy fella on the loose. Whoever pulled into the nurse's driveway around the time of her murder can be connected to the Pecan Grove hunting camp when that hospital guy was shot at!"

As Chief Agee listened intently to Lamar's investigative update, he was hesitant to believe his sudden good luck — the first real breakthrough in solving that poor nurse's murder. Startled by the telephone, he jerked the receiver to his ear. "What? Yes, yes, this is Chief Agee ... And you're certain? I see ... Great! You'll send me written determination as well. OK ... Good work. Oh, and thank you. Thank you very, very much!"

Before the chief could thrust the receiver back on its base, he looked at Lamar with wild excitement. Not in an extremely long time had Lamar seen such a wide smile on Chief Agee's broad face.

"What do you mean my titer is over eight thousand? I can't be pregnant. For God's sake, I've gone through menopause. At least I'm going through it now!" a shocked Aslyn Hawes whispered forcibly back to Britton Stewart, although what she really wanted to do was let out a blood-curdling scream.

As an ER physician, Stewart was thoroughly accustomed to dealing with physician patients and their various ailments. After all, she had realized long ago that just about everyone, no matter who they are or what profession they profess, sooner or later ends up as an emergency room patient. At times when dealing with these peers in a treatment situation, Britton felt that her formal education had been stretched to the point that common sense became her overriding strength.

Of all of her previous emergency room experiences with physicians involved in all kinds of acute medical straits, this particular incidence was becoming one of the most intriguing, if not the most humorous. Here, the lowly Britton Stewart, a mere salaried ER physician, had obviously flabbergasted an intelligent, specialty-trained, and well-recognized physician with the most personal of medical news.

While trying not to bite her bottom lip, Britton inquired, "Dr. Hawes, tell me; when was your last period?"

Aslyn had looked off across the room in bewilderment but rotated her head back in a snap to respond, "I don't know when it was. It's been so spaced out over the last year that I assumed I was through with it." Lowering her voice even more, "Besides, I've had some hot flashes and lots of mood swings." Adding a tone of self-deprecation, "No one who has been around me lately would argue that I haven't had the mood swings."

With this remark, Aslyn let out a subtle laugh at herself. Britton followed with a tension-reducing chuckle. Mesmerized, Hawes gazed away toward the window on the right side of the room and summarized her predicament. "I just never believed that I could get pregnant again. During the final years of my marriage, my late husband and I never used any birth control, and I never conceived."

Stewart returned the uncomfortable discussion to the medical follow through. "Let's see, Dr. Hawes. Your problem must be a case of severe hyperemesis gravidarum and not viral gastroenteritis. As soon as you're feeling up to it, we should send you for an obstetrical ultrasound. I'm sure you'd like to know the gestational age of your fetus since your menstrual dating is so uncertain."

"Oh, Britton, for gosh sakes, please call me Aslyn. After sharing my dilemma with you, I think we can be on a first name basis. But I would like to know this. Who else knows about my pregnancy?"

"Only the lab technician, of course, but I don't think that he is one of the regulars. Undoubtedly, the hospital-imaging department that will do your sonogram will know, but those technicians don't gossip either. If they did, they'd lose their jobs."

Aslyn's emotions drifted for a moment to her nineteen year-old sexual partner, with whom she had partnered repeatedly. Judging from his initial inexperience during their encounters, she had already decided that her risk of contracting a sexually transmitted disease from him was almost non-existent. As Jimmy became more skilled with her and she more enamored of his performances, birth control was never mentioned by either of them. Aslyn had not thought it necessary since she prematurely believed that she had ceased ovulating. Dr. Hawes wanted to sink down into her emergency room bed and put the pillow over her head, now realizing that she had without a doubt been sexually reckless and should have known better.

Sibley Paige was waiting for him so Knox left the hospital complex quickly, but not before stopping by to check on Madelyn Gwinn. Pleased to learn from the talkative Neuro ICU nurse that she was physically progressing well, Knox was also apprised of Mrs. Gwinn's development of amnesia. Per the neurosurgeon's assessment, the memory loss was expected to extend back to shortly before Dr. Gwinn's death.

Still feeling embarrassed over passing out on their first date, Sibley had enthusiastically accepted the second chance when Knox called her the day before. Within the last year she had taken only a few days off from her work in the hospital social work department, thereby leaving plenty of vacation time. Plus, she was dying to go to that marvelous hotel in Larkspur since reading about it in a recent edition of *Southern Porch*.

Knox had seen the same magazine article, which raved over the recently expanded luxury accommodations located in the nearby town. Once a deteriorating, abandoned textile warehouse home to countless vagrants, drug dealers, and pigeons, the hotel now known as the Rexford was first renovated by a once prosperous plastic surgery firm. The feature detailed how the plastic surgeons originally opened the facility as a recuperation site for their patients, convenient to their attached modern medical and surgical center. At that time, no expense was spared in transforming the nearly condemned structure from an eyesore into a much sought after treatment and recovery compound for the pampered. However, the present owners had enlarged the hotel, taking it and its restaurant to another level of decadence while the long-closed adjacent surgical facility was subdivided into small corporate offices. What currently remained was the plush Rexford Hotel situated in the heart of Larkspur, Mississippi, which undeniably rivaled the amenities of the Memphis Peabody. The magazine's color pictorial drew Knox to the resort's extreme comfort and rich seclusion, all at a price even a doctor on severance pay could afford. To be on the safe side, Knox had booked two separate rooms there for Sibley and himself, but he was guaranteed by the reservationist that they would be adjoining.

Soon after leaving Madelyn Gwinn and her Neuro ICU nurse, Knox went by his condo for a change of clothes and some toiletries before picking Sibley up at the house she rented with some other girls. The traffic immediately out of Montclair was sparse; however, after driving about twenty miles up the interstate, all the while in flirtatious conversation, their junket was slowed to an unexpected snail's pace. Having noticed no signs warning of highway construction ahead, the couple assumed that they were approaching a major traffic accident.

Just off the upcoming exit Knox and Sibley spotted no wrecked cars but instead a tattered appearing mobile home, completely surrounded by the police and highway patrol. A few ambulances with flashing lights completed the ominous entourage. Several uniformed figures could be seen scampering between the vehicles, and as Knox lowered the driver's window, gunshots were heard coming from the direction of the commotion.

Following the line of traffic cautiously, the pair soon came upon a stern patrolman, who was motioning drivers to keep moving along the interstate highway. As Knox resumed speed and raised his car window, Sibley simultaneously scanned the radio for details about what they had just witnessed. Finding none, they buried their curiosity, concentrating on the road ahead and their night out.

Their night out turned into the night together that Knox had hoped for. The romance persisted into the next morning as he remained convinced that Sibley had longed for this same experience. As they lay in the king-sized bed in the corner room, which was the larger of the two he had reserved, Sibley asked him if he thought he could get his money back for the unused adjoining one. During the night, she let it slip that she had assumed they would share the same room and bed; nevertheless, she told him that she still appreciated the gentlemanly gesture. Knox wasn't worried about the well-spent, unused room rental.

The hotel's room service included a complimentary Montclair daily with their breakfast in bed for two. Knox picked out the sports section, while Sibley opened Section A. There displayed across almost the entire top half of page one was a color photo of the house trailer scene that they had witnessed the afternoon before.

"Knox!" Sibley's excited moves promptly him to reflexively put the basketball feature down on the bedside table and reach to put his arm around her. "No, that's not what I meant," she responded somewhat stiffly. "Look at this article! It's about what we saw driving by the Pecan Grove Exit yesterday. The police say they got who killed Taylor Richards. You know who she was, that obstetrical nurse. A few days ago I heard that the police suspected her ex-husband of stabbing her in her bathtub. However, they still had not been able to prove anything against him."

Sitting up in bed closely propped up together by thick, comfortable pillows, Knox and Sibley each silently poured over the newspaper article written by a Montclair reporter. Chief Chevelle Agee of the Montclair police department was quoted as saying that the conclusion of the case resulted from his department's diligence and resolve in fighting crime. Being rather boastful, he even seemed to share much of the credit with the Montclair mayor. The final break in the case came when fingerprints on some beer cans and a newspaper were traced to a thumbprint on record of one Abraham Perry, who resided in an isolated mobile home near Pecan Grove.

"The late Mr. Abraham Perry is believed also to have been involved in an attempted murder case at a hunting camp in Peace County. Furthermore, my department has successfully assisted in that investigation," Chief Agee was also quoted.

Both reaching for the remote and switching to the television, Knox and Sibley found more details on the local morning news. The police standoff outside a dismal-looking house trailer, which quickly turned into a shoot out, had left two individuals dead: Abraham Perry and another male later identified as James Perry, believed to be his cousin. Only one weapon was found inside the trailer, a hunting rifle, lying near Abraham Perry's body.

"The police and highway patrolmen tell me that, based on evidence discovered at the scene, Abraham Perry was the lone shooter in the trailer during this deadly exchange of bullets. Even though the sharpshooters with the police and highway patrol departments consistently aimed only at the shooter, both occupants of the trailer were killed during the gun battle. It is thought that the younger Perry was probably fatally wounded by a stray bullet which pierced the walls of the mobile home," Alexandra O'Toole Cummins of Television Channel 24's 24-Hour News Team shared with her captivated audience. Cummins went on to explain that at this point of the investigation the detectives were uncertain as to any criminal involvement regarding James Perry.

From her hospital bed Dr. Aslyn Hawes was also watching the same local news channel, although with even greater interest than the average viewer. Her pregnancy-related nausea and vomiting had diminished to a tolerable degree during the night, except that now she was nauseated for another reason. Understanding that she had known practically nothing about Jimmy Perry's family and had never met nor seen any of them, she recalled his fond references to his cousin as well as to his mother.

Jimmy could not have suspected her pregnancy, just as she had not. The mental anguish Aslyn had experienced last night and earlier this morning over whether or not to share the shocking news with her baby's father had been suffered in vain. The intense television feature about the Pecan Grove shootout had informed her of that. The excited reporter was now displaying copies of drivers' license photos of the two men shot in the filthy, run-down trailer. Aslyn was tearfully looking away from the monitor when his cousin's photo was shown but turned her head back to the television coincidentally as Jimmy's picture covered the screen.

Of the definite opinion that the broadcast likeness did not do her handsome late lover justice, Aslyn once again stared away from the television. She had no difficulty in refining Jimmy's picture in her mind, admiring his pleasing, well-defined features, and firm, well-proportioned build.

Between uses of the emesis basin by her bed, Dr. Hawes was convinced that from a physical standpoint a child fathered by Jimmy Perry would be either handsome or beautiful. At any rate, since monetary support of her and a child would never have been required of Jimmy, Aslyn decided without question that she could handle what she had been given.

As she lay there over the next hour or two anticipating discharge from the hospital, Aslyn Hawes cried softly for her secret lover, Jimmy Perry. Accidentally, he had made real for her something that she had assumed would never again be possible. Here was a chance for her to re-experience motherhood, this time successfully. Feeling a sense of peaceful confidence that this second baby would develop normally and be born healthy, she felt a basic human excitement that she would go through alone.

Chapter

19

♦♦♦

THE TREATMENT

Two days later Dr. Aslyn Hawes was back hitting full stride at the Montclair Center for Women's Medical and Surgical Services. An office overflowing with impatient patients, the theatrics of two overwhelmed assistants, and stacks of paperwork awaited her when she returned to work. After starting some samples of prescription prenatal vitamins and a non-drowsy medication for her nausea, she had begun to feel healthier and was physically tolerating her first trimester of pregnancy.

To no one's surprise, Aslyn experienced exacerbation of her nausea when Nell Lowery broke the news to her about the unavailability of Dr. Gretchen Tinsley. To make the nausea more severe was the distressing news from the headhunter that there were no other prospects to replace Drs. Gwinn or Chamblee. Nell even explained to Dr. Hawes that she had conducted her own local, but fruitless, search for new physician prospects.

Likewise disturbing for Aslyn were the brief but separate confrontations with both Drs. Langley and Edmund about the

Center's physician manpower shortage. Both of them insisted that the Center rehire Knox Chamblee.

"I don't care if we have to beg him or double his old salary," Langley had shouted to the pregnant Dr. Hawes, "but we have to hire him back; that is, if he'll come back!"

Beginning more diplomatically, Faye Edmund reasoned with Aslyn that neither of them could physically or mentally carry a heavier patient load. "We need the manpower, Girl, and Knox Chamblee is available to take up the slack. Besides, I realize now that the Board rushed into voting Knox out of his contract. It was during the last meeting before Cullen died, and I remember that he wasn't even there for that really important vote. Cullen was on call that night and had to run back over to the hospital after the two of you had stopped arguing. I bet he never even knew that we decided to fire Chamblee."

Edmund then pointed a firm index finger between the still unwavering eyes of Aslyn Hawes. "Listen, I have checked around. Every hospital employee and every patient I talked with likes Knox and thinks he's capable. What's more," she added with more volume, "he's all we got, and we'll be lucky to get him to take **us** back!"

Cognizant memory rehabilitation, the term developed by a specialized Manhattan neurologist had lead to the bright green color scheme, mixed with yellows and pale orange. Recently the neurosurgery step-down unit had been redecorated upon the specialist's vivid recommendation. Earning a lucrative place on the medical lecture circuit with his progressive theories on brain damage and peripheral nerve injuries was not enough. The New York physician had assumed another prosperous position as hospital construction consultant. The space with its stimulating décor had been home to Madelyn Gwinn during the days following her discharge from intensive care. Once the intracranial pressure-reducing devices had been removed and her head quit aching so much, she tried in vain to remember her last few weeks. She had simply waked up in the hospital, neither recalling the fit of seizures in her garage nor any of the other events leading to that day.

During her stormy hospital recuperation, she would awake at early hours with the vision of a young man's face: someone she thought she knew, the face obscuring that of her husband, whom the doctors had told her was dead. Even though the strong masculine features in her apparition were balanced with kind, soft eyes, she could not penetrate through them to her husband, her Cullen. On other occasions after deeper sleep, she would regain consciousness with her hands and forearms extended, fretfully reaching for the handsome face, at first almost clawing it away, trying to dig for that of her husband. During one episode she was successful, finding Cullen behind the eyes, only to see him sink in a pool of water, dropping motionless as though he were willing.

Madelyn listened everyday to the therapists, the pale man and woman who worked with her muscles and her speech. They told her she was getting better, and she forced belief. The tall doctor who was her neurosurgeon admitted his surprise over her lasting physical and mental limitations, as well as in her tremors and muscle wasting. Remaining puzzled over her incomplete recovery to date, he explained that most patients who survive her particular kind of cerebral aneurysm do not have these residual ailments. Although she would not confide it to her doctor, the nurses, or the therapists, Madelyn knew what would make her better. She had envisioned them in other dreams as she tossed in more superficial sleep: light pink capsules, shining in a pile on a counter or stacked high in an enormous bottle before a mirror. She would leap for them, quickly scooping up the capsules and looking with immense pleasure at her thin reflection — a youthful face on a slim figure, a body free of pain.

Several weeks later Dr. Aslyn Hawes again lay on an exam table, this time a patient in wonder as she closely observed the diminutive figure moving wildly on the video monitor. It seemed to her as though the baby's extremities were flapping around almost as rapidly as its heartbeat. While she, of course, had performed and observed countless obstetrical ultrasounds, witnessing the growth and development of her own unborn child was awe-inspiring. Her obstetrician was personally performing the sonogram for her, using the new four-dimension unit that the practice had recently purchased.

Aslyn had told everyone, including her obstetrician, that she had conceived utilizing the services of an infertility clinic in New Orleans. She embellished the tale with a successful first-attempt artificial insemination procedure using a donor whose characteristics she selected from the sperm bank. Since she was a widow and at the extreme end of her biological clock, she hoped that both the medical and patient community would hold no moral grudge against her for being single and pregnant. So far, she had detected none.

"Aslyn, it's reassuring that we can see that all the fetal development up to this point appears normal. Are you still comfortable with your decision not to undergo any invasive fetal genetic testing, even despite your advanced maternal age?" her obstetrician asked.

They both chuckled a little at the age question, an obstetrical and medical consideration that could not be ignored. "Dr. Chamblee, I have ruled out genetic testing. I don't want to put my baby at any unnecessary risk," she answered without hesitation.

Over the last several weeks, Knox had become more comfortable referring to the infamous Aslyn Hawes, MD, by her first name. While her pregnancy had apparently not slowed her working pace, she had become somewhat more likable in the eyes of other professionals, including him.

Shortly after her brief, but to the point, discussion in the hall with Faye Edmund, Aslyn had personally called Chamblee, offering to reinstate his previous employment at the women's center. Proving that even naïve physicians can learn from their mistakes, Knox subsequently invested another hour in the services of Cable Tate, Esquire. That additional $125 of legal expense (Cable J. Tate, Esq., P. A., had undergone a price increase since the last time Knox had met with Tate.) led Dr. Chamblee to be reinstated at the women's center, not as a physician employee, but instead as a full managing partner with a substantial salary and benefits increase. Knox even got a new expensive car out of the deal in addition to Dr. Gwinn's old, spacious office with the nice view.

During his contract renegotiations, Aslyn began to develop a true appreciation for Dr. Knox Chamblee as she understood and respected his attributes. She realized that his seemingly forthright but gentle mannerisms would naturally transfer into an excellent patient bedside manner. She understood that more and more patients would grow to like him and use his services. He genuinely had seemed pleased, almost honored, when she also requested if he would personally care for her during her pregnancy.

As the months progressed, Aslyn's pregnancy flourished while her general health remained excellent; no high blood pressure and no gestational diabetes complicated her advanced maternal age. She regularly thought of the baby's father, her sperm donor, Jimmy Perry. Aslyn could not hide from her recurring physical feelings and desires for him. In her mind she occasionally formed similarities between Knox and the late Jimmy Perry. Those feelings neither worried her nor Knox Chamblee.

DARDEN NORTH, MD
310

POINTS OF ORIGIN
is hot with readers

"... one of the most heart-stopping, spellbinding endings I have read in a long time. A perfect book for suspense lovers."
—— Susan Pettrone, *Reader Views*

"Similar to William Faulkner's Yoknaptawa County, Mississippi, ... North's strengths are his memorable characters."
—— Lee Gooden, *Foreword Reviews*

"In North style, readers are again invited into the lives of the rich and not-so-rich."
—— Denise Grones, *Delta Magazine*

"Deceit, greed, affairs, death, love, guilt and revenge ... flows together to a superb ending."
—— Mary Emrick, *Bluffs and Bayous Magazine*

"*Points of Origin* takes the good and bad of small town wealth and wraps it in suspense. *Who done it?* becomes *Who all could have done it?* North reminds readers that things are not always as they appear."
—— Susan O' Bryan, *The Clarion-Ledger*

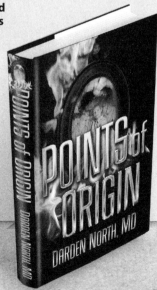

"... an intricate, suspenseful tale ... the author grabs the reader immediately."
—— Nan Graves Goodman, *Portico Jackson*

Available at booksellers everywhere.

About the Author

Darden North, MD, is a board-certified obstetrician/gynecologist who lives in Jackson, Mississippi, where he practices medicine at Jackson Healthcare for Women, PA. He and his wife Sally have two college-aged children, William and Anderson, as well as two dogs and a granddog. North's first novel *House Call* was published in hardcover in 2005. His second novel *Points of Origin* was recognized in Southern Fiction by the 2007 Independent Publishers Book Awards.